THE SEVEN YEAR ITCH (A J.J. McCALL NOVEL) BOOK 1

"The Seven Year Itch" is a mystery thriller from S. D. Skye ... hard to put down for lovers of spy fiction, highly recommended." ~ *Carl Logan, Midwest Book Review (April 2013)*

"Thick with layers, THE SEVEN YEAR ITCH is filled with strife, deceit, lust, pain, mystery, and humor."~ *OOSA Online Book Club*

SON OF A ITCH

THE FBI ESPIONAGE SERIES

A J.J. McCall Novel (Book 2)

S.D. Skye

FRANKIE V BOOKS
AN IMPRINT OF LADYLIT PRESS

SON OF A ITCH
A J.J. McCall Novel (Book 1)

Frankie V Books
An Imprint of LadyLit Press
Cheltenham, MD 20623

October 2013

First Edition

To Mommy

Acknowledgments

Thank you God. I'm still writing because of the gift You gave to me, and my earnest desire to use it to tell the stories you put on my heart.

Thank you to the men and women of the FBI who lay their lives on the line for this country every day. The United States is safer today than ever because of what you do.

Thanks to my beautiful son, William.

To my Dad. Without his love and support, I couldn't have brought J.J. McCall this far.

To my dear friends and beta readers Lisa and Becky. Thank you for suffering through my early drafts.

And last but never least, thanks to my cousin and graphic designer RheQuan Robinson for yet another couple of great book covers.

PROLOGUE

PROLOGUE

Friday, November 6th – Irving Street NW

Mist crawled through the darkness as the sound of revenge echoed with Lana Michaels' every step along the quiet residential street. It was lined with a mix of neglected and pristine darkened row houses. Her body teetered on the edge of collapse since she'd broken free from the hospital. She'd grown tired of riding the metro, looking over her shoulder, flinching at each splashed puddle, paranoid that police cars stalked her in the darkened side streets. Still, she kept her pace swift and determined, pressed into the fog, ready for battle. She tightened her paper-thin jacket around her neck as the wind wrapped her in a shivering blanket. Nothing could quell her insatiable thirst...nothing except that bitch's tears. And J.J. would very soon shed tears for the murder of her most dearly beloved.

She had no doubt J.J. McCall was now a hard target. FBI protocol demanded it. Lana suspected the Bureau had already retrieved her personal files from the laptop at her home and would be lying in wait. The director had probably assigned a detail of Special Surveillance Group personnel to tail J.J. and ensure Lana didn't get within five feet. That's the reason Lana selected a softer target, one easier to kill. And Lana planned to savor his death, and the untold pain inflicted on her nemesis.

For too many years, Lana had labored tirelessly in virtual isolation, sacrificed her body, and risked her freedom, all to end up with nothing. No small thanks to that meddling so-called star FBI agent and her bitter ex-lovers.

When Jack Sabinski, Lana's lump of a boyfriend, was freed from Alexandria jail, he went into seclusion and hadn't been seen in public since. According to *The Washington Post* clenched beneath her arm, Chris Johnson, her moronic stooge, was now keeping Jack's cot warm. He sang like the Harlem Boys' Choir during his Bureau interrogations and confessed each and every one of their sins, still angry that he'd been played for a fool and that the baby she claimed to be carrying had never spawned. She had no one to rely on except the Service—which was stifled by diplomatic protocols and bound by the Embassy compound gates.

Then her mind flashed to *him*, and tears for Jake McGee's spilled blood flooded her eyes. She tightened her lids as the memory of his lifeless body bolted from the catacombs of her mind. He lay in a scarlet pool, murdered by the merciless bullet fired from J.J.'s Glock.

Lana's TV photo, the one in which she played the blond FBI agent, now fueled intensive manhunts for the so-called Red Honeytrap across six states. Her treachery had been splashed over headlines from LA to Moscow, and the FBI had issued every all-points bulletin, short of the Amber alert, dangling a million dollar bounty to sweeten the pot for greedy hunters. Her dyed black hair and green contact lenses couldn't conceal her for long. But by the time they figured out her location the deed would be done. Her work would be complete. And she wouldn't be the only one left suffering a crippling loss.

Head down, shrouded in her hoodie, she rounded the corner onto Irving Street and pulled the folded newspaper from beneath her arm. She glanced at the address, then strained to see house numbers through the night fog. Halfway up the block she'd finally arrived.

"Here it is." She opened the rickety gate to the three-story duplex, trotted up the steps, and rang the doorbell. A tall, older gentleman with cotton-colored hair answered moments later. He stretched inches above her head, but his frame was thin, frail.

She peered up at him and noticed the hearing aid and thick bifocals. "Hi. I'm here about the room? I called earlier."

He inspected her, squinting his eyes and leering skeptically. The dead air gave Lana pause. For a moment, she believed his expression revealed a glint of recognition. How she hoped she was wrong. Exhausted, she grimaced at the thought of using her last shred of energy to slaughter the old man. Her right hand tensed when she imagined tightening her grip around his neck until his motionless body slammed against his pristine wood floors. An easier feat than convincing him she wasn't Lana Michaels when, in fact, she was.

"You don't remember? I told you…my apartment caught fire, and I need a temporary place to stay." She flashed a sheepish smile and nervously swiped her bangs from her forehead. Then she glanced down at the newspaper where she'd scribbled the name beside the advertisement. "I believe I spoke with a Mr. O'Leary? I'm Katherine."

He hesitated for another moment then patted his chest. "Katherine, ahhh yes, yes. Come in." He stepped aside and his smile warmed. She scanned the foyer and waved to the matronly woman poking her head out from the kitchen. "I'm sorry, but I've been getting so many calls, it's hard to keep all the names straight."

She exhaled, and the rigidness in her body released. "No problem, I understand. The room is still available, right?"

"Yes, yes. Do you have the deposit?"

Lana pulled a wrinkled white envelope from her pant pocket and counted out five one hundred dollar bills. "This should do it."

He held a bill up to the light and stretched it at the ends. "Can't be too careful. You'd be surprised by how much counterfeit money is floating around D.C. these days."

He pulled a key from the drawer of the side table near the door and led her outside.

"My wife and I live in this half. We rent out the rooms on the other side. There is a gentleman sharing the home with you. Nice guy. Respectful. Very quiet. You'll be perfectly safe. We've got bolts on both bedroom doors so no one can get inside." He escorted her back outside, opened the door and led her up the wooden steps inside the home next door. "You two will share a kitchen, but you each have a bathroom. Yours is here," he said pointing to a water closet-sized room containing an old-fashioned pedestal sink and footed bathtub with a shower.

"Here's where you'll be staying. Rent's due by the fifth of the month. All utilities included." The cramped space was clean, old fashioned, contained the basics. A bed, dresser with mirror, and a nightstand were positioned against the longest wall. Lace curtains hung from the windows, covering the venetian blinds.

She walked over and peered out. "I like it. You've saved my life."

"You're welcome," he said, easing toward the doorway. "Will that be all?"

"What about the neighborhood? It's not dangerous, is it? I mean, I'm, you know, single. I'll probably be alone a lot, sometimes at night."

"Oh yes, yes, perfectly safe. Most of the residents have lived here for twenty years or more. Except one. Max McCall. He lives in the red-brick house right across the street. He's been here longer than any of us."

"Is that right?"

"Yeah, keeps to himself mostly. Doesn't go out much except to check on his business."

"Oh?"

"Yes, he owns a corner store a three blocks down 7th street. You can pick up eggs, bread, milk, and the basics there. A Giant grocery store is located near the metro," Mr. O'Leary said. "Now, if that's about all, I'll be getting back to the house. Time for Law & Order."

He grasped the rail and descended down the stairs. "Oh, by the way, not that I'm rushing you out or anything but how long do you think you'll be staying? The wife and I are going on Caribbean cruise for two weeks starting tomorrow."

Lana smirked as she once more peered at the house across the street. "Not much longer than a week or two. The minute I finish my business, I'm going home."

And her business was sinking hot lead into the skull of J.J.'s father—Max McCall.

CHAPTER 1

"Character cannot be developed in ease and quiet. Only through experience of trial and suffering can the soul be strengthened, ambition inspired, and success achieved."
Helen Keller

Monday, November 16th – G.W. University Hospital

Exactly three moments defined the entire course of J.J.'s being—the day she got "the itch," the generational curse that sparked random irritating tingles through her body anytime she heard a lie; the day her mother died; and this one, the day in which she grasped the fragility of life and how it could slip away in an instant.

The ambulance siren blared down Pennsylvania Avenue through the remnants of rush hour traffic as she stared down at his tearful eyes, his face shredded with pain, his body curled with anguish. Slowly, his lids opened to expose a bloodshot blank stare. She saw her mother's eyes in his, and his last breath whispered in the distance, drawing ever near.

"I'm here. You're going to be okay. We're almost there," she said as her voice shook.

George Washington University Hospital was just a few minutes away and had one of the best trauma centers in the D.C. area.

He placed his trembling hand on hers and struggled to speak. "There...*something*...you should...kn—"

"Shhhh. Save your strength," J.J. shook her head to dissuade him from speaking. She stroked his fingers and tried to maintain a steady front. "You're gonna be okay. You can tell me everything when you're better."

Her mind whirred as the ambulance zipped into the circular driveway beneath the overhang and masked emergency personnel in blue and green scrubs swarmed the doors. They out pulled the gurney, wheeling him inside beyond her view. She'd never felt so alone in her life. She had calls to make, people to notify, but her mind was still foggy from the shock.

She searched her purse for the flask, the reminder of just how far she'd come and how much further she had to go.

J.J. walked into the waiting area and slipped onto one of the cold, cramped seats near the television, hoping to check the news for signs of a press leak. Instead, the hospital station replayed loops of doctors giving prevention tips on high blood pressure and heart disease.

Disappointed in the dearth of distractions, J.J. allowed her eye to drift from one ailing patient to another. She gazed at her feet until her vision blurred and left her wondering how she got to this place of confusion and despair. She was irresistibly drawn to this duty to her country, but with every day that passed she longed to understand her true purpose, the one that perhaps wasn't tied to her mother's legacy.

Even still, she was committed to seeing the task force through until every Russian spy was caught despite, once again, being neutered by the FBI.

The first Monday after Lana's escape—seven days ago—J.J. had arrived in Director Freeman's executive conference room, the one he had personally reserved for Task Force Phantom Hunter. The team, comprised of DIA, CIA, NSA, and FBI, had been established under DNI authority to identify members of a suspected Russian illegals network operating throughout the U.S. intelligence community. After getting passed over for well-deserved promotions and years of second-class, stepchild treatment, Freeman had entrusted J.J. with leading this critical mission, and the significance did not escape her.

But the gratification didn't last long.

Not even a day passed before the Bureau reneged. The offer that kept her from quitting that Friday was off the table. The shocking reversal, prompted by political machinations occurring in pay grades way above hers, left her wondering why in hell she didn't pack it in while she had the chance.

She didn't even have time to plan out the agenda for the first task force meeting before the next order came down from on high. President of the United States high. The directive was clear and unwavering, and J.J. had the dubious honor of breaking the news to the team.

She trudged through the drab, hollow corridors at FBI Headquarters to arrive a half hour before the rest of the group. Needed a quiet moment to collect her thoughts. It was her first day back to work since Tony Donato, the sexy co-case agent with whom (in diplomatic terms) J.J. had hoped to explore significantly warmer, friendlier relations, caught Six's lips parting from hers.

J.J. emptied a large bag of M&Ms into a plastic candy dish on the oversized mahogany conference table to dig in whenever the alcohol cravings became too intense to bear. She peered up, hearing footsteps pad toward the door. Walter Lowenstein, the NSA representative, straggled inside toting an attaché and pushing his Coke-bottle, wire-rimmed frames onto the bridge of his nose. His ill-fitting suit sagged from his shoulders and waist as if he'd pilfered the ensemble from his father's closet.

She tried to mask her exhaustion to no avail. "Good morning, glad you made it." J.J. greeted him with a cheerful but forced smile. She gestured her hand toward empty chairs on her right. "Grab a seat. The others should be here in a few."

"Thanks," he said, his toothy grin mirroring hers. He worked his way to the other side of the table, dropped his briefcase onto the floor, and gawked as if her feeble attempts to mask her disappointment had failed. "Looks like you need coffee as much as I do. Will we have time to grab a cup?"

She smiled weakly. "Fret not. Director Freeman's secretary Mrs. Whitehouse will be bringing in a carafe after we get started I hope. I think most of us will be more effective with a caffeine fix in this morn—" J.J. began, interrupted by the next team member's arrival.

Tony's wannabe girlfriend bounced in the door with all the cheer of a drunken valley girl, gazelle graceful in her four-inch stilettos and body-hugging cranberry-colored pantsuit. After flipping her irritatingly thick Pantene hair behind her shoulder, she smiled and sang a bright, "Good morning!"

J.J. grabbed a handful of chocolate with the quickness of a hungry toddler. "Gia, you made it," J.J. replied in a flat tone, offering a polite but grudging head nod. Her ears and cheeks warmed as she soundlessly growled and narrowed her eyes. "Please make yourself comfortable," she said as the words "on Mars" flitted through her mind. She stuffed a handful of M&Ms in her mouth and waited for the next arrival.

"Wouldn't miss it for the world," Gia replied, carefree and nonchalant, full of herself. In the contest for the heart of Tony Donato, she'd scored a major victory over J.J. by all appearances. A flirtatious grin edged the corners of her lips upward when Tony arrived seconds later, in all his muscled Italian glory. A towering hunk of olive-colored fine. Her voice bounced as she sang, "Ciao, Signore Donato."

Show off, J.J. groused as she shifted in her chair, cocked her head to the side and shook it in disbelief at Gia's shameless pandering. J.J. had sensed an attraction between the two. Her fears were confirmed by Tony's first lie. If Gia had the heart of Mother Theresa, J.J. still wouldn't spit on her if the spark between the two set her Pantene hair on fire.

Tony revealed an uncomfortable grin. He exchanged greetings with Walter and Gia before turning to J.J. "Agent McCall. Morning," he said, his voice devoid of its usual lightness and affection, the cold greeting she had been expecting.

Caught off guard by Gia's earlier gush, J.J. could only manage a weak, "Hi."

"Well, well, well, the gang's all here," Six bellowed, strutting inside dressed tack-sharp in a navy pinstripe suit custom-cut to every bend and curve of his frame; the tension borne from his impulsive kiss sucked the air from J.J.'s lungs. The aroma from his cologne wafted across the room, blurring J.J.'s thoughts for a brief moment. He locked eyes with J.J. and asked, "Everybody ready for round two?"

J.J. pulled back sharply and squinted until the pulse of heat-seeking missiles fired from her pupils. With the warmth Six radiated, he'd be dead before he could kiss his own ass goodbye. Although no one else would get the subtext of his comment, nothing escaped her. His late Friday night visit to her house still lingered on his mind…and hers too. For different reasons.

"Come in, gentlemen," J.J. said, her face stone. "Please take your seats, and let the meeting begin. I've got an announcement to make."

"Somebody die?" Six asked facetiously. "Your expression is pretty damn grave."

"No, nobody's dead yet…but give me a couple of hours," J.J. responded, feigning amusement. "Freeman, per orders from the President, has directed the entire Russian program to stand down offensive counterintelligence operations targeting Russian intelligence personnel, including Taskforce Phantom Hunter. The Gs can still conduct low-profile surveillance. However, the rest of us apparently must wait until a Russian intelligence operative straps a Top Secret-cleared U.S. government employee to the roof of his car and drives past FBI headquarters before we can conduct an investigation."

"What!" Gia said, bolting upright in her seat. Her body stiffened. Six expressed little-to-no surprise and Tony heard the news from Assistant Director Nixon on the same day as J.J. "I don't understand. What happened?" she continued.

"Thank the CIA Director and the President. They somehow managed to convince Freeman. Since the Mikhaylova Affair blew up in the press, the Russian FSB has arrested two U.S. businessmen in Moscow, accusing each of being CIA NOC officers. The Station fears more arrests if the FBI becomes too aggressive."

Tony turned to Six. "She in the ballpark?"

Six cleared his throat and slumped back in his chair. "Unfortunately, yes. These provocations of CIA personnel might be the tip of a Titanic-sinking iceberg and we have a much more important asset to protect— one that is key to operations in the entire community. So, yes, the stand-down is painful…but it's necessary to protect national interests. The Agency can't afford any more retaliatory expulsions."

"How'd the Russians assume the position of power here? *We* should've been expelling *their officers*, not the other way around," Tony said.

Walter clasped his hands together and leaned forward. "So, maybe this is a moot point, but what's next? Sounds like we're no longer needed here."

"Yeah, what the hell do we do now?" Tony asked. "Sit around playing with our balls, eatin' tea and crumpets?"

"Well, we've been downgraded from a task force to an analytical working group," J.J. said. "We get no investigative resources. No Gs. Any cases referred for preliminary inquiries must be vetted through AD Nixon, who will probably send them to WFO for action. Put in layman's terms—we're no longer the hammer, we are the nail. Quite frankly, I wouldn't blame any of you if you wanted to bail."

"How long this will last?" Gia asked.

J.J. responded with a shrug. "The Russian National Security Council Director is supposed to visit next week and the President's trying to smooth relations. Once he's gone, we may get some breathing room. Until then, nothing."

"I'm still in, but what do we do now?" Gia asked.

J.J. opened her mouth to answer when the song "Gettin' Jiggy With It" blasted from her cell phone. She recognized the ringtone given she'd heard it a thousand times over the past week. It was her favorite G. "Uhhh...if you'll please give me a minute. I should probably take this."

J.J. answered the phone as she stepped outside the conference room and closed the door behind her. "Hey, Jiggy. I'm in the middle of a meeting."

"You and Tony need to get down the Ellipse right now. It's urgent."

"The Ellipse? That's Secret Service territory. What interests could the Bureau have there?"

"With all the shit hitting the fan right now," Jiggy said, "you may not want to know."

"Then why'd you call?" J.J. replied.

"Because I have a sneaking suspicion the Russians have somehow gained access to a U.S. government agency communications network in this area…and judging by the close proximity to the White House…I think it's in the White House."

J.J. released a heavy sigh and shook her head. "You're right. I didn't want to know."

Her mind immediately shifted to her last remaining source in the Russian Embassy—Aleksey Dmitriyev. Only days before, he'd volunteered his services to the FBI, offering to help identify American traitors working for his Service to avenge the suffering inflicted on his falsely accused family by a ruthless KGB general.

He was promoted to Security Chief, and his new, expanded access meant he might have knowledge of an existing op.

Problem was J.J. didn't know whether he was still cooperating with the FBI. In their last conversation, he severed ties because of the impending danger of being discovered by the henchmen of Colonel Anatoliy Golikov, a counterintelligence officer at Moscow Center with the personal mission to ensure the gruesome death of anyone who betrayed the Motherland. He'd ordered his minions to Washington to determine whether there was a Russian traitor in the embassy that required his brutal brand of justice, and, had J.J. not executed the operation that saved his and his brother's life, he would be face down in an unmarked grave. He owed her, but he was spooked and J.J. had no idea as to whether she could still count on him.

They weren't scheduled to contact one another for another week, a task made nearly impossible by reports of tightened security and travel restrictions for embassy personnel. She needed to tap Dmitriyev for information—but until they could speak, a trip to the Ellipse might yield the information she needed to determine whether Russian intelligence had stuck it to the United States yet again.

CHAPTER 2

Russian intelligence officers expected to be watched, but hated to be seen. Operating in the black—in the unseen—was the difference between running a successful operation under the nose of the FBI and getting arrested and scuttled back to Moscow Center in a humiliating and career-ending expulsion or spy trade. For that reason, Russian intelligence officers had a hate-hate relationship with the Gs, the Special Surveillance Group. The Gs' sole purpose was to prevent officers from getting in the black—unless the Bureau wanted them there. And few Gs were better at this job than Jiggy, Jazz, and Money T. They were determined to prevent the Russians from providing any shred of support to the traitor Lana Michaels—the Russian illegal who posed as an FBI Agent, prompted the deaths FBI sources, and recruited and murdered a senior executive.

"Jazz, do you read me?" He clung to the bumper of his new target—the stout, weasel-like new head of Russian counterintelligence operations, Yuriy Filchenko. Jiggy smelled the burn of Filchenko's tires across the asphalt through a slight crack in the window. The force of the fall wind pulled his Malibu toward the median line, but his tight grip on the steering wheel kept his car steady until he grabbed his radio. "I've still got the eye on Filchenko. This is the fourth day in a row I've spent forty minutes outside Potbelly's while he scarfs toasty sandwiches and then gets back in his car and drives as if his steering wheel only turns in one direction. Could've at least offered me something to eat."

Jazz laughed, looking at spattering of brake lights in the three lanes of traffic up ahead along the Wisconsin Avenue's bourgeois boutique district. He was trying to decide how he'd maneuver through them to stay with his target. He covered Lana Michaels' father, Aleksandr Mikhaylov, one of the most senior Russian officers serving in Washington. "Jot that down. We'll note it in our justification to get him declared persona non grata."

A clearing in the silver sky exposed a sliver of blue as Jiggy eased his foot off the gas pedal. He hooked a sharp left onto K Street, the Wall Street for D.C.'s lobbyists replete with grids of mostly charmless, dwarfed concrete boxes that stretched from downtown to Georgetown.

"Now we're back on the road driving in circles. Just turned onto 17th Street. We usually head north. This is a new route from yesterday and his driving's erratic."

They had departed the Russian embassy compound nearly two hours before and the Gs refused to allow an inch between bumpers. The Russians were trying to exploit the FBI stand-down to provide to extract Lana Michaels from the United States safely—and the Gs remained determined to prevent it.

"Something tells me he's lost and can't drive a stick. What's your twenty?" Jiggy asked.

"I'm heading west on Wisconsin. Traffic's crawling up ahead," Jazz replied. "Looks like Mikhaylov's going back to home base. Same route."

"Keep me updated. I'm gonna need Dramamine if he loops around this block again. All these one-way streets are throwing him off. Maybe I should pull up beside his car and give him a Welcome to Washington tip—don't fuck with the Gs."

Both chuckled.

As Jiggy trailed Filchenko onto a cramped 17th Street, his stomach rumbled. The early morning start left him little time to eat breakfast. He scanned the food trucks lined along the northbound curbs next to the Ellipse, the circular tree-lined field of grass that crowned the south side of Presidential Park and afforded a direct-view of the White House. Thought he might pull over and grab a street dog and a bag of chips to hold him until he could eat real food after his shift.

When he stopped at the red light at D Street, he glanced out the driver-side window, froze, and did a double take. The man's face was familiar as was the beige Toyota Corolla with diplomatic plates. It was him—the Russian signals intelligence officer serving under diplomatic cover as a Third Secretary in the Russian Embassy. Boris Gusin—the Gs called him Goose. He dropped a handful of quarters into the parking meter, which immediately struck Jiggy as odd. Russians were notorious for racking up parking fines and not paying them. They considered free parking anywhere in the region, metered or not, a right devoid of penalty—a privilege. The hair on Jiggy's arm stood on end. Goose was up to no good.

Chris Johnson and Lana Michaels were his first case agents and they often debated about whether Goose was truly an intelligence officer. Lana said he was a nobody, but Chris finally convinced her he must be in a technical operational line—a signals collector, an eavesdropper, roughly analogous to an NSA contingent. His job was identifying and decrypting U.S. government communications channels and exploiting the information collected to the advantage of the Russian government— the more secure the network, the more damaging to U.S. national security, the better.

Gripping his cell phone, Jiggy glanced down to check the time, wondering what the hell a signals collector be would doing at the Ellipse before noon, no less? The lookouts hadn't called him out. How'd he get out the gate without anyone noticing?

The light turned green and Jiggy didn't budge. He'd gotten lost in his thoughts, wondering if he should break coverage on Filchenko and pick up Goose. The horn blared in the car behind him, jarring Jiggy out of his daze. He threw up his middle finger and grabbed his radio.

"Jazz, this is Jig, do you copy?" he asked.

"Yeah. What's going on?"

"I'm breaking coverage. Filchenko's lost…but I've spotted Goose dropping money into a parking meter near the Ellipse."

Jazz paused. "That's against Embassy rules, isn't it?"

"All day, every day. That's why I'm staying with him. Going on foot."

A lengthy silence fell between them. "While I'll admit that something's off, I gotta advise you not to do it, Jig. We're under strict orders."

"I know," he said, letting the static crackle in the void. "I'll consider myself advised. I'm shadowing him on foot until he leaves the area so I'll be going radio silent. Text my cell to contact me."

"Roger that, but if something goes wrong the only pedal you'll be pushing is on that 21-speed Trek collecting dust in your living room."

"It's probably nothing," he lied. "I'll be in and out in no time."

"You've been warned," Jazz said. "I'm riding this out with Mikhaylov. Hit me up when you figure out what's going on."

Jiggy called an audible and hoped he wouldn't live to regret it. Filchenko would spend the rest of his morning finding his way back to the compound; following him would be a waste of time. He pushed Jazz's lecture of doubt from his mind and made the command decision to break off and pursue Goose. His gut feeling verified his resolve.

Jiggy hung a right at the first corner near Constitution Hall. Nothing but rows of metered spaces. He grunted, parked in an empty one closest to 17th Street, and emptied his cup holder of all the change. After loading the meter, he scrambled through the rush hour traffic toward Goose's vehicle, pulling his hoodie over his head. He slipped on his sunglasses to conceal as much of his face as possible. He'd been assigned to cover Gusin before, a few weeks after he arrived in the United States for his second tour, so Jiggy feared Goose might recognize him. He didn't want to risk it.

Once next to Goose's car, he peered into the passenger windows.

A red-bottomed cooler with a white lid and square handle rested on the back seat. A thin silver wire hung out of the rear corner. Looked like an antenna…which were usually attached to receivers. Why would he keep a receiver in a cooler?

"That's no picnic lunch," Jiggy mumbled under his breath. He picked up his pace, scanning from left to right before he spotted Goose resting on a park bench, holding a newspaper with one hand and fiddling inside his bulky jacket with the other. He bobbed his head to the music presumably pumping through the buds plugged in his ears. As Jiggy passed by him, his eyes traced a thin, coated wire protruding from

Goose's sleeve. Why would he conceal electronics equipment beneath his clothes?

After circling the walking path once, Jiggy found a park bench within eyeshot of Goose. He pulled out his cell phone and began to send a text just as his phone rang. Jazz's number flashed on the caller ID. He rolled his eyes. The next time he saw Jazz, he'd explain the difference between a text and a phone call.

"I told you to text me!" he whispered.

"I lost him. Mikhaylov's in the black."

"What? What the hell happened? You said he was running the same route."

"Yeah…the son of a bitch pulled up to the embassy gate, waited long enough for me to break coverage. Then he threw the car in reverse and took off toward Wisconsin."

"Damn! He's probably making the drop as we speak," Jiggy whispered.

"Probably. If Michaels shows up in Moscow, I'll never live this down," Jazz said. "What's going on with Goose?"

"He's wearing headphones, fidgeting with electronics inside in his jacket and he's got a possible receiver in his cooler. He's targeting something. I mean this area is pretty target rich. The question is what…and, more importantly, how?" he said as he scanned the area. He gulped hard when his eyes locked on the White House grounds.

"You might want to find out who his new case agents are. There may be a clue in his file."

"Will do. See you back at the command center later."

After Jiggy hung up, he immediately scanned his contacts to find her number. Only took twenty seconds to figure out J.J. was the only agent who'd have the balls to take on the case in the *current environment*. He glanced at his target once again; Goose appeared in no hurry to vacate his position. If she and Tony joined him at the Ellipse, they could confirm his well-founded suspicion that an intelligence officer engaging is this kind of activity a few hundred feet from the White House had to be conducting an operation.

CHAPTER 3

Monday, November 9th—FBI Headquarters

J.J. could hardly believe Jiggy's tale—the Russians monitoring U.S. government communications from the Ellipse? Maybe even the White House? Jiggy rambled as he spewed out the chronology of the events leading up to his presence in the park.

"The M.O. looks familiar. This whole situation takes me back a few years—1999 to be exact."

J.J.'s forehead wrinkled in confusion. Took her a moment to catch his reference. The case. The thumb in the eye of the U.S. government delivered by a couple of quarter-sized electronic listening devices found in a State Department conference room, only doors down from the Secretary's Office. And inside the walls of the very Agency whose existence allowed for the Russian diplomatic presence in the United States, no less. The story was all over the news.

"199— You mean the— get out! But…how?"

"How in hell should I know? I drive cars for a living," he said. "I, uhh, hesitated to call. I'm sure you're on ice because of the stand-down."

"You got the memo, huh? I wish I was on ice," J.J. said. "The water's hot as hell over here and Director Freeman's got more eyes on me than a two-headed spider. I can't step a toe out of line or the CIA will roast my head on a spit."

"What gets me is the Russians don't give a shit about a memo," Jiggy said. "The Bureau is the only one playing by the freakin' rules."

J.J. agreed. Bad guys didn't care about the concept of "fair."

"Listen, I hate to put you in a compromising position, but…"

The pits of her arms began to burn; his lie made her itch. She smirked and shook her head. "Give me a freaking break, Jig. You knew exactly who you were calling."

He chuckled and continued, "All right, all right. You got me. But if I'm correct about the similarities, this discovery could be the beginning of something big."

J.J. quieted and sunk into her thoughts.

"Hello?" Jiggy said.

"I can't do it. My job's on the line, and I'm not sure whether I want to lose it yet."

"Then don't think of it as an investigation. Think of it as an…exchange of ideas," he said.

J.J. remained silent.

"C'mon, wasn't it you who told me 'Do your duty and damn the consequences'?"

Ugh. General Patton. She hated when her motivational speeches came back to bite her in the ass.

"That was low, Jig. All right. All right."

"Great! But you need to get down here now. Gusin's still in the area so try not to draw attention."

"This is me you're talking to, Jiggy. Low key is my middle name."

J.J. hung up, swept back into the office, and interrupted the mumbles. "Uhhh, sorry to break this up everyone, but Tony—we've got some important business to attend to," she said, cutting her eyes to signal that he shouldn't question her in that moment. His twisted expression revealed his confusion; however, he didn't say a word.

"Since we're still a task force, when are we going to prioritize and conduct our analyses?" Gia asked.

"I'll email you all tonight. By then I'll have more direction on where we go from here." J.J. expected that if events unfolded as she anticipated, the cases may prioritize themselves.

As everyone gathered their things to depart, Gia lingered awkwardly, waiting for Tony until she finally realized he wasn't leaving. A few moments later, she drifted out of the door.

Tony eased beside J.J. and in a hushed tone asked. "What'd Jiggy want?"

J.J.'s eyebrow lifted. "He was following the new counterintelligence line chief, Filchenko. The guy gets lost and Jig runs into Gusin at the Ellipse with equipment and a possible receiver. He wants us to go check it out."

Six's glance volleyed between Tony and J.J. He tilted his head to one side, pursed his lips, and said, "Wait. Gusin's a radio intercept guy, right?"

Tony looked surprised at his interruption. "What? You put your hearing aid in? We were havin' a private conversation here," Tony snapped. "As a matter of fact he leads the entire signals group, the most senior guy in Washington."

"You're not going down there to conduct an operation," Six ordered, drawing side glances from his colleagues. His expression grew serious, his voice stern. "Or do I need to define 'stand-down' for you? Too many lives are at risk for you to run out playing Dirty Harriet because some signals guy landed in the wrong place at the wrong time."

"Oh really?" Tony snapped, sneering at Six and defending J.J. "This…from Shaft?"

"Okay, you two. Watch it or I'll take you both to the principal's office," J.J. said, locking eyes with Six. "We're not conducting an investigation at this stage. We aren't making any arrests. We're only talking to the Gs. If I recall correctly, Title 18 gives me the authority to do so on behalf of the American people without regard to any of this political bullshit."

"And you wonder why you can't get a promotion," Six barked.

His words stung, especially coming from someone who knew first-hand how she'd suffered under Jack Sabinski's reign, but she bit back. "And *you* wondered how I could question your loyalty."

Six's eyes widened. He opened his mouth to speak, but remained silent.

"Okay. Okay. Now who needs a trip the principal's office?" Tony said. "Let's get outta here, J.J. Time's a' wastin'."

"I'll be right behind you," Six said. "Somebody's got to protect our interests."

J.J. rolled her eyes. "You're an American citizen. *Our* interests are *your* interests," she growled before mumbling, "asshole."

"I heard that!" Six said.

"Uhhh, I don't want to intrude," Walter piped in. "But if signals intelligence is involved, as the only NSA rep in the group, I may be able to help."

"Good thinking! You're in," J.J. said, a slight smile emerging from her scowl. Walter might have more balls than she gave him credit for. "We'll walk. It's only a few blocks away."

CHAPTER 4

Monday Afternoon, November 9th—Russian Embassy

Yuriy Filchenko was reminded of just how much he needed to take exercise as he lugged his girth in a slight jog to Embassy entrance. He paused before he started up the stairs, trying to slow his racing heart. Although tired from running, the day's events certainly had contributed. He feared he had blown a major operation—and on the third day of his first U.S. tour, no less. His career flashed before his eyes in an instant. He'd go from being a Golikov protégé and the promising new Counterintelligence Chief to nothing more than a cocktail joke in the time he took to pour a shot of vodka.

What a stupid, stupid mistake. One wrong turn had led him and his FBI watcher on a direct path to RAPTURE, one of Russia's most successful eavesdropping operation since they delivered to the Great Seal to the U.S. Ambassador in Moscow in 1946. He was not aware of the full details, but he knew the operation was so critical the Center had ordered no one to drive within a ten-mile radius of the operational area.

This would quickly become his last tour if he didn't find a way to cover his ass. Such a mistake at this tense critical time in U.S.-Russian relations might end his career. If his actions compromised the operation, he must find someone else onto whom he could pin the blunder, deflect the blame. Confessing the truth was not an option.

Only one person came to mind – Aleksey Dmitriyev.

Many influential officers already questioned his loyalty to the Service. Colonel Golikov had entrusted Filchenko to monitor the Washington Residency in general…and Dmitriyev in particular. Said he believed Stanislav Vorobyev, the departing Security Chief, had been covering up Dmitriyev's misdoings, making the two equally culpable. Gave Filchenko the responsibility to expose the new Security Chief for the duplicitous hoax he was. He greened at the thought of Dmitriyev's and the Resident's, Andrei Komarov's, fortuitous climbs up the ladders of success, their GQ dress and mannerisms more reminiscent of cartoonish, self-serving James Bonds than the real intelligence officers who served at the will and pleasure of the state.

Filchenko paced through the corridor leading to the Resident's office. He cleared his throat as he approached the door and steeled his nerves. The Resident was perceptive, perhaps too much for his own good—certainly too much for Filchenko. The impression he left must leave no doubt the operation went according to plan and he must also plant the seed that Dmitriyev was not to be trusted.

When Filchenko peered inside, the Resident looked up from a file on his desk. "Ahhh, Comrade. Come in."

"Uhhh...thank you."

The Resident lowered his voice to a hush to avoid the ears of unknowing passersby. "I've been hearing positive things about your support on this current operation. You've been a great help at a critical time."

"Thank you. I'm merely doing my duty."

"Have a seat. Anything you needed to discuss?"

Filchenko remained standing shifted his gaze from the Resident and rubbed his hands down his pant leg to dry. "No, I was wondering if Comrade Dmitriyev has returned from his meeting downtown yet. I haven't seen him all morning," he lied, knowing the Resident had forbidden all officers from leaving the compound without his expressed consent.

"Hmmm. He reported no such meeting."

"Perhaps I misspoke. I could've sworn he mentioned something to that effect the other day."

After checking the time on his wrist, the Resident said, "He should be at his desk. He passed by only seconds ago."

Filchenko nodded. "I'll let you get back to work."

"Thank you." The Resident eyed him suspiciously. "Close the door behind you."

Filchenko lengthened his stride toward Dmitriyev's office, changing his colors like a chameleon to play his new role. He was taking a major risk. He tugged at his collar to release the stifling sensation from around his neck. He needed to appear panicked, afraid, so Dmitriyev would snatch the bait and shift into protection mode when this frightened first-tour officer confessed his mistake. Then he'd convince Dmitriyev to allow him into the space beneath his wing to be his mentor, if not friend. It was important to keep his enemy close. As soon as Dmitriyev let his guard down, Filchenko would strike for the kill, boosting his star into the stratosphere and driving Dmitriyev into the muck where he belonged.

He rapped his knuckles against Dmitriyev's door frame. "Hello, Comrade. May I speak with you for a moment?"

Aleksey smiled and pushed himself from his desk to stand. "You look concerned. Something wrong?"

He was comforted by Dmitriyev's strained expression; Filchenko's ruse had kicked off as planned. Counterintelligence officers were trained to detect problems and then investigate them. Only those vulnerable to engaging in corrupt activity failed to report, an observation which gave him pause. Filchenko felt confident he'd selected the ideal stooge. "The truth is, I don't know. That's why I'm coming to you."

"Is this about today? When you showed up later than usual, I figured you'd gotten lost. If you're concerned about your performance, you shouldn't be. You've done well for someone who's been here less than a week. Some officers who've been in D.C. two years can't go from here to the corner without Sat Nav."

Filchenko chuckled before his smile evaporated. "They gave me a car with a manual transmission. I can barely keep it from stalling, let alone pay attention to the street signs. Before I realized my location, I had passed Comrade Gusin's car and drew FBI surveillance into the area. They could've seen him. I'm almost certain they did."

"Gusin? I don't under—" he began. "Wait...to which operation are you referring?"

"RAPTURE. The White House operation. Certainly you're aware of it."

"Ah, of course," Dmitriyev leaned forward on his desk and dropped his head into his hands. Then glanced up at him. "He's involved in another as well. I get them confused. Have you told anyone else?"

"No, just you."

Dmitriyev locked eyes with Filchenko. "I hate to belabor the obvious but I don't need to tell you that the ramifications could be significant. My God, if the FBI shuts it down, we will lose our only window into the White House and a critical source of reports during the embassy lockdown. No reports to the Center means more negative attention for the Residency. Komarov won't be happy," he said. "On the other hand, the chances that the FBI spotted Gusin are infinitesimal at best."

"I agree, and I'm relieved to be working with someone so … calm and reasonable."

Dmitriyev nodded. "We'll say nothing at the moment. Let's monitor the situation and see what happens."

Filchenko nodded and smiled as he stood to leave. "Thank you for your assistance in this matter."

"Well, let's just hope you won't need it," Dmitriyev said as his eyes followed him out. "Please close it behind you," he said, motioning toward the door.

Dmitriyev sat back hard in his seat as a wide grin subsumed his face. His scattered thoughts began to coalesce. Thanks to that sniveling sack of scum *Filth*chenko, he now had the intelligence he needed to prove his worth to the FBI—RAPTURE. However, if the longstanding operation was shut down within days of Dmitriyev finding out about it, the Resident might blame him for the compromise and his life would be over. On the other hand, his clueless underling had unwittingly provided him with a scapegoat if he needed one.

Dmitriyev now needed to contact Agent McCall and warn her, but he would have to ask her to do the unthinkable—find a way to leave it in place until he could ensure he would not be a suspect. The optimal means of contacting Agent McCall was via the disposable phone she had provided him during a previous operation. Yes, she had ordered him to get rid of it, but the Mikhaylova Affairs and Moscow arrests had distracted him. He would destroy it the minute he sent the text. He couldn't afford the risk of keeping it in his possession any longer anyway.

He slipped out of his office, passed the administrative assistant, and announced that he was heading out for his daily Starbucks run. Then he made his way to his flat. Pressing through the chill air, he trekked across the parking lot and up the steps to the 4th floor of the residential building. He flung open the door to his place, clambered to his closet, and grabbed one of the Nike boxes from the sea of shoes on the floor. He dug his hand into the left shoe, pulled out the ball of tissue paper, and unraveled it.

Nothing.

He searched the other shoe.

Nothing.

His brow furrowed as he stared at the sea of shoes on his closet floor. The thought of searching each one of the minimum fifteen boxes at that moment left him feeling a little exasperated, and he'd already had a long day. While he needed to find the phone, he didn't need to find it at that moment. He decided to take a break and find it later.

CHAPTER 5

Late Monday Afternoon—The Ellipse

By the time J.J. and the rest of the team had arrived at the expansive patch of field south of the White House called the Ellipse, Gusin was gone. They trekked through the line of trees, majestic oak limbs barely clinging to the last remnants of fall circling the sphere, onto the walking path that led them to Jiggy, who had clocked the Russian out two hours and fifteen minutes after his arrival. Still she felt jittery. She was more than well known to most D.C.-based Russian intelligence officers and if any one of them spotted her, the jig was up—and at the worst possible time. Each time dead leaves crunched under the feet of passersby, J.J. scanned over her shoulder to watch for stray intelligence officers in the area until they reached the Zero Mile Marker. Their position afforded a direct view of the bowed columns of the White House's south front façade just a few hundred feet away.

"So, Walter, what do you think?" J.J. asked, as he squatted on the ground next to her. He whipped out his laptop with swiftness of a gunslinger's Colt 45 and zealously tapped his fingers across the keyboard. When the map of the Ellipse appeared, he touched the screen, pushed his digits together and pulled them apart until he'd zoomed in. The satellite image labeled every nearby street and building.

J.J. leaned forward hovering over his shoulder like a watchful mother hen while flanked on either side by Jiggy and Tony. She scoured the map of the area surrounding the Ellipse, shifting her stance to avoid the sun's harsh glare.

"It's tough to say," Walter said, pushing his glasses on the bridge of his nose. "But the fact that he comes here and physically sits in this location suggests he's targeting a very specific mode of communication or device in close proximity. It can't be more than a few hundred feet away." He traced the surrounding streets with his index finger. "In that distance, the most logical target according to my calculations...."

He froze. Silence weighed down his face.

"Where?" J.J. urged.

"Can't be that bad." Tony chuckled and swiped his brow. "I mean it's not like they wired the friggin' White House."

Walter glance dragged slowly from J.J. to Tony, his face wrenched. The glare reflecting off of his glasses barely shielded his bulging eyes.

"The White House?" Tony asked

Walter nodded. "It could be anywhere. The private residence. The West Wing. Can't be certain without more information."

"The West Wing?" Tony asked. "What's there? Secret Service, the uhhh…what else?"

J.J. eyes protruded from her head. "Cabinet Room?" She moved around and collapsed beside Walter, eyeing the screen to get a closer look. "But there's no way in hell they could get inside. No way."

"Well, that's not true," Walter said, his expression and tone questioning J.J.'s assertion. "It's a long shot but they could feasibly install a listening device with a remote switch. They've done it before, and it would explain why he physically visits this location."

"If you're Russian intelligence and you wire the President's residence," Six said, "would you bother trying to plant it any place else?"

"How in the hell could the Russians get a fucking listening device in the White House?" Tony asked. "You can't change your mind in that place without bumping into Secret Service."

"A highly placed source for starters. You know, like a recruitment, a mole, or…*an illegal*," said Six.

"An asset and opportunity," J.J. added.

Walter glanced up. "Well, they've been undergoing periodic renovations for the last six or seven years now."

J.J.'s head snapped toward Walter. "Did you say six or seven?"

He nodded. "We helped install their secure comms networks in the Situation Room. The space had been totally gutted and remodeled. There are a couple conference room spaces and video teleconferencing rooms."

"With all this new technology, seems like they would've installed sensors or something to detect electronics activity in the room, right?"

"Yes, they did," Walter ran his fingers through his hair. "But they sense high frequencies. If the Russians used a low-frequency device, the sensors probably wouldn't pick up the signal."

"I'll be damned!" Tony said.

"On the bright side," Walter said, "if the device must be turned on and recorded remotely, that works in our favor. Not only does it limit the information they can collect, we have a better chance of catching them in the act and locating the device."

"Maybe," Six said. "But I think it'll be pretty tough to find."

"Seems like Secret Service would've caught Gusin by now if he made a pattern of coming down here too often, especially at night or odd hours. They must be spacing out the trips and showing up at different times during the day," Jiggy said. "Or they think U.S. security is too stupid to notice. Either way they'll be back. We need to be here so we can trace the signal."

"With the entire residency still on lockdown from this Lana business, I'd bet my soul, if we're right, that this is probably their only source of high-level intelligence. They can't meet their sources without a team of Gs on their asses. They'll be back...and sooner than later," J.J. said.

Jiggy looked at J.J. "We've got to go to WFO tonight and get authorization from MacDonald to use the MCC so we can find the signal and determine where the hell it's coming from. I'll bet the Goose will be back tomorrow."

"MCC?" Walter asked.

"The Mobile Command Center," Tony said. "On second thought, we may need to go a little more low key—it's going to stand out like shit on cotton over there parked with the food trucks."

"I can find it with my laptop," Walter said. "Just tell me where you need me to be and when."

Six interrupted, "I don't mean to pry..."

"Of course you do," J.J. snapped.

"But, uhh, this doesn't sound like you're *standing down* operations as ordered by *your* director."

J.J. tightened her lips and rolled her eyes. "You're right, Six. Let's call the whole thing off. But you might want to consider what happens to your all-important source if the Russians overhear the CIA briefing the Prez about him."

Six froze in his thoughts and said, "Point taken."

J.J. smiled. "We'll brief Gia tonight," J.J. said before turning to Tony and then back to Walter. "Looks like Task Force Phantom Hunter has a new target. Walter, we'll see you back here at 6 am? We need to set up early."

He glanced at his watch. "Sure thing. Now, I should be getting out of here. Traffic on the BW Parkway's gonna be a bear."

Within minutes, Tony, Six, and J.J. were pacing back to FBI head-quarters. Since Director Freeman had ordered them to stand-down, they required his consent to pursue the investigation further, an authorization she feared she would not receive. At that moment, with only conjecture and analysis to support their theory, the case was sure to fall victim to politics. J.J. looked upward, her eyes drawn to the flags billowing around the Washington Monument as they turned onto Constitution Avenue. Her mind was jolted by an epiphany. She thought back to the contents of Cartwright's letter that she received on Saturday—the words that he told her Lana spoke to him.

We moved from Foggy Bottom to 1600…

"Doesn't it seem odd to you?"

"What?" Tony asked.

"Well, in the State Department operation, they targeted an unclassi-fied conference room. Probably didn't get much of anything from the wire from the information I read."

"So?"

"Think about it. Why would they waste that level of time and effort, put the life of their agent and his support network at risk, to conduct a flawless installation of a listening device in a room where they'd get no classified intelligence?"

J.J. turned to Tony. The sound of their footsteps against the red brick filled the air between them for a moment while he appeared to collect his thoughts. "One possibility is the agent got the wrong conference room. Based on its proximity to the Secretary's Office, may be the jerkoff thought the space was classified," Tony said.

J.J. looked at him askance and shrugged. "I suppose so."

"Yeah, I know. That theory's got more holes than Swiss cheese. You think Lana had something to do with this, don't you?"

"I think we've got a bigger fish to fry right now than Lana," she replied.

"Who? The President?"

"Worse," she said. "An angry Director Freeman."

CHAPTER 6

Monday Night, November 9ᵗʰ—FBI Headquarters

The team returned from the Ellipse convinced they had sufficient justification to pursue the case further. Next, they met with Director Freeman to do the impossible—get authorization to conduct a preliminary inquiry which was contrary to the President's orders.

"Absolutely not!" Freeman roared, like the thunder firing up outside in the night sky. "Look under my desk. You see my foot? It's down and it's not budging. Yes, you have a valid lead. Yes, you will pursue it. No, not tomorrow. We'll put more Gs on Gusin and increase the FBI presence in the Ellipse when the lookouts call him out of the compound. He won't get within a hundred feet of the park, at least not until we can conduct a thorough investigation."

J.J. shook her head in frustration.

"But, Sir, if I may interject," Tony began. "If we increase FBI presence, the Russians will know the op, whatever it is, is blown. If you will recall, we have a source in the Embassy. Shutting down the operation will put him at risk, especially with Golikov's hoods running roughshod. We should sacrifice an FBI source to avoid pissing off the President, who I guarantee you will be more ticked off than *any of us* when he finds out the Russians have wired his house…and the FBI suspected a problem but didn't do anything about it…because we didn't want to piss him off?"

Freeman massaged his left shoulder, trying to ease the ache radiating through his arm. The stresses of the job were wearing the tread on his body thin, as was listening to J.J.'s tale of bugs and the White House. Impossible problems in even more difficult times. J.J. reminded Freeman of himself during early days in his career, running Organized Crime cases out of the FBI Philly office. He understood her dogged determination, her commitment and patriotism. Her persistence.

Ugh, her persistence.

But he'd like to strangle her with her blatant disregard for the rules and stubborn inability to follow protocol. She had a knack for doing the *right* thing for sound reasons at the *wrong* time. And with the President-ordered standdown, her timing couldn't be worse.

"J.J., consider one thing for a second. What do you think is going to happen when a team of FBI agents show up to sweep for bugs, right down the hall from arguably the most aggressive press corps in the *world?*" Freeman said, animated, his hands flailing about. "The Coast Guard couldn't save us from the splash from those headlines. And all from the office of the man who issued the order to stand down in the first place. Do you not see that?"

"Yes, sir," she said, running her fingers through her shoulder-length hair. "I hadn't considered the press corps."

"Of course, not. That's why they pay me the big bucks. To take into consideration situations that very smart agents forget to consider." He stood, walked to the front of his desk, and took a seat on the edge. "With that said, there's a reason the FBI Director cannot be fired. We're a law enforcement organization first and we operate without regard to political machinations. But the ripple effect of throwing this boulder in the water has implications for every agency in the intelligence community."

"What if we could find a way keep the inquiry low key? Find out what we're dealing with."

"If you seriously believe you can conduct a low-key investigation in the West Wing, you're more naïve than I thought," Freeman said.

"But—" Tony said.

"Thank you for stopping by this evening." Freeman returned to his seat and clasped his hands together. "Now, if that will be all. My wife would like me to arrive home sometime this century."

J.J. and Tony stood in defeat and nodded before shuffling toward the door. "Okay. Thank you for your time, Sir."

"Always a welcome visit," Freeman said as he watched them leave. He leaned back in his seat for a moment and shook his head. A half smile inched the corners of his mouth upward. He grabbed the phone and buzzed his secretary, Mrs. Whitehouse. "Catch J.J. and send her back in here."

He'd all but killed the task force, barred her from supporting the Michaels' investigation. The dejected look on J.J. face told him she was at the edge. Somehow he knew he'd live to regret the decision, but for J.J. to ask him for permission was much more difficult than for him to ask for forgiveness. While *his* misstep would certainly require a few days on the Hill, it wouldn't cost him his ten-year tenured job.

A slip-up might cost J.J. hers—and she didn't appear to take issue with the prospect.

She poked her head in the door. "You asked to see me, Sir?"

"Yes," Freeman leaned back in his seat, elbows against the armrests, and steepled his fingers. "Twenty-four hours and low key, do you understand me? I don't want to see a blip on my radar in any way attributed to you. If you so much as turn up in the *credits* on the six o'clock news, if I see you in the society section of the newspaper, you won't have to worry about turning in your resignation. Am I clear?"

"Crystal," J.J. said, unable to restrain her smile. "You won't regret this, Sir."

"Famous last words," Freeman said with a nod. After she disappeared, he grinned. He knew he wouldn't. He turned to his desk and faced his monitor. As he reached to shut down his computer, an email appeared from SAC MacDonald. An update on the Michaels investigation.

> Metro Transit Police called. They're inspecting subway footage from last Thursday and Friday. Think they've identified Lana. Will send to WFO first thing in the morning.

He exhaled and dropped his head against the neck rest. He had a gut feeling the information would bring them a step closer to catching Lana, but any woman who could successfully operate as a foreign agent within the walls of FBI Headquarters could not be underestimated. If they didn't find her soon, she'd be halfway to Moscow before she blipped on the FBI's radar.

. . .

FBI Headquarters – Monday Night

J.J. removed her suit jacket and tugged at shirt label which now grated like sandpaper against the skin on the back of her neck. She stood next to the whiteboard as she surveyed the brood of stone faces glaring back at her under the harsh fluorescent light. The room was thick with uncertainty and she could barely conjure the energy to motivate herself, let alone the rest of the team.

She hadn't slept well the night before. How could she after the eventful Sunday brunch? Now her day had gone into double overtime and the exhaustion had taken her near the edge. Her eyes felt grainy and hot and her lead-heavy body was drawn to the chair, but she had to stand and take charge, while the rest of the bleary-eyed team sat hunched around the conference table waiting for J.J. to impart direction.

Except Six.

He'd been in rare form the entire day. The contemptuous gazes he periodically shot in hers and Tony's directions confirmed his frequent interruptions and doubt-casting was meant to stall the meeting, keeping her at headquarters and in his sights.

"You've all been briefed. Now, we need a plan of action. We've only got 24 hours to collect enough evidence to pursue a full investigation. I've got some ideas, but I'd like to hear yours first. Anyone?"

"Well I—" Walter began before Six rudely interrupted.

J.J. rolled her eyes and gave a polite nod to assure Walter she would solicit his opinion after Six turned off the hot air.

"As long as the embassy's on stand-down and they don't find out we know about their operation," Six interjected. "Gusin will be out tomorrow, mark my word. We better be ready for him."

Gia and the rest of the attendees agreed before silence settled in.

Walter waited a few moments speaking his peace. "My equipment can detect the frequency and, if we narrow down the correct one, I can record the transmission."

"In downtown D.C.? Yeah, right. Do you know how many signals are transmitted through that area every day?" Six said. His skepticism was as evident as his disregard for Walter's abilities.

Walter's shoulders slumped before he snapped to attention, his posture board stiff. "Hello! I'm NSA and I've got over ten years of experience in signals collection including Russian operations. So, *no one here* understands what we're dealing with better than I do," he retorted, kindly putting Six in his place. He turned to J.J. and without taking a breath, rambled, "I have a computer-based spectrum analyzer, UHF/VHF receiver, and historical knowledge of Russian operations. As long as I have Bureau authorization, I can configure the receiver and analyzer to conduct full spectrum targeting of the RF signals, intercept, demodulate, and record them…as long as the device is activated and within my target range—which is between 9 kilohertz and 3500 megahertz."

"Uhhh," J.J. said, blank-faced and open-mouthed.

"F-Y-I, that's a broad range. I also developed a cloaking software to disguise the system. No one passing by will detect my activity," Walter added.

A hush fell over the room.

Gia was the first to break the silence. "I'm no expert, but I'll take his word for it."

"I didn't unda'stand half of what he just said which means it'll probably work," Tony said.

Six's eyebrows raised and his lips pursed. "A couple of hours? Yeah right. We need a Plan B."

"Plan B?" J.J. was too exhausted to even think about devising a Plan A. "Why don't' we bet on it?" J.J. suggested, leaning forward with her shoulders hunched. "If Walter can't narrow down the signal and record the transmission in an hour?" she looked at Walter who nodded in the affirmative, then she continued, "I'll buy you a new hat. Judging from the hot air emanating from your area, the one you wore today probably won't fit."

Everyone chuckled.

"I'll take that bet," Six said as they shook on it.

J.J. pointed to five positions on the map. "Okay, everybody knows where they'll be posted. Radio communication and cell phone back-ups. The Ellipse, 7 am sharp. Dress warmly. It's gonna be a chilly morning."

As the rest of the group proceeded to leave, Gia hung behind and made a bee-line toward J.J. and then she slipped beside her, patted her arm, and said, "I wanted to let you know that you're doing a great job, but you look exhausted."

"Thanks?" J.J. looked askance as Gia continued.

"Tony and I were talking over coffee this morning and he told me you're probably not getting much sleep with that Lana Michaels still on the loose, huh?"

J.J. blood steamed instantaneously. "Hmph. Tony said, huh? Well I'm fine…and WFO's got the Lana Michaels' investigation under control. She'll slip up. It's only a matter of time."

At that moment, J.J. was less concerned about Lana and more concerned about her source—Aleksey Dmitriyev. She prayed he would survive the arrival of the new Counterintelligence Chief. Whether the knife plunged into his back or sliced across his throat, Dmitriyev better be prepared to fend off Filchenko's attack. All available information on Golikov's protégé indicated that a confrontation between the two was inevitable.

CHAPTER 7

Tuesday Morning—Russian Embassy

The palpitations in Aleksey Dmitriyev's heart rumbled in his ear, but he mustered enough calm to keep a steady hand before the java flowed. Early morning visits from the Resident did not bode well for the day. Either he was in trouble or about to be. Still donning a t-shirt and pinstriped pajama pants, he dragged his bare feet across the cold linoleum floor.

"Ugh, Comrade," Dmitriyev grunted as he shuffled into the kitchen. The sun had barely emerged over the hazy horizon when the Resident arrived at his flat, which was sparsely decorated with a sofa and table and chair in the breakfast nook. He grabbed a mug and pot and started to pour. "I can't wait until Olga returns from Moscow. Maybe you'll go back to sleeping past the cock's crow. Coffee?"

The Resident waved his hand in refusal. "No, too early. Gives me the shits."

"So what brings you down to the fourth floor so early in the morning?"

"A favor…and a question," he said, surveying the room before turning to Dmitriyev.

"A favor? Or an order?" Dmitriyev asked.

"Both."

Dmitriyev took a seat on the sofa opposite the Resident. "What can I do for you?"

"I need you to back up Comrade Gusin today," he looked down at his wristwatch. "And I don't have a lot of time to explain why."

Dmitriyev froze, his face turned from flush to pale before he could form his next sentence. He shook his head feverishly and with eyes widened, lowered his voice above a whisper. "No, Comrade. You can't mean that. I can't. Filchenko…why can't he go alone?"

If the FBI caught Dmitriyev supporting an operation—a security officer and one of only two declared Russian intelligence representatives working in Washington—his career was effectively over. He would not only be expelled, he'd be declared persona non grata in the United States and unable to serve anywhere in the West, not to mention compounding the damage already done by the "Mikhaylova Affairs."

Even more problematic was the fact that he had no time to alert Agent McCall. God forbid she or someone she worked with caught him conducting countersurveillance in an operation she is yet unaware of. With their relationship still tenuous, he had no doubt she'd believe him to be a double agent playing against the FBI. He feared she would withdraw support from him immediately, destroying any hope he had to settle his family comfortably in America. The Resident's order couldn't have come at a worse time.

"First, he's not ready, but our choices are limited and the FBI is unfamiliar with him," Komarov began. "The minute he or another officer leaves the compound they are immediately followed by a hoard of surveillance personnel. Because you are declared and cannot participate in operations, you are the ideal person to cover this operation. You will not draw coverage," the Resident insisted. "We need you on this. Just for today."

"But—"

"Stop, please. I understand the position I'm putting you in, but it's not as bad as you think," the Resident insisted. "You do not have to participate. Just monitor. Watch out for FBI surveillance. Signal Gusin if you see anything suspicious. We've been running this operation uninterrupted for almost two years and based on our success, we'll be running it for the next five—or longer—if we are successful today."

Though feeling more like an exercise in futility, Dmitriyev took one final shot at convincing the Resident's his idea was a bad one. "If I get caught, the FBI will have a field day. It's too risky to the Service. Not to mention the problems it would cause for *you* if I'm caught. You are the only one who could authorize my participation in such an operation. You would be kicked out directly behind me."

He let out a long drawn out breath, pressed his elbows against his knees, and dropped his face in his hands. "I understand your concerns, Comrade. And I do not argue that they are valid…under normal circumstances. In this instance, I'm confident your participation is a mere formality and you will not encounter any problems whatsoever—we never have. You'll be back in within a couple of hours. End of story. I will brook no more opposition," he said.

Dmitriyev took another sip from his cup and scrunched his face. "Well, this shit won't do. I'll definitely need Starbucks this morning," he said. "Is that all or did you have something else you needed to discuss?"

The Resident pressed his lips together. "I was wondering…what do you think of Filchenko?"

Dmitriyev felt the blood rush to his face. He wondered if the Resident's request, which felt like a test, came about because *Filth*chenko had already attempted to turn the Resident against him. Counterintelligence officers were notoriously two-faced, and it would not be beneath *Filth*chenko to twist his own mistake to Dmitriyev's detriment in order to posture himself for the Resident's favor.

He shrugged and said, "It's too early to tell." He cautiously examined his boss's expression and calculated his next statement. "We should keep an eye on him."

"Very perceptive," the Resident's said, "and I agree. If ice runs through your veins, seltzer water must be sloshing through his," he said. "When you first arrived at the embassy, you were cool, calm, didn't make mistakes. He seems a little uncharacteristic of the counterintelligence line. Too jittery…nervous."

Dmitriyev nodded, relieved by his boss's revelation. The Resident didn't trust *Filth*chenko anymore than he. "This is his first time facing the Americans on their own turf. We'll find out what he's made of soon enough."

"I know we will. That's why I want you to keep a close eye on him. Personally, take him under your wing and set him up…for success, of course."

"Of course." Dmitriyev chuckled. The Resident was already looking for an excuse to rid himself of *Filth*chenko. Nobody wanted Golikov's people lurking around, and *Filth*chenko would make life miserable and uncomfortable until he left. But no one except Dmitriyev understood

Filthchenko had placed himself in a position of weakness, and Dmitriyev held the keys to his inevitable doom.

"You should be ready to leave in an hour. So hurry and get your coffee fix," his boss said as he headed to toward the door and opened. "But for God's sake please don't put any vodka in it. You'll need to be on your toes…just in case."

Dmitriyev nodded and stared at the door until the latch clicked. His desperation swelled like an eye at the end of a prize fighter's uppercut. He needed to speak with Agent McCall before he set foot outside the compound. If caught at the operational site, it'd be too late explain his presence there.

He scrambled to his bedroom and scoured through the mass of clothes and shoes boxes from his many outlet excursions covering his closet floor. In one of them, he stored the burn phone Agent McCall told him to throw away after he helped identify the FBI mole's drop site, taking a page from his brother's handbook. He'd use it one last time to warn her of the impending operation then destroy it as originally instructed. His breathing grew frantic as he opened box after box to no avail. After minutes of desperate searching he opened the final pair. He pulled out the left shoe.

Nothing.

He pulled out the right shoe and dug his hand inside.

Nothing.

At once he collapsed into the floor, covered his face with both hands. Minutes passed and his thoughts fluttered in spastic turns before he pounded his fist into the floor. "Shiiiit!" he cried out.

His recollection in that moment would seal his fate.

He'd given them away and the phone was on the way to Moscow in the hands of a man trained to detect and arrest Russian traitors.

Dmitriyev shuddered. If he discovered the phone, he would waste no time ordering Dmitriyev's immediate arrest. And based on Golikov's new world order, there would be no show trial, no 20-year stint in Lefortovo high security prison. After being beaten beyond recognition, he'd be hacked by Mashkov's blade in the belly of some Russian organized crime safe house outside Moscow.

It was only a matter of time.

Dmitriyev needed J.J.'s help more than ever. And if she caught him in the act of supporting RAPTURE, he'd never receive it.

CHAPTER 8

Tuesday Morning—The Ellipse

A cold wind pierced J.J.'s windbreaker as she glanced up at the auburn sky. The ominous clouds portended rain and threatened the operation, but the team forged ahead. With just over twelve hours left to justify a full investigation, they could ill-afford any delays. The Ellipse was fairly tranquil except for the beat of joggers' shoes against the asphalt, spate clumps of morning commuters, and a vagabond dragging garbage bags filled with his wares across the busying streets. After scanning the park to ensure Gusin hadn't arrived, the entire team, including Gia (to J.J.'s dismay), began moving into position.

"Everyone wired in? I'm on 18th checking for countersurveillance. If they sent an officer out, he has to pass by here or Constitution Avenue."

"Yeah, everything's good here," Tony said, "I'm next to the Boy Scout statue. Was messing around on my iPhone and got a text from the lookouts. Gusin was called out of the embassy about 25 minutes ago. He should be here any minute."

"Messing around already? Didn't take long, did it?" Six said.

J.J. huffed. "Save it, Six. What's your position?"

"You want me to disclose something so personal to the task force?" Six said, suppressing a chuckle. After a long pause he said, "I'm kidding, I'm kidding. Loosen up, people. I'm at 17th and Constitution, and I think we're all good."

A hard silence fell over the radio, and then J.J. growled in the throat. She patted her jacket pocket and pulled out her cellphone out to make sure the ringer was on. Then she looked down at her wristwatch before volleying her glance left and right along 18th Street as if impatiently waiting for some form of transportation, performing for any passersby who might question her presence.

"Who's got eyes on Walter?" J.J. asked.

"I just passed him. I'm sitting a couple benches away," Gia said. "Looks like he's playing Galaga or something on his laptop. Hey Walter, did you make it to stage six?"

Silence.

"Walter?" Gia said.

"Hey, enough with the freakin' game already," Tony interjected. "It's time to look alert!" He waited for a response. "Walter?"

Silence.

"Walter?" Gia asked again with no response. "Something must be wrong with his radio."

Through broken waves of static, Walter said, "I can bare—hear—guys."

"Ugh. Bad signal. We are so screwed," J.J. said.

"Tony, can you go over and—" No sooner than the smile disappeared from her face she spotted him. "Incoming! Gusin's car pulled up to the light." J.J. turned her back toward him and glanced over her right shoulder until his Corolla passed by in her peripheral vision. "Okay, guys. This is it. He's parking and should be entering the park in a few minutes. Stay alert. If countersurveillance is out they won't be far behind. Tony, text the lookouts and find out if any other intel officers were called out."

A few minutes later, he replied, "Only Dmitriyev. But he's declared so if he shows his face down here, he's going back to Moscow."

"Hmm. Strange nobody else is making a run….unless one of 'em managed to slip past the lookouts through another gate. Wouldn't be the first time. Tricky bastards."

J.J.'s senses sharpened as she scanned the area for Gusin. The warning signal at the crosswalk sounded forcing a barrage of morning commuters to run across the street. She knew he'd be carrying a bag of some kind with him so she focused her attention on spotting it. Before she could inhale, the treacherous Russian son of a bitch passed her.

And it wasn't Gusin.

"Aleksey? You can't be here!" They froze in each other's gazes. His eyes were empty, emotionless, as if looking straight through her.

He said nothing.

The bright red flashing in front of her eyes when she saw him had little to do with the crisp new Washington Capitals baseball cap he donned, the bill pulled close to his eyes. Her anger swelled in a surreal frenzy and he seemed to move in slow motion.

After a few moments that seemed like an eternity, he jerked his guilty mug toward the pavement and rushed past J.J. Once on the walking path, he headed to the right, in the direction opposite the White House. J.J. stood in utter shock, waited for him to glance over his shoulder and give her a sign, any sign, that his presence at the site of a damaging operation potentially targeting the highest levels of U.S. government was a mistake, mere happenstance. But he made no such move.

While her distracted mind churned over the implications, she'd missed Gusin's approach; he rambled across her path a couple of minutes later. As Dmitriyev strolled toward Constitution Avenue, Gusin continued his trek onto the trail toward the left.

J.J. was paralyzed, didn't know what to react to first. She closed her eyes for a moment and let her instincts take over. Pressing her hand against her ear, she said, "Heads up, Gia. Gusin's coming your way. Just passed me. He's headed north."

"I've got eyes on him—he's coming toward me. Looks like he's got an earphone plugged in. Why the hell is he walking so slowly?" she said.

After a brief pause, she continued. "Okay. Just passed me. He's…oh shit! Looks like he's walking in Walter's direction. Repeat, he's walking toward Walter."

J.J. scanned the park and saw Walter in position. She gasped and through clenched teeth said, "Listen, Walter, can you hear me?"

Silence.

"Walter?"

More silence.

"Walter, our target's approaching you from the left. The guy in the dark slacks and ugly shoes. Get that fucking earpiece out. If he sees any hint of a wire, this operation is over before it begins!"

Still no sound. Just the crackle of static.

J.J. hoped like hell Walter's computer game was still on the screen. While J.J. waited for Gia to respond, she called Tony on his cell.

"What's up?" he answered.

"You're not gonna believe this. Our *friend* just passed me!"

"Our friend. What friend?" he asked. Before she could respond, Tony growled in a loud whisper, "What the hell is *Dmitriyev* doing here?!"

"Ahhh, saw him for yourself, huh? That's the million dollar question, isn't it?"

"He's declared now. Can't engage in operational activity," Tony said. "If that piece of shit's been playing us, he just fucked himself royally."

"Well, if we wait a few minutes, we'll know exactly which side he's on," J.J. said. "If he signals that FBI's in the area, and he knows I'm here, then Gusin's outta here and we may never know what they're targeting."

"If he fucks this op, I'll pinch his ass right here. State Department's only a couple blocks over. He can grab his PNG papers and take them straight to hell for all I care."

The radio went silent as J.J. watched Gusin tread slowly around the circular walkway. She studied his movement; he appeared to be searching. Perhaps he was looking for the ideal position to get the best reception, just as Walter had done earlier. It occurred to her, they performed the same job, probably had access to much of the same training and technologies. So they probably…

Picked the same freaking spot!

She pressed the push-to-talk button. "Walter! Walter!" she said in a whispered scream. "Can you hear me? I need you to move. Now! Get out of there!"

Walter didn't budge. No hint of reception on his radio. As Dmitriyev made his way around the path, the entire operation rode on her gut instinct, which was failing her like a mofo.

Her stomach wrenched as her nightmare materialized. Gusin found a spot on the bench adjacent to Walter—and Dmitriyev was only fifty meters away. If he signaled Gusin and called off the op, she'd know she'd been played, and Golikov's rage would pale in comparison to hers. After she finished raining down the fury of her wrath, Aleksey wouldn't know what country he came from.

Six buzzed in. "Uhh…I might be seeing things, but the man who walked past me resembles the new security officer."

J.J.'s eyes popped wide and she cleared her throat. "Don't be ridiculous. He's declared," she lied. "You're getting old. Might be time for a glaucoma test."

J.J.'s phone vibrated in her hand. Tony called again. "On my mother's soul, if he makes one freakin' wrong move, his balls will get back to Moscow before he does."

"Depends on what's left after I get through with him."

The moment was upon them. Dmitriyev passed Gusin. He ran the palm of his hand across the back of his neck and tipped the bill of his baseball cap with this index finger. Then he paced quickly out of the park, avoiding J.J.'s position and disappearing into the morning crowd.

"Looked like a signal to me," Tony said.

"Yeah me, too," J.J. replied. "The question is what did it mean?"

Suddenly, Gusin reached inside his jacket and bolted up from the seat.

"Son of a bitch! He's leaving!"

As he began walking, J.J.'s blood boiled with Gusin's every lumbering step. Her mind replayed the meetings and conversations with Dmitriyev in quick time. How could she of all people be deceived? Her gift of lie detection was the reason she held out a glimmer of hope, at least until Gusin rose to his feet.

Her gaze swept across the pavement in frustration. A barrage of thoughts rushed through her mind, including every method of punishing Dmitriyev for his betrayal.

She would leave no diplomatic sanction unexploited—splash his name through newspaper headlines worldwide. Have him declared PNG, maybe even start a rumor of how he'd volunteered his services to the FBI, but was rejected because the Bureau believed it to be a blatant provocation. That would teach him. She knew exactly who to call and scrolled through her cell phone contacts…Gill Bert from *The Washington Times*.

When she returned her gaze street level, Gusin was still there. Seated at the opposite end of the bench, the side furthest from Walter.

He didn't leave, after all. He just shifted positions. She expelled a long breath and swiped her forehead with the back of her hand.

Dmitriyev wasn't a double after all—or he made the move that would save his ass for the moment. His loyalty was now in question. And he'd have to prove his worth before she gave him one shred of assistance.

"Lucky bastard," Tony bellowed through the fog in her mind. "Looks like the op is still on. Walter's fingers are going a mile a minute. He's onto something."

"Yeah, lucky bastard indeed. We'll deal with him later. For now, let's hope Walter can intercept a transmission."

"No, J.J.," Tony began, "if you think about the implications, we better hope he doesn't."

Tuesday Afternoon—The Ellipse

Three hours later, the team took refuge in the FBI Mobile Command Center that had arrived shortly after Gusin left the premises. J.J. had ordered back-up in case Walter was unsuccessful, but she felt confident she wouldn't need it. Inside the modified interior cabin, rectangular table tops affixed to the either side of the van's wall served as desk areas for five personnel. Receivers and recording equipment lined the shelves as Walter's fingers flitted across his laptop's keyboard. J.J. and the team huddled around, waiting for him to process the signal intercepts. A large pair of what appeared to be commercial-grade noise-cancelling headphones pressed into his curly black mane, as line after line of computational gibberish scrolled down his screen. His mind was in the zone and he blocked out everything beyond the complicated world in his laptop…at least until the burn of four sets of eyes seared through him. Jolted out of his intense concentration, his glance darted nervously around the room.

"Uhhh…is there a problem? I feel like a guppy in a fish bowl," he said.

"Sorry," J.J. said. "How much longer before you find something?"

"Just a couple more minutes. I've isolated one low frequency RF signal that started emitting about the time Gusin arrived. I'm trying to determine whether it's from the White House. It's hard to tell."

Gia spoke up. "How will you differentiate the intercepted signal from any other telecommunication signal?"

"Well, I won't know for certain until we conduct a sweep to verify. But classified conversations should take place over encrypted lines. I can intercept encrypted signals but they'll sound garbled. However, if I understand what they're saying, if I hear a classified conversation, I know the signal is coming from an unsecure line or a transmitting device. Does that make sense?"

She nodded.

"But how can you tell whether or not it's classified?" J.J. asked.

"Well," he said, looking around at the doubting faces. "We're all cleared here. I'll play them out loud and we'll all take a guess."

"Good idea," Six piped in. He looked down at his watch. "But we need to step this up. We've been at this all day and I need to get back to Langley before heading home."

"Okay." Walter yanked out the headphone cord from its laptop jack and cranked up the volume on the speakers. "Here's the first one."

The sound of static hummed through the speakers occasionally accentuated by a few pops and crackles more reminiscent of morning breakfast cereal than a signals intercept.

"Uhhh…am I missing something here?" Tony asked.

"If you're missing it, we all are," Gia said, with a shrug. "Maybe there's no op after all."

Walter shook his head. "No, no, something's wrong here. I…I'm not sure what's going on. I captured the recording. It's here."

His fingers rattled against the keys, focused and determined.

"Sweet baby, Jesus. I hope we don't have to run this op again. I can't handle another close call," J.J. said, wishing she could choke her words back down. She glanced at Tony whose eyes were returning to their sockets.

"Close call?" Six asked, his eyebrow raised.

J.J. hesitated while she conjured up a response Six would believe. "With Gusin…sitting right next to Walter and all. I'd hate to…have to get a new team out here. That'd…be a…pain in the ass," she said haltingly, before clearing her throat. She craned her neck to check out the laptop. "Anything yet, Walter?"

"I'm ready. Let's try it again."

They stood and listened.

More static. More clicks.

"Fahrvergnügen!" Walter yelled. Everybody's head snapped to attention before they bubbled up with laughter.

"I'm sorry. Did he just use the 'F' word?" J.J. said.

When he slapped his hand against the desk, another pop rang out then voices emerged through the crackle of static. A burst of laughter—males, females, a group of voices. Then a man spoke.

J.J. gasped and her breath grew heavy. As she scanned each face, everyone stood frozen. Not a single movement. Not even a blink. "Director Miller," Six said, remarking on the voice familiar to him—the head of CIA.

The recording continued to play.

"Oh my God, DIA. That's General Ronaldson. I'd know that Southern accent anywhere," Gia said.

"That's definitely Director Freeman," Tony said as the talking persisted. He ran his fingers through his hair. "And that one sounds like the DNI."

"This…is a…*National Security Council* meeting." Walter stood, turned his back to the desk, and leaned against it. His face went beet red and his voice sounded as if his throat had constricted. He gulped hard and said, "Do you know what this means?"

"I'll tell you what it means," Tony said. "The Russian's have ears in the White House."

J.J. shook her head. "No, this is much bigger than ears in the White House—this has to be coming from the Situation Room. And we couldn't hear this conversation over a communications line."

"*Somebody* planted a listening device," Walter said.

"Which means the Russians have a mole in the White House," J.J. said, glancing at her watch to gauge how much time they had left before the Director-issued deadline was up. They only had a few hours to get authorization for a full investigation or they'd potentially have to wait weeks to pursue this lead. "We've got to get in there and do a sweep—tonight."

"Isn't the White House Secret Service jurisdiction?" Six asked. "I don't think they'll be thrilled about FBI encroaching on their turf."

"The White House may be their turf in terms of security and presidential protection," J.J. began, "but inside the United States, any activity involving counterintelligence and counterespionage is the FBI's turf. But we probably should walk softly. Who do we know over there who can maybe help ease tensions?"

She looked to Tony first. He always hadda guy or knewa guy.

Tony thought about it and shrugged. "I've got a lot of contacts but nobody high enough at Secret Service to help us," he said. "Sorry, I got nothin'."

She turned to Gia who also shrugged and tightened her lips. "We've got analysts who brief the White House most days, and one of my friends works in the Navy Mess, but I'm afraid no contacts in Secret Service."

J.J. turned to the one person who would usually be the first to speak but hadn't made a peep of a sound since the discussion on Secret Service contacts began. "Six? What about you?" J.J. asked.

He tightened his lips and looked at the ground, avoiding the curious gazes of his colleagues. "I, uhhh, I-I-I-I don't think using my connection is a good idea."

"What's the problem?" J.J. recognized the look of anxiety on his face. As much as he liked to be the aggressor in confrontational situations, he hated when such instances were out of his control. His expression betrayed his fear. "Or should I say *who*?"

"I don't—"

"C'mon *two-point-seven-five*, can't be that bad, can it?" Tony chimed in.

Six rolled his eyes. "You might want to stay out of this one, Stallone. Trust me," he said.

J.J. cranked her neck toward Six and cocked her head to the side. "Why get snippy at *him*? He has nothing to do with your contact."

"No," Six said, "but *you* do."

"Me?" She appeared incredulous at the suggestion when the complication finally struck her—the only person in the world who wished for her demise more than Lana Michaels. "Ah, hell! I thought she went to State…to Diplomatic Security."

"She did, right up until she left to head up the White House Security Detail for Secret Service."

J.J. cut her eyes at Six and dropped her head. She cupped her forehead with the palm of her hand. "Somebody kill me! Just put a bullet between my eyes right now. Our probability of obtaining an authorization for a full investigation just went from impossible to 'You must be fucking kidding me,'" she growled. Through clenched teeth, she hissed at Six. "We're in a major pickle, and this one's all *your pickle's* fault."

"Kendel might beg to differ," Six said with a chuckle, which disappeared at the sight of J.J.'s scowl.

Gia, Walter, and Tony looked at each other confused and then at J.J. and Six.

"What on earth did I do to deserve this?" J.J. let out a long breath and rolled her eyes up at the ceiling. "Six, go ahead and make the call. Tony, record a short clip of the end of the meeting, so we have a sample that isn't classified. We're running out of time. If our twenty-four hours runs out, this case is tanked no matter what we do."

CHAPTER 10

Late Tuesday Afternoon—The West Wing

Butterflies fluttered through J.J.'s stomach as she, Tony, and Six approached the Marine in dress blues standing sentry outside the West Wing entrance. His presence signaled the President was on deck. The air of majesty was both awe-inspiring and intimidating as J.J. trailed up the circular driveway at the grand, columned north entrance; it was accented by precision-manicured shrubbery. The sense of honor and history enveloped her, brought goose bumps to J.J.'s forearm as the crisp wind coiled around her.

She'd only been to the White House once before, in what seemed a lifetime ago. Ronald Reagan was president and she was a patriot-in-the-making, rolling eggs across the South Lawn. How times had changed. This day she wore a suit instead of a ruffled blue dress; had a holster with a Glock over her shoulder rather than a patent leather white purse, and the President and she shared more than a love of country—they shared the same skin color. J.J. sensed her mother's smile in the glimmer of sun peeking through the clouds; the warmth gave her confidence to forge ahead.

In a few choreographed motions, the Marine opened the door and they paced across the threshold, Six leading the way and J.J. and Tony trailing in close behind. J.J. eyes roamed the foyer, which was formal and painted in welcoming neutral tones. She marveled at the light shimmering against the chandelier dangling overhead when Tony's voice jolted her from her daze.

"Good afternoon, I'm Special Agent Antonio Donato," he said as he flashed his credentials to the stiff, brown-haired uniformed Secret Service police officer in a starched white shirt, black tie, and dark pants. He was posted in a room at the foyer's edge leading out of the entryway and into the West Wing. Tony gestured toward J.J. and Six, introducing them in kind. "We're here to see Kendel Phillips."

The officer stood up from his desk, examined their IDs, and mumbled some jibberish into a mic attached to the wire dangling behind his ear. "Afternoon. I'll escort you all downstairs and get you a visitor's badge."

"Thank you," J.J. said, following close behind him. He led them through a narrow hall and then down a short flight of steps, each pristine room and entryway accented with rich mahogany wood accents and Victorian tables and seating wrapped in soothing blues and neutrals.

"So, what's the purpose of your visit today?" he asked, the sound of his voice somewhere between attempting small talk and collecting facts.

J.J. glanced at Six and Tony and replied, "We're here to coordinate on an urgent matter. Can't really disclose more than that." Just past the stairway was a security post on the right and a second lobby area ahead and toward the left. "So, uhh…the President's in?"

"Yes, ma'am. He's attending a meeting in the Sit Room on a VTC…with Putin. Should be leaving shortly."

He nodded. "This way please." He spoke to another agent briefly who handed him three visitor's badges. He passed them out and they each clipped them to their lapels. "Agent Phillips will be out momentarily. I'll make sure she's on the way." He disappeared down a short corridor. J.J. spotted the Secret Service shield on a wall in the back.

Moments later, a stylish black woman clad in a sophisticated navy suit and rimless eyeglasses, about J.J.'s height, sauntered up the hall. The tight bun in her hair gave her a stuffy but elegant appearance. The closer she got to the group, the more her eyes narrowed. She barely glanced at J.J. before locking a searing gaze on Six. In her heart of hearts, she knew things were about to get ugly. And fast.

"Agent McCall. Six," she said tersely without ever shifting her glare from him. "What brings you here…*today of all days*? This couldn't wait?"

Six looked down at the vintage Omega beaming from his wrist and backed out of arm's reach. "I…I, uhh, didn't realize the date."

Kendel tightened her lips. "Wouldn't be the first time, would it Z?"

Tony leaned over to J.J. and whispered, "Z?"

"Zero," she whispered through clenched teeth. "It was Zoro before the break-up."

"Sorry," Six interrupted, his expression one of genuine angst. "But, no, this couldn't wait."

After noticing Six's flustered demeanor, J.J. glanced down at the date on her own watch—November 10th. She closed her eyes briefly and shook her head. In a flash, a colossal white elephant soaked up all the oxygen in the room…and it was dressed in a strapless, floor-length Vera Wang with a lace veil.

"I think you're the only one I've not met," she said turning to Tony, flashing a fake smile. "I'm Agent Kendel Phillips. Secret Service. You are?"

"Special Agent Antonio Donato." He extended his hand. "Tony's fine."

"Yes you are," she mumbled in a voice inaudible to everyone except J.J., whose face crumpled.

She cut her eyes at Kendel before catching herself and relaxing her tension.

"Uhhh, thank you Agent Donato. Shall we step into my office," she said leading them back through the cramped corridor. They passed a few offices on the left and right until arriving at the Secret Service section in the rear.

Kendel led them into her constricted office with oversized mahogany furniture that took up precious free space. J.J. and Tony took the two seats in front of her desk while Six remained standing. She waited for everyone to settle in, then leaned back in her seat and defensively folded her arms over her chest. "So," she said scanning each face at the table before returning her gaze to J.J. "This must be a serious matter for Six to risk coming to see me. What's going on?"

J.J.'s gaze darted to Tony and back at Kendel. "Well, one of the Gs tracked a Russian intelligence officer conducting an op at the Ellipse a few days ago. Long story short, Russian intelligence has installed a listening device in the White House."

Kendel let out a sharp breath, sat forward in her seat, and shook her head, incredulous at the notion. "You mean you suspect."

"No, it's here," J.J. said.

"Impossible!" she yelled, appearing insulted, yet unsure. "My security team conducts weekly sweeps."

A crawling sensation started in J.J.'s hand, seeping up through her arm and shoulder. She jerked back and bit her lips to maintain her composure. Kendel was lying—J.J. didn't know about what and didn't have time to drill deeper. She made a mental note of it and moved on. Her most pressing challenge was to get Kendel's cooperation with the least stink possible, and doing so without applying excessive pressure now appeared unavoidable.

Six said, "Well there must be a problem with your sweeps. Otherwise, we wouldn't be here. We all heard it."

"You all heard it, where?"

"Here. Coming from the Sit Room," Tony answered.

Kendel stood to her feet and slammed her palm against the desk. "We've got dozens of officers on this property every day and an upgraded security system. There's no way in hell a Russian installed a bug in the Sit Room."

J.J. waited for a reaction, but none came. "It's funny, you know, how you phrased it," J.J. said, "because we don't believe *a Russian* did."

Tony continued. "Based on the evidence we've collected so far, Director Freeman's authorized a full investigation. We have the authority to conduct our own sweeps right now, but we'd appreciate and frankly expect maximum cooperation from your office," he bluffed.

"I'm sure you do," Kendel said as she returned to her seat. "But if anyone's going to conduct a sweep in the Sit Room, it'll be Secret Service." She bent forward and, with her index finger, pointed to the nameplate on her desk that read Chief of White House Security. "In case you hadn't noticed, this is *my house.*"

J.J. jerked her head backward, looked down at the floor, and started to bark out a reply but choked down her initial response. She only had a couple of hours left to gather the evidence she needed to justify the full investigation. Her patience was wearing thin and her time short. While her second-thought told her she might catch more bees with honey, a voice vaguely sounding like her ornery Auntie Adelaide said, "Sometimes you've got to be a bitch to check one."

She leaned forward, rested her elbows against her knees, and oozed a forced calmness as she retorted, "I don't mean any disrespect, Kendel. I realize this situation must be difficult for you. After all, Six is, well…Six. But I must remind you that Tony and I are FBI Special Agents conducting a possible espionage investigation involving Russian intelligence on U.S. soil."

"And?" Kendel snapped with a slight roll of the eye.

J.J. suppressed the "Oh no you didn't" and snapped, "Well, according to the United States Congress, when a case involves Russian intelligence and espionage on American soil, *my house* is bigger than *your house*—and it includes the Situation Room."

Kendel froze, clearly taken aback by J.J.'s brashness.

"Now I can have my director call your director," J.J. continued, "or you can put on your big girl panties, lose the attitude and escort us to the Sit Room. Then you can report to the President that because of your cooperative spirit, Boris the Russian diplomat won't be able to listen in the next time he and the National Security Council are deciding what *not* to discuss with the Russian National Security Chief during an upcoming visit," J.J. cocked her head to the side. "And since this is *your room* in *my house*, I'll let you decide where we go from here."

J.J. had crossed a major line of engagement and prayed her no-nonsense approach would work. If Kendel picked up the phone and called FBI Headquarters to kick up a stink with Director Freeman—all their effort would be for naught. Freeman would put the kibosh on the entire operation and she'd go back to leading her analytical working group until she quit. The Task Force had a mission to accomplish and there was no time for the stone-wall, ball breaking that plagued cooperation between law enforcement agencies. Besides, Kendel's frustration had more to do with the fact that Six fell in love with J.J. than any legitimate beef about jurisdictional encroachment.

"Play the clip for her, Tony."

He pulled out his cell phone and played back the information from his voice recorder.

Her eyes widened before her face contorted into a scowl. Her lips curled as she seethed and stewed in her own anger. She'd made it painfully clear she had no intention of extending anyone an olive branch except to beat Six over the head with it…and maybe J.J. too.

"Well?" J.J. asked.

After a few moments of focused thought, she ran her fingers through her hair before hissing, "What do you need?"

J.J. exhaled and concealed her relief. "We've got a sweep team on standby not even ten minutes away."

"Fine!" Kendel said. "But when they don't find anything, I expect an apology for your lack of professionalism."

"My lack of— Listen heif—" J.J. began before Tony nudged her.

He leaned over and whispered, "We got what we came for. Leave well enough alone."

J.J. cut her eyes at him and tightened her lip.

"May I use your phone?" Tony asked.

Kendel nodded. "They'll need White House clearance or we can't give them access today."

Tony looked a J.J. then back at Kendel. "Uh, Walter Lowenstein from NSA counterintelligence is cleared. He can conduct the sweep. We just need you to get him in the gate."

"I'm on it," she stood, walked to the door, and opened it. "Now if you'll all step outside for a few moments. I'll make the necessary arrangements and escort you downstairs."

After stepping outside and shuttering at the slam, Six said, "That went better than I expected."

Tony shot him a side-eye. "Well, what the hell did you expect? To get shot? Because that meeting was just slightly less painful than death," Tony said before turning to J.J. "Now, somebody wanna tell me what's so freakin' special about today's date?"

Six and J.J. glanced at each other, then at Tony, and in unison replied, "No!"

Tony strode into the corridor and shot back a blank glance over his shoulder. "I'm going to step outside to make a call. I'll be back in a couple minutes."

Standing outside Kendel's office, J.J. smirked and turned to Six as he studied her expression. "What is it, Six? You keep looking at me like I have spinach in my teeth," she said running her tongue along the top row.

"No, no. Trying to figure out what's up with you and the Italian Stallion. The air between you two was so cold I think my balls caught frostbite."

J.J. chuckled and shook her head. "Is your brain in any way connected to your mouth?"

"Don't try to deflect the question. Answer me."

"If I wanted to talk about it, I would've." She shrugged and paced ahead. "Let's just say, what happened between you and me last Friday was a game changer. Things between Tony and I will never be the same."

CHAPTER 11

The Smirnov's burn in J.J.'s throat served as a coarse reminder that she had knuckled under at the first hard blow, leveled by the human upper-cut called Grayson "Six" Chance. In five minutes, her life had taken a calamitous turn. One minute, she'd crossed the threshold into the FBI Headquarters Executive Conference room where Director Freeman had announced she'd be leading the Phantom Hunter Task Force along with her new love, her co-case agent Antonio Donato. By minute five, Six's lips were parting from hers and Tony walked in just in time to catch an eyeful of the remnants of their embrace, one J.J. neither invited nor welcomed.

After Sunnie left and her nerves calmed, J.J. set off to find Tony. She needed to make things right. Overcoming Tony's stubbornness would be a difficult feat. Walking in on the disturbing scene no doubt ignited his ire and put a chink in his macho Italian armor.

She paced back to the office, rehearsing her speech with every step. *You didn't see what you thought you saw...Okay, you did, but it's not what you think...Okay, it is what you think, but he kissed me first...Okay, I kissed him back, but not much.*

Nothing sounded reasonable. If the shoe were on the other foot, she wouldn't have believed a single excuse. Any attempt at explaining would've been met with a detailed description of the many express routes he could take to hell. In her final analysis, only one truth mattered. Whatever her wayward lips succumbed to at the moment, her *heart* belonged to Tony—and Tony alone.

J.J. flung her purse over her shoulder and gathered her inner strength as she twisted the doorknob. She stepped inside her office and scanned the area for Tony. Most cubicles were empty except for a couple of voices mumbling back near Tony's space. She wasn't surprised. Everyone tended to cut out early on Fridays if they put their hours in throughout the week. J.J. stood on her tip-toes to view over the top of the cubicles and noticed a brunette hovering around. A burst of jealousy quickened her steps. Just as she suspected—Gia Campioni, the DIA counterintelligence specialist and member of Task Force Phantom Hunter.

J.J. growled in a low steady rumble as her stomach hardened. From the moment the interloper laid eyes on Tony, she knew Gia had put a target on his back. Her eyes were filled with the hope of a woman who longed to take the bull by its horn so-to-speak. As J.J. made her way up the aisle, Gia did a double-take before sidestepping to allow J.J. to enter

"Hey, Tony," J.J. said. "You ran off before I had a chance to explain what happened. Can we talk for a minute?"

When Tony glared at J.J., eyes narrowed, Gia's gaze shifted nervously between them before she grabbed her purse and jacket from Tony's guest chair. "Uhhh, I know you two have a lot of work to do. Tony, if you get time tonight I'm heading up the block to Gordon Biersch. Maybe you'd like to stop by and have a drink." She turned to J.J. and with much less enthusiasm said, "Of course you're welcome too."

"I'm sure," J.J. snapped as she returned the cold sentiment. "But, no thank you. As you said, I've got work to do."

J.J. watched Gia leave, waiting until she heard the door to shut before turning to speak to Tony.

"Seriously? Gia? The corpse of our relationship isn't even room temperature yet," J.J. whispered in aggressive hushes.

"Really, J.J.?" Tony responded, his expression tightly pinched and his cheeks visibly flush. He lowered his voice. "Don't even try to turn the tables on me. What you experienced is nothing compared to what I walked in on!"

She slipped into his guest chair and pulled it close to him.

With his face crumpled, Tony closely examined hers.

"Something in my nose?" she asked.

"No, something's missing," he said. "Ohhh, yeah. Six's lips!"

She released a heavy sigh. "That's how you're going to carry this?"

He turned from her, aligned his fingers to the keyboard, and tapped annoyingly loud. His bullheadedness never ceased to amaze her. She never believed the day would come in which she'd bear the brunt of it.

She struggled to find the right words to say. She opened her mouth and hoped they would come.

"Look at me," she said, her eyes chasing his. She needed him to believe her sincerity and hear the truth in her tone. Still he refused. "Please, Tony. Look at me."

He didn't turn around. Just kept typing up his report.

"Okay, fine. The only reason I even stayed behind is to tell him in no uncertain terms that I don't love him anymore. Whatever he wants or believes, my heart belongs to someone else. Before the words formed in my mouth, bam! On my mother's grave, I didn't welcome it. He caught me totally off-guard."

He abruptly stopped and turned to her. "What about the picture on your entertainment shelf?"

"It's gone. Last night. In about fifty pieces at the bottom of my trash can, along with the Belvedere bottles. I'm trying, Tony. I'm trying."

He shifted his gaze back toward the computer. "Well, if I was the right man for you, maybe you wouldn't have to try so hard."

Her rapid blinking was followed by an open stare. "Or perhaps this situation presented the excuse you needed to pursue more *family friendly* options at the bar tonight."

He cut his eyes at her. "You must be freaking kidding me. Man, you've got a hefty pair given that we're here because of you."

"No, Tony, we're here because of Six," J.J. replied. Then she disobeyed her mother's biggest piece of advice—she asked the question she didn't want the answer to. "You're attracted to her, aren't you?"

Her stomach plummeted. She knew there was a possibility her gift would tell her much more than she really wanted to know. But she needed to know.

"How do you expect me to respond?" he asked.

"With the truth."

He rolled his eyes and hesitated before barking, "No!"

A sharp stab jabbed at her heart, which was unrelated to the intense itching sensation permeating her feet. He did have a thing for Gia. For the first time, he'd deliberately lied to her. She rose to her feet sullen and defeated.

"I'm going to my desk. Director Freeman expects our report by close of business."

"Whateva," he mumbled under his breath.

J.J. sulked with every step toward her cubicle and collapsed into her chair. She hadn't anticipated this level of anger from him. She hoped Tony would cool down and drop by her desk later, but she realized convincing him that Six meant nothing to her would be difficult. The question was how to convince him that he meant more? And even if she managed to convince him, did she mean anything to him? If he could switch his feelings off like a light switch, maybe his words to her last night were as empty as her heart felt that moment.

She wondered if this conflict was a sign they weren't as compatible as she'd hoped. Maybe Gia would be a better match. An attraction that crumbled under the weight of one week's turmoil may suggest they weren't meant to be together. The mere thought gave her a migraine, so she rejected the notion by refocusing her attention on other pressing matters—like her own safety.

She needed to plan her next steps.

Lana was still on the streets, no doubt drowning in rage, desperate, and vengeful, which made her a very insidious threat to both J.J. and Tony. J.J. would need to be extra vigilant about her safety with every move she made, on guard every moment of every day. While J.J. had no clue about Lana's strategy to strike back at her, she knew Lana's success would culminate with one of two events—J.J.'s admission to a hospital or burial in a casket—unless she got to Lana first.

As J.J. stirred in her thoughts, the phone rang. She eyed the caller ID and hesitated to answer. She didn't recognize the Northern Virginia number and feared Six might be trying to woo her. After second-guessing herself, she picked up the receiver.

"McCall."

"Uh, J.J.? This is Debbie. Debbie Cartwright. We met last year at the Christmas Party," the woman said as her soft voice trembled. She was the wife of James Cartwright, the former FBI Assistant Director of Counterintelligence and father of two who Lana murdered before attempting to make her escape to Moscow. "I hope I'm not catching you at a bad time."

"Oh my goodness, Mrs. Cartwright. I hardly know what to say. I'm...I'm so deeply sorry for your loss. Jim was a good man."

"Thank you for those kind words at this difficult time. I hope he's remembered that way. He just..." Her voice cracked then trailed off. Moments later J.J. was deflated by a barrage of sniffles.

"Are you okay?" J.J. asked as if she had the power to ease what she could only imagine must be crippling grief.

"I'm sorry. It's all so overwhelming. News reporters camped outside on the front lawn. FBI Agents turning my house inside out. It's all just ... so overwhelming," she said, collecting herself.

"How are you and the girls holding up?"

"We're all devastated of course. The girls are struggling to understand. I'm trying to help them understand situations I can't even begin to grasp myself," Debbie said. "But we do what me must, right? With God's grace and mercy, we'll make it through."

"Yes…you certainly will," J.J. said, still confused as to the reason Debbie had called to speak with her. After a lengthy, uncomfortable pause, she continued. "Is...Is there something that I can do for you? As you can imagine, things are pretty crazy here."

"Oh, of course, dear," Debbie said. "I called because I was going through Jim's things. He had the forethought to collect his insurance policies, retirement accounts, and such. And among the paperwork, I found a letter specifically addressed to you. His secretary, Sue, gave me your number."

J.J.'s eyebrows scrunched. "Jim left a letter for me?"

"Yes. Marked 'For J.J. McCall Only'," she said. "It's thin, one or two pages at the most. I thought you might want to come by and pick it up."

J.J. shifted in her seat and sat back. Her mind began to spin, wondering if he wrote the confession she suspected he'd planned to deliver before his death. She was tempted to ask Debbie to open the envelope but decided against it. She didn't want to add anymore to Debbie's hurt and confusion than humanly necessary. J.J. sensed her struggle to come to grips with the man she loved and the man she was now discovering him to be. "I can't imagine what it could be. I'm finishing up a report for the Director today. Would it be possible for me to stop by tomorrow?"

"Absolutely. We're having family here about noon, following the memorial service. Any time later would be fine."

She fell back into her seat, curiosity piqued. He died before he and she could meet. She had an inkling about the contents, but she'd have to wait until Saturday to find out for certain.

Chapter 12

Later that Friday

Took her a little over an hour but J.J. had finished her report when the office door opened and closed.

She stood up, and called out, "Hello? Tony? Anybody?"

No one responded, so she grabbed her report and made her way to Tony's space. His desk was dark and clean except for a short stack of paper. He'd shut off his computer and hadn't so much as bothered to leave a Post-it note saying goodbye. She grabbed his stack, scanned them, and headed to Director Freeman's office. She'd drop them off with Mrs. Whitehouse.

Her heart ached. Tony had left to meet Gia for drinks. How could she compete with Pantene hair and Sicilian genes? Seemed their relationship had ended before it began. Tears welled behind her eyes, but she stubbornly refused to let them fall.

She entered her cubicle and printed out her section of the report, placed both in a folder, and delivered them to Mrs. Whitehouse's desk in the director's office and paced quickly to her car.

As she pulled out of the FBI garage and waited for the guards to lower the barrier, she wondered what more she could've said or done to make him understand and believe her. At that moment, an epiphany told her to take the leap and say the one thing she had not yet said.

She grabbed her cellphone and called him, expecting his voicemail. When she heard the beep, she spoke the words her head could not force her heart to silence.

One last thing...I love you.

Her greatest fear, more painful than outright rejection, was deep-seated dread that his behavior reflected the fact that he did not share the same feelings. It struck her, the courage she'd displayed, baring her heart to a man who might be in the arms of another. She had no regrets, though, and she'd done everything possible to prevent it.

There was truly nothing left to do.

And even less to say.

CHAPTER 13

Late Friday Afternoon—FBI Headquarters

Director Russell Freeman released the tie from his neck and collapsed into his office chair. He stared out the window and watched the cloudless sky succumb to dense mounds of silver. The dizzy spell had passed but he was still a little short of breath. He'd regretted bumping his doctor's appointment three times in the last four week to handle the massive fallout from Assistant Director Jim Cartwright's murder, Agent Chris Johnson's arrest, Jake McGee's death, and Agent Lana Michaels' escape. But the powers that be refused to wait for answers. His confidence in leaving agents McCall and Donato in charge of Task Force Phantom Hunter eased his angst, particularly given the mettle they'd demonstrated in identifying the ICE Phantom, but Lana Michaels' disappearance troubled him.

He sifted through the stack of phone messages that his secretary, Mrs. Whitehouse, had left for him. Two from the DNI. One from Rayna, his beautiful wife. One from SAC MacDonald, who headed up the Washington Field Office. And the last from US Marshall Service Director. Deputies from his department had been working non-stop alongside WFO agents in a joint effort to hunt down Lana. He hoped the bounty on her head might yield some loose tongues, but he didn't care whether they located her dead or alive. After the cold-blooded murder of his dear friend Jim Cartwright, he wanted her off the streets, and would exhaust every resource in the entire law enforcement community if he must to ensure she'd pay for her actions. He only hoped John had positive news to report.

"Hey, Russell?" Acting Assistant Director John Nixon called out in his blustery Southern twang from the threshold of Freeman's office door. Freeman turned to his voice, his eye drawn to Nixon's his coal-colored coif that had somehow escaped the stress-born grey peppering in his own hair. "Can I speak with you for a minute? I've got an update on the Michaels investigation."

Freeman waved him inside and asked him to have a seat. Nixon, the lone senior executive holdover from the previous administration, was a solid counterbalance to Freeman's own easygoing manner. But his inability to separate his personal leanings and agendas from FBI business might cost him more than Freeman's trust. "Good news, I hope. After this week, I'd be excited to hear the FBI still had the authority to conduct investigations."

"Well, we can conduct investigations," Nixon said, pressing his lips together in a tight grimace. "But I'm afraid there's no sign of her anywhere. Apparently, we trained her well. Metro Police located footage of her entering the Alexandria metro station. They're still reviewing to find out where she exited."

"What about her house? Any activity?"

John shook his head. "It's cordoned off and we've had ERT at the premises around the clock recovering evidence. That's the last place Lana will turn up."

"So she could be anywhere," Freeman said. "I think we can all agree her primary objective at this point is to get the hell out of the United States. She won't risk buying travel documents from an FBI snitch."

"No, we think the Russians will attempt to make a drop with money and travel docs."

"What about the Russian Embassy? Any intelligence officers been spotted outside the compound?"

"No one's left the embassy since the news broke. Security's locked down for the near future," Nixon said. "Stanislav Vorobyev is still scheduled to depart today. Dmitriyev, who we believe will take over as Security Chief, will probably drive him to Dulles and pick up Yuriy Filchenko, the new Counterintelligence Chief."

Freeman nodded. J.J. had already revealed she'd recruited Dmitriyev. If any op had been planned J.J. would find out before anyone.

"Think they'll attempt to fill a dead-drop for Lana?" Freeman asked.

"Doubt it," Nixon replied. "Dmitriyev's a declared officer and can't engage in operational activity, plus we'll have them covered like wax on a hairy ass. They'll wait a few days before conducting any operational activity. The heat's high and the Bureau smells blood," John reasoned. "Lana's the wildcard. They won't disavow her so they'll attempt to provide support at some point. Even so, the question is whether she'll risk returning to the grid to receive it. In the meantime, we've got a potentially more critical issue to deal with."

Freeman rolled his eyes and took a seat on the edge of his desk. "God, what now?"

"Lana kept a journal, random thoughts, in an encrypted file on her computer." John rubbed his forehead. "To say she harbored great resentment toward Agents McCall and Donato would be an understatement. And hate was an accurate description before Agent McCall killed the love of her life. With Jake McGhee dead, we think Lana's going to avenge his death before she's extracted to Moscow."

"You mean she's going to try to kill J.J.?"

John nodded. "She's bitter, angry, and desperate. J.J. recruited her countrymen to spy against the Russians and was attempting to decimate Lana's plans to return to Moscow as a hero to her country, according to the journal entries. And she's got one hell of an ugly temper. She'll be hell bent on getting revenge."

"So, what's the plan?"

"Obviously, we have to protect Agent McCall," Nixon said. "And, if I may speak frankly, McCall is a loose cannon and shouldn't be authorized to support this investigation. She needs to sit this one on the sidelines. Doing so might offer us key opportunity to find Lana."

"Opportunity? Explain."

"Lana's coming for her, but we don't know when or how. We'd like to put a small team of Gs on J.J. until Lana's caught. Maybe rotate two or three of our best personnel. Unobtrusive twenty-four seven coverage. If the Gs spot anything suspicious, if she makes any attempt on J.J.'s life, they can call in support."

"We can't spare a team. Resources are thin right now. I'll authorize one during third shift. Best I can do." Freeman gave a tentative nod and let out a strained chuckle. "You ever met Agent McCall?"

"Once or twice. She's a good agent, don't get me wrong. But you give her entirely too much latitude."

Freeman pinched his lips together; his brow furrowed and released. "Interesting. She and Agent Donato have worked side-by-side on every investigation, yet you're not complaining about his latitude."

Nixon swallowed hard, his eyes shifted to the right.

"You and I both know this has nothing to do with *latitude* and everything to do with her genes," Freeman snapped.

"That's not—"

"Please." Freeman threw up his hand and stopped him before he began. "I haven't been director for very long, but I've been here long enough. Bottom line is Agents McCall *and* Donato get latitude because *they* get results," he said. "With that said, this is for her safety. The plan is not optional, no matter how much she balks. Let her know that when you break the news."

"I'm happy too."

"I'm sure you are."

John chuckled. "Anything else, Director?"

"Yes. You'll need to deliver one more piece of bad news."

"What's that?"

"I had a meeting with the DNI and CIA director today. They've requested we stand-down all Russian operations until further notice."

"Stand-down?! Do they realize we're in the middle of a man…woman-hunt for a Russian intelligence officer who killed an FBI agent? The daughter of an intelligence officer working in the Russian Embassy? I mean, c'mon."

"I understand and trust me, I conveyed as much myself," Freeman said. "But the CIA is conducting a sensitive operation with a high-level SVR recruitment. If the CIA handler is expelled or PNG'd, the entire community will lose a critical source of intelligence."

A misplaced smile overtook Nixon's face before he asked, "So, that's it for the task force?"

"Easy, John. Your Alabama is showing," Freeman said, gently reminding Nixon of who he was…and what he knew.

"Russell, you know this has absolutely nothing to do with race."

"And everything to do with genes…neither of which Agent McCall can do anything about," Freeman replied. "Regardless, it's out of my hands, at least until the CIA asset makes the next drop and Lebed returns to Moscow." The Russian National Security Director who was scheduled to visit in a week and the President had tied Freeman's hands until it was over.

"What are you going to do when she quits?"

"She won't. The FBI is in her blood. She can't shake it. By the time she cools off, she'll be operational again and Task Force Phantom Hunter will proceed as planned."

"If you say so. I'm just marching to orders," John said, offering a playful salute.

"I do," Freeman agreed, his mind shifting to J.J.'s latest recruit, Aleksey Dmitriyev. "In other news, what do we know about this Filchenko, the new CI Chief?"

"Our intel says he's one of Golikov's most trusted officers, an ambitious backstabber who would cut his own mother's throat to posture himself for a higher position. On the other hand, it's his first tour and operating against the FBI is no picnic," Nixon said. "I've gotta say, I'm relieved J.J. doesn't have any recruitments in the embassy right now. If Filchenko even got a whiff that we had recruited an intelligence officer in the Embassy he'd be a Golikov victim before we could say, 'espionage.'"

"Last and final question," Freeman said. "Who at WFO is on the Michaels investigation?"

"The only FBI agent who wants to takedown Lana more than J.J."

CHAPTER 14

Special Agent in Charge of the Washington Field Office, Greg MacDonald, made head turns with his imposing presence as he rushed through the Counterintelligence squad bay. His Eastwood attitude and ceaseless thousand-yard glare outstripped the timidity of his lanky frame and conservative suit. He quickened his pace, zigzagging between cubicles until he reached his favorite supervisor, trained by MacDonald himself. Twenty- years before, Kyle and his best buddy strutted out of Quantico, both cocksure, hard-headed rookies eager to make their first arrests…at least until MacDonald schooled them. Years later, Kyle would learn his most important lesson from Mac: controlling an operation could often yield more long-term success than a quick arrest and a little press—the soul of counterintelligence.

Kyle's office was off to the left and to the rear of the squad bay. Although one would never use the word spacious to describe its size, an array of family photos and Redskins paraphernalia coating the walls and desk made it his home away from home. MacDonald, peered inside the office and knocked on the door frame.

Kyle's back was turned to Mac as his fingers tapped furiously against his keyboard. So deep in his thoughts, he didn't realize anyone was standing behind him.

"Hey Kyle, how're you holding up?" Mac asked, knowing he, more than anyone else in the Bureau, was still reeling from the stunning loss of his best friend. Raw grief is the reason Mac selected him as the agent best-suited to arrest Lana Michaels and take her off the streets. Kyle was someone he could trust, someone with the right connections on both sides of the law, and one thing no other agent had.

Startled, Kyle jumped and snapped his head toward the door. "Jeez, you scared the shit out of me," he squelched before pressing his hand against his chest. "I'm not. I feel like a piece of shit, my wife's giving me hell, and you may not want to come too close. Think I caught the bubonic plague."

"I'll take my chances." MacDonald took a seat in the guest chair and leaned forward, elbows to knees. He eyed the pile of used tissues cluttering his old friend's desk. The consummate anti-bureaucrat, Kyle shunned the standard Brooks Brother uniform for Dockers and plain button-ups. Despite the slightly contorted pained expression furrowing Kyle's brow, Mac proceeded, knowing he'd be compounding his friend's present miseries.

"Bet I don't need to ask what brings you down from the throne," Kyle said. "It's my fault. From day one, I had doubts, concerns. Never followed-up on them. Now look at what's happened," Kyle said, his voice faintly above a whisper. "*I* created the bomb. Lit the fuse. The explosion was inevitable … I just never dreamed it would take my best friend's life."

"Jim made choices neither you nor I could control," Mac said. "You did your job. We all did. We're all culpable. After chasing our tails for a decade after Hanssen, nobody in the entire community took the intel on the second mole seriously."

"RAZOR was right all along, and we all but marched him to his death."

Mac's voice tensed. "We accepted the word of an agent who conducted an asset validation and provided full justification for her findings. We had no way of knowing Michaels was playing executioner. The fact of the matter is, it's done. To sit here and stew in our missteps would be yet another mistake we don't have time to make. We need to get her off the street—now."

"Of all the agents in the Bureau…you picked me?" Kyle said, chuckling to himself. "No ulterior motives there, huh?"

Kyle could anticipate Agent Michaels' every move and beat her at the game the FBI had taught her—the game Kyle himself had taught her as her mentor during her rotation at Washington Field. Since the news of her treacherous fall from grace, Kyle had been laden with sadness and guilt, hitting a tailspin into a pit of internal despair. Mac hoped this assignment would pull him out of it…eventually.

"You've got eyes where most people won't think to look, and you've got one quality no other agent in Washington Field has."

"What's that?"

"Strong personal motivation," Mac said. "With you at the helm, we'll get her safely tucked away in Super Max before she hits another agent."

Kyle settled in his thoughts as the room grew quiet. "All right. But I'll do it on my own. My way."

Mac raised his eyebrow and waited. "Uh, not exactly. I'm assigning a co-case agent. Whether you realize it or not, you need help on this."

After a few grunts, Kyle considered the proposition. "Okay, who're you thinking about, Davidson? Smith?"

MacDonald shook his head. "Hopper."

Kyle's back slammed against the chair and his eyes widened. "You've got to be fucking kidding me! He's a hardheaded 12 year old know-it-all whose only concern is bagging bank robbers."

Mac laughed out loud sparking Kyle's apparent confusion. "Remind you of anyone? That's exactly why picked him."

"I was different," Kyle said, shaking his head, realizing he was the butt of an unfunny joke. "I listened. I followed instructions. And even if that's all a lie, at least I could take a joke."

"Yeah…not so much. Someone cared enough to set you on the right track. Pay it forward."

Kyle stood up and walked to the window. He stared out into the distance. "I'll do this under one condition," he said, his eyes locked on the auburn sky. "I want the death penalty. No bullshit plea bargains. Ten consecutive life sentences wouldn't be enough to make up for this."

Mac's lips pinched together as he exhaled. He understood Kyle's pain better than anyone else; he also knew his limitations. However personally driven, the investigation must adhere to the rule of law. "I'll do what I can, Kyle, but the Bureau avoids trials on Espionage cases for a reason. We have sources to protect. Just between you and me, though," he lowered his voice to just above a whisper. "I told you to get her off the street…I didn't say *how*."

Kyle nodded and a slight grin edged corner of his mouth upward. They exchanged approving nods and MacDonald stood to exit the door.

"Great. Keep me updated. I want daily briefings." He stepped through the threshold, froze, and leaned back to add his parting words of advice. "Don't let your emotions get the best of you, my friend. Control them…or they will control you."

CHAPTER 15

Friday—Russian Embassy, Washington, D.C.

The day after Svetlana Mikhaylova's escape from custody, Aleksey Dmitriyev, and the other senior Russian intelligence officers, gathered in their secure conference room. Now that their operative had been caught operating under deep cover in the FBI, they needed to discuss their strategy. He dreaded attending the meeting or helping their precious Svetlana. It was because of her that the man he called brother was recalled from Washington back to Moscow and tortured at the hands of Mashkov. His close friend Vorobyev was nearly beaten to death by Golikov's goons at her behest. If she rotted in an American death chamber, it would be more than she ever deserved. He wanted her to die, and he wanted to choke the life out of her with his bare hands.

"No one is to leave the compound without my authorization. No meetings, no nothing if I have not given my expressed consent," the Resident ordered. Andrei Komarov served as the most senior Russian intelligence officer posted in the Washington Embassy. He met with the key members of the staff involved in the debacle termed by the media as "The Mikhaylova Affairs."

A member of the more sophisticated political operational line, his English skills had been perfected such that he could speak with no detectable Russian accent in the company of Americans. He also relished in his lady-killer reputation, nicknaming himself the *bunny trap* for his ability to successfully target assets of the female persuasion and corrupt them into cooperation with relative ease.

"The FBI must have six teams posted outside. Every gate covered. They're not even trying to disguise their activity anymore," said the Resident, pinching his squared jaw as he peered out the tinted conference room windows into the streets surrounding the compound. He feared the increased traffic stream in the area was no coincidence.

"Mikhaylova—the Red Honeytrap as the American press calls her, as well as the NOC arrests in Moscow, have caused quite a stir."

"The FBI views Svetlana as an American agent of a foreign power and she murdered a senior FBI official on behalf of a foreign service. In their eyes, she's a traitor of the worst kind," said Dmitriyev, hoping with every shred of his being that the FBI found her before she managed her escape to Moscow. "They will not stop searching until she's in custody or dead."

The senior intelligence officers circling the table all nodded in agreement.

"Without question," the Resident began, as his azure glare cut across the table and caused his underlings to shrink in his presence, "but we cannot stand down our operations and our ability to provide her with the necessary support is limited at best. We are paralyzed and mobilizing our deep cover personnel to support her will put them in equally grave danger and that's unacceptable."

"I agree. We cannot afford to shut down our critical operations," said the Political Chief. "Our contacts refuse to meet with us until this controversy dies down, which elevates the priority of the intelligence we're collecting from RAPTURE. We must extricate Mikhaylova from the United States soon. I needn't remind anyone here that inspections are underway."

If higher-ups determined the Washington Residency was ineffective during inspections, they risked losing personnel and funding for their missions.

"I agree," said Lana's father, Mikhaylov. He had only one goal—to ensure his daughter's safe travel to Moscow. "Svetlana can't stay underground much longer. The more time we take to conduct the dead-drop and provide her travel documentation and money, the greater the risk she will be apprehended. She devoted her entire life to conducting this operation on behalf of her country. We *cannot* fail her."

Dmitriyev sighed. He understood that Mikhaylov was speaking with a father's desperation.

"How do you propose we service the dead-drop and arrange travel, Comrade?" Dmitriyev asked only because his position required it. The words tasted like acid in his mouth. "Even if she retrieves the package from the drop location, American authorities have blanketed the area. Comrade Komarov has said so himself. We can hardly take a shit without some surveillance team handing us toilet paper. Our chance of getting her out on a flight to Moscow is non-existent. Impossible."

Lana's father tapped his temple with his index finger. "I've come up with an idea. While somewhat risky, it's much less so than the usual routes." He clasped his hands together as he cleared his throat. "She's booked to travel to France on a freighter ship that accommodates passenger transit. Our trusted agent is a crewmember who can ensure safe passage. The crews are usually foreigners; only small groups of five to twelve people can board at a time, so it's unlikely that she would be identified. Our agent will keep her name off the manifest and ensure they conduct only a cursory check of her documentation if at all."

The Resident nodded. "This sounds like a very good idea, Comrade. When is she set to leave?"

"She *must* leave next Sunday—nine days from today—otherwise he will not return for four months. I'll work with Dmitriyev on a plan to get her the money and a new passport. We have a very small window of time to extract her and it is quickly closing."

"Agreed," he responded. "We must act now. I'll contact the Center for final approval."

"I foresee another significant problem," Dmitriyev interjected, as it was his job to do, being the new Security Chief. "The Americans probably suspect we will attempt to deliver instructions, money, documentation, or some combination of the three. You need only look outside the compound to see the amount of surveillance they'll assign to anyone who exits the gates, intelligence or otherwise."

"Yes, this is a problem, and we cannot count support from our Ministry brethren either," he replied, referring to the diplomats assigned to the Ministry of Foreign Affairs. They were often antagonistic toward

Russian intelligence, too many hardened memories of the KGB. "How do you propose we address this?"

Dmitriyev pinched his bottom lip and tapped his finger against it. Then he stood and paced the room, his crisp white sleeves rolled to the elbow and the razor sharp creases in his slacks slightly buckled after enduring third meeting that morning.

He carefully considered his options. The thought of supporting her made him want to projectile vomit, but in order to secure his access to the critical intelligence he needed to provide the FBI, he would need to demonstrate his competency, even though temporarily complicating FBI efforts to find the witch. So, he said, "We should take the Americans on...uh, how do they say it, a *wild duck chase?*"

"Goose," Mikhaylov said. "I'm sure it's goose.

Everyone at the table sat at attention waiting for him to expand on his explanation.

"Go on," the Resident said.

"The FBI is expecting us to conduct an operation, this is no secret. So, let's give them what they're looking for," he scanned around the room and locked eyes on Lana's father. "We'll, send comrade Aleksandr out. Svetlana is his daughter; they will expect him to support the operation. We should also include counterintelligence; it will appear as if they are providing security or countersurveillance," Dmitriyev continued, more pleased with himself. He knew the FBI would catch on quickly and likely devise a counter-operation to neutralize them. "Perhaps the new Counterintelligence Chief—they will assume he is little more than a decoy because he's new. We'll take them on a few surveillance detection runs and then return immediately to the embassy without conducting any hint of an operation. We'll repeat this daily; it won't take them long to identify the pattern. In two or three days, they will assume we're playing with them and back off. That's when we can fill the dead drop. But if we get an opportunity to conduct the operation earlier, we'll seize it."

A wide grin spread across the Resident's face as he let out a throaty chuckle and pounded his fist against the table. "That just might work," he said to Dmitriyev, shaking his index finger. "You! You've been a little off in recent days but by all appearances, you're back on track."

Dmitriyev nodded and smiled, as his mind shifted to. J.J. McCall. He needed to find a way to help her without compromising his present position. He was indebted to her. The operation she devised saved his brother Plotnikov from a gruesome untimely death at the hands of Mashkov. He wanted revenge on Mikhaylova as much as he wanted to repay J.J. for her loyalty, but attempting to do either at this time was too risky, too dangerous.

Lana's father asked, "Now that we've resolved that issue, how much longer must we endure Golikov's . . .*inspections*?"

"Why, you're not ready to send Igor and Vasiliy packing already, are you?" the Resident said facetiously of the Crooked Twins, the hulking henchman sent to tattletale on insubordinate colleagues. He scanned each face as if verifying their loyalty before speaking. "I've rather enjoyed having my every move scrutinized, walking on eggshells. Let's not pretend. We all understand that generals conduct *inspections*. They were sent here as watchdogs, bullies...thugs."

"Perhaps, we can ask the American State Department to declare them persona non grata," Lana's father joked.

Everyone laughed.

"As a matter of fact, they are expected to visit New York next week since Golikov selected Yuriy Filchenko, Dmitriyev's replacement as line chief, as he assumes the Security Officer position," the Resident continued. "We can all be certain Golikov has identified someone who shares his zest for identifying traitors."

Dmitriyev's back stiffened and he sat board straight. His new position as Security Chief provided him with access to files that would allow him to turn over more Americans to the FBI. However, with a new Golikov thug en route, he must be even more careful and vigilant. And divulging the details of support for Lana to the FBI would implicate everyone sitting in the room—including himself. He wanted to find a breadcrumb to pass to the FBI but he didn't know how…or what.

"Congratulations, Comrade Dmitriyev," Lana's father said first as his colleagues followed.

Dmitriyev bowed his head in contrived thanks.

The Resident checked his watch and glanced at Dmitriyev. "About time for you to take Comrade Vorobyev to the airport, isn't it?"

"Right, you are," he responded, and turned to Lana's father. "We can discuss the details of the plan to neutralize FBI surveillance when I return."

CHAPTER 16

Friday Evening—The Russian Embassy

Stanislav Vorobyev, the beleaguered outgoing Security Chief, served out the final day of his Washington tour reflecting on his career as he packed his family photos. The thought of returning to Moscow left him hollow. He was thankful to be leaving the Embassy on his own accord after being beaten nearly to death a couple days before. The gash beneath his eye and the bruised ribs were sore but the pain of each thrash from the Crooked Twins' fists still reverberated in soul-deep wounds that would *never* heal. Although he'd been cleared of the false charges alleging he'd cooperated with the FBI and would arrive home a free man, he felt stigmatized, ruined by the accusations. Overgrown strands of grey concealed the worry creases in his forehead and he'd tightened his belt extra notch since the week began. His once illustrious career would be forever colored by a traitor's mistake.

If not for his family, he might stay in the U.S., and but for his two children going to university in a few short years, he might have retired. He could not afford to quit working with that expense looming over his head. Unless….

He shuddered at the ill-timed thought, at committing the ultimate crime against his country that mere months ago would have been unthinkable. Alternately, he considered seeking a lucrative position in the private sector. He'd spent years developing contacts throughout all sectors of Russian society, including hobnobbing with a few oligarchs. So many of his colleagues begged him to quit the service and join any number of privatized companies after the fall of the Soviet Union. He believed in a life of public service and wanted to make a difference, wanted his work to help Russia evolve into a strong democracy. Now, word of his troubles preceded him, and the gossip would reach Moscow Center before he could defend himself.

Three sharp knocks jolted him out of his thoughts. He pulled his suitcases into the living room before answering the door.

"Stan, it's me, Alek."

"One moment," Vorobyev replied, as he rushed to open the door.

His dear friend, whose tall frame dwarfed his own, greeted him with a tenuous smile. "You almost ready?" Dmitriyev said, toting a bag containing two tennis shoe boxes.

"Is that a trick question? Come in and sit. I'll be ready to leave in a moment."

Dmitriyev scanned the sparse room, spotted a half-full duffel bag, and proceeded to pack the shoes inside. "These are the Keds I promised your boy. You're checking this one, right?"

"Yeah, yeah. Go ahead and put them inside. That's fine."

After securing the lock on the bag, Dmitriyev took his comfort on the worn brown sofa. "Looks like you're about ready to go. Any idea how long you'll be stuck at Center until your next tour."

Vorobyev shrugged and pursed his lips. "You and I both understand I'm not likely to get another slot for some time, if ever again. I can't believe my career has devolved to this."

"What do you mean? You've done nothing wrong. The agent admitted he made a mistake. You're over-thinking this, comrade."

"Oh, you think so?" Vorobyev said. "If you believe that, perhaps I've been in this business too long...or you haven't been in long enough."

"I have enough experience to know one thing," Aleksey said. "We serve. We don't question, right?"

"Yes. We serve," Vorobyev said. "The question is whom? The people? Does our work benefit the least among us in our so-called democracy? Or do we support a system that celebrates its thieves and betrays its faithful?"

"You're asking questions, and questions are not a part of the job description," Dmitriyev said as he pulled the handle on the larger of Vorobyev's suitcases. "Especially not those we can't answer. As the world changes, so will Russia. We need more time."

"You say that to yourself long enough, you'll believe it," Vorobyev said. "If I've learned anything in this ordeal, it's that nothing has changed, not really. Same bullshit, different day. That's how it is and always will be."

"Well, if you ever need anything, brother, contact me. Anytime. I will help you in any way I can. While you have an extensive pool of people to whom you can reach out, I too am...*well connected*."

Vorobyev froze mid-stride and tilted his head to the side. The tone in Dmitriyev's voice had piqued his curiosity.

"What?" Dmitriyev said. "You think you're the only one who's met an oligarch?"

He studied the precision of his friend's expression before taking a final look around his flat. Anticipating the treatment awaiting him when he returned home left him numb; he shuffled as if weighed down by cinderblock. "Did you hear Golikov found a new replacement for you?"

"Yes, Yuriy Filchenko. Komarov told me this morning," Dmitriyev said, leading Vorobyev down the hall. "You ever worked with him?"

"Unfortunately. He's, for lack of a better phrase, a piece if shit," Vorobyev replied, "fresh from the shithouse."

"That bad?"

"Worse," Vorobyev continued. "He's nothing but a power-hungry tattletale. Be careful. He will study your every move, exploit any opportunity to cast you under the proverbial bus, and report everything back to the Center to ingratiate himself to Golikov who I hear is being promoted to general."

"Figures," Dmitriyev said.

"Watch your drinking...and *other vices*," Vorobyev warned. "You will find him far more intolerant than yours truly...and even less forgiving than Golikov himself."

Dmitriyev reached the end of the hall and pressed the elevator button. "Didn't think anyone could be worse than Golikov."

Vorobyev eased up beside Dmitriyev and locked eyes with him. "They aren't."

CHAPTER 17

Friday Night—J.J.'s Place

J.J. stepped into her condo, exhausted from the day's emotional roller coaster and ready to lick her wounds. She'd lost Tony to Gia and wanted a drink more than sleep, food, or anything else really. Pouring out the entire contents of her elixir bottle in a rare fit of sanity now seemed a bit hasty in hindsight. Yet, she was too tired to make a liquor store run. So, she decided a warm bath, hot tea, and Star Wars would suffice.

As she looked around her empty space, she remembered how differently day was supposed to proceed and her night was meant to end. In the version she'd envisioned, she stumbled through the door attached semi-permanently to Tony's lips while stripping bare as they released a year of pent up passion in a perspiration-filled body rock. They'd both prepared to face society, their families, their friends, but neither were ready for the walking nightmare that was Six.

Schlepping into her bedroom to change into her pity pajamas, her cell phone rang. Her heart leapt at the misplaced thought that Tony might have come to his senses. She practically dived toward her purse and began an ungraceful scramble to grab the phone. When she finally fixed her eyes on the caller ID, to her disappointment, a headquarters number flashed. She started to ignore it, but if the search for Lana had yielded some results, she wanted to know before crazy showed up on her doorstep.

It was John Nixon, the next worst thing to Jack Sabinski even though Freeman kept him in check…mostly. And the conversation didn't last long. With barely concealed pleasure, he delivered three swift blows, sucker punches to the gut, and left J.J. not only impotent but drowning with regret. J.J. didn't know what axe Nixon had to grind with her, most likely the sudden unemployment of his good ole boy buddy Jack Sabinski. But she was thankful Freeman directly led the charge. God forbid she should ever have to answer to Nixon—he would make her life hell.

"So let me get this straight. We're standing down all Russian operations indefinitely, I'm off Lana's investigation, Task Force Phantom Hunter is now an analytical group, and you've ordered the Gs to watch me like a Secret Service detail on the President's grandmother while I serve as bait for a bat-shit crazy woman hell bent on revenge. Does that about sum it up?"

"Uhhh..."

"I should've quit today while I had the chance."

"Maybe you should've."

"Gee, thanks. Now if you'll excuse me. I need a cup of tea…with hemlock in it." Her mouth salivated for the heat of vodka but tea, minus the hemlock, would have to do. It was all she had in the house and she was too exhausted or depressed to go out.

Everything she longed for—Tony, the task force—had slipped in and out of her hands so fast she hardly had time to form a memory. She resolved then to quench her thirst Saturday if it lasted through the night. She had nothing else to lose.

After hanging up the phone, J.J. walked out onto her patio, tightening her robe around her neck to fend off the chill. She looked down on the street, spotted the familiar silver Malibu, and waved.

Money T.

He flashed his high beam to acknowledge her greeting before she returned inside and secured the lock on the patio door.

She dawdled around the room, trying to focus her mind on the drama that lay ahead in the week to come. She paced the floor trying to think of something else she could do to appeal to the adoring man she'd fallen for, but the stubborn ass was his current gatekeeper and her hopes faded by the second.

She hated the sense of powerlessness, defenselessness, the inability to force her enemy's hand…or even her own. For once in a long time she'd been forced to accept that every person and event threatening to impact her life over the coming weeks lie outside of her control. At times like this, she missed her mother, the calming voice, the soothing hand. The force who could break down the seeming enormity of her troubles to withering dust, to make her wonder why she allowed fear to dominate her outlook at all.

To escape the pain and frustration of the man she couldn't have and the career she couldn't escape, she sought consolation with the remote control. No sooner than she flipped to the Spike network and scooped up enough M&Ms to soothe her alcohol cravings through the next century, she caught one of her favorite scenes in *The Empire Strikes Back*.

Yoda asked Luke Skywalker, "Why wish you become Jedi?" And Luke replied, "Well, mostly because of my father, I guess."

The words struck her like a hammer to the head of a nail. She repeated the words out loud, except one. "Well, mostly because of my…mother, I guess." J.J. questioned whether choosing to join the FBI was ever what she wanted for herself—or some misguided attempt to keep a piece of her mother alive. At that moment, she realized she had only made one decision in the last thirty years that was uninfluenced by anything except the desires of her own heart—her choice to love Tony.

A hard, rapid knock at the door made J.J.'s heart beat wildly. She wasn't expecting anyone. Although she hoped Tony had come to his good senses and had arrived to kiss and make up, her enemy was on the move. She grabbed her gun from the holster, then jetted to the bathroom, checked herself in the mirror, and did a ten-second primp before bounding for the door.

Steps away, she yelled, "Just a minute!" before pressing her eye to the peephole and her finger firmly against the trigger. A coif of spiked blond hair barely reached her line of sight. Definitely wasn't Tony. She latched the chain for added security and pulled the door slightly ajar.

"Yes? Who is it?" she asked with a quizzical tone in her voice.

"Ma'am, I have a delivery," he said, holding two large shopping bags with Maggiano's printed on the front of the peephole, "for a… J.J. McCall?"

"Uhhh…that's me," she said, confused and excited, her earlier troubles disappearing into the night. She tucked her gun in the small of her back, opened the door, and eyed the load of foil containers sealed with thin white cardboard lids. "What's this?"

"Judging from the smell, I'd guess dinner."

J.J. smiled. "But who sent—"

The courier threw his hand up to stop J.J. mid-sentence and handed her the gift.

"Give me a second to put these down and I'll get you a tip."

"No, thank you, ma'am," he replied. "Already taken care of. Enjoy your meal."

The grand gesture had Six written all over it, although a poisoning would be a smart move on Lana's part. In a different time and state of mind she would've tossed the food in the trash at the mere possibility of Six's involvement, but this night she welcomed the distractions. J.J. rushed off to wash her hands before sampling the delights. Spinach and cheese manicotti, artichoke dip, gnocchi, spaghetti, an entire family-style meal with all the trimmings—and every sweet treat from cheesecake to cannoli. She'd decided to sample the desserts first when there came another knock at the door.

She paused and smiled, anticipating yet dreading the presence on the other side. She looked out the peep hole hoping beyond hope to see curly black locks. Instead she saw a tall black man…of the non-Six variety. He delivered a bottle of wine, a 2008 Spottswoode Cabernet Sauvignon, and refused the tip.

"Now what did I do with the corkscrew?" she asked herself aloud, admiring the Napa Valley bungalow gracing the label. Whoever sent the hundred dollar bottle of wine was trying to make a lasting impression. By the time she poured out enough to fill two bowls half way, the doorbell rang once more.

She began the routine again, hoping the admirer would reveal himself this time. When she cracked open the door, two black, beady little eyes met hers…and a round stomach with plush, brown fur. Judging by the hands, a gentleman was concealed behind the top-shelf, carnival-sized teddy bear. In a not quite familiar voice, he said, "Delivery for J.J. McCall!"

J.J. laughed when she finally noticed the red T-shirt covering the midsection of the enormous furry creature. "Kiss me I'm Italian" was written in the colors of the Italian flag. The delivery man lowered the bear from his face and her heart melted the way it had every day since she met him.

"So, *you're* the guilty party." J.J. grabbed the bear from his arms and backed up to allow Tony inside. "Thought you had an engagement after work this evening."

"I do. That's why I'm here with you." He stepped in and glanced at the dining room table, noticing the two full glasses of wine waiting on the table. "You were expecting someone?"

"As a matter of fact, I was." J.J. grabbed his hand and led him to his offering. "Denzel is on his way and likes his wine pre-poured," she turned sharply toward him and peered into his smiling eyes. "You, Mr. Donato, better make this quick. Now, to what do I owe this honor?"

Tony laughed and shook his head. "I got your message...and couldn't stay away."

"So it would seem," J.J. replied, beaming as she handed him his wine glass. "How about a toast? To new beginnings."

He raised his hand. "Salut."

J.J. nodded, tilted the glass back, and let the Cabernet Sauvignon slip down her throat and smooth the edges off of her jagged day.

"Listen, sorry about earlier. It's just...when I saw *him* there...with *you*... Well, let's say he'd better thank his lucky stars I'm not in my family's business."

"I know that's right," she said. "Trust me, I put him in his place. But I will warn you now, he isn't one to give up easily."

"Can't blame the guy, I guess. I wouldn't give up on you either," he said. "But don't worry, I can handle *Three*. He's not a problem for me."

J.J. sighed in relief. "Thank you...for all of this," she said as she reached for his shoulders, ready to pull him into her embrace. "Didn't know you had it in you."

"Is 'at right?" he said, as he lowered his voice to a low, throaty rumble and cupped her face in his hands. "Well, I'm planning to let you see a lot of stuff inside me."

"Is that a threat...or a promise?" she asked.

Before he could answer, his mouth covered hers and together they dissolved into a sensuous kiss.

For so long she'd hoped for the moment in which to release all the passion she'd repressed. She craved him, hungered for him, needed him. And there he was, in her arms. Home.

As their lips intertwined, J.J.'s fingers crawled around Tony's waist, up the firmness of his back, and down again. She wanted to feel him, all of him. Outside her, inside her, everywhere his touch could reach. The warmth of his firm embrace enveloped her as they shuffled across the floor toward the bedroom, connected and caressed the entire way. He lifted her at the threshold as if she weighed no more than a feather and carried her inside until he laid her on the bed. The moon was their only light.

J.J.'s desire had swelled, bubbling to the point of explosion; she want to rush and devour him in one delicious bite. But Tony shook his head no, demonstrating with his slow measured pace that he wanted to take his time and savor every second. Each caress, each touch, slow, purposeful, and mind-bending. She loved the way he looked at her, studying her frame as a connoisseur of beautiful art would a Rodin, Bernini, or Michelangelo. His hands roamed the breadth of his newfound territory. He allowed his fingertips to help him memorize the softness of every bend and curve until they were engrained in his mind beyond forever.

He gently slipped off the clothing from her longing body, layer by layer, until she was down to her stark glory, kissing every inch of her natural form in a delicate appreciation. After removing his clothes and protecting himself, he eased beside her, then inside her. As their eyes locked, he whispered, "I love you."

Then love had its way.

As their mouths met, their bodies joined together as one, rocking in the sweetest rhythmic dance, her penetrating moans driving the force of his intensity. The ebb and flow of their figures swayed faster and faster, each delicious stroke lengthened and strengthened until their souls trembled and both cried out in a satisfied song.

Face to face, J.J. held Tony, pressed herself against him until she caught her lost breath, until her frame descended from his heavenly command. Their damp bodies glistened in the moonlight filtering into the blinds covering the window. J.J. exhaled and smiled as she traced her fingers through the strands of curly black hair on his chest and admired the beauty in the contrast of his skin against hers.

She clamped her eyes shut and shook her head before turning onto her back as the beauty of their evening slowly succumbed to the burgeoning reality. "I hope you realize what we've gotten ourselves into."

Tony purred and nuzzled his lips in the crevice between her shoulder and neck. "I sure do," Tony said. "And I'm hoping to get into it again in another fifteen minutes."

J.J. chuckled and turned to look him in the eye. "I'm serious, Tony."

"So am I," he said, caressing her cheek.

She gave him the stink eye and turned her back to him, this time in frustration. She understood the black and white of their new reality in a way he never would.

"Oh, don't be mad," Tony said. "Listen, I hear what you're saying, babe, but trust me when I say my understanding is deeper than you might think. You know my father is a boss in the Bonanno Family. La Cosa Nostra. How do you think he reacted when I told him I was accepted to the FBI Academy in Quantico?"

She snickered and faced him once more. "Really, Tony? You know my father is an ex-Black Panther…which is kind of like being an ex-Marine; there's really no such thing. How could you think I wouldn't understand?" she said. "But let me guess…he congratulated you on your noble choice of profession and threw a party?"

Tony lay on his back and clasped his hand behind his head. His lips drew downward and he looked out the window as if trying to conceal the vulnerability already exposed in his expression. "Oh, they threw me a party all right. A moving party. Accused me of ratting out a member of my father's family—which I would never do. Called me a traitor and cut me off from everybody I knew. Pop said I couldn't serve two masters, especially when my master was hell bent on pinching him and his family and putting him behind bars," Tony said. "I was told in so many words that if I ever returned to New York or Jersey, I would never leave. Every day I'm looking over my shoulder thinkin' somebody might order a hit."

J.J. gasped. "You don't mean…"

Tony nodded. "Yep. Two in the back of the head and they'd probably send someone who was once a friend…or even a relative. Tell you what, though, they better hope I don't see them first."

"I can't even imagine. I mean, we've always been close. Dysfunctional but tight-knit."

"I realized Pops would be upset, but I never thought…actually I don't know what I was thinking. Maybe I got sick of living a life where my father spent more time in the streets and in prison than with us. Swore I would never let it happen to me. The FBI was my escape, my ticket to ensure I'd always be around for my kids, my family."

J.J. placed her palm on his chest and rested her cheek against the back of her hand. "You will, Tony. You're a better man than even you realize," she said of the man who never made her itch except the one time she was now willing to forgive. He had an honesty and goodness to a depth at which no one would ever understand except her. Perhaps grasping his true value is what drew them together.

"And you do?"

"Yes," J.J. said, nodding her head eagerly. "I do."

He wrapped both arms around her and pressed her close. "I gave up my entire existence to live on my own terms," Tony said. "So the way I figure it—if I could give up so much *to live* on my own terms, then I can sacrifice as much or more *to love* on my own terms…to love you."

J.J.'s stomach curled into knots, as it had done the last time those words glided across his tongue, penetrated her weakened defenses, and embraced her heart. As his palms caressed her hips, urging her to join him for round two, her stomach rumbled.

"Hungry much?" Tony asked with a chuckle.

J.J.'s cheeks warmed from the embarrassment. "Perhaps it's time to warm up something from the massive buffet you bought. Want something?" J.J. asked playfully with an eyebrow raised.

Tony eyed her with a sexy gaze that said the only food he wanted was the contents of her "cookie jar."

"Besides that," J.J. said, tapping his arm playfully.

"A bottle of water," he said, sucking his tongue. "I'm dehydrated."

"I bet you are." J.J. winked as she slipped on her robe and headed for the kitchen, closing the bedroom door behind her. She held her arms up as if to waltz and then glided across the floor when a knock at the door startled her out of her blissful haze. She glanced back over her shoulder and smiled. "Gee whiz, Tony! Another surprise?"

"You say something?" Tony called out, his voice muffled.

This time, without fear, she whisked the door open and froze.

"Did I catch you at a bad time?" Six said in his warm tenor.

There he stood once more in all his chocolate glory, a bottle of Grey Goose in one hand and brown paper bag filled to the brim with red and white boxes of Chinese food and chopsticks. The scent of Kung Pao chicken made her stomach growl. The last time Six stood in this hall, she wanted nothing more than for her eternal source of hate and discontent to disappear for good, and not much had changed. His gaze pierced her as if he was using his X-ray vision to invade J.J.'s private places.

J.J. noticed his intense stare and clenched the neckline of her robe shut. "Jesus, Six! What the hell are you doing here?"

"Who's 'at, Babe?" Tony called.

"Someone knocked on the wrong door!" she yelled before returning her voice to a whisper. "You can't just pop up here whenever you feel like it. I'm with someone else now. Whatever you have to say to me can wait until 9 am Monday!"

The corners of Six's mouth turned down. Although stymied for a moment, he recovered quickly. He always did. "Yes, you will," he said, sauntering down the hall like a magician with another trick up his sleeve. "I'll give him round one. But the fight isn't over until the final knockout. Until our next encounter."

She shut the door and leaned her back against it while she gathered her thoughts.

"I'm dying in here," Tony yelled. "Where's the water?"

"Coming right up," J.J. said, hopping nervously to the kitchen. "Coming right up."

CHAPTER 18

Friday November 6th—Irving Street
9 Days Left...

Santino Castellano glanced at the calendar thumbtacked to the peeling floral wallpaper of his rental. His time was running out. He found it hard to believe he'd been in D.C. for nearly two months already, but he couldn't wait to vacate Irving Street and return to Jersey. He'd had enough of living in exile while he repaired the damage caused by his explosive temper. He wanted to learn the truth and settle his business once and for all.

He regretted the fallout for the family, the Bonannos, but he wouldn't change what he did. From his wallet, he pulled out a picture of Rosa, his childhood sweetheart since first grade; he kissed her forehead to complete his daily ritual. He couldn't believe she was gone. The victim of a hit and run, her mangled body had been mowed over and left for dead like road kill in the middle of Jersey's Jackson Street. Only one night before the soul-shaking incident, he'd put the three-carat ring on her finger. He barely finished asking the question before she said yes. Their dream of forever, however, came to an abrupt, bone-crushing end.

After a lingering stare, he pushed the picture back in his wallet; he headed downstairs to grab a beer when his cell phone rang. He looked at the caller ID and recognized the number from the payphone his crew boss Nicky Mumbles used. He was a capo and called Santino once every couple weeks, both to check he was okay and ensure he was on task. After all, Nicky's ass and reputation were also on the line.

"Hey Santino, how's tricks?" Nicky asked. When he spoke, he always sounded like he had half a sub sandwich in his mouth.

"Everything's good," he replied, the sound of his voice less certain than he meant it to be.

"You makin' any progress on your, uhhh, lesson?"

"Yeah…yeah. Almost complete. Just a little bit to go," he lied. Santino needed to earn quick money. He had a few blood ties in the area and some contacts who dealt a blow on the streets to hook him up with some product to distribute.

"Good. Glad to hear it, 'cause word is our friends are losing patience. And if you don't finish up school soon, by next Monday to be exact, you might get expelled *if you get my drift.*"

When Santino received the news of Rosa's death, he hadn't cried so hard since he was a baby in diapers. His body collapsed in an epileptic tremor and the tears streamed hopelessly down his cheeks. He asked a couple guys from his crew to find out what they could. Days later, word on the street was that fucking douche bag, *stunad* Cappi Merendino had a shitload of blow in the trunk of his Caddy and left Rosa for dead so he wouldn't get pinched. Of course, once Santino found out who did it, he whacked him. Cappi took three shots right in the side of his sorry mug, parked inside the truck still damaged from the collision with Rosa. Any man in his position would've done the same, which turned out to be his only saving grace when word later got around that Merendino was the nephew of a made man.

Since Cappi was a piece of shit dealing weed and Ecstasy to high schoolers under the table despite the boss's repeated warnings, Santino's uncle Sal was able to broker an agreement with the families—financial restitution in exchange for forgiveness. With ten grand on his person, Santino was still fifteen in the hole and trying to dig his way out. His Uncle could've easily fronted him the money, but a loan would defeat the lesson's purpose. So he forced Santino to tough it out.

Santino ran his hand across the back of his neck. "The situation's handled already. Should be home Tuesday."

"You sure, now? Cause I don't wanna hear any bullshit 'I ain't got it' at test time, ya hear me?"

"Loud and clear, Nicky," he said. "Loud and clear."

After a brief exchange, he was glad the conversation ended. Truth was he had barely earned two grand since he arrived in D.C. and clearly his time was running out. His contact, a man nicknamed after Santino's new adopted city, was still days away from connecting him to the gangbanger who would buy his product for the right price. If he didn't find a way to earn soon, he might be forced to make a choice, one that would save him from the pan, only to land him deeper into the fire. He took a deep breath and descended down the steps to get a drink—a stiff one—to help him forget.

D.C. was as good a place as any to lam it until he could come up with the balance of the money he owed. Mr. O'Leary's place was clean, cheap, and as long as you paid the rent on time, he was a ghost and minded his own business, just the way Santino liked it. His new room-mate, whoever it was he heard creeping around, had better follow the same policy.

• • •

Lana allowed the hot spray to wash over her aching body until the water turned cold. The shower gave her a chance to think, find some clarity. If she had any hope of moving around the city undetected, retrieving the drops containing the money and papers she needed to travel, she needed some help. Preferably someone whose silence could be bought for the right price. She stepped beyond the curtain and nourished her skin with oil. It had begun to harden to a leathery roughness, as the remnants of her heart. She wrapped the towel around her torso and prepared to return to her room for some much-needed rest when hard footsteps tapped up the stairs. She cracked open the door.

She touched her lips and took in the entirety of his tall form as he entered his room. Her eyes roamed from his thick black curly hair to his broad shoulders, into the curve in his tight waist and perfect backside, down his sturdy thighs and rather large feet. An appreciative smile edged her lips upward.

"If you take a picture it'll last longer," the man said, craning his head over his shoulder to glimpse his admirer.

Embarrassed, Lana snatched the door shut and pressed her fingers against her cheeks. Her face warmed to a flush rose color. "I wasn't staring, if that's what you're thinking. Just waiting for you to get inside your room. I'm not dressed."

"Yeah, yeah. Any excuse will do," he said. He flipped the light switch, closed the door within a sliver, and peered out.

She found his New York accent as sexy as he.

"I'm in my room. You can come out now."

She poked her head out and noticed a fluorescent glow slice through a thin crack. "I can see you, ya know. If you're gonna pretend you're not looking at me, you should probably try again with the light *off*."

"Hey, one good stalking deserves another." He pushed the door shut and the latch clicked. Through the door he yelled, "Go ahead. It's closed now."

Lana tipped across the floor, her towel barely large enough to cover her naked frame, peering back over her shoulder just in time to see the glow disappear. She shook her head and chuckled.

Her thoughts lingered on the stranger in the other room as she slipped into a pink camisole, matching silk pajama pants, and dried her hair. A sense of humor, a little charm, and he was a special kind of hot, but he could serve only one purpose in her life at the moment. For the first time, she needed help and she despised her position of weakness. With Jake barely cold in his grave, she would only flirt with purpose. Her first goal was to find out why he was in a D.C. rooming house and how he could help her escape from this God forsaken country.

Checking herself in the mirror once more, she hadn't yet gotten used to the new look, which she termed Goth chic. The black strands contrasted starkly against her sun-shy skin. Still she favored the color because the coal-black tint looked as coarse as she felt. Just as she reached to twist the doorknob and introduce herself, there was a knock. She opened the door and hung her hand on her hip.

"You look smart enough to appreciate the value of a cold beer," he said, carrying two bottles of Heineken. He snapped his head back, blinked, and hungrily eyed her. "Thought I should introduce myself since we're going to be roomies and all. I'm Santino."

"Santino, huh? You got a last name to go with that?" she asked grabbing a bottle from his hand and taking a seat on her bed.

"Santino," he said. "We just met, so you oughta know I follow a strict 'don't ask, don't tell' policy. I don't ask you about your business, and I don't tell you mine."

"Works for me, Santino Santino." She took a long sip from her bottle to stall until her mother's name, Katerina, came to mind and crossed her lips. "I'm Katherine Katherine."

"Katherine?" His brow drew in and his face tightened. "You don't look like a Katherine."

"Oh, really?" she said. "If not Katherine, then what?"

"I don't know. I expected something a little more exotic. Maybe Lola...or Giselle. Giselle's good."

"Giselle. Hmm," she said, crossing her legs Indian style. "You can call me Giselle. But only if I can call you…" she looked him up and down, "stud muffin."

He laughed. "You're funny. No, Katherine and Santino will do fine."

Lana studied him as he leaned against the wall, his tailored slacks, the silk sleeves on his long-sleeved shirt, how the pomade stiffened his perfectly sculptured hair, the gaudy gold chain around his neck, and pinky ring glimmering on his left finger. "So what do you do?"

"For a living?" he replied, clearly hesitant to answer.

She nodded.

He paused before unbuttoning his cuffs at the wrist. He rolled up his sleeves as he considered his response. She'd made him uncomfortable. "I guess you could say . . . I do favors for family and our associates."

"Favors? You going for sainthood?" she asked.

"Not even close," he said with a slight grin.

"So where would I fit in…in this scenario?"

He glanced down at his lap. "I could think of a few places where would you fit quite nicely."

She chuckled. "So what brings you to D.C.?"

"Let's say I owe someone a few favors," he said. "Twenty-five thousand of them."

"That's a lot of favors," she said, the discomfort looming between them.

"So, what's a nice lady like you doing in a place like this?"

She exposed a flirtatious grin and purred, "What makes you think I'm nice?"

He smiled. "Touché. So what's an evil bitch like you doing in a place like this?"

Her smiled disappeared and she turned away. "My husband died. I lost my job and my house. I needed a place to stay...to take care of some unfinished business before I return home."

She looked around the room nervously.

"Wow. Don't I feel like a piece of shit? You've been through hell, huh?" he asked. His expression was nervous, uneasy.

"The depths of which you can't imagine," she said, with a strained chuckle. She waved him over. "You look tired. You should come have a seat. I don't bite...*much*."

He made his way to the bed and took his rest at a respectful distance. When he drew in a drink of his beer, she glimpsed artwork on his forearm and leaned forward to examine it more closely. With that she'd gathered all she needed to know about the kind of man he was, the company he kept, and how she could use him. "Nice tattoo."

"Yeah," he said as he pushed up the sleeve to expose the full view. It was small and easy to keep concealed—the picture of a flaming cross with an Italian flag draped around the full length. Beneath, in an old-world cursive script, the words "Morte Prima di Disonore" were written.

"Hmm. Death before dishonor." Her eyes locked on his. "Where I come from, tattoos can tell you a lot about someone. Where they've been. The kind of company they keep. All sorts of interesting things."

"Why do I feel naked all of a sudden?" Santino joked.

"Because I see you. Don't worry, though, we're all thieves-in-law, right?" she said with a wink.

He smiled and lifted his bottle to her in toast.

"Do you outsource...your favors, I mean?" she asked.

He shrugged. "Occasionally. Depends on what my customer requires."

"I suspect you can handle my *all of my needs*…and I'd certainly be willing to make it worth your while."

CHAPTER 19

Friday Night—Washington Field Office

Kyle sat back hard in his seat, glanced out the window at the red bricked façade of the National Building Museum across 4th Street, and chewed on Greg's order to hunt down his former protégé. He wondered whether he should recuse himself from the case because his emotions ran so high. Mac was right in warning him. His actions were not subject to reason, but the investigation he needed to conduct must be nothing but. He drew in a deep breath and clenched his eyes shut until he forced the doubt from his mind.

The time for second-guessing had ended and the time to work had begun. A necessary evil to take Michaels off the street was schooling the rookie.

Hopper Mack.

He'd already shown his proclivity for counterintelligence work when he located the intelligence files and money cache in Jack Sabinski's basement. He was a natural, had the makings of an exceptional agent. Unfortunately, he also had the ego of a kid who might quickly find himself in Duluth taking squirrel bite reports if he didn't reign in the self-righteous attitude. Kyle decided to let Junior cut his teeth on this case. If he survived, he'd help groom him along as Mac had done him so many years ago. If not, he'd get him transferred to Duluth.

Kyle stuck his head out the door and scanned the office. "Hey Junior, you out here?" After waiting a few moments with no response, he called out again. "Anyone seen Hopper Mack?"

"Yes, sir," Hopper replied, running down the hall chewing on half a street dog with a fresh glob of mustard adorning his navy Polo shirt. Cheeks bubbled with beef franks, he mumbled, "Sorry, I was hungry."

He was always clean-cut and fired-up like a Marine fresh out of boot camp.

"Who ordered you to eat?" Kyle barked as he walked back into his office. "Maybe I should start calling you Grey Poupon instead of Junior."

Hopper stood paralyzed, as if confused as to whether Kyle was pulling his leg again. His guesses were usually wrong.

Kyle cast a glance over his shoulder. "What are you gonna do, stand there with your mouth hanging open and let the grass grow under your feet? Get your hungry ass in here. I've got a case for you."

Hopper dunked the remainder of his lunch into the trash can and slipped into the guest seat before Kyle could sit firmly in his. He sat forward, ready to listen.

"MacDonald requested my help on the Michaels investigations, and I, ahem, need some assistance. You up for it?"

His eyes widened. "Wait. You....picked *me*?"

"You'd prefer me to select someone else?"

"No...no," he said, shaking his head. "I'm ready to go. How can I help?"

"Our job is to locate Agent Michaels and bring her in," he said. "You're familiar with the case, right?"

"Yeah, who isn't?"

"So, what are your thoughts? Where's a good place to start?"

Hopper rubbed his face repeatedly, then cleared his throat. "Well, if I'm Lana Michaels, the one thing I want to do more than anything else in the world is get as far away from the United States as possible. I'm going someplace where I won't be extradited, so Mexico and Canada aren't options."

"Where would you go?"

He thought for a few seconds and scratched through the scruff on his chin. "Back to Moscow, especially if I were Russian. Maybe France. Any place where there's no extradition treaty…which means I'll be trying to find some travel documents, a passport in Lana's case because hers is in evidence."

"What do you do in the meantime?"

"I'd lie low, except…"

"You're an attractive, high profile target. Probably have money stashed but not a lot...and law enforcement has blanketed every cheap or seedy hotel east of the Mississippi."

"Hmmm. I'm gonna find an empty house and break in. But if the neighbors see me they'll call the police. So if I've got any money at all I'll find a room."

"Good thinking, Junior," Kyle said. "You might make a halfway decent agent yet."

Hopper bowed his head in thanks. "You think she'll try to get to the embassy? If she makes it inside, she'll technically be on foreign soil. There'd be no arrest."

"No, she won't go there. We've got the embassy covered—Uniformed Secret Service, FBI lookouts, Gs, and agents. She couldn't fart without law enforcement smelling the stink. I don't doubt the Russians will try to make a drop though."

"Money?"

"And travel documents. They'd probably try to get her a new identity and book her on the first flight out of here. But the likelihood of her passing through the checkpoint with all this heightened security is pretty much non-existent."

"She won't cross any borders. The only other way for her to get out of here would be by ship."

"You think she's going to take a Caribbean cruise?"

Hopper chuckled. "Doubt it, but the Counterterrorism Task Force issued an interesting report a few days ago. Lemme go grab it."

He dashed out and returned a minute later with a two-page document in hand. "Check this out. What do you think?"

Kyle scanned the page from top to bottom, leaned back against his chair and clasped his fingers behind head. "Hmmmm. Passenger travel on cargo ships. This is interesting. We'll send a lead up to the Baltimore office and ask them to inquire."

Hopper smiled.

"Don't get beside yourself. She's still on the streets, remember? Why don't you start working on a plan to investigate D.C. boarding rooms."

"Did Metro Police ever determine which subway station she exited?"

"Do I look like Metro Police to you? You've got a few calls to make. Report back to me when you've got facts. First thing tomorrow morning, we hit the streets. I'm going to put a feeler out with some of my informants to see if we can get a lead on the travel docs."

Kyle grabbed his cell phone, the one he used for his more seedy contacts and scrolled through the numbers; Hopper watched his every move without budging.

"Uhhh… private call, Junior. I'll holler when I'm done."

Hopper nodded and disappeared out the door. Kyle pressed the name "D.C." and pushed his door shut. The phone rang twice before he answered.

"What's up, man?"

"Well, well, well…long time, no speak. Thought you traded in your street clothes for a cushy desk job."

"I tried," Kyle said. "But the Bureau's got me on some *Godfather* shit. Every time I get out, they pull me back in."

D.C. chuckled. "You a funny motherfucker. What can I do for you, man?"

"I need a favor. I'm sure you've seen reports about this agent on the run."

"Have I? The streets are hot. A few people wouldn't mind cashing in her location for seven figures."

"Is that right?"

"Hey, she's a cop. Ain't no loyalty, even if she did kill a fed."

"Do me a kindness. If you get word on a white chick trying to cop a passport, I need to be your first call."

"What's in it for me?"

"The usual, of course."

"The usual? Try again. Do you really think my contact won't suspect I'm asking for five-oh? He'll charge me triple for that reason alone."

"Trust me, you get this done for me and you can name your price, but there's one catch."

"Oh, here we go," D.C. said. "Always a catch with y'all, what is it?"

"I supply the docs and you only sell them with my okay."

"What do I care? Same price for me no matter who supplies the docs."

He glanced up in time to see Hopper's frame moving closer to his office door.

"I gotta go. Hit me up the minute you get wind of anything," Kyle said as the phone clicked against the cradle.

Hopper knocked and Kyle waved him in.

"What's going on?"

"Metro police just called. Nothing yet on Lana's location. Maybe early next week."

CHAPTER 20

Saturday Morning, November 7th—J.J.'s House

The heaviness of the down comforter surrounded J.J. as she eased out of her restful slumber. The rumbling tones of Tony's snores jarred her back into an acute state of awareness of the long night behind her…and the long days ahead. While she would like to cover her head and bask in the here and now, between Nixon's news about the stand-down and the pending visit with Cartwright's wife, work was determined to yank them back into reality. With that thought, J.J. decided to roll out of bed and get her day started.

"Where do you think you're going?" Tony said, gripping J.J.'s waist as she attempted to slip away unnoticed. He laid a soft kiss into her back and pulled her into his spoon; she loved to sink between the broadness of his shoulders, to feel the warmth of his body against hers. She wanted to him to live inside her. "Don't even think about getting dressed. It's Saturday and we've had a hellish week."

She turned to face him and planted the softest of kisses on his naturally cherry lips. "As much as I'd like to make this a lazy day, I got a call from Debbie Cartwright yesterday."

Tony's expression turned serious. He propped himself up on his elbow. "Oh, man. What did she have to say?"

"She's holding a small memorial ceremony today for his family, but she wanted us to stop by afterward. Apparently, Jim left a letter addressed to me."

"Hmm. Did she say what's in it?"

"I asked," J.J. said. "But she didn't open it. Told me to stop by her house after the memorial around noon to pick it up. It's already 10:30."

Tony snuggled his cheek against J.J.'s and gave her a quick peck, then turned to get out of bed. "All right. Hate to do it, but work calls. Maybe he gave you something to help the task force…or an apology."

"Oh yeah…about the task force," J.J. began. "I got a call from Nixon last night. Not only have I been barred from Lana's investigation,

Task Force Phantom Hunter is dead in the water…sort of. We've been ordered to stand down offensive operations."

"You're freakin' kidding me!" Tony yelled. "What genius came up with that bright idea? I'm sure Freeman's not responsible."

"Nope. We can thank the President for this one," J.J. said, explaining the complexities involved including Lebed's visit and ongoing CIA operations. "I'm sure Freeman fought the good fight, but you know what they say about the needs of the many…"

"Yeah, they're ignored whenever the Agency cries source protection," Tony said with a shrug. "It's a shame this has become the rule more than the exception."

J.J. got quiet for a moment, lost in her thoughts and experiencing a bout of guilt over missing Jim's memorial service. Without realizing it, she was still torn between the agent and father she admired and the traitor murdered while meeting his Russian handler. "Jim and I were supposed to meet the morning before he died. He'd planned to tell me something. I had always thought he'd confess, but maybe there's something more."

"You think?"

She sat up and leaned her back against the headboard then shrugged. "I can't say. But I always suspected Jim had more intel than he let on. Time will tell, I suppose. The sooner we get over there. The sooner we'll know."

• • •

Two hours later, J.J. and Tony pulled up in front of Jim Cartwright's house in Burke, Virginia, which sat in a small cul-de-sac lined with perfectly maintained brick-front colonial homes. A slew of cars crowded the streets as they paced up the walkway and approached the entryway. They exchanged mischievous smiles before the door opened.

"May I help you?" a stout matronly woman in a navy suit asked as she eyed them from head to toe.

"Yes, ma'am," J.J. said. "Mrs. Cartwright, Debbie is expecting us."

She gave J.J. the side-eye and stepped aside to allow them in. After closing the door behind them, she began moving down the hall and said, "Right this way."

As she weaved through the crowd, J.J. looked for signs of a spy's extravagance, but she found none. His home was quaint, normal. The artwork, though complimentary to their décor, was comprised of simple landscapes one might find in an advanced art class, not Winslow Homer's, but nice nonetheless. The furniture had a modern country feel. The size was just large enough for a family of four. Although Jim's car would likely be held in evidence until the unlikely occasion that Lana was caught, an older model minivan parked in the driveway showed signs of wear. They lived modestly. He'd been getting paid by the Russians, but signs of how he spent the money were few and far between.

As they rounded the corner of a small hallway and arrived at the kitchen, J.J. saw Debbie staring into the backyard amidst of what appeared to be a small grouping of close friends or family members, dabbing her eyes with a floral-embroidered handkerchief.

"Deb," their guide said, calling for her attention. "You have some visitors."

She turned toward the voice, her eyes red, the bags beneath betraying her sleepless nights. She attempted a slight smile. "J.J., Tony. Thank you for coming."

She excused herself and they exchanged hugs before she led them back to the bedroom.

"Follow me," she said. "It's in my bedroom."

She entered the room and reached out for a jewelry box sitting on top of a dresser. She pulled the bottom drawer out and slipped the letter out from beneath a small pile of papers. "Here you are," she said, placing the envelope in J.J.'s hand.

J.J. observed the handwriting which appeared to be Jim's penmanship. "With the ongoing investigation, I'm not certain whether I can share the contents with you, Debbie."

Debbie shook her head. "Please don't worry. Given what's happened, that's probably for the best."

J.J. stepped beside Tony, opened the envelope, and unfolded the paper inside. The short letter began:

Dear J.J.

I hoped you wouldn't need this letter, but wrote it in case you did.

As you probably know by now, Lana Michaels is an agent of the Russian Intelligence Service, an illegal. I helped her obtain her position in the FBI and when asked, I've supported other tasks. It is because of that work that I can leave this letter to you.

Lana is part of a network of moles who not only provide classified information but directly support Russian intelligence operations. Each operates a cutout, code named Bumazhnaya Kuklas—Paper Doll—who serve as go-between to make drops and pass materials. Chris Johnson was Lana's paper doll. Find the paper dolls and you'll find the spies.

Lana didn't make many mistakes, but allowing her ego to run her and her mouth was one that might have given us a window into her operations. She showed up at my office one day, drunk on Stoli, bragging about how she'd made her father proud with the success of her network. I recorded it on my iPhone. The following is a translation: "American arrogance astonishes me. So smug that you cannot see the thief who waves hello with one hand while picking your pocket with the other. We have eyes and ears everywhere. We moved from Foggy Bottom to 1600 without raising an eyebrow. We harvested gold from your farms, marched soldiers on ground zero, and took the cores right from under Liberty's skirt, and you Americans remain mesmerized by the friendly hand."

Her meaning will be as apparent to you as it is to me. She obviously wanted me to know the severity of the breaches, to know how badly her service was sticking it to us. Perhaps she believed we'd figured it out too late. I don't know.

Of all the agents I've worked with, I left this to you. She despised you because you were never mesmerized by the friendly hand. She's cold-blooded and dangerous, J.J. And she won't hesitate to kill you or anyone who gets in her way.

Don't ever forget what I told you. Sometimes to get the King, you have to sacrifice the pawn. But you are the queen—the most powerful piece in the game.

The Bureau owes you a debt of gratitude for your service and so do I.

Your friend,

Jim Cartwright

Tears watered J.J.'s eyes as she read his closing salutation. *Friend.* Tony placed his arm on her shoulder and pulled her close to him in a brief embrace. She glanced at his widow and forced a smile.

"Whatever happened, Debbie, remember that in his heart of hearts, he was an honorable man and a good father."

"I know," Debbie said. "I only wish that he knew that too."

J.J. hung her head as the matronly woman again called Debbie to greet more guests.

"I should return to my guests," she said. "If you two will please see yourselves out, I've got to muddle through the next few hours."

They nodded and made their way through the crowds and out the door.

J.J. stopped short of stepping down the porch steps and took a seat on the landing. She opened the letter and read Lana's passage again. "Foggy Bottom—State Department. 1600—."

"That's easy. The White House," Tony said sitting beside J.J. and peering over her shoulder."

"Gold from your farms?" J.J. said. "Hmmm."

Tony thought for a second and snapped his fingers. "Gotta be CIA. The Farm."

J.J. closed her eyes and said, "Cores from Liberty's skirt. I don't know about the cores, but Liberty's skirt means what? The liberty bell? Statue of Liberty? An operation based in New York or Philly?"

"Maybe two operations in New York. Ground Zero's got to be the World Trade Center."

J.J. shook her head. "Hmm. Probably so. But a little-known fact is Ground Zero's also a Cold War reference to the Pentagon. So it may be right across the river."

Tony propped his elbows on his knees and dragged his fingers through his hair in exasperation. "What the fuck have we gotten ourselves into? An entire network of Paper Dolls and illegals?"

"Appears so…and other than Lana's cryptic drunken confessions, hardly a clue about who they are or how to find them."

• • •

Saturday Morning, November 7th – Surveillance Detail

"I can't believe those jack offs drove us in circles again today!" Jiggy said to Jazz as he slipped his classic Raybans into the breast pocket of his black leather biker jacket. He removed his toboggan, revealing the smoothness of his bald head. Jazz and he could pass for brothers except for a couple inches in height in Jazz's favor and a slightly darker complexion. They complained as they walked to the Special Surveillance Group Command Center, based inside an old warehouse near a seedy industrial district off of New York Avenue in D.C.

"This is the third day in the row, and Filchenko is proving to be one slick son of a bitch. Another forty-five minutes at Potbelly's, down to the millisecond. He's barely been in the United States long enough to inhale and he's already establishing cover stops and performing surveillance detection runs. You know they're screwing with us."

After being jerked around for three days, they decided to seek guidance from the most senior member of their team. Jiggy followed Jazz through the large steel double entrance doors of the bland white structure and they paced down a narrow hall leading to the offices. The walls were papered with security posters warning against espionage, depicting convicted spies like Hanssen, Ames, and Walker in shackles. They were not-so-subtle hints to stay on the right side of the law and a reminder of why their work was so critical to the FBI.

To the right of the main area, a separate enclosure with 30-foot ceilings housed the Gs mechanic shop. It was visible through a large picture window. Five cars hung in the air on lifts while those awaiting service were lined up as far as the eye could see. Most were specially equipped with tracking devices, kill switches, specialized headlight controls, and supped up engines to ensure they had the speed and equipment to conduct evasive or defensive maneuvers while trailing their targets during surveillance runs.

On the office side, partitions filled the area where the Gs desk-hopped to draft reports at the ends of their shifts. Jazz and Jiggy scanned each one apologizing for interrupting their colleagues who were deep in concentration. Jiggy knew Money T and Cham had to be around the base somewhere. Money T had much more experience in Russian operations than either he or Jazz. They hoped he could offer some explanation or objective opinion on how to handle recent events.

As he turned the corner and headed toward the back of the room, he noticed the top of Money's head poking up from behind Cham's workspace wall.

"Hey!" Jiggy called out.

Money peered out from behind the wall and smiled, the pricey haircut and two signature gold teeth that earned him his moniker (short for Money Teeth) glimmering against the halogen light on his desk. "Thought you two were on duty this afternoon."

"We had the first shift this morning. Look, we need to talk to you about something. You got a minute?"

"Yeah, step into my office," Money said as he led them into an empty conference room and closed the door behind them. After taking their seats, he leaned his chair back and clasped his hands behind his head. "What's going on?"

"It's the Russians," Jazz said.

"Putin? Medvedev? Mind being a little more specific?" Money asked.

"It's Lana's father and this new guy, Filchenko," Jiggy inserted. "They're out at the same time every day. Hit a couple of cover stops, and then head back to the compound. At first I thought maybe Filchenko was just attempting to get acclimated to the area, but this is starting to set my teeth on edge, especially with Daddy Dearest involved. You had an experience like this before?"

Money shook his head. "No, I haven't," he leaned forward on the table and rolled his eyes up to the ceiling. "What'd the lookouts have to say? Anybody else leaving at the same time?"

"Nope," Jazz said. "Just these two. As matter of fact, they're the only ones who have been out of the compound since the Agent Michaels went missing."

Money snapped his gaze toward Jazz. "First, that bitch is no agent. Secondly, have you spoken to anyone else about this?"

"No," Jiggy said. "Not yet."

Money grabbed a stack of Post-It notes and a pen from the center of the table and begins to scribble. Then he ripped off the top sheet and handed the slip to Jiggy. "Call these guys. They're leading the investigation to find her."

Jiggy scanned the note. "Kyle Oliver and Hopper Mack?"

"Yeah," Money said. "They're co-case agents. They've been flooding this office with requests for information on activity at the compound. I'm sure they'll more than welcome your call. And Oliver is old school, whatever he tells you to do, that's what you do. He won't steer you wrong."

"Roger that."

"Now if you'll both excuse me my shift's about to begin. I'm on the detail to cover J.J. McCall until you find Michaels, so the sooner you guys figure out what the hell is going on, the sooner I can get back to the team."

CHAPTER 21

*Saturday Morning, November 7th—Irving Street
8 Days Left...*

A brisk wind iced Lana's core as she rounded the corner from Irving onto 7th Street and headed north for six blocks. Max McCall's store was open and Lana had business with the new men in her life, but no one would die—not until she'd been extracted and was on her way to Moscow.

She'd exploit this opportunity to test Santino, to gauge the level of his felonious tendencies and the lengths he would go to pay back his twenty-five thousand favors.

She'd also introduce herself to Max McCall in a way that he would never suspect she had entered his life *to end it.*

With her hoodie drawn over her head, she trudged face-down to minimize witnesses and pressed forward to meet her target eye-to-eye. The luminescent glow from the sun ensured no-one would question her dark sunglasses. She was, after all, a woman on the run.

Five minutes later she found it, McCall's Grocery and Wine, a converted corner row-house with painted gray brick only three blocks away.

She peered through the beveled glass door before pushing her way inside, the jingle alerting her arrival. Then she took a moment to scan the layout before entering the fray. If all went according to plan, she only had moments to spare before the op went down. To the left of the narrow walkway, a tall black man with pepper colored hair tapped the keys of the cash register behind the checkout counter. To the right, seven chest-high cramped aisles loaded with grocery stock while glass-door refrigerators and freezers were lined up along back wall.

Lana grabbed one of the black plastic hand baskets and pulled her grocery list from her hoodie pocket. Max McCall peered at her with a skeptical eye before they exchanged silent nods to greet one another. She perused each aisle, glancing at the door periodically and looking down at her watch. At 10:15, she grabbed a bag of Utz in the snack food aisle and dropped it on the floor. As she bent to pick it up, she heard the bell ring and a slam after a burst of cold air washed across her face. Seconds later, heavy footsteps padded toward the counter and stopped.

"Get your hands up!" the frantic man yelled. Lana scuttled to the end of the aisle, concealed behind a potato chip rack. She peered around the corner. The robber's hands were jammed in his jacket pocket, and the distinct form of a barrel pointed toward Max McCall's head. "Gimme everything you got! Now!"

Keeping one palm raised, a panicked McCall fumbled to open the cash drawer but couldn't open it.

"Something's wrong! The drawer's stuck!"

"Shut up and hurry, old man! Don't make me pull the trigger," he growled.

The caramel-skinned thief, dressed in black from head to toe, hovered nervously, his hand shaking. His face was largely concealed beneath his hood, and he stood about her height, maybe fifty pounds heavier. Obviously an amateur. Didn't even bother to check and see if anyone else was in the store. She shook her head.

Lana eyed the overhead shelf above McCall to assess the security system. With an FBI agent for a daughter, she felt certain one had been installed. She spotted two small white cameras, one trained on the door, and the other on the cash register itself. She wouldn't be seen.

"Move it! Now."

With the silence of a light wind, she stooped down and tipped behind the robber. Before he could turn to face her, she leaped, pulled her leg back, and with full power landed a front snap-kick with board-splitting force into his crotch, the crunch of his testicles almost audible.

His legs buckled as he howled like a wounded wolf and crumbled to his knees. Curled over and still gripping his nuts, she landed a second kick to the back of his head; he slammed face-first into the floor. Blood spurted from his nose, and his howls grew silent. She felt the outside of his pocket for the gun, careful to stay out of the camera's view or leave finger prints. Through the fabric, she felt the plastic weapon.

Max rushed to survey Lana's damage. When the robber began to squirm, Lana slammed her fist into his jaw, silencing him once more.

"Sweet Jesus Almighty," Max yelled, thanking Lana profusely as he grabbed the handset from the phone behind the counter and dialed 9-1-1.

"You're welcome," she said coolly, looking at her watch again. 10:20. "I'm...I've got an appointment. Trust me, he's not moving."

"The police will want to talk to you," he said. "You're a witness."

"You don't need me," she pointed to the camera. "Just pull the tapes. You'll be fine from here."

Still standing behind the man sprawled in the floor, Lana pretended to avoid stepping over him as she walked toward the refrigerator section before cutting sharply toward the door.

"Wait!" Max said, raising his hand in the air to gesture her to stop. "Please, take everything you need. It's on the house."

Lana smiled. "That's very generous of you." She stuffed her hands into to her hoodie pocket and lowered her head before reaching the camera's line of sight. "But I've got to go. Good luck. And do yourself a favor and get a panic button installed. There's a lot of shady characters in this neighborhood."

He nodded and waved goodbye as she exited.

As the sound of police sirens drew closer, Lana steps quickened and her breathing grew heavier. She broke into a slight jog and cut into an alleyway roughly three blocks away from Irving.

Minutes later, she burst through the front door of her temporary abode and leaped up every other step until she reached the upper level landing. She bent over and craned her neck to look beneath Santino's door and listened.

Is he here?

The door snatched open, startling Lana. She grabbed her chest. "Shit!"

"You shouldn't lurk outside people's rooms like that. Someone might think you're up to something."

She exhaled and chuckled. "They'd probably be right."

He waved her inside, backing up to his bed before taking a seat. "So, uh, how'd everything go?"

She leaned against the wall and examined her bruised knuckles. "Pure genius," she said as she glided toward him stripping the hoodie over her head to reveal a form-fitting black camisole with her breasts seeping out of the cups. She relished in the power of her sexuality and never hesitated to leverage her looks against witless men. "Plastic gun. Nice touch."

"We try. You'd be surprised what people will do for a couple Gs when they're desperate for cash. I'll have my people spring him later today. You didn't hurt him too badly, did ya?"

"I could've done worse…oh wait, I almost forgot." She disappeared to her bedroom and returned moments later with an envelope thick with 50 dollar bills. She slinked next to him and ran her fingers across the width of his chest before slapping his payment against it. "Can't thank you enough for your help."

Santino opened the envelope and flipped through the cash. "This is more than double what we discussed."

"Yeah," Lana said. "You're strapped for cash right now, so let's call the extra a token of my appreciation and the beginning of a beautiful relationship…if you're willing to lend me your services again, that is."

Santino locked his eyes on Lana's cleavage and his voice rumbled, "If this is the way you show your appreciation, I'm here for *whatever* you need."

He slipped his fingers beneath the straps on her shoulder then flashed a wide smile as he tried to expose her.

"There will be plenty of time for that later. Right now, I need another favor."

CHAPTER 22

Sunday Brunch November 8th—Max McCall's House

The wind spiked and whipped around the otherwise listless Irving Street. Dressed in slacks and a button up suitable for a first-time meeting with his girlfriend's father, Tony squinted as he craned his neck to see past J.J. through the passenger window. He surveyed the area as the rain slammed against the three flights of concrete steps leading to Mr. McCall's front door. The dark clouds hung heavy overhead like the doubt in his mind about whether this visit was a good idea.

"Do we have to?"

"Yes," J.J. said as she glanced down to check the time. "Ten more minutes and it'll be time to eat. Listen, I realize you're a little anxious, but it's best to just *rip* the Band-Aid."

Few situations made Tony nervous in his lifetime, which spoke volumes given the nature of the family business. Meeting the Black Panther father of the woman he loved would rank somewhere in the top ten.

"Okay, okay. Let's do it," Tony said. Before he swung his feet onto the ground he peered up to see a man hawking over him like a shadow from his past.

The man lurked from the front door of the house directly across the street.

Tony locked glares with the familiar olive-skinned dark-haired figure before the slick New Yorker disappeared inside. Tony froze and his eyes widened as he surveyed the area, looking around for any untoward movement. After all the years of doubt and suspicion, Tony feared the order had been given and death was breathing down his neck. Maybe he'd wait until he caught Tony alone, with nothing between them except the truth and death—the family didn't like witnesses.

He stepped out of the car and put his hand on the gun in the small of his back.

"Tony? Uhhh…everything okay?" J.J. asked, jarring him out of his thoughts. Her eyes were locked on his hand.

Shaken, he turned to face her; she was already near porch landing. He sharply turned back to the door across the street, jerking his head left and right. But the street was as bare. He shut the car door and ran up the stairs.

"You okay, Who was that?" J.J. asked.

"Probably nobody," he lied. "Thought I recognized him, but I can't place his face right now. It's nothing. Fuhghettaboudit."

"Agh!" J.J. yelled, as she shot him a side-eye glance. The discomfort in her face was palpable.

He touched her shoulder. "*You* okay? You really need to get that thing of yours checked out."

As J.J. stuck her key in the lock, Tony peered over his shoulder. A curtain in the upstairs window stirred as the thunder cracked, Mother Nature's warning that another storm was brewing. And without his father's protection, he would perish alone.

• • •

J.J. drew in a few deep breaths as she waited for Tony to make his way up the steps. He'd certainly piqued her curiosity, glaring at the handsome stranger across the street as if it was high noon at the OK Corral. She'd spent nearly every weekend at her father's house for brunch and had never noticed him or anyone moving in. Mr. O'Leary rented out the place from time to time, so she figured the guy must be a new tenant. But with what she now knew about the Bonannos and Lana, she'd be on guard for Tony's sake and hers.

The moment they stepped inside the McCall's humble abode, Tony asked, "You sure about this?"

J.J. dropped her purse on the couch and ushered him in. "Please stop worrying. We're fine." She attempted to convince herself as much as Tony. She patted his chest and rose to the tips of her toes to kiss him on the cheek as a symbol of reassurance. "Trust me, he's going to love you...*someday*. And don't be alarmed by the pictures," J.J. said, pointing to her father's Black Panther photos blanketing the walls. "He doesn't hate white people nearly as much as he used to."

His eyes darted around the room, bulging as they scanned each pho-to of the rifle-toting, fist raising black men in black. Max McCall's home looked more like a civil rights museum than J.J.'s childhood home. "Used to?"

"Is that you, J.J.?" her father called.

"Yeah, Dad. Just a sec," she said before returning her voice to a whisper. "So, three things. First, please don't step into the kitchen without washing your hands. He's fanatical about bacteria. Powder room is on the left."

He nodded. "Gotcha. My mother's the same way."

"Always address him as 'sir.' It'll reduce the number of reasons he has to pick with you."

"And third?"

She smiled. "I love you," she said before mumbling, "and I hope you still love me when this is over."

Moments later, J.J. watched Tony suck in a deep breath as he stepped out of the bathroom. He smiled at an awaiting J.J.; the smell of bacon and warm bread wafted through the air and drew them into the kitchen.

"All right. Here we go," J.J. whispered. "Your gun's in the car, right?"

He chuckled.

They entered the kitchen, greeted by Malcolm's smile and Max McCall's skeptical glare. "Well, well, well."

"Hi, Mr. McCall. Pleasure to meet you," Tony said, extending his hand. A wave of relief appeared to wash over him when Max returned the favor.

"I'm sure," Max said. "Come on in and have a seat. Finishing up breakfast right now."

"Everything smells great. Appreciate you having me ova." Tony sur-veyed the table for empty seats and took the one nearest to Malcolm, his other ally. He was the slightly younger, male version of his sister, equally brown and trim, but with a few inches above her five-ten frame and close-cut hair. "Hey Malcolm, good to see you again."

"So, you work with J.J., huh?" Max asked, his eyes fixed on Tony.

"Yes, Dad," J.J. answered. "We're co-case agents. I told you."

"I know. I know. We're making small talk, J.J. Settle yourself down. This is the easy part."

Tony shook his head at Max and then turned to J.J. "What he said. Go ahead and fix your plate. You look hungry."

J.J. patted his arm and moved toward the stove.

"So, Tony," Max said, pointing his spatula in Tony's direction. "*You're* Italian. What did *you* think of *The Godfather*?"

"Daaaad!" J.J. cringed as she whined. His question was wrong on so many levels but sadly not surprising.

"Relax," Max said. "At least I haven't asked him about his credit score…*yet.*"

She clenched her eyes shut and prayed for a distraction. Anything to change the subject of this conversation before he or Tony spoke a single syllable they couldn't take back. No sooner than the thought crossed her mind, the doorbell rang.

"I'll go grab that," Malcolm said, jumping up from the table seemingly as relieved by the interruptions as J.J. Before leaving the kitchen, Malcolm leaned into J.J. and whispered, "Don't let them finish without me. This is getting good."

"I wonder who's visiting at this time of morning," Max said. "Nobody in our family interrupts brunch day."

A few moments later, Mike entered the kitchen his eyes wide, his expression sheepish. He slipped into his seat and began to cough uncontrollably.

"Who was that, Malcolm?" J.J. asked.

Her brother held up his hand and grunted, attempting to clear his throat. "Grayson," he coughed out in a muffled grumble.

J.J.'s eyes narrowed then bulged wide open when the large chocolate frame appeared, her favorite cologne now choking the oxygen from her lungs.

M&Ms, she thought, *I need M&Ms.*

"Good morning! Good morning!" Six bellowed. His voice fell on J.J. like a sledgehammer. He sauntered in dressed to the nines in his tailored suit and fresh haircut, his cologne arriving thirty seconds before he did. "Hope I'm not intruding."

"Yes, you are!" J.J. snapped. Six moved toward her and attempted a kiss on the cheek, but she snapped her head back out of range, gave him *the hand,* then gently nudged him back a step or two. "What the hell are you doing here?"

"Watch your language Jasmine Jones McCall!" Max said. It was never a good sign when Max barked three of her four names. All four names was the worst. "Ain't nobody in this house grown but me. Besides, what kind of way is that to treat our guest?" Max said. "Six! I can't tell you *how happy* I am to see you…but I'll give it a shot if you pull up a seat. We're just fixin' to eat."

"How is the beautiful McCall family doing on this fine Sunday?!" he asked, smiling like a Cheshire cat in a cardboard box.

"Fantastic…now that you're back in town." Max beamed from ear-to-ear. Unlike everyone else in the room, he seemed completely unsurprised by Six's appearance.

Her father's profuse joy struck a bell. J.J. realized what happened. She'd been set up by "the man." Her father was on a mission to rid himself of Tony. She wouldn't have taken her father for the unscrupulous type. The nerve and the gall. Merrily extending an invitation to Tony and inviting the snake. She cut her eyes at her so-called father, a cold expression that was met by Max's wide grin.

"You know I wouldn't miss this for the wor—," Six's eyes locked on Tony. "Ohh ho ho, we have company this morning. Good to see ya again, man." He held out his hand to shake Tony's, who reluctantly returned the favor. He shifted his gaze between Tony and J.J. "What brings you here? Wait a minute, wait a minute. You two are a…" he began before Tony interjected.

"Uhhh, we're on our way to…take care of some Bureau business," he lied.

"Oh? Anything I need to be aware of? After all, we're in this together now. Partners in crime, so to speak," he said, finishing with a hard, fake chuckle. *He he he.*

"It's strictly need-to-know…and you don't," J.J. said to Six. "Now, back to my question. What the hell are you doing here?" J.J.'s jaw tightened as she tapped her foot heavily against the floor.

"I'm hurt, J.J.," he said pressing his hand to his heart. "You know I'd never miss one of Mr. McCall's breakfasts if I'm in town."

Angry enough to punch the pigment out of his cocoa-colored skin, she couldn't force him to leave but she could make him sufficiently uncomfortable to ensure he didn't prolong his stay. "Well, since we're used to seeing your back as you run out the door, how soon can you make that hap—"

"Uhhh, so how long you in town for?" Malcolm asked, in an obvious attempt to keep the conversation light and his sister at bay.

"Depends on how long it takes for your sister to come to her senses," he said, laughing. Then he locked eyes with Tony and forced that annoying laugh again. "Just kidding."

A series of beeps sounded from the coffeemaker.

"Coffee's ready. Who's pouring?" Max called out.

"Let me do the honors," Six said, lifting the steaming carafe. "Mmm. Smell that aroma. Comes from only the darkest, richest beans. I suppose we should serve our guest first. Coffee, Tony?"

"Mmm...you're right. Thanks, man," Tony said. "Steaming hot and black. My favorite."

Six stopped pouring mid-cup. "You sure you can handle it?" he asked Tony. "Mr. McCall makes his coffee pretty strong. It's not for the weak and weary. Keeps you going all day long."

"Oh, I can handle it," he said. "I drink it at all times of the day and night."

Six's eyes rolled before they narrowed. "Coffee for you, J.J.?" Six said. "You still take yours *black*, don't you?"

"No, not anymore. Makes me sick to my stomach. Now, I take mine with *cream*. Lots of *cream*." J.J. said, glaring at Six. "In fact, the *creamier* the better!"

"We don't keep no *cream* in this house," Max interjected, his eyes squinted at J.J. "Cream weakens the coffee. Black coffee is strong, better for you too."

Six exposed a wry smile. Max was on his side and always would be against Tony. But unfortunately for him, Max's vote didn't wasn't powerful enough to take Tony out of the running.

"You're mistaken, Dad. Cream doesn't weaken the coffee, only gives it a richer flavor."

Six cleared his throat and eased around Tony. He held the carafe over Malcolm's cup. "How about you, Malcolm?"

Malcolm's eyes darted back and forth between each of them, the subtext apparently not lost on him. The final vote was his and his alone. Who would it be? The guy who made her crazy or the guy he hardly knew? J.J. narrowed her hardened gaze as if to dare him to pick sides. He placed his hand over his cup. "Uhhh...orange juice for me. Thanks."

* * *

The sound of forks clanking against her mother's china was the only noise that broke the strained silence. J.J. simmered as she quickly plowed through her breakfast and Tony followed her lead, gobbling down their eggs and gulping their coffee in a manner that would impress a Marine recruit on the first day of boot camp.

The nerve of her father imposing on her life...as usual. What did she expect really? Open arms and an invite to the Panther meeting? Perhaps she hoped beyond reason he would display a sliver of the respect he and her mother had spent so many years instilling in her as a child.

She struggled to stifle her emotion, to not speak the words she wanted to say, to walk out the door and try again next week with lower expectations.

But she couldn't.

After all, she was the daughter of Max and Naomi. Neither had made a habit of holding their tongues.

"Dad, can I speak with you in the living room for a moment...please," she said, her voice stern, her back stiff.

"Sure, excuse us," Max said as he dabbed the napkin along the corners of his mouth, dropped it beside his plate, and slipped out of his chair. "We'll be right back."

J.J. tromped in front of the fireplace and crossed her arms across her chest. "All I want to understand is why? Why would you do this? And don't tell me you didn't know he'd be stopping by because I have no doubt you did. Next time you could at least pretend to be surprised."

"I'm sorry, baby, but you understood how I felt before you came," Max said. "Listen, for what it's worth, he seems like a perfectly...decent guy."

"Then what's the problem?"

"The problem is, J.J.—he's not for you."

"Hmph. Same thing Grandma Jackson said about you. Mr. Black Panther marrying her upright, FBI agent daughter. As I recall, society wasn't wrapping its arms around you either. But you survived together... right up until the end," she said, choking up.

"Yes, you're right," he said. "But we were different."

"No, you weren't," she fired back. "And until you can see that, you and I will be standing on opposite sides of the fence."

He lowered his head. "So...you won't be coming to Sunday brunch anymore?"

"I said fence...not wall." She glanced at her mother's photo. "I'll be here, but I won't enjoy it as much. Neither will you...because every time I come here, he'll be right beside me! So there."

Max shook his head. "You got that snippy attitude from your mother's side."

"Yeah...I also got her sense of curiosity too. Which brings me to my next question...do you know Jack Sabinski?"

"I've heard you mention his name once or twice. Your mother too, but that was years ago. Trust me when I tell you, I know more FBI personnel than I ever want to know," Max responded. J.J. waited for a reaction but got none. His answer was the truth, even if only half of it.

"He told me I should ask you what happened to Mom. No more beating around the bush, Dad. Every corner I turn leads me back to you. What are you not telling me?"

Max stood to his feet and walked over to the window. He pulled the curtain back and stared out into the distance. "This was your mother's favorite kind of weather. She loved the rain...nature's cleansing, washes away the old and makes life new again."

"Dad, please. What happened?"

"J.J., it's complicated. What you must understand is—"

"What's going on in here?" Malcolm interrupted, his smile the mirror image of his father's. "Had to make sure there was minimal bloodshed in this room because I don't think I can hold those two off much longer."

"Oh God," J.J. said. "What's Six doing now?"

"Being Six," Malcolm said. "You better get in there or only one's coming out alive. My money's on Tony."

J.J. chuckled. "That's a good bet," she said to Malcolm before turning to Max. "Dad, we'll continue this another time. Soon."

He nodded in agreement. "Don't I know it."

CHAPTER 23

Monday Night—Irving Street
6 Days Left...

The sun burned red beneath the horizon and the rain clouds had begun to move in when Lana returned home from checking the signal left by her embassy handler, her father. He had somehow managed to evade FBI surveillance and fill the dead-drop containing her travel documents and money. Now she had to find her way to the location to retrieve them so she could get the hell out of the United States.

And not a moment too soon.

Unfortunately, the drop must be cleared under the cover of night and she had no car to drive to the location, Henson Creek Neighborhood Park, off a windy walking trail in the heart of Prince George's County. It was supposedly accessible by metro, but such a lengthy trip would leave her too vulnerable to being detected.

She glanced out of the window. Santino's car sat parked in front of the house. Maybe she could convince him to let her borrow it. Wouldn't take her much more than an hour or two to retrieve the drop. Surely he would accommodate her.

She unbuttoned her blouse down to her cleavage, exposing the heaping mounds of flesh and silicone beneath. After slipping on her jacket, she skulked to his room.

She knocked. No answer. Again. No answer.

He must've gone out for a walk. She noticed he did so from time to time when he didn't want to smoke his stogies in the house. Helped keep Mr. O'Leary's complaints to a minimum. She quickly paced back to her room, poked her head out the window to see if he was on his way down the block. Then she retrieved her Metro Smart Card and returned to Santino's door. It only took her a minute to slip it into the door jamb and pop the lock. Once inside his room, she searched through every drawer and closet, hoping to find an extra set of keys.

She heard sound, froze and waited. Perhaps it was her imagination. She dashed to the door and peered downstairs. Nothing. She returned to her search, her frustration increasing. She couldn't find them. Maybe he only had one set of keys. Perhaps he'd taken them with him. One last ditch effort to ensure all was clear and she checked the pocket of the two coats still hanging in the closet.

A jingle sounded when she slid one hanger aside She dug her hand inside the pocket.

"Yes!" she screamed in a whispered tone.

She bounded for the door, scanning the street up and down before jumping in the car and taking off. Lana left nothing in her wake except fumes.

Once the package was in hand, she'd be on the ocean and back in Moscow by week's end. However, not before exacting revenge against J.J. McCall. Her game required a pawn, and Santino had proven that he would serve well. He helped set up a fake robbery in a matter of hours. And the final deed, the one that would seal both of their fates, would free Lana from the United States and all suspicion in the death of Max McCall.

• • •

Meanwhile, a furious Santino had rounded the corner in time to hear the rumble of his engine and spot the flash from his brake lights as his car passed by.

"What the f—" he barked to himself, cutting himself off. He grumbled with a vicious sneer and tromped back to the house as the rain began to pour. "I can't believe that cunt stole my car with all that shit in the trunk! Ohhh, if she has the balls to show her face back here, she's as good as dead!"

CHAPTER 24

Monday Night—Washington Field

Rain pounded against the office window by the time Kyle finished filing his 302s for the day. He scrolled through the caller ID for the fifteenth time hoping to see D.C.'s number. With each passing minute, the Russians' chances of delivering the travel documents to Lana increased exponentially. Wouldn't be long before some other priority subjects threatened to shift Gs resources to different investigations, a threat which loomed heavily. Everybody knew it...including Lana.

Kyle turned off his desk lamp and headed to Hopper's cubicle. Maybe Junior's conversation with the Gs had yielded information that would indicate whether or not the Russians had resumed operational activity. When he rounded the corner, Hopper held up his index finger, gesturing Kyle to wait a minute as he finished up a phone call.

"All right, Jiggy," Hopper said. "I'll discuss it with Kyle and see what we can do. We'll call you back." He hung up the phone and his face crumpled; he pulled out his guest chair. "You may want to sit down for this."

"Uh oh. The expression on your face says it all."

Kyle grimaced as Hopper recounted Jiggy's bleak report from the Gs. Not only had the Russian not stood down operations—they'd ramped them up a notch, in their own special way. After more than 15 years in the field, Kyle learned most intelligence officers avoided antagonizing surveillance; they strove to stay under the radar and off the Gs' shit list. Only a critical operation would make them do so intentionally. With only two officers making runs, it was clear the rest of the residency was probably on stand down. So why send out Lana's father and the new counterintelligence officer? Only one reason for their bizarre surveillance detection runs made sense—to support Lana Michaels.

"Your thoughts?" Kyle asked.

Hopper shrugged. "I dunno. It's obvious they want to establish a pattern. Maybe they're trying to gauge how many surveillance personnel we've posted on the streets. At a minimum, they want us to believe they're just fucking with us."

"You nailed it. That's what they want us to believe. The question is why? I'll tell you this...if an FBI agent went on the run after a sanctioned op went bad, we'd stop at nothing to get them home...even provoke the local security service."

"Yeah, I agree," he said. "But what do we do about it?"

"I think it's pretty obvious."

"Obvious?"

"Yeah. We need to fight fire with fire. They think they've faked us out. So we need to use that to our advantage. We need to use these fake runs to get the information we need to disrupt their operation."

"I was going to suggest backing off, but it sounds like that's the last thing we want to do."

Kyle shook his head, then scraped his fingers through his grey infused strands of blond. "No, can't back off now. But we need to find a way to make them believe they evaded our coverage and are operating in the black when in fact we still have eyes on them."

"Problem is, we have no way of letting them get in the black...without letting them get in the black."

"Ahhh, not necessarily," he said. "We could go through air, a plane or a drone, but we don't have time to get the authorization."

Hopper jerked his head back and popped his right eyebrow up.

"They've timed their stops perfectly, you say?" Kyle asked.

Hopper nodded. "That's what Jiggy said. Each stop's predictable almost to the second. Leave the same time, stop the same time, return to the embassy at the same time. Like clockwork. About 45 minutes for the longest phase."

"That means we've got a forty-five minute window. That's plenty of time," Kyle said rubbing his hands together sinisterly. "I've got an idea for the next run."

"What is it?"

"Weeeellll," Kyle began, "it's a complicated operation and you'll play a critical part. The Gs have done it before. It's old hat for them," Kyle said. "First things first. We need to get SAC authorization. Then we've got to go to Special Projects to get some toys."

"Toys?" Hopper said, rubbing his hands together eagerly. "Okay, I'll start the paperwork now."

"No, no. I'll get a verbal and we can do the paperwork later. It's been a long day and we've got a tough few days ahead of us," Kyle said. "Why don't we grab a beer and discuss your upcoming meeting with Filchenko?"

"Filchenko?" Hopper froze and locked a confused glared on Kyle, eyes wide. He shrugged and said, "Okaaaaay." Just as he stood to leave, his phone buzzed. He checked the caller ID, opened the line, and mouthed the word. "Metro."

"Mack," he answered. "How can I help you?"

Kyle twiddled his thumbs as he waited for Hopper to wrap up his conversation.

"Okay, thanks." Hopper hung up the phone and turned to Kyle. "They think they've got footage of Lana leaving a D.C. metro station. We'll have it first thing in the morning."

"Great. Another good reason for a beer. Let's go."

As Kyle led Hopper to the Capitol Grille, he questioned whether he could pull off the op he'd conceived, especially given the current climate. Such operations were simple in theory but much harder to execute on the streets. Things could go very right or very wrong—and very wrong would be very ugly for the FBI and the country. Kyle wanted no part of the *Washington Post* headlines.

He resolved not to spin his wheels for too long. At the end of the day, the move would get him closer to finding Lana. She'd already taken down his best friend and had her sights set on another agent. Any op designed to put a stranglehold on support for her escape was worth a shot.

• • •

Back at Irving Street…

With the drop contents resting on the passenger seat of Santino's Mustang, Lana pressed the gas pedal through the floor, the tires screeching on every turn back to Irving Street. There was no time to open the package and ensure everything she needed had been provided, but with her father at the helm she trusted with blind faith. It's thickness suggested it contained the cash, passport, and travel tickets. She'd stopped at a drive-through carwash to quell Santino's inevitable anger and ease his suspicions. The cash she'd pay him, now that she had resources to do so, would ensure his expedient forgiveness. She didn't much concern herself with the potential blowback from her brief pilfering; after all, he was just another silly little man. She'd tangled with men much more foreboding than an Italian thug and always came out on top...so to speak.

Once home, she crept upstairs to the landing and slipped the key beneath the mat and approached her bedroom. Before she could grip the knob, the door had flung open and Santino's large hand tightened around her neck. He yanked her inside and jammed her back against the wall. She could feel the rush of blood turn her face plum red as she gasped for air. Thickened veins popped out of his arms as she struggled to release his stone hands from her neck, but his limbs felt as solid as concrete.

"What the fuck are you playin' at Katherine?!" he growled through clenched teeth. "You take my car without askin'! You tryin' to get me pinched? I could break the bones in your neck with one squeeze!"

She shook her head feverishly, her face beyond purple, as she tried to respond. "Money. Mo-ney," she gurgled and mouthed as she yanked at his fingers.

He loosened his grip and she sucked in a breath through the eased constriction. "Please. Please. I can explain," she gurgled as tears streamed down her face. She'd underestimated him for the last time whether she died in his grip or changed tactics. "I promise," Katherine squelched. "Just listen."

He released her from his chokehold, stepped back, and pulled a pistol with a silenced tip from the small of his back. He dug it into her temple. "You fuck with me, you make one wrong move and your brains will be sliding down this shitty wallpaper!"

She grasped the nape of her neck as she sucked in deep breaths, her appreciation for air increased exponentially. Holding one open palm up and facing him to reassure him her movement was non-threatening, she bent her knees slowly and descended toward the floor. "Please, I needed to pick up my package. I'll show you."

He backed up, only a half-step, and turned his gun toward the bed.

She grabbed the bag, sat down, and ripped out her words out in rapid succession as if each syllable cost might cost her something more precious than the money she planned to sacrifice. "I've got to leave the country. I was going to pay you," she explained as she ripped off the mounds of duct tape and pulled out the contents.

An envelope thick with cash. A ticket. And a note.

No passport.

She fanned the cash on the comforter beside her. "See? I'd planned to give you half."

Santino pursed his lips and returned the barrel to her head. "What would stop me from putting a bullet in your head and taking the whole thing?"

"Because, if you help me," she said as she divided the money up and tossed at the end of the bed. "I can get you triple this amount. You'll have enough to pay off your debt and pocket the rest."

His eyebrow popped up. "Triple, huh? You got my attention. I'm listening."

"First I need to check something." She pulled the ticket from the envelope and reviewed the travel plans. "Maris Freighter Cruises. Le Havre, France. This Sunday," she looked up toward the ceiling and remembered France had no extradition treaty with the United States, and she'd always wanted to visit Paris. She smiled and turned to Santino. "I'm going to need a ride to Baltimore."

"Hell, I can handle that."

She opened the note.

We will drop your new passport at the emergency location on Thursday. Once you retrieve the package and mark the signal indicating receipt, we will sever communications until you return to Moscow. Safe travels and your courageous service shall be rewarded.
Andrei Komarov

"Is that all?" he asked.

She shook her head no and hesitated before speaking. "What would you say if I told you I needed...to *take care of* someone?"

"Take care of?" he said, jerking his head back. "Who?"

She smiled and rolled her eyes. *Dumbass*, she thought. It wasn't his fault she was the only one between the two of them who knew precisely with whom they were dealing. "Does it matter, *mudak*?" she sang sweetly as if using a term of endearment. "It means darling one," she lied.

"Hmph, Sounds like a sissy name. If you're gonna give me a nickname, at least make it something with balls."

She let out a hearty laugh at his expense. Dare she tell him the name had more balls than he knew? "I'm sorry, Santino Santino, but you didn't answer my question."

He shrugged. "Nah, what do I care? As long as your people aren't my people, we're good." He smiled. "So, is this about your husband? You want to get revenge on the person who off'ed him?"

"Please. Revenge is for children bullied out of their lunch money. I want justice," she said, her voice flat and cold. "If I can't kill the one responsible. I'll kill someone she loves. Let her live with that pain, as I have to, for the rest of her miserable days."

CHAPTER 25

Tuesday—The Situation Room

"How this could've happened?" Kendel asked, staring at her reflection in the glossy mahogany conference table anchored in the center of the Situation Room. On it laid one of the square removable panels concealing the wires and telecommunications and video equipment installed along the perimeter walls.

Burrowed into the rear of the panel were two circular inserts containing the devices.

With gloved hands, Walter and Tony carefully examined each component, while Six and J.J. stared at Kendel's stupefied expression. "The space underwent renovations in 2007 and has undergone a few sporadically since. I mean, it had to be somebody on the security or construction teams. Had to be."

"Tony, J.J., you see this?" Six asked. "I'm not a betting man, but I'd say this looks almost identical..."

"To the device found in the State Department?" J.J. asked.

"Yeah, even down to the precision-cuts. This panel isn't removable like the others that cover the cabling. They cut this panel especially to plant the bug. Look, you can't even tell the difference. Whoever did it had expert carpentry skills," Tony interjected. "At best the White House has a mole. At worst..."

"A sleeper," Six said.

They each exchanged glances and turned to Kendel, whose scrunched brow served as a clear indication that her mind was spinning.

From the midst of her haze, she continued speaking as if she hadn't heard anything but the sound of her own thoughts. "But we conduct sweeps regularly," she urged, her shock apparent as her eyes shifted nervously.

J.J. waited for a reaction, but none came.

"We installed electronics sensors during the last renovation. Why didn't our equipment pick them up?"

Walter looked up with his glasses low on his nose and his eyes peering above the rim. "The sensors installed in this room scan for high-frequency devices like cell phones. This device operates," Walter said, holding up the panel, "on a low frequency. The sensors wouldn't detect it," he said. "But there's another possibility to consider. If I'm right, you may have a much bigger problem. Can I take a look at your equipment?"

Kendel froze as if she was momentarily paralyzed. Then she picked up a phone and made a call, mumbling something indiscernible under her breath. After hanging up the receiver, she said, "They're on the way. Hawk will be here in just a few minutes. He's fully cleared."

"So, what's next?" Six asked.

J.J. turned to Kendel. "Do employees badge both in and out of this space?" she asked.

Kendel nodded. "In, not out. The system maintains a log which goes back to 2003 when we installed it."

J.J. asked, "Are there hours in which the room is regularly not in use?"

"Most nights, unless there's a major operation going on. We run a 24-7 watch desk, but that's located in the space next door."

"Okay, we'll need a printout of the log. All entry records from the date of the last renovation."

"Are you kidding me?" Kendel said. "You have no idea how much paper you're talking about, but let me give you a clue. With the volume of information in this system, we could build a bridge from here Moscow."

Walter shook his head. "If you can download it to a drive, our VECTOR program can conduct the analysis and identify patterns. You'd need an intel analyst to run down leads though."

The face of Sunnie Richardson, her favorite go-to intelligence analyst, popped into a J.J.'s head. "No problem. I've got someone who can handle the job."

A click sounded and the door opened. A well-groomed, middle-aged Caucasian man in blue coveralls pushed in a cart with an array of handheld frequency scanners. With eyes narrowed, and mouth twisted into a smirk, he scanned the room before staring down J.J. and Tony in a scornful glare. He had prominent European features, a strong jaw-line, cleft chin, and the worn skin of a man familiar with alcoholic beverages.

"Thanks, Hawk," Kendel said, pointing out the visitors in the room. "Please meet FBI special agents McCall, Donato. That's Grayson Chance, a career officer at the Agency."

"Six, please," he responded.

Kendel looked at Hawk askance. "Everything okay?"

"Couldn't be better," he answered. "I'll be over here if *you* need any-thing."

He stood with his back against the wall, monitoring as if he was on watch duty.

J.J. frowned in confusion. "Excuse me? What's *his* deal?" she asked Kendel. She couldn't help but notice the obvious disdain and look-that-kills sneer from this man who didn't know her from a can of paint. While she understood "F-B-I" didn't always engender feelings of light and love given it's long and often tumultuous history, his 'tude was over the top by all standards. This was going to be a long investigation.

"Technical security contractor. FBI made him jump a bunch of hoops to get his clearances," Kendel whispered to J.J. "He got them but I don't think he's over it."

J.J. smiled warmly and turned to Hawk. "The line for people with a grudge against the FBI could wrap around the Earth twice. You've got a long wait," she said with a chuckle, trying to break the ice.

He forced a fake chuckle before baring a sliver of his teeth like a rabid dog. "Perhaps."

Hawk's attitude took up more space than he did as Walter stood up and walked over to the cart, palming a few of the devices. He examined them closely while removing a jackknife from his pant pocket. He slipped the blade into the scanner's seam, cracking it open.

"No, you can't do that!" Hawk said, loud enough to draw Kendel's attention.

"Are you nuts?" she said. "That's a $500.00 device."

"Just as I suspected," Walter said, facing the circuit board toward her and pointing to a small grouping of wires. "You see this?"

She nodded as everyone nearby turned their attention to Walter.

"Someone disabled the sensor. This $500 scanner isn't worth 5 cents. It'd make a better Christmas decoration," he said, pointing at the blinking light. "And if my suspicions are correct the others aren't worth a nickel either. Someone's been tampering with your equipment. That's why you never detected the bug during your sweeps."

"Jesus!" Kendel braced her hand on the table before taking a seat. "Who would… There's no telling how many bugs are in the building, or how long they've been here."

"Unfortunately, we don't have time to think," J.J. said. "Let's check for other devices so we can determine the magnitude of the breach."

"Use our equipment," Tony said to Kendel. "Your officers can conduct a sweep of the entire residence so we can see if we need to expand the crime scene."

"Yeah, meanwhile, the first thing we need to do is get the ERT in here," J.J. said, speaking of the FBI's Evidence Response Team, slightly uncomfortable with Hawk staring down her throat. "They may find prints or anything else we've overlooked. Although, if the spy is shrewd enough to pull this off, I doubt we'll find much."

"ERT can't show up with the van or raid jackets or the Press Corps will be all over the story like stink on shit. We've still got to keep this under wraps, remember?" Tony said.

"We don't want to risk tipping off the Russians either," Six added, before continuing, "which begs the question, what are you going to do with the bug? The minute you remove it, the Russians will shut down the op and begin an internal investigation."

As J.J. thought about it, Six had a good point. An internal investigation would be disastrous for all involved. Dmitriyev, although he had made a major error in judgment, might still pull through with some critical intelligence. With him supporting the op at the Ellipse, he'd come under immediate suspicion if the Bureau shutdown the device. Yes, the bug had to go, but they couldn't afford to throw Aleksey under the Golikov bus. Losing yet another source, by her own hand nonetheless, was not an option. Once Director Freeman understood the consequences, he would have to agree.

"We'll need to get authorization from Freeman, but it's got to stay, at least for now."

"Have you lost your mind?" Kendel asked.

"No, my mind isn't the loss I'm worried about," J.J. said as she glanced at Tony and conjured up an excuse, hoping he would put two and two together. "I've got to confer with Director Freeman to ensure we don't compromise our sources and methods. Once the ERT arrives, nobody can use the room, not even the President. So, barring the discovery of any new devices, there's no danger of leaking any more intelligence to the Russians once it's sealed."

Kendel reluctantly nodded in agreement and scanned the room. "This situation feels incredibly surreal. I mean, any number of things should have tipped us off to a problem. How did the perpetrator mitigate the risks and pull off what appears to be a flawless operation? It's not like you can practice this."

At once, the deafening blares of a fire alarm sounded. Everyone in the room jumped, then froze amid the muffled grumbles and chaotic footsteps pounding outside the conference room. FBI personnel looked at J.J.; Secret Service looked at Kendel.

J.J. scanned the room and yelled to Kendel, trying to raise her voice above the screeching bonks. She inhaled but smelled no smoke in the air. "What the hell's going on?"

"Fire alarm! We've got to go."

J.J. shook her head. "I'm not going anywhere. We've got to secure the scene."

Kendel smirked. "I'm sorry, but if the President has to leave the premises, so do you," she said. "Hawk is fully cleared. He will secure the room."

J.J. hesitated for a moment, staring down Kendel. Finally, she conceded. "Let's go," she said to Tony and Six. She looked back and watched everyone leave, then stood outside the door as Hawk brought up the rear and secured the room.

"Don't worry," he said, waiting for her to follow the crowd heading outside. "Go ahead. I'll lock it up."

She waited for a reaction, but none came. He appeared sincere in the eyes, but a slight edge in his voice left her with a strange chill of uncertainty. Seconds after she exited the building, Hawk appeared in the doorway and headed toward a group of White House personnel. He hadn't lingered behind for as long as she suspected he might—but long enough.

Standing outside in the driveway, just beyond the Presidential cavalcade, J.J. pondered Kendel's question. It was a good one. How in hell do you conduct an operation of this magnitude so flawlessly? It was almost as if they had… *Oh my God! That's it!* J.J. stepped away from the bustling crowd and motioned Six and Tony to follow her.

They paced toward her and huddled up.

"You remember the State Department case? The listening device was placed in a conference room down the hall from the Secretary, but the space wasn't classified. They probably got nothing in terms of valuable intel."

"Yeah?" Tony and Six said at the same time.

"Well, what if they never meant to collect intelligence? What if the operation was practice, a dry run? What if the Russians had another target all along?"

"The Sit Room," Six said.

"Interesting theory," Tony said. "And if that's the case, narrowing down the list of suspects should be a matter of finding the person in the White House who also worked at the State Department."

J.J.'s eyebrow popped up. "Well, off the top of my head, I can think of *one person* who fits the bill on all counts."

Tony and Six glanced at J.J. and then, one by one, each turned toward Kendel.

With their gazes burning holes into her back, Kendel spun around, appearing confused. She shifted her gaze between the trio and with a bemused expression said, "What?"

"Uhhh, nothing," J.J. said. "We're going to let the team wrap up here and go back to headquarters. Our analyst needs to get started on the deep dive. Who should we call to coordinate interviews?"

"Me," Kendel said. "I'll get you access to whomever or whatever you need."

J.J. knew the answer before she responded. She suspected that if the case implicated Kendel in any way, she'd want to be alerted as early as possible.

Based on the itching sparked during the discussion in the office, J.J. was certain Kendel knew much more than she'd let on—but expert carpentry was probably not her forte. At worst she was a mole—at best, a Paper Doll. Thus, the questions lingering in J.J.'s mind circled around the depth of Kendel's involvement and who, if anyone, had helped her.

CHAPTER 26

Tuesday Morning, November 10th—Irving Street
5 Days Left...

Lana woke up earlier than usual, peering through the black strands of wild hair shrouding her face from the sunlight bursting through the window. Her vivid, rampant dreams allowed her little rest. The more her mind churned over the inevitable, the death of J.J.'s father, the more difficult it became to still her mind. She'd come to the sobering realization that she would much rather see J.J. screaming in pain as she watched Tony bleed out from shots to the head and chest than Mr. McCall. But getting close enough to slaughter them without risking capture was nearly impossible. And leaving the United States without making J.J. suffer was not an option. No, though his only fault was his genetic connection to J.J., Max McCall must die.

But a spirit haunted her, perhaps her guilt, and an eerie, uncomfortable darkness consumed her every time she looked at the front of his house. She quickly shrugged off the thoughts as paranoia born from stress, and, fortunately, she had no time to stew. With hardly three hours of sleep, she needed to leave and check the signal as soon as possible. In the last dead drop, her father had instructed that he would leave one when her travel documents were prepared. Once in her possession, she would escape this godforsaken country.

Santino had posed a minor threat to her plan but not anymore. She had him right where she wanted him...dependent on her for his safety, just like all the others. Her newest Paper Doll—her cut out. As long as he needed money and she had it to earn, he would do her bidding to save his own hide. In the mafia, whether Russian or Italian, the only principles that ranked above anger and revenge were money and self-preservation. He would forgive her the minor transgression to pay his debt and return home.

Lana checked her closet, which was woefully bare, and selected the day's outfit. Nothing to wear except the identical jeans, shirt, and jacket she wore at McCall's store two days ago. The rotation was short and would remain so until she left the country. After winding her hair into a bun and tucking it into the Washington Nationals' baseball cap, she swiped from a vendor near the metro, she moved quickly to the window and scanned up and down the block. The neighborhood was funeral-home still. The only light poured from tall street lamps.

She quietly crept down the stairs and slipped outside, turning her back to the street as she pulled the door shut and locked the bolt. She threw her head back in relief and drew in a long breath before trotting downstairs. Just as she stepped beyond the gate a deep voice called out, "Hey!"

It sounded familiar. "Uhhh…excuse me?" Her eyes searched the darkness for the body connected to the voice, but nothing appeared. Before she could turn to run inside, fast-paced footsteps padded toward her. Her eyes darted around the area. The voice was close. But she couldn't see the body attached.

"I'm over here," he said, his dark figure appearing on the sidewalk. "It's me. You were in my store the other day."

Max McCall. She stared at his front steps until his body appeared beyond the darkness of his porch door and into the beam shining down from the street lamp.

She gasped and grabbed her chest. "Oh my God! You scared me."

He had a warm, gentle smile, and his tall frame hovered high above her. Except for his pumpernickel skin, his girth and the strength emanating from eyes reminded Lana of her own father. "Thought I recognized you. I never forget a face…although you don't have sunglasses today so that threw me off. But the hat…and…you know, the clothes," he said uncomfortably. "So, you're bunking with Mr. O, huh?"

"Uhhh…yeah. Just for a couple of weeks. Had a little trouble at home. Needed a place to stay."

"You don't have any family in the area?" he asked.

"No, not in the area." She shook her head and looked down to check the time. "Anyway, I should get going. I've got an early appointment. Nice seeing you again," she said pointing in the direction opposite of his store.

"Oh okay. Well, thank you again…for the other day. If you ever need anything, stop by the store. Your groceries are on me." He turned to walk away. A few steps into his stride he stopped and said, "Hey, what are you doing for dinner Saturday?"

"I don't know," she answered in confusion. "Why do you ask?"

"Well, my daughter and her friend from work are coming to dinner for my birthday. It would be great if you could come by…and meet *him*. You two would be perfect for one another. "

"Well, I don't—"

After staring at her expression, he shook his head and chuckled. "Ohhh…no no no. He's not …like *me*…he's more like…*you*. So, what do you say? 6 pm?"

"I say…," she began, as an evil smile edging the corners of her lips upward. "6 pm would be *perfect*. I look forward to it."

As Lana paced toward the metro station, a sense of calm enveloped her body. Max McCall's life had been spared. In an instant, her main enemy was back in her sights and headed for the slaughter. The tips of her fingers tingled with anticipation. Just as Lana's heart would forever ache for Jake, J.J.'s would ache for Tony—right before her own death. A miserable and just way to die. And after Santino finished the crime, collected his money, and Lana locked the vision of J.J.'s expression into her mind, Lana's well-timed call to the police would shift the focus of their manhunt from the Red Honeytrap to the new agent killer—Santino Santino—while she sailed the high seas onto France, and finally to Moscow.

Saturday evening couldn't come soon enough.

• • •

Tuesday Morning – Washington Field Office
Hopper walked briskly through the vacant hallway to Kyle's office tucking in the tail of his shirt while he replayed the conversation with the Metro Police in his head—a 7 am breakthrough. Lana was still in D.C.

He was certain of it. The long-awaited call came just as he bit the sole hunk out of his morning bagel. The noise from his stomach growls muffled his thoughts as he tried to anticipate what Kyle would ask him to do next. He'd learned the hard way to stay two steps ahead of him if at all possible. This morning he was ready.

He knocked on the door frame and poked his head past the threshold. "Hey Kyle, you got a minute?"

"Yeah, come in. What's up?"

He stepped inside and plopped down in the guest chair. "Metro called this morning."

"They said they would," Kyle said. "What's the good word?"

"The footage is fuzzy but looks like they found a clip of Lana leaving the station. Green line, U Street area. Not far from Howard University, right?"

"You work in this city. Do you get out?"

"Yeah, just not U Street. Wonder what the hell she's doing over there?"

"The fact you ask is no doubt the precise reason she exited at that stop," Kyle said as he rose from his seat. "I doubt her bestie lives in the area."

"Certainly nothing in her file."

"So, tell me, hot rod, what do you think we should do?"

Hopper blew out a long puff of air and a pressed his lips together in a slight grimace. "Well, if she's laying low in the area near Howard, she's got to find a place to stay. And there's probably plenty of rooms to rent in the area—no shortage of college kids looking for local housing."

"Now you're thinking, Sparky."

"My sister has a dog named Sparky." Hopper frowned. "A labradoodle."

Kyle chuckled. "Fair enough, Junior, how do you propose we follow-up this brilliant theory of yours?"

Hopper thought for a second, flashed a cocky grin and squared his shoulders. "Check the *Post*, school newspaper, see who's renting rooms in the area. Then go door-to-door."

Kyle pursed his lips. "Is that your last and final answer?"

He thrust out his chest and with over-confidence said, "Yeah. Last and final."

"Figures," Kyle said flatly. He scribbled on a Post-It, which he tore from the pad and thrust at Hopper. "Here. Start with the *Post*. Call my contact. He'll get you a list of all the renters who have *pulled* their ads since Thursday. If anyone's rented a room…"

Deflated, Hopper's chin dropped to his chest as he finished Kyle's sentence. "They don't need the ad anymore."

"Lucky for you, the list should be pretty short. Now scram. The timer's winding and we're running out of time."

CHAPTER 27

Tuesday—Russian Embassy

Like the sunless afternoon sky, a dense gray cloud loomed over Aleksey Dmitriyev's life, threatening to unleash a furious storm that would drench him in conflict and accusation. He didn't often lose his cool, but between the panic-induced heart palpitations and sweaty palms, he found himself on the verge of a nervous breakdown.

Agent McCall had spotted him at the site of Gusin's operation, and her distempered glare burned through him like a laser knife. He had no refuge—he couldn't run and was scared to stay. To compound his troubles, the ultimate snafu, Vorobyev and the missing tennis shoe. He had no idea whether Vorobyev had discovered the FBI burn phone and reported him to security. Or even worse—to Golikov.

His own guilt gnawed at him. He should've dumped the phone. He shouldn't have been at the op site, especially as he'd only days before been declared to the State Department as the new embassy security officer. Now, he only questioned whether or not she would expose his activity. And if so, how long before she lodged her complaint? He had no idea and her decision was beyond his control; however, contacting Vorobyev to find out whether the Crooked Twins would be snatching him up in the dark of the night was well within his control, so that's what he set out to determine.

Dmitriyev's feet pounded against the steps as he jogged up the Embassy stairwell leading to his office. He felt as if his heart had exploded in his chest, anticipating the consequences he'd suffer for any one of his many transgressions. He avoided the elevator to remain unseen and slipped past the Resident's closed door, practically unnoticed. It was lunch time and the office area was empty with the exception of a couple of the officer's wives who were working as secretaries.

Once inside his office, he picked up the phone and tried Vorobyev's number again. If he could just speak to him and hear his voice, he could gauge from the tone whether or not he'd been cast to the traitorous hell he deserved. The secure phone rang five times before a female voice answered.

"May I help you?"

"Ludmilla, this is Aleksey Dmitriyev calling from Washington," he said in Russian. "Is Stan available to speak?"

"Ah yes, hello, Alek. Did you forget the time difference?" she said.

Dmitriyev looked up at the clock on the wall. 3:00 pm. He grunted. It was 7 am in Moscow. "I don't know where my mind is today. Perhaps he arrived early?"

"I'll check. Maybe he's in."

While waiting, Dmitriyev stewed in his thoughts. His new fear was that the FBI might discover the bug and immediately pull the plug on the operation and expel Gusin. If Agent McCall was pissed off and acted as expected, as he would have himself, the focus of the Russian intelligence inquiry would point the finger directly at Dmitriyev himself. His presence was the only new variable in an operation, one that had been conducted without incident for at least five years, maybe longer from what he could gather. Yet, refusing to participate could've sparked the Resident's suspicion. He'd be no better off anyway.

"I've checked his schedule and he's in already, scheduled for an all-day meeting with General Stepanov. Some big, new operation."

"New operation? Hmm. Sounds fascinating."

"Between you and me, I heard they're trying to catch someone spying for the Americans."

Dmitriyev gulped hard and swiped his hand across his brow. Sweat beads had burst through his pores before he realized he was warm. He tried to shake off the nervousness and suppress the tremble in his voice. He cleared his throat and said, "Not again. Fucking assholes!" he said, cringing as the words spilled from his mouth. "Any idea which residency?"

"No, that information is very tightly held," she said. "Anyway, I must get going but I've left a message on Stan's desk. Watch yourself. You never know who may be lurking about."

"Indeed, you never know."

The silence was now deafening. Was Stan sufficiently disenchanted with the Service to cover Dmitriyev's ass as he had so many times before? If not, it would be only a matter of time before Komarov called him to attend a "special" or "urgent" meeting. Golikov's goons might return from New York; they had more experience than Filchenko in the art of torture. They would subject Dmitriyev to a gruesome beating before summarily shipping him back to Moscow and feeding him to the vicious wolf called Mashkov.

He had but one sliver of hope. J.J. McCall. He did not signal Gusin to abort his operation—nor blow hers—and his quick thinking may have spared their relationship from damage he could not repair. His heart rate and pulse slowed. The heat withdrew from his neck and ears. He had reasoned himself into relative calm. He glanced at the time. 8:00 pm. He was ready to pack it in for the day. He'd start fresh early tomorrow. After grabbing his jacket, he reached for the doorknob to leave when a knock sounded. He opened it to see the Resident standing there, his face mashed into a fatigued grimace.

"Good, you're still here. I need you to come with me. We have an urgent meeting to attend."

"Urgent meeting?" Dmitriyev asked, blinking rapidly, his heart almost exploding through his chest. "It's late and I was headed to my flat. What is it about?"

Komarov snapped his head toward Dmitriyev and growled. "Don't worry. You'll find out everything you need to know when we get there!"

Dmitriyev followed his boss down the narrow hall to a conference room just at the end. When the Resident pushed the door open, Dmitriyev's glance darted from face to face. *Filth*chenko. Lana's father. The Crooked Twins. His judge and jury stared at him blankly as he entered.

Dmitriyev's face felt flush, the temperature suddenly felt like a thousand degrees. He jammed his trembling hand in his pocket and proceeded inside trying to maintain his cool exterior as the door slammed behind him.

"They're here," Dmitriyev thought to himself, oddly craving one last sip of Starbucks dark roast and a long drag from a Newport. *"I'm dead."*

CHAPTER 28

Tuesday Afternoon—Washington Field Office

"We got it!" Hopper bellowed, as he rushed into Kyle's office flapping the printout in his hand. "Seventy-six ads dropped from the two major newspapers. Forty-one in the vicinity of Howard University."

Kyle peered upward, stone-faced, his brow furled. "Uhh, Junior? The architect who designed this building went through a lot to put doors on the offices. The least you could do is knock on them."

Hopper glanced over his shoulder and pointed back at the door with his thumb, then returned his confused gaze to Kyle. "You mean, you want me to—"

He nodded. "Four years of college and you did learn how to detect a hint."

An incredulous expression covered Hopper's face as he tromped away. He knocked on the threshold and waited for an invitation inside.

And waited.

And waited.

He pounded again.

"Who is it?" Kyle sang. After a long pause and no activity, he said. "Hello? Junior?"

Kyle dashed to the doorway and peered outside. His pain-in-the-ass subordinate was gone. "I don't fuckin' believe this kid," he growled beneath his breath, thundering through the aisles at a breakneck pace until he reached Hopper's desk. Junior was furiously clearing his desk, shutting down his computer and locking his overhead cabinet.

"Where the hell do you think you're going?"

"Ohhhh, I'm no longer invisible," Hopper snapped, securing his gun in his holster. "I don't have time for these fraternity hazing games. If you'll excuse me, I have an investigative strategy to execute."

"Are you kidding me? I pull your leg a little and you stomp out of my office like a grade school girl who got her ponytail yanked? Let me explain something to you in little words that you can understand—when you step into my squad bay check your sensitivity bullshit at the door."

Hopper stood paralyzed, his chin dropped to his chest, and shoulders hunched. Yes, perhaps Kyle had been giving him the blues since before the Sabinski probe, but he had been a little too sensitive and his skin needed some thickening.

In his first smart move, Hopper sat down in an obvious capitulation. "Sorry. Guess I'm a little *passionate* about my work."

Kyle sat in the extra chair and leaned forward, elbows on his knees. "Hey, I appreciate your enthusiasm, and I'm sure you're about as excited to be assigned to me as I am about you. But how about you lighten the fuck up for five minutes so we can catch Michaels before she high-tails it to Moscow, huh? Let's try that for an investigative strategy!"

Hopper conceded and threw his hands in the air.

"Good. Now, while you were on the phone with Metro, I got a call from Jiggy. You've worked with him before, right?"

"Yeah… couple times. What'd he say?"

"A new angle. Two intel officers engaged in some suspect surveillance detection runs. He thinks they may be attempting to make a drop for Michaels."

"You think they're onto something?"

"That's what we're going to find out later today. We'll split this up and go door-to-door on a few of these addresses for a couple hours, then meet the Gs at their command center later this afternoon."

"Sounds like a plan," Hopper said, grabbing a sheet from the desk. "I already organized the list and divided the addresses so the houses are located in the same relative area."

After an eye roll, Kyle grabbed the paper from his hand and scanned it. "Hmmm. Gresham Place, Harvard Street, Columbia Road, Kenyon, and Irving Streets. This'll work. I know the area pretty well."

"I'll hit the ones near campus. Probably will take a couple of days."

"If I need to, I'll request a few extra bodies. For now, I think we can handle it. Let's get out of here."

CHAPTER 29

Tuesday Night—Russian Embassy

The Crooked Twins whispered intently and cut their eyes at Dmitriyev as he made his way to his seat. Aleksey felt the heat of every eye burn through him, his guilt barreling over. Although his intestines would surely melt from the excessive acid bubbling in his gut, he maintained a calm exterior and tried his best to behave as if the meeting was a matter of routine.

"Good evening," Dmitriyev said, giving a respectful nod as he occupied the empty seat adjacent to his boss.

"Before we address the severity of the problem we are facing tonight," the Resident began, locking his eyes on Dmitriyev with a hardened glare. "Comrade, do you have any news or developments to share with the room?"

His eyes widened; he feigned bemusement over the Resident's request. "Excuse me? To what are you referring?"

"One of our esteemed colleagues informed me that you recently attended a special meeting," he said. "Thought you might want to share with us any events relative to our current operations…before we proceed."

Relative to our operations, he repeated to himself. *Does he know?* His ears burned white heat. Now he was not only afraid, but genuinely confused. He didn't know how to respond, what to do. His thoughts raced.

He swallowed hard and a new level of panic kicked in until he recalled one critical factor. He'd last met with J.J. well over a week ago. He hadn't spoken at length to anyone outside of the residency—not even during the brief interlude with J.J. McCall. Onlookers couldn't suspect him of anything other than asking for the time, if that.

Dmitriyev opted to play stupid and said, "Perhaps if I knew which colleague mentioned it…right now, my memory is failing me. I must be having what the Americans call, a senior moment."

A few chuckles erupted through the room.

Komarov turned and looked directly across the table and tilted his head forward. "Filchenko?"

Filchenko cleared his throat and loosened his collar and tie. "Oh, I, uhhh…must've been mistaken," he mumbled, avoiding Dmitriyev's gaze. "We have far more important matters to discuss. Mikhaylova."

Figures! Dmitriyev thought. His boss's motive was clear now. *Filth*chenko must've told the Resident that Dmitriyev conducted an unreported meeting with an unknown source to stoke suspicion. Komarov had sent a clear message to *Filth*chenko—his tattling would not be tolerated, and Dmitriyev hoped he'd learned his lesson.

"Agreed," Dmitriyev said, narrowing his gaze at the scum to his right. The tension between them was now palpable. Aleksey knew from this point forward Filthchenko could not be trusted. "A much better use of our time than mindless gossip I should think."

Lana's father sat forward in his seat and spoke with urgency. "I've been informed that Svetlana's travel documents are ready for delivery. We have a very short window to make the next drop."

"What do you need from us?" Filchenko asked.

"A perfectly executed operation," Komarov replied. "Dmitriyev's plan has been highly effective to date, but the more times we attempt to make the drop, the greater the likelihood that the FBI will discover our activities. So, I'd like to conduct one more dry run of the operation tomorrow and make the final drop on Thursday," he turned to Filchenko. "There is no room for mistakes. The timing must be on point. And I'm making a couple of changes."

"What's that?" Filchenko asked.

Lana's father turned to him. "You and I will switch cars—and routes."

"Switch?" Filchenko responded to Mikhaylov, confused by the suggestion. He'd already told Dmitriyev that he had a difficult time adjusting to driving in the U.S. already without compounding the issue. "I don't underst…"

"It's simple," the Resident interjected. "Aleksey told me you had problems driving the manual transmission. We want to avoid any mishaps. Mikhaylov's car is an automatic and his route is much simpler. You can practice on the manual sometime when our work is not as critical."

"Exactly," Dmitriyev said. "I'm sure the FBI will complain to the State Department but we'll be ready to stand down our operations by the time the Ministry admonishes us."

"I understand," Filchenko said. "I'm certain we can conduct the operation without making any critical errors."

"We?" Lana's father asked with a slight chuckle, as if insulted by the inclusion. "As I was saying, Igor and Vasiliy are running countersurveillance at the drop site. You both will leave an hour ahead of us so you have plenty of time to get in the clear if you're followed. If you see any watchers in the area, draw them away from the site."

"Okay," Vasiliy responded. Igor nodded in agreement.

"I cannot stress enough that we need to extract her this week. She's not just my daughter; she's a loyal officer in the Service, and she will not be left behind," he urged.

"Agreed. This is our top priority." The Resident again turned to Filchenko. "You should prepare to leave at the usual time," he then faced Dmitriyev. "I have a meeting at the Syrian Embassy tomorrow morning, so you will supervise until I return sometime late tomorrow afternoon."

"No problem, I'll be in my office at six a.m., if I'm needed for any reason. We should all return to our flats and get some rest. Tomorrow will be a long day."

After everyone was dismissed, Dmitriyev and the Resident exchanged knowing glances as the Resident passed by to catch up with Lana's father. The Crooked Twins grinned at Filchenko and followed closely on Komarov's heels. Dmitriyev hung back and called out to Filchenko, "Yuriy? May I speak with you for a moment? After everyone leaves, of course."

"Certainly," Filchenko replied, flashing a cocksure smile.

Once the room emptied, Dmitriyev closed the door and turned to stand face-to-face with his new enemy. He squared his shoulders and growled, "What the fuck was that all about?"

"To what are you referring?" Filchenko responded snidely.

"You know exactly to what I'm referring. Leave your infantile games to children. You have no idea with whom *you're* dealing!"

With a menacing glare, Filthchenko moved so close Dmitriyev could smell the scent of his last cigarette. Through clenched teeth, he spat, "On the contrary, Comrade. I know exactly who *you* are. Golikov knows too. It's only a matter of time before you're exposed for the traitorous pig you are." He stepped back as if suddenly fearing his words might get him slugged. "So, take *my* advice and find out who *you're* dealing with!"

Dmitriyev was stunned by his boldness. As the Security Chief, he could devise any number of ruses to prompt his recall to Moscow. He was clearly stupid, and Dmitriyev planned to use that to his own advantage. "Listen to me you sniveling little piss-ant. You are stepping way up in weight class, you lightweight."

"Is that right?

"Yes, that's right. I already know everything I need to know about you. You're nothing but a glorified snitch serving at the pleasure of your Master, merely a slave to Golikov's bidding."

Filthchenko's jaw and lips tightened. Dmitriyev had touched a nerve. He patted Filchenko's head like a dog. When Filchenko took a swing, Aleksey gripped his arm and twisted it behind his back to the breaking point. The scum's face turned plum and his knees buckled slightly as he grunted in pain.

"You are little more than an irritant to me, a thorn in my foot. Continue your silly little games, you will quickly find your neck crushed *beneath* it!"

After Dmitriyev released his arm and stepped toward the door, Filchenko shook it out and barked, "We'll see about that!"

Dmitriyev held the door open and stepped aside to let the scum exit first. "After you." He slipped into a condescending tone. "Enjoy your evening, son. Leave the threats to the real men, and study your maps so you don't fuck up another critical operation."

He slammed the door behind Filthchenko, collapsed into a chair, and dropped his head into his hands. That was close. Too close. His every fear had nearly come to fruition in a matter of minutes. This time he escaped the situation unscathed. Next time he feared he would not be so lucky. The matter had gone from serious to urgent. He needed to find a way to contact Vorobyev.

His life depended on it.

CHAPTER 30

Tuesday Evening—Irving Street

After returning home from a long day of monitoring the dealers finally pushing his product in the streets, Santino hiked up the creaky stairs to his room and noticed a sliver of light shining through a crack in Lana's bedroom door. Usually, he would respect her privacy and mind his own business. For some reason, he couldn't bring himself to ignore the muffled sobs and sporadic sniffles echoing into the hall.

He walked to her door and peered inside, seeing Lana wearing only a pink camisole and cotton shorts, curled up on the bed in the fetal position, clutching a pillow to her chest. The intoxicating scent of lavender drew him inside; the soft sheen of her freshly oiled skin begged for his touch.

He tapped on the door with the knuckle of his middle finger and softly said, "Hey, you! Everything okay in there?"

Her back faced him so she didn't even notice he'd been standing there, watching over her as if she'd morphed into a helpless child.

Lana didn't respond or move her position, nor did her sobbing cease. He was a bit stunned by her behavior. She'd always seemed like a rock, as if she had it all together. And before his eyes she had crumbled into a remnant of the woman she was only one night ago. He slowly pushed the door open and inched toward her. "It's me, Santino. Just want to check and make sure you're okay."

She remained motionless, except for her stomach which constricted with each sniffle; her body began to tremble with every drop of sorrow released.

A surge of emotion overcame him, one he hadn't experienced in a long time. Almost instinctively, he wanted to make her pain disappear. As his eyes traveled up the curve of her hip, to the dark strands of hair shrouding her face, easing her suffering became his only concern.

He sat down at her side, afraid his touch might be unwelcome. "Hey. We don't know each other so well, but I'm here for you…if you ever wanna talk," Santino said, waiting to see if and how she responded.

Her sniffing subsided but she moved nothing except her hand to wipe her eyes. Santino almost felt suffocated in the silence. Patience had never been his best virtue. He figured if she wanted to say something, she'd have spoken up. He decided to leave her to her tears. "Okay…well, if you decide you wanna talk, I'll be in my room."

He planted his fist against the mattress to brace himself as he stood up when suddenly she gripped his wrist. He turned back toward her as she slowly spun her body around to face him.

Her glistening eyes were red and puffy and she had cried the make-up from her skin. Yet, she was still a remarkable beauty. The intensity of her baby blues held him spellbound and he knew, now more than ever, he should run before he couldn't turn back. After all, he'd been in this place before. "Please, don't go," she said patting the now empty space beside her. "I need you here."

She scooted to the opposite side of the bed pulled him toward her. As he lay next to her, she guided his hand around her waist until he felt the small of her back. Then he tightened his arm around her, drew her close.

She laid her head against his chest and let out a long deep breath. "You ever have one of those days when the light at the end of every tunnel is attached to a train waiting to barrel over you….and all you want to do is *give up*?"

Santino chuckled, not at her, rather in the irony of it all. On his own since his mother kicked him out of the house for dealing drugs and running with gangsters, he'd been living in a continuous state of chaos for so long that he didn't whether people lived any other way. "I think you've described every day of my life since I turned 17."

"Some days I can't shake the memory of him…lying in the floor, the life literally blown out of him. You make plans for your life," she said, her voice vibrating with distress. "Things are supposed to go, you know, according to a plan. Then, in a split second, it dissipates like smoke vanishing into air, and you know in that instant that nothing will ever be good again," she continued. "With each day that passes, you become consumed with ensuring the person who robbed you of your happiness pays…for the past, for the present, and the future you'll never have."

An image of Rosa drifted through his mind. He understood her words in a way that few could. Some actions can never be forgiven. And there are some tragedies inflicted upon us that we are bound by our very nature to avenge.

He glanced down and lifted her chin with his index finger until her eyes, sad and soggy, met his. "My grandmother used to say *'Male e bene a fine viene.'*"

Lana propped her head up with her hand. "What's that mean?"

"Evil and good come to an end," he said, pushing her hair from her face and caressing her cheek. "Everything passes away with time, the positive and the negative. You just gotta live long enough to see it through."

She glanced down and up again. "Your grandmother sounds like a smart woman," Lana said. "What other words of wisdom did she leave you with?"

Santino's eyes roamed the room as he searched his memory for something appropriate to the occasion. "I've got one. *'A chi non beve birra, Dio neghi anche l'acqua'* which means, 'may whoever doesn't drink beer be denied by God water also."

Her face scrunched she asked, "What does that mean?"

"I dunno. I think it's some fancy excuse my Uncle Paulie used to get loaded back in the day," he said, as they both broke out in laughter. He was happy to see her smile.

"Reminds me of home. Where I'm from, we say, 'There cannot be too much vodka, there can only be not enough vodka.'"

"Just thinking about this stuff is making me thirsty. I've got a couple Heinekens in the fridge and Grey Goose in the freezer. You want some?"

"French vodka, hah! You would be less insulting to offer me a bottle of piss," she said, tongue only slightly in cheek. "Anyway, I'm not thirsty for anything French or German. I have something Italian in mind."

"Is 'at right?"

She gently ran her fingers down his chest and until she reached his waist. Then she tugged on his belt buckle.

Santino purred through his smile. "I like the way you think."

CHAPTER 31

A hollow silence surrounded J.J. and Tony as they padded along the quiet corridors in the J. Edgar Hoover building. There was no sound except the clack of their heels against the linoleum and the annoying hum of the trash cans wheels being pushed along by the third shift cleaning crew. Pounds of exhaustion weighed her body down as she stopped, grasped the nape of her neck, and arched back into a stretch.

"It's rough, but at least we've got a week," Tony said.

"At least? These investigations usually take months, sometimes years. You really think we're going to find an illegal or a mole by next Tuesday…before the Russian National Security Advisor's trip to Washington?"

"What choice do we have, except to try?" Tony asked. "The current stand down's nothing compared to the one we'll be on during Lebed's visit. By then this jerk-off will figure out we're onto 'em and can use the investigation-free week to cover his ass and maybe even skip the country. That ain't gonna happen on my watch."

"Agreed," J.J. said. "We've got authorization for a full; I hope like hell Sunnie and Walter came up with something. Even one identification based on our initial instructions will help us pin this asshole down sooner than later."

"Come 'ere," Tony eased behind her and gripped her shoulders. "Anybody ever tell you, you work too much?"

"Yes. You. But then you go and set bad examples every day by working as many hours as I do," she said. "If you think about it, my work-a-holic behavior is really all your fault."

"Anybody ever tell you, you talk too much?" he said with a chuckle. He spread his fingers across her shoulders and moved them in a firm circular motion, unbinding the tight muscles in her neck and shoulders.

"Mmm, that feels soooo gooood," J.J. moaned, her eyes practically rolled in the back of her head. "But, uhh, we shouldn't be doing this here."

Tony stopped and leaned around her side until she faced him. "What? You ashamed of me?"

"Don't be ridiculous!" she said, jerking her head back in disbelief. "We mutually agreed to keep the masses out of our business, remember?" She turned to face him, pulling his shirt collar down toward her until his face met hers. "Besides, wouldn't you like to hurry up and get out of here so you can do that in bed?" She laid a soft, sweet peck on his lips him and continued down the hall.

"I'll take that as a 'no'," he said, smiling as he picked up his pace to keep step with her. Their office was only a few steps away.

When they rounded the corner, J.J. grabbed her badge, swiped it across the infrared light, and punched in her code. She barely got the door open before Sunnie and Walter dashed to greet them at the door. J.J. froze and struggled to stifle a chuckle as she took in the sight of Sunnie standing before her wearing a black headscarf with pink and green hair rollers popping from beneath.

"Really?"

"Hey, at 8:00 a.m. you get *Gone with the Wind* fabulous. At midnight, you get this," she said. "Now it'd be great if I could pass on this intel so I can go home and get my beauty rest. Clearly, I need it."

"No, bella," Tony said with the flirtatious accent that always made Sunnie melt. "You're lovely just as you are."

Her cheeks blushed school-girl red as she looked down at the notebook in her hand. "Okay, Walter ran a query using the NSA's VECTOR program and the three criteria you gave us—people who regularly entered the conference room during third shift hours, worked in the State Department in 1998, and in the White House from 2006 to the present." She ripped off the top sheet and handed it to J.J. "Here's what we've come up with so far."

J.J. grabbed the sheet and held it out so both she and Tony could scan it. "Kendel Phillips, Bryer Scott, Edward Tomlin, and Maddix

Cooper. Only four people," J.J. said. Then she mumbled to herself. "And I already get the feeling Kendel has something to hide."

"At least based on the initial scrub," Walter piped in. "Sunnie came up with some ideas about how we can drill down a little deeper, but this will get you started."

"Sweet," Tony said. "I gotta say, I thought we'd be up to our earlobes in 302s. I won't say you've made our jobs easy, but you sure narrowed down the list."

Sunnie handed J.J. a stack of thin files. "We don't have much, but based on the information available, my money's on Bryer Scott. Former Science and Technology Officer for the CIA and worked at INR," Sunni said, referring to the Department of State's Bureau of Intelligence and Research. "He's also pulled duty as a contracting officer. His last financial report indicates he's up to his eyeballs in debt. Divorce, wife took half. Yet, somehow he had the money to purchase a Sea Ray."

"A fish?" J.J. asked.

"Not sting ray, Sea Ray," Sunnie said. "It's a boat."

Walter shook his head. "No, it's more like a McMansion on water. They can run upward of a half a million."

"A five-hundred thousand dollar boat? And he's an FS-what?" J.J. asked, referring to the Foreign Service pay scale.

"If he's an FS-anything, he shouldn't make enough money to purchase THAT boat," Tony said. "Unless he inherited it from a rich uncle or something."

"Yeah, or received a payment from Uncle Sasha," Sunnie added.

"Who are the other two?"

"Edward Tomlin is a former diplomat, defense attaché. He served two tours at the American Embassy in Moscow."

"CIA?"

"DIA," Sunnie said. "He's now serving as one of the President's key military advisors. His wife's a foreign national—Ukrainian."

"Interesting," J.J. said. "The last one?"

"Maddix Cooper. Ex-Navy. Former CIA and Diplomatic Security. He served as a Security Officer in Moscow, preceded Grayson Chance. He's now on the White House security detail."

"Anything interesting on this Cooper guy?" Tony asked.

"Well, Kendel filed a change of marital status form a little over a year ago. Maddix Cooper was the intended spouse. She rescinded it 5 months ago. Guess the wedding's off. And now they're stuck working together too. That's gotta su—" Sunnie said, shifting her eyes between Tony and J.J. She cleared her throat. "Ahem. I think I need some water."

Tony tightened his lips. "Or a snack."

"Okay," Walter said. "We've done all we can do tonight. I'm heading home and I'll be at Fort Meade tomorrow. Call me if you need anything."

"Thanks, Walter," Sunnie said. "You were brilliant," she turned to J.J. and flashed a wide smile. "He's a smart guy."

J.J. gave Sunnie the side-eye that said, "Let me find out you've got a thing for Walter."

"It really is time for you to get some sleep," Sunnie said in response to J.J.'s look. "The long work day has officially made you delirious."

J.J. laughed. "Get out of here…and thanks for all your hard work. I'll expect you here looking *Gone with the Wind* fabulous at 9 a.m."

Sunnie whisked away to her desk, snapped up her jacket and purse, and bounded for the doorway. "If you see me at 9 a.m., you better go home sick," she said as she eased out the door. "You're hallucinating."

J.J. and Tony both chuckled. Not only was Sunnie pretty sharp, she was good for keeping otherwise heavy nights light.

Tony said, "We'll call Kendel tomorrow and set up the interviews."

"Yeah. And to ensure she remains cooperative for as long as possible, we'll save hers for last."

"Good thinking," he replied, looking around the empty office. "Well, we should hit the road. We've got a long day ahead of us."

J.J. arched her neck to the side and pointed to her shoulder. "That's the least of your concerns." She batted her eyes suggestively. "You've got to make it through a *long night* first."

Tony smiled and popped his eyebrows upward. "Have I ever told you I like the way you think?"

CHAPTER 32

Wednesday Morning, November 11th—The White House

J.J. and Tony returned to the West Wing sufficiently early to get the jump on their investigation before the previous night's personnel cranked up the rumor mill. No matter how tightly they intended to cap the lid on the probe, word would seep throughout the staff before long, and once the staff got a hold of it, the press wouldn't be far behind.

The sand in the hourglass was draining quickly; they only had a week and a day to get the subject off the streets—and at least four initial interviews to conduct.

Hawk, the salty contractor with a heaping grudge against the FBI, met Tony and J.J. at the entrance; he and his contempt escorted them up the hall leading to Kendel's office, grumbling beneath his breath the entire way.

"You know, Hawk. Anger causes heart disease, diabetes, and strokes," she said.

He halted abruptly in his tracks, turned to face J.J. with a sneer, and snapped, "Agent McCall, anger is a futile, and would suggest a level of interest in you that I don't have." When they reached the closed door, he said, "Wait here. She's on a call and will be with you in just a moment."

"All righty then," J.J. said, before mumbling under her breath, "cranky son of a bitch."

They nodded and eyed him until he disappeared around the corner.

"She kind of took a shine to me yesterday," Tony said, seemingly oblivious to the tension. "Maybe you should let me do the talking."

"You noticed that too, huh? Clearly you have an effect on the estrogen-dominant among us."

Tony chuckled. "You should know."

J.J. jabbed him in the arm, when Kendel's door opened.

"Morning," Kendel said, bearing a tenuous smile. "You're here early." Her tired eyes bagged, strands of her hair had escaped the tight bun, and her suit appeared twice-worn. She locked her eyes directly on Tony's bright beam, only acknowledging J.J.'s presence with a head jut.

"Ciao," Tony said in his Italian lilt. "Long night, huh?"

J.J. rolled her eyes and tried to suppress the gag reflex induced by his shameless flirting.

"You don't know the half of it," Kendel said, her voice flat, droll. She glanced nervously over J.J.'s shoulder, now avoiding both of their gazes. J.J. turned around to see what she was looking at. There's was nothing except a clock on the wall. "We conducted sweeps through the entire residence. The breach is limited to the Sit Room which isn't a surprise. If the Russians could plant a bug there, where else would they need to put one?"

"You okay, Kendel?" J.J. asked. "You don't seem like…*yourself*."

"I'm fine," she said. "This is what happens when you begin the day with three hours of sleep and no coffee."

"I know that's right," J.J. replied. "So, where do we stand this morning?"

"The Sit Room is still locked down," Kendel said, her eyes meeting J.J.'s for the first time. "ERT finished up collecting evidence a couple of hours ago."

"How many people do we need to neuralyze?"

Kendel let out a strained chuckle. "Men in Black. Glasses. Funny," she said. "We managed to keep the stir to a minimum. There was minimal staff on duty, and the watch desk staff is cleared Top Secret with special accesses." Her voice turned urgent. "But I'm not certain we can contain this fiasco much longer. Has your Director indicated when we can remove the device?"

J.J. shrugged and shook her head. "Freeman's coordinating with your director. They'd both like to find out what we turn up in the investigation. We should know something one way or the other inside of a week, depending on how much cooperation we receive."

She huffed and let out an exasperated sigh. "So, what do we do until then?"

"Issue a notice and post a sign indicating the communications systems are under repair. This *is* the U.S. government. That shouldn't be too much of a stretch."

"I'll take care of it today."

J.J. glanced down to check the time. "In the meantime, time is tight. We've identified a few subjects we'd like to interview. Who can we work with to review the personnel files and coordinate the interviews?"

"Can I see the list?"

"Sure," J.J. said, digging the list from her pocket. She'd rewritten the list before they arrived, omitting Kendel's name from the one she carried. "The list is short. Only three people for now. Anyone you know?"

Kendel scanned over the list, while J.J. watched closely for any discernible reaction. There was none. "All of them," she said, her voice growing more coarse.

"All right then," Tony turned to J.J. sensing her increasing hostility. "We should get started. Where to?"

"Sheldon Vance is our Senior White House Staff Assistant." Kendel's gaze shifted nervously between the two before she pointed down the hall. "Make a left at that corner; his office is the last on the left. I'll call and let them know you're on the way."

A crawling sensation permeated J.J.'s scalp. She tried not to scratch herself but the itching intensified by the second, driving her mad.

"Stop by and see us before you leave for the day," J.J. said, scraping her nails through her hair. She tugged at Tony's arm and motioned her head. "We may need to speak with you later."

Kendel rubbed her arms and shifted her weight from one leg to the other. "Why don't I just strap on a GPS? Save your special ops guys the trouble."

"Excuse me?" J.J. snapped.

Tony grabbed J.J.'s arm and pulled her down the hall before she could unleash the response on her tongue.

"Did she give me attitude?" J.J. asked. "That was uncalled for."

"She's obviously tense. This all happened under her nose."

"No, no. Something more is going on with her. Couldn't you tell how nervous and irritable she was? She rubbed her arms and shifted her eyes and legs so much that I'd think she was coming off of a high…if I didn't know better."

"I can't argue with you on the strange behavior," Tony said as they rounded the corner. He pointed down the hall. "His office must be right there."

"Yep. That would be the last door on the left," J.J. said and then chuckled. "Sheldon Vance, ha! I'm picturing a cross between Steve Urkel and Newman from Seinfeld."

"You can't tell anything from a name."

"You wanna bet? I always win."

"Twenty-bucks," Tony said as they approached the entrance. "Shhh. Here's the door."

He tapped on the doorframe and walked inside. The room was split by a service counter with four waiting chairs lined against the wall to the right and six empty cubicle spaces in the back. J.J. longingly eyed the M&M dispenser on the countertop.

She tapped the head of the bell with the palm of her hand and a man appeared. A tall gorgeous man with bronze skin, a square jaw, and at least a hundred bucks worth of precision-cut layers in his dirty blond locks. His steel-silver eyes and a chiseled body made his custom-tailored suit sing Amen in the Hallelujah choir.

"Good morning. May I help you?" he said.

"You're," J.J. gulped, "Sheldon Vance?"

He smiled and replied, "Kendel said you were on the way. I took the liberty of calling for the files already. They'll be delivered in maybe another five minutes."

J.J. reached into her pocket, pulled out twenty bucks and passed it to Tony who snatched it from her fingers midway.

"Thanks! We really appreciate your cooperation." J.J. said with a little too much enthusiasm judging from Tony's sneer which was visible in her peripheral vision. She looked at him and noticed what appeared to be a circular birthmark at his neckline. "Is everyone in the office today?"

"Except Maddix Cooper," Sheldon said. "He's out of the country. All the contact information you need is in the files."

A stinging crawling sensation crept up the back of her knees into her thigh causing her legs to buckle briefly. Tony grabbed her arm to steady her gait.

"You okay?" Sheldon asked, clearly concerned with his scrumptious self.

"Ohhh, I'm fine. Skipped breakfast." By then, her smile had disappeared and the professional agent kicked back in.

"Out of the country, huh? When's he due back?" Tony asked.

His eyes shifted behind J.J., he wouldn't make eye contact. "A week or two. I'm not sure. Should be..."

"In the files. Got it. I'm pretty quick on the uptake." In her mind, she rolled her eyes in disappointment. Sheldon was lying about something, but if Maddix Cooper was out of touch for any reason, the case would be stalled until his return.

Sheldon glanced the clock on the wall behind J.J. and paced quickly toward the door. He rapid fired, "I've got a meeting to get to, but here's my number if you need anything else. You've got time before the files arrive to grab a cup of coffee or something and return here to review t in these empty cubicles. Call Kendel when you're ready to leave."

"Thanks, man," Tony said to Sheldon's vapors. He high-tailed out of there before they could blink. "Well, at least he was helpful."

"Was he?" She reached her hand to the desk behind the counter, grabbed the handset from the desk phone, and dialed. The phone rang twice and voicemail picked up. "Sunnie, do me a favor? I need everything you can find out on Maddix Cooper including his travel itinerary, and see what you can find on Sheldon Vance too."

"What was that all about?" Tony asked. "No, lemme guess. More of your women's intuition."

"Don't hate, Tony," J.J. said, knowing Tony wished he had her gift. "Call me crazy, and I know you will, but my gut tells me Sheldon's not exactly 'keeping it one hundred' if you get my drift. I aim to find out what he's hiding."

Chapter 33

Wednesday Morning—Irving Street
4 Days Left...

Santino's stomach fluttered as he approached Lana's door. He'd reminisced about their liaison through the night and the memory lingered with him into the dawn. He closed his eyes in the shower and the scent of her hair overpowered him as if still swaying across his face in the midst of their passionate throes. He cringed as his emotions dragged him kicking and screaming to a place he had no desire to go, a place where he couldn't stay even if he wanted to. Inside the recesses of his mind and the fragment of his heart still beating after Rosa, he recognized the upsurge of passion, the longing sensation threatening to drive him to distraction. Still he found himself drawn to her door. Once he peeked through the crack, there was no turning back—maybe not ever.

"You packed yet?" Santino asked, his voice more animated than his expression. Truth was, he wanted her to stay, not forever but a little longer, until he'd had his fill. There was no hunger worse than craving more of a sweet fruit you could never taste again. "By my calculations, four days from now, I'll be taking you to catch your slow boat to France. You packed yet?"

"Are you kidding me? My entire life practically fits in my purse now. I can be packed before your stomach growls again."

He rubbed his abdomen. "You heard? Somehow I worked up a pretty big appetite. I was thinking, maybe we could get out this hole for a while and go grab a bite," he said. A boyish bashful expression seized his face. "I don't know about you, but I'm becoming a hermit. I could use some air."

"Me too," Lana answered. "But, uhhh, why don't I cook breakfast here instead? I'm not big on restaurants these days."

"Ohhh, too many people, huh?"

"No, last week I watched a 20/20 restaurant exposé where the cooks drop your food on the floor and waiters spit in your food," she said making a hock spit noise.

Santino frowned. "Ugh, thanks for the visual," he said. "Way to help me work up an appetite."

Lana paused in silence and fell back on the bed, laughing deep from her belly. She laughed so hard she began snorting like a nerd, which made Santino collapse in laughter on the bed alongside her. His comment and her retort weren't as funny as the levity would suggest; it just felt good to let loose, to live two minutes without the weight of the Cappi Merendino murder and the heat from Nicky Mumbles bearing down on him. As their chortles withered to quiet laughter and dissipated, Lana propped herself up on one elbow and looked down on Santino's face. "Thank you," she said. "I haven't laughed so much since…since…"

"*Him*, right?"

She nodded.

"Glad I could make you smile," he said, "especially with all you've been through."

"No. Thank you. I needed that so much," she said. "Listen, about last night."

He glanced at her with a confused expression. "I have no idea what you're talking about?"

"You know exactly what I'm talking about. It's why your stomach sounds like a broken Harley."

"Ohhhh, *that* last night. Go ahead."

"Well, I'm very vulnerable and our…you know…was probably a mistake," she began. Then she laid her head on his chest and continued, "but I don't care. Meeting you couldn't have happened at a more perfect time and I can never thank you enough for what you've done."

"Oh, yes you can," he said, with a wry smile. The warm and fuzzy feelings of the moment hadn't subsumed the memory of the fact that he was helping her largely because she was paying for his services. Even still, he continued, "I know we don't have much time together, but whadaya say we make the best of the time we have left. Deal?"

"Deal," he said taking her hand in his. "Now that we've got that settled," she said, popping up from her seat. She grabbed the ink pen and notepad resting on her dresser and began to scribble feverishly.

"You're not writing up a contract, are you?" Santino asked.

She didn't respond until she finished and handed him the sheet. "No. It's the grocery list. The faster you pick up the food, the faster we lose the Harley."

He leaned over and pecked her on the cheek, before bolting up from the bed and preparing to leave. "You're coming with me, right?"

"Why? You need me to help you carry the bags?"

"Ha ha." He said with a fake laugh. "I'll be back in a few."

Lana sat motionless, waiting for the door shut. She jumped up peered out the window and watched until Santino's car pulled off. Then, with her camera phone in hand, snuck into his bedroom, which he carelessly left unlocked. Already his instincts were off; he'd started slipping. She smirked smugly and began her search. She needed some insurance. She wasn't sure exactly what she was looking for, but she'd know when she spotted it.

As she rummaged through his space, she was methodical about leaving everything more orderly than she found it. After she checked the bed, she made it up, pulling the sheets tight and fluffing the pillows. As she ran her hands beneath the folded underclothes in his underwear drawer, she felt a thin stack of papers under her fingers. She pulled them out and sifted through each one by one.

Old love letters from a woman—Rosa.

The paper was wrinkled and worn as if he'd read them a thousand times. At the bottom of the stack was a *Hudson Reporter* newspaper article. The headline in the read, "Hoboken Woman Mowed Down by Drunk Driver."

Lana pulled the cell phone from her bra, snapped a picture, and returned the stack beneath his unmentionables, lining them up military style. She hated using email. The Service taught them that the FBI monitored communications like the Russian Security Services. That's why Russian intelligence minimized the use of landline phones, electronic communications, and the postal service. They preferred the old ways, dead drops and face-to-face meetings in foreign countries. On a chair in the corner, she noticed the jeans he wore the day before.

She lifted them, squeezed to check for pocket litter, and felt a large square bulge in the back pocket.

His wallet.

"Shit!" she yelped. Her hands quivered as she took the wallet in hand, folded the pants, and returned them to the chair. She spun around to return to her bedroom and screamed, "Oh my God!" She pressed her trembling palm over her pounding heart. "You scared me to death!"

Santino hulked over her, seething with his face twisted in a scowl and his fists balled. "What the hell are you doing in here?!"

• • •

Wednesday Morning — Surveillance Detail

At o'dark thirty in the Surveillance Group Operations Center conference room, Kyle conducted his pre-op brief in front of a band of sleepy-eyed Gs chugging coffee like happy hour Budweisers. The pack of khaki-clad twenty- and thirty-somethings cast blank stares at the projector screen. He painstakingly reviewed every detail of the operation on the zoomed in map of the 19th Street area where Filchenko made his routine cover stops.

"This is our perimeter," he said, circling the five-block area surrounding the Potbelly's restaurant. "The flatbed with the switch car will be posted in this garage a few doors down from the target area. We've already cleared it with the owner."

"So let me make sure I've got this straight," Hopper said. "Filchenko parks at the meter and fails to drop money as usual. I follow him inside and engage him in conversation—a welcome to the U.S. greeting from the FBI."

"Yeah, it's routine. They all know we're coming at some point. Little does he know today's his lucky day," Kyle said. "But wait until he starts eating. Cheap bastards won't leave an unfinished meal, even to get away from the FBI."

Hopper nodded. "Okay, the special ops group switches cars, circles the block, installs both GPSs and then returns and swaps them again."

"Here's the trick though, his back's gotta face the window—which goes against every instinct of an intel officer. You've gotta make him not only comfortable with sitting with you, but with being positioned with his back to the door, you understand?"

"Yeah. And as long as I keep him distracted for the couple minutes it takes to get the car on the flatbed, we shouldn't have any problems. If he looks outside, our car will be sitting in the parking space."

"You got it," Kyle said as he scanned the lifeless faces around the room. "Everybody good? Everybody know where you're supposed to be?"

Kyle stood there waiting for some energy, enthusiasm but saw nothing except a wave of half-hearted head-nods followed by muffled groans. His fingers curled into his hand and jaw tensed. His face turned 1969-Mustang candy-apple red. He gripped the base of the glossy blue ceramic FBI mug resting on the podium, his hand numb to the fresh heat, and slammed the mug against the far wall. The glass exploded then fell in barely audible thumps onto the carpeted floor.

"Does anybody understand what the fuck we're doing here today? Anybody?" Kyle screamed at the top of his lungs. Startled, his audience froze with eyes widened. "Apparently not because you're sitting around here all dead-eyed and nonchalant like this is fucking Baywatch and you're going on beach patrol!"

He walked the perimeter of the room, and, one by one, glared in every single eye as he continued his rant. "Lana Michaels isn't our garden variety Russian spy. In case your head's been jammed up your ass for the last week, she's a murderer, an FBI Agent killer. And if we don't get her off the streets, she's got *at least* one more agent in her sights.

"This operation is our single best chance of not only preventing the Russians from providing her with support, but locking her away for good. Raise your hand if you think that's an important mission."

Every hand shot up in the air, whether the sentiment was genuine or not.

"Then wake the fuck up and act like it!" he said. "Jazz and Jiggy are team leads and Cham is supporting. Everyone is dismissed…except you three," he said, pointing his index finger at Cannon, Slicer, and Hopper. "I need a word."

"Just one?" Cannon mumbled.

"You wish!" Kyle fired back.

They huddled around him at the front of the room as he took a seat on the edge of the table. "What the hell's going on here, today? It's like an army of the walking dead."

Slicer shrugged. "We've been on 16-hour shifts for a week straight. Everybody's pretty exhausted."

"Yeah. Guess the week's been rough for everyone involved," he said, "but I've got a lot riding on this case and can't afford to let it get away from me," Kyle said, unable to release his grief for the friend and agent she took.

"You mean, the Bureau, right?" Hopper asked, clearly not knowing when to seal his mouth shut.

"I don't need you to correct me, Junior," Kyle barked. "I'm the reason she's still out there. And I've got to help take her down."

He stood and walked over to the projection screen. "You two will be posted here," Kyle said, pointing to parking spaces just outside the Potbelly's L Street entrance. "Cannon—you signal me when Hopper's got our target distracted. Slicer, you conduct countersurveillance. If anything goes wrong, I need you step in and backup Hopper, you understand?"

"I thought the FBI didn't make mistakes," Slicer joked.

"We don't," Kyle said. "But if I've learned anything about the Russians, their favorite tool of tradecraft is the monkey wrench. If they throw one in the mix, we've got to be prepared for it."

Slicer's glance swung from Hopper to Cannon before he nodded. "Roger that."

CHAPTER 34

Wednesday Afternoon—Surveillance Detail

The hardened knot in Hopper's stomach had tightened enough to tether the U.S.S. Enterprise to the Boston Harbor. Parked inside his FBI-issued Malibu, he waited to commence the op to install the GPS in Filchenko's car, the op he hoped would lead them to Lana Michaels. A few minutes passed when he was startled out of his thoughts by the sound of footsteps passing him. The afternoon K Street lunch crowd wore three-piece Jos. A. Banks specials and trudged through the sea of brake lights in the stop and go traffic, seeking food and respite from their mind-numbing nine-to-fives.

A lot of lives hung on the success of this operation and, by the minute, he'd grown more painfully aware of how little operational experience he had. He found himself questioning the soundness of Kyle's judgment—pitting Hopper, an agent five minutes out of Quantico, against a Russian intelligence officer who was probably recruiting his hundredth asset while Hopper was at prom getting laid in the back of his father's Cadillac Seville. He gripped his steering wheel and tried to settle his nerves, arriving thirty minutes early to give himself time to mentally create worst-case scenarios and develop responses to each. Faked his brain into believing he was more prepared and acutely aware than would bear out in reality.

He marveled at the silver Toyota Camry identical to Filchenko's car, even down to the sun-faded Little Tree car freshener hanging from the rear-view mirror, his diplomatic license (hidden under the fake D.C. plate), and the black scratch on the left rear bumper, sitting on the flatbed. So thoroughly executed, that if the op went bad, the key would open the doors and start the car.

The Special Projects group had pulled off a major coup in less time than his kid took for a mid-day nap. The parking garage attendants, both with dark skin, curly black hair, and blue vested uniforms eyed him suspiciously even though their boss advised them the FBI would be hanging around for a couple of hours. He glanced down at his watch.

11:15. They should've been out the gate five minutes before. Hopper picked up his Motorola.

"Hopper to Blue Team. Hopper to Blue Team. I'm in position. Looks like we're running a little late here. Did the lookouts call out the targets yet?"

"Negative, Hopper," replied Cham, one of a handful of female Gs on the team. "I've got binoculars in one hand and the radio in the other, standby," she said. Only minutes passed before she said, "I've got eyes on…wait a minute. The target vehicles are approaching the gate."

"Rabbit 1 and Rabbit 2," Kyle said over the radio. "Looks like we're about to get this party started."

"Uhhh, shit…Blue Team, we've got a problem," Cham said. "A big one."

"What's going on?" Kyle asked.

"Rabbit 1, uhhh, Filchenko and Mikhaylov are out the gate, as expected, but…" She paused for a moment that seemed like an eternity. "They switched cars! I repeat they switched cars. Mikhaylov is driving Filchenko's Camry. Filchenko's in the burgundy Honda Accord. Jazz and Jiggy have the eye. Stand by."

"Damn Russians and their monkey wrenches! Everything is riding on this op. The hell we can't finish it," Kyle barked. "Jiggy. Jazz. You stay on 'em. My guess is they aren't going to switch routes, even if they switch cars. Hopper, get over here. We need to talk."

"Copy that," they each replied, one right after the other.

Hopper stashed his radio under the seat and scrambled out of the car, padding toward the garage where the flatbed was tucked away on the second level.

Panic collapsed on him like an overweight sumo wrestler.

He had no idea how they'd wrangle themselves out of this jam. Not in this world or any other would a silver Camry ever substitute for a burgundy Honda Accord.

Hopper yanked the door to Kyle's car open and slipped inside, his breathing slightly heavy from the jog. Kyle tightened his lips and slammed his hands against the steering wheel.

"Monkey wrench, huh?" Hopper said.

Kyle nodded. "Sons of bitches. Trying to give me a fucking heart attack," Kyle said. "Goddamned stand down's got us paralyzed, can't move left or right without the fear of setting off the next Cold War. But we don't have time to reschedule the op for a second attempt."

"The op is blown," Hopper urged. "You're not still going to try to go through with it."

Kyle grunted, frowned, and snatched up the radio. "Blue Leader to Cham. What's your twenty? You still on the same route?"

"Roger that, blue leader. Except Lana's father is taking Filchenko's route," she said. "Traffic's clear. We're doing thirty-five down Wisconsin. ETA 11:45. Stand by."

"Shit!" Hopper checked the time. "11:35. Only ten minutes away."

Kyle's mind was stirring, evident from the creases in his forehead. He ribbed his scalp with his fingers and expelled a hard breath. "Screw it. Help me get this car off the flatbed."

"You're not…you're going through with it? How the hell are we gonna pull this off?"

"We'll improvise," Kyle said.

"No disrespect, Kyle. And I know I'm new…but unless the guy is color blind and a complete idiot, a burgundy Honda will never equal silver Toyota. If he so much as glances over his shoulder while the car's gone, we're neck-deep in an international scandal."

"Listen, Junior. In apprehend and arrest, you ask for permission. In life and death, you ask for forgiveness. When catching an agent killer, you do what you need to do to get that bitch off the streets. Comprende?"

"Si, senor." Hopper nodded, feeling a new kind of green. "So, what now? We're just going to plant the one tracker?"

"No, we're still planting two," Kyle said. "While you help me get this car off the flatbed, you're going to think of a way to keep Mikhaylov from noticing that his car's missing for twenty minutes."

"Twenty minutes? Excuse my language but…are you fucking kidding me?" Hopper was on the brink of a major flip out. "Didn't you get the memo? This guy's one of the most senior in the residency. He was trained to look out the window...every 20 seconds. What the hell am I gonna tell him? I'm Houdini and *Abracadabra* I made your car disappear?"

Kyle shot him a blank expression.

Hopper rolled his eyes and slapped his hand against his thigh. "Oh wait. Let me guess...improvise."

"Cannon and Slicer are already inside," Kyle said to Hopper. "The minute you sit down, they will signal me. Whatever you've got planned, that's when your clock starts."

• • •

Irving Street...

Santino's were cold, empty, devoid of any of the affection he'd shown her just a few minutes earlier. For the first time, Lana feared for her life. How could she know he'd forget his wallet? She scrambled to center her thoughts. Devise an approach. A lie wouldn't work, not on Santino. She needed a truth that wouldn't get her killed.

"You forgot this." She held out the billfold in her hand with a cheesy grin. "Tough to buy groceries without money."

"You heard me! What the fuck are you doing in here?"

She started folding his jeans. "This place is a sty. I don't understand how you rest in here. When's the last time you cleaned?"

"Oh, you want to know the last time I fucking cleaned. I'll tell you!" He snarled and jutted his arm out, snapping his fingers around her neck with the quickness of a cobra strike. "I'll clean this room up with your face if you don't tell me what the fuck you're doing in here."

Lana struggled to breath, tried to release herself, but he had the strength of ten men. It was like trying to push over an oak tree with her hand. She thrashed as tears drifted from her eyes. "Don't do this. It's not what you—" she strained to speak. "Let me explain."

Santino glared at her with his nostrils flared. He slammed her on the bed; her body bounced like a rag doll. He snatched the Sig Sauer from the small of his back and cocked the gun while pointing it at her head. "Two seconds. Say what the fuck you gotta say so I can end this."

"You've got to calm down and listen to me," Lana said, desperate to find the words that would save her life. "I wasn't doing anything to hurt you. Think about it, Santino, you're all I have. Without you, I can't leave this country. I can't go home. I can't do anything without you!"

He froze for a second then lowered the gun to his side. "Then why were you snooping through my shit?"

"I hesitated to tell you because…I felt…stupid," she said. "I didn't want you to think I was some crazed stalker."

"Too late now."

"I was checking to see if there was any evidence…of other women."

"Get the fuck outta here," Santino said. "You haven't seen anyone here, have you?"

"Yeah, but you leave every day for hours at a time," Lana said, sitting upright. She shook her head and covered her face with her palms. "I'm so embarrassed, going through your stuff like a teenager. This isn't me. I don't know…I was afraid this would happen."

Santino de-cocked his gun and sat next to her on the bed. "You were afraid what would happen?"

"I came here to lay low until I could get out," she said. "I wasn't expecting…you know, us—this."

"Hey, me either," Santino said. "But you don't need to worry about me seeing anybody else. You're the first since…"

"Rosa?" she asked to his surprise. "I saw the newspaper article."

He leaned forward, elbows to knees. "Yeah, it happened the day after we got engaged. I, uhh, I don't really want to…listen, I think all this being cooped up is makin' us both a little crazy. Get your hat and sunglasses and we'll both go to the grocery store."

Lana nodded without argument. She'd barely dodged another bullet and the next one might land in the back of her head if she didn't tread carefully. "You're always right," she said, stroking his ego. "Neither one of us would do well in jail."

"Once we get the package tomorrow, we're half way home. I can get the hit over with Saturday and head to New Jersey while you're tossing down the Stoli on the way to France. Be nice to return to the real world, huh?"

"I guess," Lana said in a melancholy tone. She looked up at him and smiled in the way an angry dog bares his teeth before the bite. "But whatever will I do without your hand around my neck?"

She shook off the incident with the knowledge that tomorrow she would have her passport. Then the noose she'd fashioned from her duplicity would tighten around his neck and she'd be one step closer to home.

Chapter 35

Wednesday—Surveillance Detail

Hopper tightened his tie and brushed the car dirt from the side of his pant leg and sleeve as he prepared to enter Potbelly's. His idea was ludicrous, bonkers, so far left field that Headquarters would blast it out of the sky like a homer out of Fenway, resulting in a one-way trip to the unemployment line with a pink slip if he failed. But the situation was dire. He was at the bottom of the 9th with the score Russians—one, FBI—zero and only one at-bat remaining with two men on base.

The idea was just crazy enough to work and might net them more than the 20 minutes necessary to conduct the op. With lives hanging in the balance and an agent killer one passport away from Moscow, only an insane idea would finish the job.

The line inside Potbelly's snaked half-way around the store, as usual. The main reason Filchenko spent forty-five minutes at the stop was the twenty minutes it took to order and pay for his sandwich. With the sandwich shop sitting on the corner of 19th and L and walls of glass exposing both streets, taking the car while he stood in line was too risky. Lana's father could glance over his shoulder at any moment. No, Hopper lurked in the background until Lana's father arrived at the cash register. As his target dug into his pocket and pulled out the bills, Hopper quickened his pace, slipped beside him, and held out $20 to the cashier.

"My treat," Hopper said with an easy smile as Lana's father sized him up from head to toe. Hopper purposely dressed in the standard FBI uniform, a clean-cut, black suit, Ray Bans, beige trench coat. Didn't have to be a genius to figure out where he worked or why he was standing there.

"I wondered when one of you would show up." Mikhaylov snatched his food from the counter, but all the seats were taken except one near the rear of the restaurant with a cup resting on it. Cannon had saved it for Hopper and shifted to another empty seat as Hopper approached the cash register.

"I think this one's okay," Hopper said, speeding up his pace toward the seat so he could take the seat facing the door. "Looks like someone just forgot the cup." He grabbed it and tossed it in a nearby trashcan.

"I prefer to face the door," Mikhaylov said, placing his food on the table and waiting for Hopper to switch seats.

Hopper sat down and with his hand gestured for his target to do the same in the seat opposite his. "Trust me, if anything happens in here, you want the guy with the gun facing the door. Please sit, I won't be here long, and your sandwich is getting cold. They're so much better warm." Hopper watched Cannon jump up and head out the exit. Seconds later the flatbed had pulled up outside.

The clock had started.

Lana's father hesitated for a moment and finally took his seat.

After introducing himself, going through an excessively lengthy explanation of his counterintelligence duties as an FBI agent, and making small talk about the weather, Hopper finally paused long enough to give Mikhaylov the opportunity to speak. "So, now that I've told you who I am, who are you?"

"I'm a diplomat of the Russian Federation. I have immunity and nothing to say to you, so why are you here?"

Hopper shrugged. "To be honest with you, I don't have a clue. I'm fresh out of Quantico, and some prick supervisor who calls me 'Junior' ordered me to come down here and talk to you—of all people." Hopper's brow furrowed as he shifted in his seat. "I mean, you've got more experience in your pinky than I have in my entire career. What the hell did they really expect me to do? Recruit you?"

Lana's father arched his eyebrow and chuckled. "You don't enjoy counterintelligence work?"

"I requested something more exciting—criminal division, terrorism, organized crime, anything but this. Yet they send me here to work counterintelligence. Gotta love the Bureau," Hopper said flippantly, tightening his lips to feign regret of his brutal honesty. "Sorry. I mean no disrespect to you or anything. This work just isn't for me. The faster I rotate off the squad, the better. Six more months and I'm done with these lame ass assignments."

"You remind me a little of myself when I was your age. Young and cocky," Mikhaylov said, already making short work of his sandwich and chips. Hopper watched him bite large chunks from his sandwich. "Sounds like you're out to satisfy your adolescent cowboy and Indian fantasies. Intelligence work is challenging, some of the most difficult you'll ever do. Trust me."

"I'll take your word for it." Hopper deadpanned, looking down to mark the time. Ten minutes left. He glanced over Mikhaylov's shoulder and then reached in his trench coat pocket and pulled out a pen and small notebook. "So, if you'll bear with me for another couple of minutes, I need to check a few more boxes for the file, and I'll be out of your hair."

Mikhaylov chuckled at Hopper's droll frankness and unenthusiastic demeanor. The look on his face suggested he was intrigued by what Hopper might ask, so he allowed him to proceed. "Okay. Ask away."

"Question number one—are you an intelligence officer for the Russian Federation."

After drawing back his head in feigned surprise, he said, "I'm a diplomat. The Russian Federation has no intelligence officers operating in the United States."

"Okay," Hopper said, scribbling feverishly on the small sheet. He quickly shifted his eyes from the notebook to the watch and back. Three more minutes. "Yes, intelligence... officer... for the.... Russian ...Federation. A...very...senior...one," he dragged out as he scribbled on the paper.

Mikhaylov froze and chuckled. Then he took the next to last bite of his sandwich.

"Are you currently operating moles or illegals in the United States?" Hopper asked.

With his jaw stuffed with his sandwich. "What's a mole...or illegal?"

Hopper began to scribble again, speaking with each word he wrote. "Operates…moles…AND…illegals…in…the…United States," Hopper said. "No wonder you've been in the U.S. so long. You're really good at this. Just a couple more and I promise I'll let you go."

Hopper saw the flatbed pull up. Two minutes early. He was thankful because Mikhaylov had just swallowed his final bite and, according to the report from the Gs, would be rushing to hit two more cover stops before returning to the embassy—or attempted to conduct his operation.

"Next question," Hopper began, "do you know where your daughter is located?"

Mikhaylov froze in silence, his face reflecting more anger than annoyance. He reached for his soda and knocked the cup over, spilling the contents all over the table and onto Hopper's lap.

"My apologies," Lana's father said. "Let me get you a napkin."

Hopper blurted out, "No, that's o—"

Too late.

Mikhaylov turned to grab napkins from the counter and saw his car being lowered and detached from the flatbed. He turned around, shot Hopper a scowl, and then jetted outside to catch the truck operator, bumping chairs and tables along the way.

Hopper scuttled out behind him, his mind racing, trying to devise a Plan B. Plan A was screwed, and he was cold busted. By the time, Mikhaylov reached the door, the flatbed had sped off, screeching through the yellow light ahead before disappearing into the next block.

Mikhaylov ran to his car and peered inside the passenger window. Furious, his eyes protruded and his face reddened. Hopper didn't know what to say. What to do. How could he make this right? This was their last chance to find Lana and he was on the edge of blowing it.

"What the fuck did you do to my car?" Lana's father screamed. "Your Secretary of State will hear about this!"

"It's my fault," Hopper said, stopping his target cold in stunned silence. *Think fast. Think fast.* "I told them this stupid plan wouldn't work, that you were too good of an officer to fall for it, but they wouldn't listen to me. I'm Junior, remember? But if you report this, my career is over. I'll be chasing truckloads of Tide washing powder from Baltimore to Jersey for the next 25 years. Didn't you make mistakes when you first started out?"

Mikhaylov's breathing calmed. "So, you put a tracker on my car and you think I'm just going to let you get away with it?"

"No, no. But…if I make this right, will you please consider not reporting this…*unfortunate* incident?"

He pursed his lips and turned away from Hopper appearing as if taking a moment to gather his thoughts. Hopper knew he'd be running behind schedule if he held him up much longer. "Make it right?! How?"

Hopper wanted to kick himself for not asking where in the car they had planned to install both GPSs. If he picked the wrong one, he was dead meat. He eased to the front, dropped to his knees, and reached beneath the bumper. If they wanted Russian intelligence to find the GPS, that was the most logical position. He ran his fingers from front to back. Nothing.

"It's gotta be here. Let me check the back."

Mikhaylov tapped his foot impatiently as Hopper moved to the back of the car. On his knees again, he ran his fingers from left to right when his fingers finally moved over the square hard-plastic object. He breathed a sigh of relief, pulled it out, and held it in his hand.

"I found it," Hopper said. "I removed it. No harm, no foul, right? Please?"

Lana's father shook his head and let out an impatient sneer. "Rookie mistake. Don't let it happen again or your career will be over as fast as this conversation, do we understand each other?" he asked. He opened his driver-side door and stuck one foot inside. "Try anything like that again, and I will not be at all charitable. Now I've got to return to the embassy." He slipped inside and drove off.

As soon as the coast cleared, Kyle sprinted across the street, huffing and shaking his fist. "What the hell happened? You pulled the device. Fucked up the entire operation!"

Hopper tried to catch his breath. "Listen, I almost had—,"

"I never should've trusted you," Kyle barked. "If Michaels gets away with this or kills another agent, I swear to God you'll be taking squirrel bite reports in Duluth by the time I'm through with—"

"Will you shut up? You love the sound of your own voice, don't you?" Hopper yelled. "Give me five seconds to explain what happened before you go jumping off the cliff!"

Kyle's snarl loosened and released as Hopper detailed the events inside the store. "I almost had him, playing the disgruntled, disenchanted new guy with a shit assignment and a prick boss and he was going for it…until he spilled his soda on me. Saw the tow truck when he grabbed napkins to clean up the mess. I had to do something drastic."

"Son of a bitch!" Kyle said. "When he ran out here, I just knew the op had gone to shit. That was some pretty quick thinking, Junior."

Hopper raked his fingers through his hair to relieve the tension. "If he believes I pulled out the only tracker. It still may work…maybe."

Kyle offered Hopper a fatherly pat on the shoulder. "You either made the smartest move of your career…or you ended it. Unfortunately, we won't find out until tomorrow."

"Thanks for the confidence boost."

"Shake it off and get back to the office," Kyle said, his voice more calm and soothing. "You've got a shitload of paperwork to do."

CHAPTER 36

Wednesday Evening—The White House

J.J. glazed over as she reviewed the last page of yet another personnel file in their small temporary office in the West Wing. She rubbed her tired eyes as she prepared to interview the first mole suspect. She could hardly decipher her notes which had been scribbled so fast they resembled chicken scratch more common to medical prescriptions than pre-interview pointers.

Tony wasn't faring much better. The exhaustion from weeks of intense investigation coupled with reading volumes of personnel files had worn his patience thin. He'd rubbed his temples red, and she'd heard less heavy breathing out of him during their midnight trysts.

First on the list was Edward Tomlin, the Navy intel officer and defense attaché. J.J.'s main concern in his file was his reported bombshell of a Ukrainian wife. How he still had access to intelligence, she didn't know. To maintain his clearances with a wife from the former republic meant he was very clean or ultra dirty—the information in the file was insufficient to discern.

By the end of the day, she'd know one way or the other. The only hiccup she could foresee was an inevitable clash with Gia. While Tony's suggestion that Gia use her defense intelligence experience to highlight any inconsistencies was a good idea in theory, J.J. feared her presence would cause more dissention between them rather than unearth a few lies.

J.J. stood up from her desk and took a long deep stretch. "Gia on her way? Tomlin should be here any minute."

"Yeah, she just sent me a text. Kendel's bringing her down now," he said.

"Oh, she sent you a text, huh?"

"Yeah, because you told me to call her," he snapped. "Really, J.J.? Green ain't a good color on you. I like brown much better."

J.J. had a bad feeling about them. She didn't know why; she just did. Before J.J. could respond, there was a knock at the door. Tony rushed to grab it. "Ahh, here she is. Just in the nick of time," Tony said.

Gia walked in and looked around with an uncomfortable expression on her face. "Hey, J.J. Where should I sit?"

"In here," J.J said, ushering her inside. "Tomlin should be here in a few. This shouldn't take long."

Most agents had to conduct a battery of questioning sessions with subjects, their friends, co-workers, and associates to develop the comprehensive picture necessary to detect inconsistencies. J.J.'s lie detection ability eliminated the need—ultimately cutting down on the time it took her to solve her cases. She didn't give a shit about the stats. The more cases she solved, the more bad guys she took off the streets.

There was a second knock at the door. When Tony opened it the second time a rail-thin, bespectacled guy walked in. His features were indistinct and easily forgotten. J.J. struggled to find the words that she'd use to describe the tall, skinny man with glasses except "man."

They all dispensed with the idle pleasantries and introductions, then made their way into the conference room. After J.J. and Tony displayed their badges and credentials, Tomlin started to blink incessantly. J.J. couldn't tell whether he had a tick or the usual nerves people get when being interviewed by the FBI.

"Can I ask what this is all about?" he asked.

J.J. carefully measured her reply. Sometimes the best way to encourage honest responses was to divert suspicions to someone else. But Tomlin was nervous, his face reddened, his hands shaking. He had something to hide. In his case, she'd hit him square between the eyes. He'd either fight or flee. An attempt to flee would warrant a deeper look.

J.J. looked at Tony and responded, "We're investigating some very specific security breaches that we believe occurred in the White House and State Department during the period in which you worked in both places. We have no suspects at this time. We're just conducting exploratory interviews, okay?"

He nodded and exhaled. "Oh, I see. Well, that's a relief. I don't know anything about a security breach."

A crawling sensation began in the tip of her toes. But it didn't explode through her as it would've if he'd been flagrantly dishonest. Still, he was lying about something.

"We don't have many questions. Let's get through them so we can get you back to work," J.J. began. "We understand you served as a Defense Attaché in Moscow from 1996 to 1998. Can you tell us a little about your assignment there?"

He nodded. "I represented Naval Intelligence. Targeted the GRU— Russian military intelligence. We met regularly to discuss Iraq issues. At that time Russia wanted the U.S. to back down from Iraqi sanctions, and we wanted them to support the sanctions. It was a tense time."

"So, you regularly met with Russian intelligence as part of your job. Did you report those contacts to your security officer?"

"Yeah, I submitted AARs every day, uhh, After Action Reports."

She waited for a reaction. There was none. She hadn't hit the sweet spot yet. She'd keep poking until she struck gold.

"Were you ever approached by a member of Russian intelligence?"

"Approached? I don't understand your meaning."

The crawling sensation returned and intensified. She stomped her foot beneath the table forged ahead. The sweet spot was near.

"I'm sorry, let me make it plain," she said. "Did a member of any Russian intelligence service—or someone you suspected was a member of Russian intelligence—request, coerce, or attempt to coerce you to provide any information, to include classified information, outside of your reported contacts."

His eyes bulged. He opened his mouth but no words came. Then he shook his head no.

"Is that a '*no*'?" J.J. snapped, beginning to lose her patience. "I need you to answer verbally."

"Yes, Agent McCall," he snapped. "That's a no."

The crawl rushed into her thighs and into her backside. She wriggled in her seat before regaining composure. As usual, Tony looked at her as if she'd lost her mind. She played it off as if nothing happened. "We understand you have a Ukrainian wife. How did you meet her?"

"At a bar in Moscow."

"She approached you?"

"Yes, yes. She did."

J.J. expected him to answer in the affirmative and she also expected that response would be the truth. Honeytraps always targeted foreign service personnel very aggressively. But the sensation of ants permeating her arms signaled he'd told yet another lie. The wife was not the aggressor. *If she didn't approach him, then how did they meet?*

"I see," J.J. said in a sugary sweet voice with a venomous undertone. "Let me confer with my colleagues outside for a second and we'll conclude our discussion in a minute."

Gia and Tony shot J.J. sideways glances and followed her out of the room.

"What's going on?" Tony asked.

J.J. scratched her head, reminding herself that she had an insight they didn't. They wouldn't understand her impatience.

"How do you think this is going so far?" J.J. asked. "Because I believe he's lying like a dusty rug."

Gia glanced and J.J. and Tony and said, "He's extremely nervous, but nothing he said struck me as untruthful."

J.J. snapped her head toward Tony. "And you? What's your opinion?"

"I dunno, but I tend to agree with Gia. Although I'll also admit something isn't right with this guy. He's awfully twitchy. Can't put my finger on it."

"I also think he's twitchy, largely due to the fact that he's lying his ass off. Are you watching his mannerisms? Couldn't be more obvious to me than if we wrote 'liar' on a flag and flew the pole from his left nostril," J.J. said. "I mean he's blinked so many times *my* eyes are getting dry. And he's probably sweat out half of his body weight in the last 15 minutes."

Gia bit her bottom lip. "Yeah, but that room's a little warm."

"*A little warm.* Not the Mojave desert," J.J. said. "Listen, I'm going back in. Play along with me and he'll either fold, or we'll have to lock Tony in a room with him so Tony can play bad cop."

J.J. returned inside and took her seat. Gia and Tony followed suit.

She flipped through her papers authoritatively and lined them up in front of him. "If you could please review my notes and then sign at the bottom to verify your truthfulness. We've decided to wrap up this interview early."

Tomlin appeared confused. "Is there a problem?"

"Quite frankly I'm not convinced that your answers have been forthright, you know, truthful. And I simply don't have the time or the patience to coddle you. We're going to institute a Code Red, Level 7 investigation—that's an internal FBI code," she said. "For the record, my colleagues disagree with my assessment, but in another sign that it's not your lucky day, I *outrank* them."

"What does Code Red, Level 7 mean?"

J.J. tightened her lips and lowered her head. Her expression was grave. Then Tony piped in. "It's not good," he said shaking his head. He looked at J.J. with pleading eyes. "Do we really need to do that? I mean, think of his family. You do have a family, don't you?"

"Yeah," Gia added. "Give the guy a break."

J.J. shook her head and fiddled with the band on her Movado.

"Hmph. That's unfortunate. Your job. Your clearances. Ugh." Tony turned to J.J. again. "Are you sure you won't reconsider? I mean, look at him."

Gia, Tony, and J.J. all stared at him. He appeared as if he'd disintegrate from the stress.

"No, you're free to go, *after* you sign this paper. It's very important that we have your signature. After that, we'll be in touch…*soon.*"

"I'm not signing a damn thing!" He bolted up from his seat, his gaze volleying back and forth between his interviewers. He slowly made his way to the door, appearing deep in thought along the way. He looked around one last time, exited, and closed it behind him.

All eyes turned to J.J.

"You sure this is gonna work?" Gia asked.

"No," J.J. answered. "But nothing beats a failure, but a try."

• • •

FBI Headquarters – Washington D.C.

J.J. asked Six to hang back at headquarters and provide guidance to Sunnie, who was conducting the initial analysis on the Situation Room entry records. With his operational knowledge, he could help right her direction if she went off on a tangent, something easy to do with the sheer volume of information. After listening to several successive rounds of huffs and puffs and groans, Six circled around to Sunnie's desk. He'd seen her from time to time while visiting J.J. back when he and she were still an item. He knew that J.J. thought highly of her even though many other agents didn't. In his eyes, J.J.'s endorsement was the only one she needed.

He poked his head around her cubicle wall to find her head face down in between two heaping piles of computer printouts. In fact, her desk was no longer visible beneath the ordered chaos.

"Everything okay over here?" Six asked.

"No," Sunnie didn't budge to glance up and her voice was muffled. "Who are you?"

"Six. I'm on the task force with Agent McCall….J.J."

She popped up her head and turned to him.

"What's the problem? Maybe I can help," Six said.

"The problem is I've been staring at these printouts for 20 hours and I still feel like there's a major gap in my analysis."

"I've reviewed everything. You and Walter have done a pretty thorough analysis, especially given the volume of information you had to contend with."

"It's not good enough for J.J.," Sunnie said. "If she were here, she'd be filling my head full of metaphors right now…like leave no stone unturned. If you fall off the bike, brush yourself off and try again. Or maybe, it's the last key in the box that opens the lock."

"You forgot, fall down seven times, stand up eight. Listen, maybe a break will do you some good. Care to join me in the cafeteria for a cup of coffee or a snack?"

"Snack?" she perked up. "Now you're talking my language. I'll walk with you."

She led the way out of the office and through the busy halls as employees prepared to depart into the afternoon rush.

"So," Six began, "how do you like working with Tony and J.J.?"

She shrugged. "It's cool," Sunnie said. "But we both know that's not what you really want to ask me. What you really want to know is whether they are happy together."

"Are they?"

Sunnie started walking. "That's none of my business…or yours for that matter. But if I had a man who looked like him, there are no fewer than a zillion other things I could do with my time than find reasons to be unhappy with him. But maybe that's just me."

"Touché," he said. "She ever mention me?"

"Yeah, usually when discussing the death penalty and contract killers."

She stopped abruptly in her footsteps, snapped her fingers, and muttered the word, *"Contract."*

She'd had an epiphany.

"What is it?" Six said.

"That's it!" She reversed course and double-timed it back to the office, her mind distracted by the new stream of thoughts. "Oh my God, I'm an idiot. Why didn't I think of it before?"

Six followed behind on her heels, quickening his steps to catch up.

"Think of what?"

"The search criteria. We couldn't see the forest for the noses on our faces…or something like that."

"I think you mixed your metaphors there."

"J.J. asked me to focus on employees, and we did. Full-time government employees. We forgot one important group."

She burst through the office door. She zigzagged through the laby-rinth of cubicle spaces until she reached Walter's desk.

"I figured it out. What we're missing."

He straightened his back and leaned against the chair. "Okay, what'd you come up with?"

"We were so focused on the key employees we forgot the contrac-tors. There are only a few companies that are cleared to work at State and the White House. Let's run a query to see if any contract employees worked in both places. Let me know what you come up with."

"Good thinking," Six said. "I see why J.J. holds you in such high re-gard."

Sunnie grinned. "Ugh. Forgot I've got to pull a file for some Shel-don Vance guy...and somebody named Maddix Cooper."

"Maddix Cooper. That should make for some interesting reading."

"You know him?"

"Seen his name but I've never met him in person. You could say, he and I covered the same territory."

CHAPTER 37

J.J., Tony, Gia exchanged disappointed glances. Edward Tomlin had stormed out of the interview. And for all they knew, he might never return…at least not without an attorney. It appeared this was one of the rare occasions when J.J. gambled and lost. Her stomach sunk. Had she calculated wrong?

"Well, this sucks," J.J. said. "I was sure he wou—"

A noise at the door interrupted her impending capitulation. The doorknob twisted and Tomlin shuffled in, chin to chest. "Uhh…excuse me, can I come back inside?"

J.J.'s eyebrow arched. "Why? So you can waste some more of our time?"

"No. I remembered some details I, uhh, may have accidentally omitted some information if you'd be willing to ask me those questions again."

He squeezed around J.J.'s chair and returned to the hot seat. He weaved his fingers together as if to pray and waited for the questioning to resume.

"Okay…let's start with your wife. How'd you two really meet?"

"We met at a bar after work. Bunch of us got together and my friend Coop brought her over. She was gorgeous, most beautiful woman I'd ever seen. Of all the guys there she was into me."

J.J. eyed his scruffy hair and basset hound mug. He had a face only PETA could love. The reasons why an exotic Russian beauty would fall for this guy were obvious—his security clearances, money, and a green card.

"There was a non-fraternization policy indicating you weren't supposed to date Russian nationals, am I correct?"

He nodded. "Yes."

"So, we understand you made the mistake. Did you report it to your security officer?"

"Nope," he said. "Didn't have to."

Gia straightened her gait and leaned on the table. "Why? The policy is clearly specified."

"Coop. He introduced us. You know, Maddix Cooper—he was a security officer. CIA counterintelligence."

J.J. sat back in her seat. "Really."

"He was a real player, if you know what I'm sayin'. Worked hard, played harder. Knew all the night spots and all the hot women. Life of the party, you know the type. Didn't mind bending the rules. Nature of being a spook, I guess."

"So were you ever approached by Russian intelligence?"

He tightened his lips and lowered his eyes. "Yes. Once."

"The incident's not in your file. You didn't report it?"

"Listen, Irina invites me to her place, for…well, you know. Anyway, she takes me out on the balcony and tells me a man is coming and he will say he's her uncle, but it's not true. He's no relation of hers."

"So she *warned* you?" J.J. said, her surprise obvious. "And she took you out on the balcony to avoid listening devices. She certainly knows how the Russians operate."

"Yeah. When I finally had a chance to think about the situation, it surprised me too. Later I found out the 'uncle' was an FSB officer. You know, like one of you guys but only Russian."

"Yeah, I know what the FSB is," J.J. said. "Continue."

"Well, she hated them because the old guard tortured her grandfather during the Soviet days. She sees Putin's government as oppressive as it was during the Cold War," he said. "Not long after she warned me, some hulking guy appears at the door. He doesn't threaten me directly but suggests it'd be a shame if I was arrested and his people made a big splash in the papers. I refused and had resigned myself to quit and be recalled from Moscow."

"Interesting. So you reported this to Mr. Cooper?"

"Yeah. Bright and early the next day. He thanked me for reporting it, said he felt bad for introducing her to me in the first place. He then promised to make it go away. And he did."

His revelation took some air out of the room…and J.J.

Clearly, Maddix Cooper was dirty. But was he a Paper Doll? Or was he the real mole?

"Well, I appreciate your candor. We're finished for now, but we'll contact you if we need to follow up."

He thanked J.J. for her understanding and left the room. They took a moment to process what happened. An employee had just told them a security officer encouraged him to break the rules and then covered for him.

"Well, the second time around was a charm. Enlightening."

"How do you do that?" Tony asked looking at J.J. curiously.

Gia frowned, her face green with envy at Tony's unintended show of admiration.

"I told you…it's a gift." She glanced at Gia and cleared her throat. "Well, I for one don't think I can take another interview today. Gia, if you don't mind stepping out for a second? I need to discuss a few things with Tony in private. Bureau business."

Gia eyed Tony and disappeared into the adjacent room, closing the door behind her.

"Interesting, huh?" J.J. said. "We have to ask ourselves why a security officer, a counterintelligence officer, would hook-up a cleared military attaché with a Russian woman, knowing it would break the no-frat policy, and every security policy ever written."

"Either he's dirty, or he's an idiot."

"Let's see, he was serving as a CIA security officer in Moscow. Idiot is definitely not off the table." J.J. said. "Speaking of Six, he should know Mr. Cooper. Russia House isn't very big."

"Yeah, he's also Kendel's ex," Tony said. "Maybe his 'activities' had something to do with their break-up. Seems like we've got some poking around to do."

Tony laughed, stood up, and opened the door for J.J. When he stepped into the office area she ran smack into Kendel, who was waiting to escort them out.

"Long day. Are we ready to go?" Kendel asked, everyone nodded and followed her lead. "You guys unearth anything interesting today?"

"Tomlin was quite informative," J.J. said. "But I was wondering when Maddix Cooper is expected to return."

Kendel began to fidget with the badge dangling from the chain around her neck. "He's taking some much-needed time away."

"I see," J.J. said, feeling a slight sensation behind her left ear. *Still lying.* Kendel continued to dig a deeper hole of deception and J.J. was no closer to the truth than when she started. The vision of paper dolls danced in J.J.'s head and made it ache.

The second she cleared the West Wing entrance, J.J. retrieved her phone from her purse and dialed Headquarters. She needed answers and at this stage there was only one place to get them.

"Did you find any intel on Maddix Cooper?" J.J. asked Sunnie.

"Not yet but I found a new angle on that query of the entry and exit records," Sunnie said. "I think I'm onto something."

Chapter 38

Thursday Morning—Surveillance Detail

Hopper Mack's stomach roiled as he dragged his hands down the length of his jeans from his thighs to his knees to dry the clamminess. He then chewed his last remaining nail while pacing the floor, a ritual he'd performed at least nine times since he arrived that morning. He had a lot at stake, his professional reputation, his career, his sanity.

His gut instinct had ruled him for so long that he didn't know how to shut it down and think through the consequences of his actions.

Some called it genius, other called it recklessness. A whole lot of people would call it the reason he got canned if the Russians swept Mikhaylov's car and yanked out the last GPS unit. In one fell swoop he may have wrecked the single chance the Bureau had to find Lana before she killed another agent and absconded to Moscow.

Before Hopper could return to his seat, Kyle straggled in bearing his trademark snarl and two steaming cups in his hand.

"Have a seat and drink this," Kyle grumbled. "It'll take the edge off."

Hopper waved in refusal. "Coffee gives me the jitters. No, thanks."

"Well, today's your lucky day. It's not coffee."

Hopper held the cup to his face and sniffed. His nose wrinkled. "What is this…hair of the dog? Eye of newt? Hot arsenic?"

Kyle chuckled. "You should be so lucky. It's tea. Zen. It'll help calm you down. Give you something to do with your mouth other than bite your nails to the nub." Kyle's eyes darted around the room, finally locking on the radio sitting silently at the end of the conference table. "Got a call from my confidential informant last night. Still no takers on the passport but I'm holding out ho— Something wrong with the radio?"

Other than the fact that I didn't turn it on? No," Hopper replied. "I couldn't stand to listen. The wait is killing me. Thought you'd leave the room long enough for me to catch the tail end."

Kyle rolled his eyes, stood up and stretched his arm to the edge the table until his palm wrapped around the unit. "Look on the bright side, Junior," he said as he flipped the switch to the on position, "Things always get worse before they're completely shot to hell. You've still got a little further to fall."

Hopper shook his head in disbelief, thankful he wasn't suicidal.

"Boot up the computer and let's get the tracker up."

A few pressed switches on the projector and a web browser appeared on the wall screen. Hopper's fingers tapped against the keyboard until a map of the perimeter of the Russian Embassy appeared.

"Still in the compound," Kyle said.

Before the momentary distraction ceased and the tension kicked back in, Jazz's voice boomed through the radio. "Heads up, Blue Team. Rabbit 1 is approaching the gate. Repeat, Rabbit 1 is approaching the gate. I've got the eye."

"It's Filchenko," Kyle said. "Shouldn't be long now before we know your fate."

Hopper locked his eyes on the red arrow, his heart thumping like rapid succession sonic booms. Beads of sweat began to form on his forehead. He sat paralyzed, waiting for the moment the Gs would call out Lana's father's car. "It's not moving. It's not moving. He usually leaves right on Filchenko's bumper," he said in despair.

"Relax. Give it a minute. The lookouts haven't called him out yet."

The radio fell silent. The sound of static filled the room.

Minutes later, the radio popped.

"Rabbit 2 is slowly approaching the gate," Jiggy said. "Rabbit 2 is slowly approaching the gate.

"The arrow's not moving!" Hopper yelled as he crumbled into a pool of anxiety. "Fuck!"

He blew his big chance. His career was over before it began. Nobody would ever trust him to run an op again. Even if they didn't immediately fire him, they'd probably treat him as if they had. His gut had steered him wrong and he had no one to blame except his stubborn, hard-headed self. He ribbed his fingers through his hair and stared at his feet until his vision blurred. "I can't believe this shit!"

"Look!" Kyle yelled, pointing at the screen.

Hopper looked up and inhaled until the air filled his lungs to capacity. The arrow moved toward Wisconsin Avenue. "Yes!" He smacked his fist into the other hand in a loud pop before placing his hand over his chest. Within seconds, his breathing slowed. "Whew! That was close!"

Kyle gave him a fatherly pat on the shoulder. "You must've put on one helluva a performance, Junior. Not many could pull one over on Mikhaylov. He's damn good." The corners of his mouth lifted. "We're getting close to Michaels. I can feel it."

"We'll know by the end of the day."

Kyle palmed the radio and called out, "Jiggy, this is Blue Leader. The tracker's working. Pull it up on your iPhone. When he goes aggressive, hang back. We need to give him some time in the black so he'll make the drop."

"If he makes a move, I'm on him," Jiggy said. "Time to focus. I'm out."

Hopper stood up and grabbed his tea from the table. "I need coffee now."

Kyle shut down the computer and the screen went dark. "Get it to go. We've got work to do."

"I thought we were gonna monitor the op today."

"We've got more important matters to attend to than playing watch the arrow," Kyle said, waiting for Hopper to follow him to the door. "Grab your radio and we'll get on the road. I want to finish up these interviews before the end of the week."

"The end of the week is tomorrow."

"Exactly," Kyle said. "We've been sidetracked too long. I've still got a couple of addresses on Kenyon to hit before we finish up at Irving Street."

"What if she left the area?"

"Then we find someplace else to search. We're closing the walls in on all sides and we need to keep bringing the heat. I want her to feel claustrophobic from the pressure. That's when she'll make her biggest mistake."

CHAPTER 39

Thursday Morning – The White House

J.J. had nearly drowned in testosterone by the time she, Tony, and Six approached the West Wing entrance. The boys had been volleying insults for an hour, going at it like male pit bulls vying for Alpha supremacy. She'd have preferred to exclude Six from the trip, but they needed him, whether Tony wanted to admit it or not.

Based on what she could glean from his personnel file, Bryer Scott wouldn't make the interview easy. Despite his stellar work performance, he'd been cited numerous times for his brash attitude and inability to play well with others; he took issue with authority. Spending the early hours of his morning glaring at the twisted faces of two FBI agents and a case officer would not fill him with light and sunshine. The mere presence of CIA counterintelligence would, however, keep Bryer from going too far off the reservation with any tall tales.

In the meantime, she had her own demons to deal with—namely, the one shuttling toward the door with red-veined eyes and a vacant stare. Kendel had descended yet another step from the day before. Her countenance and attire lacked their usual elegance. The fresh-from-the-dry cleaner freshness had been replaced by crumpled fabric and a face creased with worry. Dark circles betrayed her sleepless nights. The investigation was surely taking its toll, but J.J. wondered why it had impacted her to this degree—unless she was culpable.

Granted, she'd have to answer for the breach in the Situation Room, but insider spies were an evil every government agency with secrets worth selling struggled with. Even under the tightest, most stringent security measures, those determined to do harm would always find a way to burrow into Government secrets like treacherous termites, silently causing unseen damage until the walls crumbled. No, Kendel's issue ran much deeper. She'd already lied to J.J. on multiple occasions. With each passing day, the stress wore her down, and J.J. could only hope Kendel's inevitable breakdown would lead her closer to revealing the truth.

"Back at it this morning, I see," Kendel said, her voice flat. She stopped short of the entranceway and flicked her hand, gesturing for the group to follow her. Six fell in beside Kendel as she led them down the narrow aisle to their temporary space.

"We just can't seem to pull ourselves away," J.J. said. "Any idea when Mr. Scott's expected to arrive?"

"Yes. He's on the way," Kendel said. "*Any idea* when you're going to get the bug out of my conference space?"

"Director Freeman has briefed the President on the issue," J.J. replied. "When the time comes to remove it, you'll be the fifth to know."

Six turned to Kendel, paused to take in her worn expression, and whispered, "Are you okay?"

She nodded weakly and stepped aside so the team could enter. "Home again," Kendel said. "Call me. If I'm not here when you're ready to leave, Hawk will escort you out."

Before she disappeared from sight, J.J. asked, "Will you be around to talk later? You know, so we can update you on the investigation." She immediately sensed Kendel's reticence from the uncomfortable look on her face.

"I'm not well. I may not be here," she answered.

"Try to be," J.J. urged.

Once inside, J.J. closed the door behind her and glared at Tony and Six in a way that made each stiffen their gaits. They understood she meant business…and not monkey business. "I don't know what's going on between you two today, but it's time to knock it off." She turned to Tony. "Do you have a problem with that?"

"Hey, I'm not the one walking around here acting like this is the dating game. If *he'll* man up and grow a pair, *I'll* keep it professional."

Six rolled his eyes and glared at Tony. "What's the matter? My presence threaten you? Thought you two weren't an item anymore," he said. "Besides, I'm a complex man and fully capable of multi-tasking. If you've got a problem, step aside and let the grown men get to work!"

"That's enough you two," J.J. said. "This whole behaving like five year olds comparing the sizes of *your popsicles* thing is getting old."

The door opened and Sheldon Vance appeared, wearing the hell out of the sleek, black double-breasted number that accentuated the guns bulging through his sleeves. Each time she saw him she was wondered what they called him in his previous life. Maybe his name was Hunkeus, the Greek god of Fine.

"Good morning, Agent McCall," he said, stepping aside to usher in their interviewee. "This is Bryer Scott. Your next interview."

An early 40-ish Caucasian man cloaked in blue polyester slacks, a casual tieless button-up, and a surly junkyard dog expression stepped inside the office. He scanned each face until he locked on Six's. "What's *he* doing here?"

Six sneered but didn't speak, as instructed.

"I've been asking myself the same thing all morning," said J.J. "Unfortunately, my boss says we had to invite him along to keep us honest. You know, ensure the Agency's interests are protected. Don't worry, though, he's been ordered to observe."

"Step into our office and have a seat," Tony said. "We'll get you out of here as quickly as possible."

They all entered the makeshift interrogation room and took seats, leaving Bryer an open chair at the opposite end. He sat down and rubbed his hands together. While he appeared calm from the waist up, his knee bounced beneath the table to the point of distraction.

"You look pretty serious for this to be an informal talk. Do I need to call my attorney?"

J.J. masked her intensified suspicion with a slight grin. "Not unless you think you've engaged in illegal activity. We certainly didn't call you here for that reason."

Tony nodded in agreement. "Just need to ask you a few questions and we'll get you out of here."

He nodded in agreement and waited for the first question.

"So, how do you know Maddix Cooper?"

"Coop? What's he got to do with this?"

"We have some…*concerns* about his activity in Moscow and need to clear up a few issues." J.J. glanced at Six who jutted his chin in approval. "We hear he's quite the party guy."

Bryer's shoulders dropped as if he was let off the hook after J.J. suggested Maddix was the focus of the investigation. He fell back in his seat and appeared to be enjoying a moment of nostalgia. "Heh, heh, heh. He was a rascal that's for sure. A wolf in coyote's clothing. Never met a bottle of Stoli he didn't like. Coop was the go-to guy. Need a good cigar? Go to Coop. Need a girl? Go to Coop."

"Need money?" J.J. asked as if she'd already anticipated the answer.

"Yeah," Bryer replied. "Money too."

"He's a mid-level government guy," Tony asked. "How does he get to be the money guy on his salary?"

Bryer shrugged. "Hey, don't ask, don't tell. That's what they say, right?"

"Ahem!" Six belted out, tilting his head to the side and scrunching his face. Based on his expression, it was a signal. He wanted them to ask a question they hadn't asked.

J.J. fired daggers through her narrowed eyes, tightened her lips, and sliced the tip of her index fingernail across her throat.

"Excuse him," J.J. said to Bryer, clearly annoyed. "So, did you ever go to Maddix for money?"

"I haven't done anything wrong," Bryer pulled out his cell phone and positioned the screen so J.J. and Tony could see he was scrolling his contacts. "Now, where's the name of my attorney?"

"Keep 'im on speed dial, huh?" Tony said.

"Nobody's accused you of anything, Mr. Scott. At least not yet," J.J. said, ready to carefully examine every movement, expression, and focus on each word. It seemed like the perfect time to ask about the Sea Ray, the McMansion on water. "Now, can you tell us about The Devil's Rest?"

He froze and his eyes bulged before he settled against the back of his seat, trying to play it cool. "It's a present to myself for surviving my former wife."

"That's a mighty big gift for a bad wedding," Tony said.

"With all due respect, Agent Donato, you haven't met my ex-wife."

Six guffawed from the corner and said, "Touché!"

J.J. rolled her eyes, turned to Six, and let out a heavy breath. "Really?" She turned back to Bryer, frustrated. She couldn't get a read on him because he never directly answered a question. "How'd you get the money? I mean…you're a what? GS-12?"

"Thought this was about Coop?!" he barked as his gaze flitted around the room. "I didn't come here to be interrogated."

"Ahem!" Six belted out, tilting his head to the side and scrunching his face.

"We didn't come here to interrogate you," Tony snapped, shifting into bad-cop mode. "But I'm listening to this bullshit, and you haven't directly answered a single question Agent McCall or I have asked. If I wanted to be jerked off, I'd make a midnight run to 14th Street." He grunted and turned to J.J. "He's stonewalling. I say screw this and get a warrant. Jets play tonight. I don't' have time for this."

"I'd hate to go the warrant route," J.J. said, staring Bryer down. "Listen, we came here to talk about Maddix Cooper. You don't want to talk about him? Fine. We'll talk about *you*. I can start with the work of fiction in your personnel file. Or I can open that big ugly can of worms security won't find in the file because somebody, I'm not naming any names, failed to do his due diligence in reporting significant changes in finances."

Tony faced J.J. and said, "Last I checked, that's enough justification to get the clearances yanked, right? The devil will have plenty of time to rest. Does your attorney know about the financial reporting requirements necessary to maintain your clearances?"

Bryer's face glowed red as his cool officially left the building. The cell phone disappeared into his pocket and the seeming pillar of strength dissolved into a pile of salt. His bluff had been called and he nearly choked on the truth about to ooze from his lips. "I didn't ask for the money. He offered it to me."

"Offered it? For what?"

"He was the security officer when my wife filed for divorce. We lived a caviar and champagne life on a beer and pretzel budget. Our debt was nuts. Credit card bills out the wazoo. Living in a palace because she needed a closet the size of Iraq to hold all of her shopping spoils."

"Ahem!" Six grunted again.

J.J. scowled at Six and growled. "One. More. Time."

"Tried to make her happy and the bitch left me for a broke son-of-a-bitch convenience store manager. Can you believe that? Took everything with her except the damn bills. Cost me $20,000 in legal bills to keep a $7,000 car and $5 worth of clothes. I didn't ask for help, but he knew I needed it."

"So what did he ask you to do…for this money?" J.J. asked, waiting for a reaction and getting none.

"I never turned over any classified information, if that's what you're thinking," he said. "At the time, all he said was when he needed a favor, I had to come through. I figured he's a security officer, right? What's he gonna ask that I can't deliver? So I accepted the offer. He gave me money…never asked for anything. At least until we returned stateside and I took over as C-O."

"Commanding officer?"

"Contracting officer. We were looking for a company to do the renovations on the Sit Room. He asked me to steer the business to a particular company—MCM Construction."

"And did you?"

"I led him to believe I did. In reality, they submitted the winning bid. We were looking for technically acceptable, lowest cost. They offered the best price. I figured he got a cut and that's how he paid me. Millions of dollars in renovations, even a one percent commission on that job would've put his fee at over a million. I expect he got way more."

J.J. bit her bottom lip. Based solely on appearances, she would've sworn he'd lied like a cheap rug through the entire interview. But her gift told her otherwise. Not a single reaction to a word he said.

She glanced at Six and Tony. "Just one last question. MCM didn't, by any chance, do any work for the State Department?"

He rolled his eyes up to the ceiling to collect his thoughts. "As a matter of fact, they did. I remember because they used their work at the State Department as a past performance reference. We called to verify the work they did. I had also heard they did some work on the new American Embassy in Moscow."

"You mean the Russian intelligence listening post?" Six interjected from his corner.

"Yep, the very one."

"They found so many bugs planted in the walls, they thought termites ate concrete," Six said. "But we understood the problem to be locals hired to pour the concrete, not the contractor."

"Hmmm," J.J. said before turning to Six and Tony. "That's all I have. You two got any more questions?"

They both shook their heads no.

She stood and offered a kind hand to Bryer. "Thank you for your time, Mr. Scott. You're free to leave. We'll be in touch if we need you for anything else. In the meantime, I might suggest contacting your security officer and reporting the few accidentally overlooked discrepancies before we draft the 302. Otherwise, we may be asked to return under less friendly terms."

"Will do," he responded.

Her eyes followed him until his disappeared out of the door. She waved Six over and waited for him to take a seat at the table. "Are you thinking, what I'm thinking?"

"Yeah," Tony said. "Had to be one of the contract workers. He must've recruited one. That's got to be it."

"Now to figure out which one," Six said.

"First, we need to talk to Maddix Cooper. He filed a travel notice, but he's nowhere he's supposed to be. Might be traveling on fake documents. I'll check with Sunnie to see if she's got anything from Customs."

At that moment, J.J.'s phone rang. She glanced at the caller ID. It was Sunnie.

"Speak of the devil. I must've talked you up. What's going on?"

"Remember the other day I told you I had Walter expand the search to contractors? Well, I've come up with something but it's a little complicated to explain over the phone. When are you coming back to headquarters?"

"Complicated? Hmph," J.J. said. "I'm on the way."

"Oh, oh…one more thing," she said. "ERT called. They didn't find much of anything in the Sit Room. No prints. No nothing. Said it's almost as if the room was wiped clean."

"Wiped clean?" J.J. repeated, her mind flashing back to Tuesday night. Kendel, Hawk, and the rest of the team left because of the fire alarm. There was no one else who knew about the investigation who would've been in a position to sanitize the room of evidence. So who could've cleaned up the evidence? "We're on the way right now."

J.J. disconnected the call and rushed to the outer office. She gathered her belongings and hustled toward the door, her confused colleagues dragging behind. "Well? What are you waiting on? Sunnie's got some information on the contractors. We've got to get back to HQ."

"What about Kendel's interview?"

"It's got to wait until first thing tomorrow morning," J.J. said. "Besides, if Sunnie's found what I think she has, Kendel may have to answer for a lot more than the bug in the wall."

CHAPTER 40

Thursday, November 12th—Surveillance Detail
3 Days Left...

Jiggy's heart thumped and eyes shifted back and forth from the GPS tracker screen mounted on his dashboard to the twisted, wooded road ahead. He approached the site from the south to avoid spooking Mikhaylov, who took the north entrance. He was thankful Kyle's op was successful. As an intelligence officer, Mikhaylov would expect the Gs to follow closely behind him. Someone arriving from the opposite direction wouldn't register a blip on the radar.

As Jiggy reached for his radio, the arrow on the screen showed his target had arrived at the driveway and pulled into what appeared to be a large cul-de-sac; Jiggy's eyes darted excitedly along the windy, wooded road peppered with autumn-colored leaves as he searched for the entrance. He hoped to get inside the area before his target exited his vehicle.

Finding the location of the drop was everything.

They usually marked them with benign items, pieces of trash or natural markers most passersby would mistake for litter or scenery. Jiggy knew what to look for, and once he found it, he would lay in wait for Lana, catch her red-handed, and call in the reinforcements to get her off the streets. The end was near. It was only a matter of time.

He turned into the driveway and scanned the area, his arrow getting closer to Mikhaylov's, and spotted his target's car in the center of the lot. He backed into a parking space directly facing the walking path into the woods. A large group of grey-haired women sporting sweat suits and sun visors were grouped at the entrance and most of the parking spaces were filled. Jiggy let out a hard breath and searched for an empty space at the end furthest from Mikhaylov's position. Once parked, he grabbed his radio, rested it in his lap, and reported in. Time to give Kyle an update.

"Blue leader, this is Jiggy. Do you copy? Blue Leader, do you copy?"

A static-filled hush filled the airwaves. Time dragged by like a bullet in a John Wu flick. Mikhaylov stepped out of his car, leaned against the hood, and lit the cigarette he pulled from his pant pocket.

"Copy that," Kyle responded. "What's going on?"

"Looks like we've got a possible drop site, a cul-de-sac about two miles from the zoo entrance. Bunch of civilians standing around talking though. Looks like some Granny walking group."

"How many?"

"I dunno…fifteen, twenty."

"He's not going to make that drop right now. Grannies are nosy and he's in a car with diplomatic plates. No, if he's still there, he's looking for surveillance. He's not going to make a move."

"Well, if he doesn't make the drop today, he's not going to mark the signal, so Lana won't show up."

"Unless he has a secondary site, in which case he drops the package there instead." Kyle fell silent, so immersed in his thoughts Jiggy could almost hear the gears turning. "Listen, I want you out. Sit tight nearby and follow him when he leaves. We've got a lock on one location. It's more important to find out where he goes next."

"Roger that. And when I leave ahead of him, he won't suspect that I'm FBI surveillance."

"Exactly. Keep me updated. Junior and I are conducting interviews, so if you don't get us on the radio, call my cell. You know the number."

Before Jiggy could set the radio on the seat, Lana's father had slipped back into his car, which crept slowly toward the main road. Missing the next location would blow, but following too closely behind could kill the op. Once Mikhaylov disappeared from the driveway, Jiggy pressed to keep the close-in distance short. Just as Jiggy pulled out to the edge, he glimpsed a couple passing him.

He followed Lana's father out of the park onto Tilden, a narrow street that cut through to Connecticut Avenue, one of D.C.'s busiest thoroughfares. A block down, Mikhaylov parked illegally in a metered parking space just past the corner of Upton Street, in a quiet residential neighborhood where D.C.'s upscale residents lived in charming red brick Victorians on leafy streets. Jiggy followed suit, parking a half a block away, keeping his target in his sights.

Mikhaylov eased up next to the mailbox. With an almost slight-of-hand move, he swiped his palm along the side of the box before opening the hatch door and dropping an envelope inside. He broke into a slight jog back to his car, climbed in, and sped north up Connecticut for a block before hanging a left on Van Ness. Jiggy figured he must be on his way back to the embassy judging from the direction. He was more concerned about what his target had left behind.

Once Mikhaylov drove out of sight, Jiggy jumped out. Without dropping any money in the meter, he darted to the mailbox, examining all sides until he spotted it—a six-inch chalk mark along the edge facing Connecticut Avenue.

"Son of a bitch!" Jiggy said to himself, his mind churning. Lana's father had marked a signal, but without making a drop. He started running back to his car when he screeched out, "Son of a bitch!"

The second outburst happened as he ran to the parking attendant slipping the ticket beneath his windshield wiper. "I was right there!" he said, pointing at the corner. He leaned forward and whispered. "I work for the FBI. I'm in the middle of an operation."

She eyed him from head to foot and back again and said, "Wow, the FBI, huh? Today's your lucky day!" Then she whispered. "They can pay the ticket."

She rolled her eyes, cranked her neck with a ghetto twist, and sash-ayed down the sidewalk as Jiggy snatched the ticket from the windshield.

He opened the door, flopped into his seat, and groaned as he gripped the radio. "Blue Leader, this is Jiggy. You copy?"

"We copy, Jig. What's going on?"

"He didn't go to a secondary site. But he did mark a signal."

"Wait. He marked a signal without making the drop?"

"Certainly appears that way."

"Hmmm. You sure he didn't make the drop before you showed up?"

"No way…he didn't have time and too many people were standing around. I don't think the signal is to let Lana know he filled the drop."

"Then maybe he marked it to let her know he couldn't fill it, and he'll leave the cache another day."

"If there's no secondary site, then we'll need round-the-clock surveillance at the one we've identified for a few days," Jiggy said. "The good news is the next time we can maintain stationary positions there while Jazz follows him out the gate. He won't see the same team members."

"Park's only open from 6 a.m. to 8 p.m. so he's got to make the drop during that time frame," Kyle said. "We're gonna get her. Victory favors the patient."

• • •

"This isn't good. Not at all," Katherine said as Santino wheeled into Rock Creek Park. She scanned the area for an open parking space and found one toward the center of the cul-de-sac.

"Hey! You see that fanuk in the car that passed us checkin' me out?" Santino grumbled after he'd locked eyes with a stranger staring at him. "Fuckin' rip his balls off and shove 'em in his eye sockets he wouldn't stare at me again."

Katherine rolled her eyes. She had more important things to worry about—namely the fact that she'd once again risked going out in the open and being discovered for nothing. "The package isn't here. No way."

Santino backed the car into a parking space and turned off the engine. "So, you can't get the money?"

She looked at him and narrowed her eyes. "Don't worry. You'll get your payment as long as you do the job. Just won't be today."

He chuckled in disbelief. "You expect me to just believe what you say? I'm putting my own life on the line by helping you out and the best you can tell me…as long as I do my job, I'll get the money someday? Fuck you, someday. I'll get it now."

She let her head fall back against the headrest and shook it, exasperated by the fact that she was dependent on a Neanderthal for her safety. She bit her bottom lip before eyeing his snarling expression. "Look around. What do you see?"

Santino watched the old ladies heading to their cars and one-by-one drive away. "A buncha geriatrics." He winced and shuddered. "Haven't seen this many droopy boobs since Uncle Paulie took me to the chubby chaser strip club."

"Exactly. Too many people. It's my fault. I didn't check the signal. Start the car up. We need to take a ride," she said, rustling through her purse until she palmed her wallet. She pulled out a folded slip of paper, opened it briefly and returned it to the slot.

"Appreciate you explaining the situation to me. So let me explain something to you...watch your *fucking* tone when you're talkin' to me, eh? I'm not your fuckin' kid, you understand me? This is *the last* time I'm gonna warn you." Santino turned the ignition key and cooled his attitude as fast he put the car in gear. "Now, where to?"

"Connecticut Avenue. It's not far from here. Five minutes," said Katherine.

The tires screeched as Santino sped out of the picnic area, his lips tight and nostrils flaring. His frustration had bubbled to its peak and Lana's mouth was close to shoving him over the edge.

She glanced at Santino's reddened face and quickly relented. "I honestly didn't mean to push your buttons. This is irritating to me as well. I just want this over with, and I'm ready to get the hell out of here."

His frustration might be warranted but couldn't outstrip hers. He could conduct any manner of illegal activity to earn the funds he needed to pay his bosses back. The passport and travel documents were her only chance for a one-way ticket to Moscow, to freedom, to peace. And getting them seemed as challenging as stealing the Hope Diamond.

At once, she was flush with fear and regret, two emotions she'd not been acquainted with for some time. She could've run years ago. She'd done more than enough to prove her value to a country that had hardly embraced her presence the few years she'd lived there. She'd earned her hero status the moment she stepped onto U.S. soil and went undercover without the protection of diplomatic immunity. The boys in the embassy couldn't even claim that level of courage, not even the father she so admired.

But her satisfaction from her job well done was insufficient to fulfill her as long as J.J. McCall still drew breath.

She could not leave the United States without watching McCall suffer, without rejoicing as J.J. stood helplessly over the body of the man she loved and watched him die. She would not. Whatever cost she had to pay to see that plan come to fruition, it could never be too much. And if doing so required her to make peace with Santino, so be it.

"You forgive me?" Katherine asked, playfully batting her eyelashes. He didn't respond, kept his eyes facing forward.

"All right. We're on Connecticut. Where's this place at?"

"In the next block," she said, watching carefully, pointing to the corner. "Slow down so I don't miss it."

She craned her neck as they passed the mailbox, spotted the mark. "Saturday."

"Cuttin' it close isn't it? Your freighter leaves Sunday afternoon," Tony responded, breaking the silence.

"I don't care if I have to leap fifty feet from the dock in an ice storm. I'll be shipping off as scheduled," she said. She rubbed his leg near his crotch until she felt involuntary movement. "We friends again?"

Santino grunted and locked his eyes forward. Everything about his demeanor said, "Hell no."

After twenty minutes of driving in stone silence, they finally turned up Georgia Avenue, only a block away from the house. Lana pressed her forehead against the window as her mind churned on how she could shift Santino's attitude. For many reasons, she didn't want to waste their last days together stewing in resentments over a few misspoken words. When he found out the actual mission she was paying him to conduct, he'd have a genuine reason to be upset. As she drifted out of her thoughts, and back into her present hell, they arrived at the end of their block. She sat up in time to spot an empty parking space close to the house when she saw…*him*. The hair. The walk. The icy glare.

"Oh shit!" sprayed from her mouth as she crouched low in her seat. "What the hell is he doing here?"

Kyle Oliver…and a new flunky she presumed. He stared into the window. *Did he see her?* Probably not through the heavy tint, but her paranoia told her yes.

"Who is who!" Santino yelled, turning his head left and right. In the rearview mirror, their backs faced him. Two men. "Who are they?" Santino pulled into the parking space directly in front of Mr. O'Leary's house.

"No, no," she whispered. "Keep going!"

"Why are you whispering? He can't hear you," Santino said. "He can't see you either. Tint's too dark."

Katherine pushed her back against the heated leather and buried her face in her hands. "I can't even believe this shit. Sunday can't get here soon enough."

"Katherine, who were they?"

She turned to him and deadpanned, "Trust me when I say, you don't want to know. Circle the block a couple of times to give them a chance to get out of the area."

"I take it they're not friends of yours."

"What gave it away?" She swallowed hard. "Either the world is getting incredibly small or I'm incredibly screwed."

CHAPTER 41

Thursday—Irving Street

Kyle led Hopper up Irving, the last street on their list. Two hours of teeth-pulling interviews had yielded nothing. He was frustrated that they had yet to interview a single Fed-friendly person in the entire neighborhood. Most were older African-Americans who had a deep-rooted distrust of law enforcement of any kind, a problem he was well aware of before he arrived. Snitching on a stranger with no ties to the area engendered as poor a level of cooperation as any fear of ratting on a local kid.

Frustration subsumed him, but he refused to give up. The faint, steady sound of a clock ticking down haunted him. It'd been a week to the day since she disappeared. The longer she remained free, the less likely their chance of finding her before she departed for Moscow. He couldn't let her get away. She had to pay for Cartwright. And if Karma hadn't yet stepped up to do the job, Kyle was determined to do it for her.

They carefully shifted their gazes between the lists in their hands and the address numbers, searching for the location of their next failure.

"The next house is just up here on the left," Kyle said as he opened the gate and walked up the steps. "Mrs. Merla Rae Simmons. Strong southern name. Hope she throws some sweet tea in our faces before she slams the door on us. I could use a swallow."

"I'm too busy swallowing my pride," Hopper said. "Here goes nothing."

He rang the doorbell and waited; he heard the sound of faint footsteps approaching the door then a pause. The curtains rustled when a small finger pulled open a slit in the sheer-covered side window. Kyle saw the tip of a brown nose. The fabric released and a voice screeched, "Whatever you're selling, we don't want any!"

Kyle chuckled and reached in his breast pocket. "Ma'am. Mrs. Simmons. I'm Special Agent Kyle Oliver with the FBI and this is my co-case agent Hopper Mack." He pulled out his credentials and pressed them against the window. "Promise not to take up much of your time, just like to ask you a few questions."

She cracked open the door and sunlight glistened on her long silver hair. Her narrowed skeptical sneer carved him up from beneath the bifocal line in her brown-framed glasses. "FBI. Hmph. You'da been better off tryin' ta sell me somethin'," she said, pursing her lips together. "You never see the *po*-lice 'round here 'cept to haul off one of these hard-headed chirrens."

She extended the opening, grabbed the thick leather case from his hand, and ran her finger across the golden badge before handing it back. "All the money I'm payin' Uncle Sam and that's the best the FBI can do?" She shook her head. "What brings you to the 'hood?"

"We appreciate your cooperation, ma'am."

"I ain't told you nothing yet, but go on and say what you gotta say. I'm listenin'."

"We got your name from a friend at the *Washington Post*," Kyle began. "As we understand it, you advertised a room for several weeks and then withdrew the ad."

"Is rentin' illegal now?"

"No, no, Ma'am. We were just wondering if you pulled the ad because somebody answered it."

She shook her head. "Oh…no. Uh-uh. Kids run up my light bill, sneakin' in and out the house in the middle o' night, don't pay on time, gettin' my pressure up. I could find life on Mars before any one o' dem on rent day. Decided it wasn't worth the headaches. Can't have nobody playin' with my money and I'm gettin' too old for jail."

Hopper smiled, shot Kyle a side-eye glare, and cleared his throat. "So, you never had anybody respond to the ad?"

"I got a few calls, but nobody showed up here."

Kyle pulled Lana's picture from his jacket pocket. "Have you seen this woman around here in the past week?"

She took a careful look at the photo, tightened her lips, and handed it back to him. "That's the one on TV, right?"

Kyle nodded.

"No, definitely ain't seen her," she said. "Only times you see white people in this neighborhood is to take somebody to the hospital or to jail…or every once in a while 'cause they're lost."

"Anyone else on this street rent rooms to college kids?"

"Hmm. Let me think about that for a second," she said, tapping her index finger against her upper lip. "You know. I think the Mamie Douglass rents her basement. She's three doors down. Oh, and the O'Learys too. They rent to just about anybody."

"O'Learys?" Kyle asked.

"Yeah, I know what you're thinkin' but they ain't white. They Irish," she said. "I reckon they lived here about as long as anybody. That's all I can think of. If you want to talk to somebody who really knows, you should talk to Max McCall. He's been 'round here 'bout forty years. Ten longer than me."

"Max McCall, you say?" Hopper said, jotting the name in a notebook.

"Yeah. Come to think of it, last time I heard his daughter was working with y'all. Surprised you don't know her. She was all over the news last week. Beat that lady's ass at the airport."

Kyle's eyes bulged as he turned to Hopper. "Wait! Max McCall is J.J. McCall's father… and he lives here?"

"Ain't that what I just told you?" She stepped out on the porch and pointed to a duplex midway down the block. "You see that one there? The red brick one? He lives there. Owns a little corner store a few blocks up 7th Street too. He don't miss a beat."

Kyle and Hopper shot knowing glances at one another.

"Well. I think we've got everything we need for now, Mrs. Simmons. Thank you for taking time out of your busy schedule to speak with us," Hopper said, handing her a business card. "If you think of anything else or see anyone suspicious who might fit Lana Michaels' description, please give us a call. In the meantime, we're gonna talk to Mr. McCall," Kyle said, leading Hopper out of the gate.

"He's probably at the store. Make a left at the far corner and walk three blocks up," she said after glancing from side to side to check for nosy neighbors.

Kyle and Hopper walked in silence a few steps until out of earshot of Mrs. Simmons. Then Kyle stopped in the middle of the sidewalk and dug his hands into his pocket. "Let me ask you something, Junior. Do you believe in coincidences?"

"Not like this one I don't," Hopper said. "Our assessment was wrong the whole time. Michaels was never planning to attack J.J. No, she'd plan to hit an easier target all along. But why do you suppose she hasn't hit him yet?"

Kyle thought about it for a second and then it struck him. "Of course. That's it. She can't leave," Kyle said. "The fact that he's still alive means she can't get out."

"That's gotta be it," Hopper said. "That's the only reason she'd risk staying this long. She had no choice."

"Most importantly, she's not going to kill McCall or do anything that'll draw heat from the cops until she's ready to leave the country, which means we've still got time."

Kyle threw his head up to the sky and starting pacing quickly toward the corner when a car with dark tinted windows passed by. The deep, throaty rumble from the sparkly black Mustang's engine, reminded him of his own V8 with off-road H-pipes and Flowmasters. The shadow of a head ducked midway down a passenger window. Strange. But he didn't give it much thought. Chalked it up to sensory overdrive as he followed it with his eyes for half a block. Couldn't be Lana. She wouldn't drive a car that would turn the head of every straight male within a 100-mile radius. Wrong way to lay low.

"So what's next?"

"We'll talk to Mr. McCall and then call J.J. and the Gs," Kyle said. "We've had Money T watching the wrong target all along."

CHAPTER 42

"Which room is Sunnie in?" J.J. asked, striding down the 8th corridor looking for briefing location. "There's 2,000 conference rooms in this building and she leaves a note that says, 'I'm in the conference room.' What the hell?"

"It's gotta be one closest to the office," Tony said, with Six trailing a step behind him. "Wait. You just passed it."

J.J. stopped in her tracks, took two steps back, and twisted the doorknob. When she entered the room, her eyes fixed on the wall-to-wall whiteboard filled with diagrams approaching Rorschach test proportions. Sunnie was scribbling notes alongside the diagram while Walter watched in wonder.

"Geez, Sunnie, what the hell is that?" J.J. parked herself in the seat at the front of the room closest to the whiteboard. The chicken scratch was so small in some areas she could hardly decode the words.

Six laughed and took a seat at the head of the table. "Exploring your inner Jackson Pollock? That's incredib…bly confusing."

"What the hell?" Tony added.

"Okay, Wendy Whiners. I'll explain everything once somebody shuts the door. I don't think there's a clearance level high enough to cover all the crap I've got on this board."

After everyone settled down, Sunnie circled three stick figure people and two pitiful representations of buildings.

"Okay, so to help you understand what's going on here," Sunnie said, circling her hand over the board and landing her finger on the first stick person. "I need to start with Lana Michaels."

"Ugh, Lana," J.J. groaned.

"We got diddly off of her work or home hard drives except some expressions of insanity in a few journals, not much from her house either. Interviews of Jack Sabinski and Chris yielded a little bit of nothing. And the only other person who knew her that intimately is…well…" she eyed J.J. and stammered, "Uh, er…not here anymore. So we got more nothing. I mean zilch."

"So, what's all this on the board then?" Tony asked.

"It dawned on me that if she's the nucleus of a spy network, there's one thing that she needs more than anything else."

"Money," Six said.

"Exactly. So what you see up here is what we found when we followed the money," Sunnie said. "We found a book by Pushkin called *The Daughter of the Commandant* in her house. The cover fell off when ERT dusted for prints. On the inside of the cover along the spine, she wrote a series of numbers."

"Let me guess," J.J. said. "Bank account?"

"Bingo! Linked to a limited liability company," Sunnie said. "I ordered a Treasury FINCEN analysis on the account and just got the report this afternoon."

"I don't understand. Lana owned a company?" Tony asked.

"No, Lana didn't own it, but she was a signatory on the account, using a slight variation of her name—L. Alexandra Michaelson—and a fake social security number. She could write checks and withdraw cash without ever directly linking a single transaction to her personal account. Tens of thousands of dollars transacted through this account every couple of months. Each deposit less than $10,000 to stay off Treasury's radar."

"So where did the money come from?"

"Troika Technologies," Walter replied. "I'm still drilling down but from what I've found so far, they buy and sell computer technologies and network installation equipment. Apparently, they supplied cabling to a contractor who performed the White House and State Department renovation jobs. All U.S. companies. All legal. All above board," Walter said.

"The owner is Ivan Mashkov, a naturalized U.S. citizen originally from Belarus," Sunnie added. "The money comes from his Bank of New York account."

"Mashkov?" J.J. asked. "Wait, he wouldn't by any chance be related to…"

"The one and only," Sunnie said. "He's the brother of Golikov's henchman numero uno. Been loosely linked to Russian organized crime in New York, but nothing solid. FBI New York's had a case opened for the last 8 years and this is all they have." Sunnie held up a thin file folder. "Might be ten sheets of paper in here. Can't get enough on them to request a wire."

"Until now," J.J. said. "But I still don't understand. What's the connection to the Sit Room?"

"Glad you asked," Walter said. "Our new friend Ivan didn't send the money directly to Lana's account. It made a pit stop at another company—anybody ever heard of MCM Construction?"

Everybody gasped and snapped upright in their seats.

J.J. slammed her elbows against the table and scraped her nails across her scalp before her phone vibrated. She sent the call to voicemail and returned her attention to the conversation. "Oh my God. My head's about to explode."

Tony slapped his hand against the table. "I'll be damned. It fits. They did the renovations in the State Department and the Sit Room."

"We think MCM was being used to help launder the money used to pay the agents in Lana's network. And you'll never guess who owns MCM."

"Oh, I've got this one," Six said. "Maddix Cooper?"

Sunnie shook her head. "No, his brother in law, Gary Mosin. Married to his only sister."

"Are you freakin' kidding me?" Tony said. "What'd you find on the brother-in-law?

"Based on what we have right now, he's clean. A model, naturalized American citizen. But we're still digging," Sunnie answered.

"This Cooper guy's a regular John Walker," J.J. said, speaking of the convicted former Navy officer who recruited a network of spies among his family and friends. A simultaneous release of anger and frustration overcame her. "He's recruiting his peops into his duplicitous little circle."

"I've also linked calls from Troika Tech to the company in Russia I told you about," Walter chimed in, referring to the company linked to Lana's secret bank account. "We think Troika is the American-based financial hub. Money is transferred from Russian intel into an account for the Moscow-based company, then cut-outs move the money from Moscow to the U.S. For all intents and purposes, Troika operates as a NOC."

"If we can cut off the money, it's only a matter of time before we catch the moles. The Russians will have to risk exposing new members of the network or lose valuable sources of intelligence."

"Just in time for us to cut them off at the neck," Six said.

"Our mission is clear, gentlemen…and lady…very smart, awesome lady," J.J. said, smiling at Sunnie. Her phone rang again, increasing her annoyance. "First thing tomorrow, we find and interview Maddix Cooper. He's the lead domino. We take him down and the rest will fall right behind him. Did you ever find anything on his whereabouts, Sunnie?"

"Sure did. Based on what I got from my contacts in Customs, he never left the country. Not on *his* passport."

J.J. leaped forward in her seat. "You mean he's been here the whole time?" She turned to Six. "I think your girl is dirty."

"No, kidding. She's got to be covering for him," Six said. "The question is why?"

"Hmm. We'll find out soon enough. Call her tomorrow, Six. Pour on the charm. Tell her you've been thinking about her and you want to do breakfast. When she arrives, we'll all be waiting. She'll cough up Maddix Cooper's location or she'll go to jail for obstruction. Her choice."

J.J.'s phone rang again. She finally looked at the screen and realized she needed to answer. Pronto. "Listen guys, I've really got to take this now. It's Kyle Oliver from WFO. He's been blowing up my cell, must have something on Lana's investigation." She stepped into the hall and answered.

"McCall. What's going on, Kyle?"

"Well, I've got good news and bad news. What do you want first?"

"Uhh…give me the good first. God knows I need it right now."

"Well, the good news is we think Lana has abandoned her mission to kill you."

"Hmph. The feeling certainly isn't mutual. What's the bad part?"

"We believe she may be after a softer target…your, uh, your father."

J.J.'s heart thumped so hard she lost her breath. She bent forward trying to regain her composure.

"J.J.? J.J.? You okay?"

The sound of Kyle's voice barely seeped through the pounding in her ears. Her father and brother were all she had left in the world since her mother died. The mere thought of losing either paralyzed her left her dizzy with fear and anguish. She didn't have time for the anxiety attack she so richly deserved. Her first objective was to ensure her father didn't die at the hands of that witch.

"I want protection on him," she said, forcing calm into her voice. "Like yesterday."

"Money T's on the way there now."

"What's he going to do? Follow Lana to death?" J.J. said her voice in a nervous high pitch. "Unfortunately, we don't' have time to hunt her down and burn her at the stake, and I'd prefer someone with a gun."

"J.J., I understand your concerns, but we don't have the resources to put an agent on him right now," Kyle said. "Every free body's on the streets."

"The Bureau has already failed my mother. Now you want my father too?"

"I can't even respond to that."

"You know what? I'll get my brother to stay with him," said J.J. "Forget Nixon and his orders. And as soon as I wrap up this case, I'm going to devote every second of my life to making her suffer for deigning to think she could get away with threatening my family."

Chapter 43

Thursday—Russian Embassy

Aleksey checked his watch as he rounded the corner to his office. 4 pm. Time seemed to drag this week, every second ticking by like pouring frozen molasses. But he was determined to reach Vorobyev and find out what he knew about the tennis shoes and, more importantly, whether he'd reported his find to Center counterintelligence.

He checked the residency floor thoroughly before taking a seat at his desk. Everyone who mattered was holed up in the conference room waiting for Lana's father to return from the drop. He pushed aside the stack of operational reports awaiting his approval and grabbed the handset from the cradle. After swallowing hard and taking a deep breath, he began to dial. Three rings resonated in his ear before he got an answer.

"Comrade Stansilav Vorobyev, please," he said. "This is Aleksey. Aleksey Dmitriyev."

"Ahhhh, Aleksey. I've been expecting your call."

It was his friend. Finally. "Brother! Why have you not returned my calls?"

"Things here have been quite hectic since my arrival. Paperwork. Bureaucratic bullshit. You know how it goes." When Stan paused for a moment, a faint click sounded in the phone. He feared their conversation was being recorded. After a few seconds passed, Stan asked, "Those who matter have long memories, quite slow to forget. Especially General Stepanov, who has been a particular *joy* to work with," he said, his voice molten with sarcasm. "I assume all is well in Washington? It's all abuzz here with the pending return of the so-called Red Honeytrap."

"Ahhhh, yes. She is due to travel Sunday. Won't be soon enough for us here. All eyes are on us and, of course, we don't work well in the spotlight," he said. "Apart from that, it's the same old story."

"Ah, yes, and the stories you could tell," he said. "The stuff Le Carre novels are made from, eh?"

"What do you mean?"

"Oh, I almost forgot to tell you. My son…he sends his regards and deepest appreciation for the tennis shoes. I asked him what is so special about Converse shoes. He says you can't get more Russian than Keds. Indeed, if you knew how valuable these shoes were, I think you would not have given them away."

Aleksey's heart sank. Sweat flushed from his forehead and his hands began to tremble.

"Ahh, well, too late now," Stan said. "I've got them and I plan to ensure they are put to good use. After everything that has transpired over the past week, I certainly deserve everything that's coming to me. We all do, don't you think?"

Aleksey gulped. "Listen, Stan, I—"

"Look at the time, brother. I must be going. I've got a very important event to attend."

"A meeting with Golikov?" he asked.

Vorobyev lowered his voice and responded, "A date with destiny. I'll be in touch soon." Then he abruptly hung up the phone without so much as a goodbye.

Aleksey listened with dread at the dial tone. Although he wasn't stunned by Vorobyev's cryptic tone, he was certainly disturbed by it, still unsure as to whether Stan had divulged the depth of his treachery. Wondering if at any moment the Crooked Twins would crash through the door, snatch him up by the collar, and drag him kicking and screaming down the hall to the place where Vorobyev nearly lost his life just one week before. He froze in fear, panicked. Unsettling thoughts shook his mettle.

Dmitriyev questioned whether he should run, not walk out the embassy doors, call J.J. and start a new life in the United States. Problem was he realized he hadn't provided the level of information necessary to receive a sizeable settlement from the FBI. There'd be no retirement; rather, he'd be forced to accept consultant work and speaking engagements whenever he could. He'd be a nowhere man, which was an unacceptable end. He'd slogged in the Service's drudgery for too many years to be relegated to the status of a stepchild defector. No, for everything his family had suffered, he wanted fair remuneration. And he was determined to get what he deserved by any means necessary, even if it meant risking his life. After all, in his mind, a return to living in poverty would be a fate equal to death.

Before he could inhale a calming breath, harried footsteps pushed through the hall outside his office. Mikhaylov passed by Dmitriyev's door at a determined pace in the direction of the conference room, without poking his head in for their usual greeting. Something had gone wrong. The op had failed. He hoped the FBI wasn't the source of the problem because their involvement would only intensify suspicions of a compromise within the embassy and heat up the scrutiny on Dmitriyev, all but ensuring he couldn't provide the information he needed to free himself from the bondage and deliver the ultimate blow to the Service.

He swept out of his seat and rushed down the hall, tapping on the closed door before entering. Lana's father and the Resident were seated at the conference table and both bore intense expressions.

"Aleksey, please, come inside and close the door," the Resident said.

Relieved at the invitation, Dmitriyev took the empty seat beside Mikhaylov in deference to his boss. He scanned both of their faces. Neither showed signs of mistrust, reassuring him that Vorobyev had not yet revealed anything damaging. "Judging from your expressions, I take it the drop did not go as planned," Dmitriyev said.

"No," Lana's father said, shaking his head. "We evaded the FBI well enough; however, too many people surrounded the location. I couldn't fill it without drawing undue attention."

"What's the alternate day?"

"Saturday. The freighter sails Sunday afternoon which means I need to fill the drop early if she's to have any chance of leaving as scheduled."

"Hmm. I see your problem. You risk drawing the attention of the police."

"Precisely. The park police will have nothing better to do than disrupt this operation. I'm afraid I have to request your assistance again. I cannot trust this critical task to that nit Filchenko. Don't you understand? Her life depends on my success!" he urged, his face creased with the desperation of a father terrified for his daughter's life.

He found it difficult to empathize with Mikhaylov or his daughter's troubles. He wanted her in an American jail where she could do no more harm to his family or friends. And if J.J. caught him participating in yet another operation, it would all but seal his fate with the FBI and ensure he never resettled in the United States as he'd long hoped. He must shirk the responsibility at all costs.

Dmitriyev turned to the Resident and narrowed his eyes, determined to reason his way out. After all, his boss was nothing if not pragmatic. So he turned to Komarov and said, "I've already—tell him, Comrade. As the Security Chief, my participation puts the entire residency at risk. As much as I would welcome the chance, I—"

"You'll do as he asks," Komarov demanded. "I understand your concerns, but we will stand-down most operations the minute Svetlana marks the signal indicating she's cleared the drop. It is for that reason we cannot afford any mistakes. You have my word you won't be asked again."

"You word?" Dmitriyev said. "As I recall you made the same vow three days ago. May I get your promise in writing *this* time?"

"It's settled then. Countersurveillance. Saturday morning," the Resident said to Dmitriyev. "Until then, let's see what Gusin can collect from RAPTURE. We haven't submitted a single report of value to the Center this week and we need to know what the Americans have planned for Lebed's visit."

Dmitriyev nodded.

"That will be all for now," Komarov said as he rose to leave. "Director Lebed arrives Tuesday. I'll be busy coordinating meetings for his visit until then, but I'll expect a full briefing on the outcome Sunday, noon."

As the three men left the conference room and parted ways, Dmitriyev's anxiety compounded exponentially. It was clear he could brook no opposition to the Resident's orders, not given his precarious position. His only choice was to find a way to turn it to his advantage—ingratiate himself with the FBI, while concealing his duplicity in the unlikely event that Vorobyev maintains his secret.

Divulging Lana's pending activities was not an option. No, the secret he revealed must be valuable yet give him plausible deniability. And Lana had to fulfill her mission…or at least believe she had. No sooner than the idea flitted through his mind, the epiphany struck—the idea that would protect his present and secure his future.

And Komarov's word had made it possible.

For the first time, he was thankful for broken promises.

CHAPTER 44

Friday Morning, November 13th —J.J. McCall's Condominium

Tony moaned through a long yawn as warm rays and the sounds of Luke Skywalker landing in the Dagobah system yanked him from his slumber. Each morning renewed his appreciation for the hot brown body spooned against him. His own limbs had gone limp and nothing short of a thousand volts of electricity could coax him from her grasp. He was not only shocked at J.J.'s undercover nerd tendencies, but her voracious appetite for him and her ability to drain every ounce of energy from his being.

Every day, his feelings for her strengthened. He was the best version of himself when in her presence and she knew it, which is why her apparent jealousy over Gia perplexed him. Sure, he found Gia attractive. Okay, sizzling. Any man with two working eyes could see she's hot. Didn't mean he'd sleep with her. Okay, he would if J.J. didn't exist in his world. But she did. J.J. had become intertwined in the fabric of his life and he could no longer picture his life without her. His heart was firmly in her grasp, whether she realized it or not.

She stirred, arousing from a deep slumber. She turned to him and smiled, careful to cover her mouth and avoid blasting him with hot morning breath. "Good morning, you."

He pushed her hand aside and kissed her lips anyway. "Right back atcha," he said. "I feel like a wet noodle thanks to you."

"I'm trying to earn a reputation around here," J.J. said, sitting up with her eyes glued to the TV screen. "This is my favorite part," she said, watching Yoda teach the young Jedi to hone his skills.

"What is it with this movie?"

J.J. shrugged. "I dunno. Gotta feel bad for the Luke, right? I mean the poor guy loses his parents, the only two people in the world genetically disposed to love him, and while he's living under this cloud an incredible power is thrust upon him. And rather than shrink and disappear into his small, quiet life in the hot dirt on Tatooine, he answers the call. He fights the dark side. What's not to love?"

"Hmmm. I never thought of it that way. Sounds a little like you."

"No, my father is still alive."

"So was Luke's."

"And I don't have a superpower."

"You sure? I mean, I didn't think anyone could detect a lie better than my mother. I'm startin' to think you've got something more powerful than female intuition."

She looked at him with her mouth agape. "Crazy, that is," she said in a pathetic Yoda imitation that sounded more like Grover from Sesame Street. She reached over and felt his forehead. "Sick, are you?"

His stomach tightened with laughter. "Get outta here. You're funny. And not just a little bit nerdy. But I like it."

"Good!" She glanced at the clock and slipped out of bed into the bathroom. "We need to get a move on. Big day. Six is meeting us at the West Wing for Kendel's interview in an hour."

"You think she's dirty?"

She appeared in the doorway with her toothbrush, layered a bead of Crest along the bristles, and disappeared again. "I don't think she put the bug in the wall. I'm not even certain she knew it was in the wall." The sound of water streaming into the muffled her voice. "But she knew Maddix was dirty. Something tells me that may be the reason for their break up."

"Yeah, she seems to be coming apart at the seams lately too. I mean, the first time we saw her she was so sharp and reassured. Now, she comes in looking like she ran to work in her suit. Sweating. Clothes wrinkled."

She appeared in the door again. "Yeah, I told you. It was as if she was coming off of a...."

"High," Tony said. "You said that before and now I'm beginning to think you're right. I swear to God you're brilliant."

J.J. gurgled, swished, and rinsed before making her way into the closet. "That would explain a lot, wouldn't it? If she closed a blind eye to his activities, she certainly aided and abetted, if not committing espionage herself."

"Do you think she'll rat him out?"

"You've seen her. She's not a willing participant, and she's all but melted in front of us. If we pull the right trigger, so-to-speak, she'll give up anything to make this all disappear."

"Now, what can I do to make you come back to bed?" Tony asked.

J.J. chuckled and slinked toward the bed. "Pull out your light saber. And make it quick. We've got a meeting on the dark side."

CHAPTER 45

Friday Morning – Irving Street

Hopper and Kyle wheeled their Charger into the lone empty parking space in front of Mr. O'Leary's place. His was the last on the list of rooming houses that had withdrawn advertisements from the *Washington Post* within a day of Lana's escape. The sound of rakes dragging through leaves echoed as early risers began the annual gathering of yard waste. High clouds cluttered the sky allowing the sun to filter into spike-shaped rays. After scanning the street left and right, they exited the car and ascended the steps, craning their necks to eye passersby.

Kyle rang the doorbell, then attempted to peer through the sheer curtain covering the window from the other side. No movements, no lights, only the sound of a faint bump overhead.

"You hear that?" Hopper asked.

Kyle nodded. "Yep. Doesn't look like anybody's home, though…unless they're hiding inside."

Hopper backed away from the door, stepped down from the porch and gazed at the second-story windows. "I don't see any movement. Maybe it was next door."

"Maybe." Kyle scratched his head in confusion.

"Can I help you?" a baritone voice called from across the street.

They both turned around to face the tall, dark-skinned older gentleman in a track suit.

"Sir?" Kyle responded.

"Can I help you?" the man repeated.

"Hello. I'm Special Agent Kyle Oliver and this is Special Agent Hopper Mack. We're from the FBI."

They presented their credentials and returned them to his pocket when he finished

"Max McCall." He held his hand out for both to shake. They offered firm responses in return. "My daughter's an agent. She told me about what's going on…son's inside."

"Glad to hear it. It's just a precaution for now," Kyle said. "We're going to finish up our interviews today. Hopefully we'll get a new lead. Do you know if any of your neighbors have rented out a room in the last week?"

"I've only seen one new face in this neighborhood, but she doesn't look anything like that girl on the T.V.," he said.

"She?"

"Yeah, O'Leary took her in about a week ago. He rents out the other side of his duplex. She and another gentleman stay there."

"You say she bears no resemblance to Lana Michaels?"

"Maybe she's around the same size. But definitely not the hair and eye colors. No way. I know blue from green and black from blond," he said. "Besides I doubt someone trying to kill me would save my life."

Both Kyle and Hopper were taken aback. "Save your life?"

"Yeah. Last Saturday. Some young hoodlum with a gun came in trying to rob my store. Before I knew it, he was flat on the ground. The woman took him down and walked out. Wouldn't even accept free groceries."

"You wouldn't by any chance have security cameras in your stores, would you?"

"Sure do. Although before the woman left, she told me to get a panic button installed. I saw her a couple of days later."

"Mr. McCall—"

"Max, please," he interrupted.

"No problem, Max. We'd like to take a look at the video, after we speak to your neighbors here. The O'Learys. You wouldn't happen to know if anyone's home."

"Claire dragged him kicking and screaming on a two-week cruise to the Caribbean. They won't be back for another week," Max said. "The tenants should be around, though. I've been up since five and haven't seen either of them leave, but I'm not exactly keeping watch by the window."

"We'll walk over and grab you when we're done."

"All righty," Max said as he made his way back into the house.

Kyle turned to Hopper and said, "You think it's coincidental this mystery woman saved him during an armed robbery?"

"No. But, if she's Lana, why wouldn't she just kill him herself? Or let the robber do it?"

"Good questions. I'll be interested to check out the video. In the meantime, let's see if Barbie and Ken will answer."

Kyle rang the doorbell, then attempted to peer through the sheer curtain covering the window from the other side. No movements, no lights, only the sound of a faint bump overhead.

"You hear that?" Hopper asked.

Kyle nodded. "Yep. Doesn't look like anybody's home though, unless they're hiding inside."

Hopper backed away from the door, stepped down from the porch and gazed at the second-story windows, again. "I don't see any movement. Maybe it was next door."

"Maybe." Kyle scratched his head in confusion.

They rang the doorbell and knocked several times before hearing the staircase creak under heavy footsteps. A large, olive-skinned man opened the door and said, "Yeah?"

Hopper and Kyle introduced themselves and proceeded through the standard introductory procedures. Kyle couldn't help but notice his facial features and build were familiar, but he couldn't place the face.

"What's your name, if you don't mind me asking?"

"I mind," he said. "But you can call me Sonny."

"Thanks, Sonny. Listen, we don't want to take up much of your time. Just wanted to ask you a few questions and we'll be on our way," Kyle said. "We stopped by earlier, but you didn't answer the door."

"Oh, sorry. I was in the shower."

"Okay, that's understandable." Kyle nodded and gave him the once over thinking that if the disheveled man before him had truly taken a shower he missed a few spots. All over. "We understand from some of the neighbors that you and a female tenant are sharing this place right now."

"Yeah, I've been here since June. My roommate didn't move in until last week sometime. She told me her apartment caught fire, but what do I know?"

"I see." He pulled Lana's photo from his breast pocket and handed it over. "We're canvassing the neighborhood asking neighbors if they've seen this woman."

Santino carefully studied the photograph, his face remained expressionless as he twisted and turned the paper at multiple angles before handing it back to Kyle. "Nah. She don't look familiar to me. Different hair, different eyes. The lips ain't right eitha. But I gotta admit, I don't spend much time checkin' out her face, if you get my drift?" he said, shaking his hand and biting his lower lip.

"Is she home now?"

"Nah. Left a few hours ago. Asked me to feed her fish for a few days. I think she got a job or somethin'. May be lookin' for a permanent place. I dunno. I mind my business; she minds hers. I'll feed 'em while I'm here."

"Any idea when she's coming back?"

He shook his head. "Most of her stuff is still up there so I know she's coming. I dunno when. If you leave your card, I'll give you a call when she shows up."

"We appreciate your cooperation." Hopper handed him a card. "Thank you for your time."

"Eh. Just doing my civic duty," Santino said before the door slammed.

Half way back to Max's place Hopper said, "At least he was cooperative."

Kyle smiled and shot back, "So was Benedict Arnold. Doesn't mean he was helping our side."

• • •

Friday—Irving Street

"You think that's her?" Hopper said, staring at the monitor behind the cashier counter at Max McCall's corner store. Max pulled the video tapes from the day of the robbery and hovered behind him.

He looked on as the woman disarmed and dropped the would-be robber flat to the ground in a matter of seconds. "She's no civilian. The take-down was textbook Quantico," Kyle said. "Even still I wouldn't bank my check on this being Michaels yet."

"Yeah, I know a few female cops and Marines who could've done twice the damage in half the time," Hopper said.

"Between the hoodie, the hat, and the glasses, I can't tell. Same height though," Kyle said. "The build, on the other hand, is well concealed under the baggie clothes." He turned to Hopper before saying, "Either it's not her, or she's doing a damn good job of hiding in plain sight."

Hopper stood up and walked around the store. ""If we only had a clean shot of her face, CJIS could run a facial recognition analysis. I'm gonna check and see if any place nearby has a camera outside. She had to get here somehow, right?"

"Good thinking," Kyle said. "I'll review the footage again. See if there are any other clues."

After a few minutes, Hopper burst through the door. Breathless.

"Mr. McCall…uh, Max," Hopper said, his arms flailing. "Are you kidding me? You have another camera." He marched over to a small storage closet along the wall opposite the checkout counter and twisted the doorknob. It was locked. "What's in here?"

"It's just a storage closet. Nothing in there except a mop, broom, and the dust pan, you know, the supplies we use to clean the store," he said, digging in his jingling pockets. He pulled out a ring bloated with keys and fished through until he found a small golden one. He walked over to Hopper and handed it to him. "Here you go."

Hopper nodded and proceeded to unlock the door.

"Now that I think about it, my son did tell me he installed another camera," he said. "But he didn't connect it to a monitor. Made me hook up the hidden one in case someone tried to disable the main system or take the DVD."

Hopper entered the closet and stood on the tips of his toes. Two black boxes were perched in the corner. He traced an electric and phone cord, adhered to the wall under white duct tape, to plugs concealed behind a small panel. "Score!" Hopper yelled.after taking a few minutes to examine the hardware. "Bad news is he doesn't have DVD recording. Good news—it's DVR with battery back-up."

"Fantastic. Bring it over. We'll hook the box up to the monitor. And see what we've got."

Hopper slid the flat black box and remote control off the shelf and took it to the counter, letting the video cords drag along the floor. In no time, he hooked it up and pulled up the menu which allowed him to select last Saturday's video.

"A wide-angle version that captured the area outside the door. We can almost see to the end of the block."

They fast-forwarded and watched each move in double-time. "There's you entering," Kyle said. "How long after you got to work did it happen?"

"About three hours. I opened early."

Hopper held the button down until a figure showed up at the corner. "Stop right there. That's her. No sunglasses. Play it at regular speed."

They eyed the screen as she paced up the sidewalk. Outside the entrance door, she stopped. "Freeze it. Right there."

Kyle and Hopper studied her face. "What do you think?"

Kyle nodded. "It's tough, but looks like Lana."

"As much as I want to find her, I'm not ready to make the leap," Hopper said. "Then again, I've never worked with her. You have. Before we storm the house, I say we let CJIS look at it. We'll email it. Shouldn't take more than a day to get some definitive results. With a positive ID we can get an expedited warrant."

"All right. I agree," Kyle said. "Now let it play. Let's see what's going on when the perp walks in."

When Max spotted the robber approaching the entrance, he shouted, "That's him! He's the one who had the fake gun in his pocket!"

"Fake gun? Hmmm. Rewind it," Kyle said. "Stop it, right there. Look at the corner."

A car pulled up to the corner, a black Mustang. The perpetrator got out of the passenger side. He stopped at the driver window and bumped fists with dark-haired man. The man in the car stayed parked until he walked inside the store. He then looked both ways and made a right down 7th Street, in the opposite direction.

"The face is too distorted to make out an ID."

"Yeah, but we've got a bigger problem here," Kyle said. "A robber getting dropped off and fist-bumping his best bud before he commits a crime? That doesn't make any sense. He wasn't tense or nervous."

"My son told me the kid got bailed out the next day," Max said.

"By whom?" Kyle asked.

"He didn't say. We can ask though. I'm sure he could find out in a few minutes."

"Something tells me whoever dropped him off is the one who bailed him out," Kyle said.

"So let me get this straight," Hopper said. "You think the robbery was staged?"

Kyle nodded. "It's possible, and a brilliant plan if indeed she planned it. What better way to draw suspicion from yourself than to save the life of the respected, long-time resident in the neighborhood. And the father of Michaels' most hated rival, no less." Kyle snapped his fingers and punched his fist in the air. "People talk. Word gets around. Nobody would suspect she's America's Most Wanted. If the cops come asking questions, she's the last person anybody thinks of, even if she fits the description. Couldn't have planned it more perfectly myself. And what better way to get close to her target. Did you ever talk with her about your personal life?"

"No, nothing I can think of," Max said. "I did invite her to my birthday dinner. Told her my daughter would be visiting, and I wanted to introduce her to a nice guy. Tony. J.J.'s partner."

Hopper and Kyle exchanged glances. "You're kidding," Hopper said. "Did she accept?"

"Yeah," Max responded. "She did."

"So she knows you, J.J. and Tony are expected here this Saturday." The expression on Kyle's face grew urgent. "We need to get that plate enhanced. Pronto," Kyle said. "Do you mind if we go to your house and burn a copy from the internet? We'll talk to your son and be on our way."

"That's fine," Max said.

Hopper disconnected the DVR and returned it to its place on the closet shelf. He set it back in place and closed the door behind him.

"You stick close to your son, Mr. McCall. If my suspicions are correct, we're going to have a lot of dead bodies on our hands if we don't get some answers to these questions…and I mean yesterday."

CHAPTER 46

Friday—Russian Embassy

Aleksey dry-heaved and coughed over the cold whitish commode, gripping the seat with one hand while wiping the perspiration from his forehead with the back of the other. He'd slept like a Marine on night watch ever since his friend departed Washington. And with the nebulous tone of his chat with Vorobyev the night before, his stomach wound tight into knots of distress, boiling over with the acidic bile that had projected from his mouth only moments ago. One thing was clear—Vorobyev had found the phone and probably had turned it over to Golikov.

Dmitriyev could feel the heat of death's breath on his neck. Between the vodka and his inability to hold down anything resembling sustenance, his morning spent hurling into the porcelain god was as inevitable as his fate. The time bomb ticked louder and louder by the second. Golikov's people were coming for him. He could almost hear the steps, pounding louder and louder toward him. Each step marking a moment closer to the end of his life. He was through with living in fear. It was finally time to walk away and never look back. Today's trip to Starbucks would be his last…at least from the embassy. As soon as his stomach settled, he would make his way off the compound forever.

As he rose to his feet, the bathroom door flung open and slammed against the wall, the thud resounding for moments after his company tromped in. He snapped out of his fog and realized the footsteps were real.

"Alek!" a voice yelled urgently. It sounded like that sniveling imp Filthchenko. "Alek! Are you in here?"

He wondered for a moment if he should answer, but he could see the man's shadow bending over through the slight crack in the door jamb. "I'll be out in a second." Dmitriyev adjusted his tie, straightened his clothes, and flushed the toilet.

"Komarov wants to see you in the secure conference room," he said. "Right this moment. You must hurry."

Aleksey stepped out of the stall and studied Filthchenko's expression. His face was red, flush with distress, anger. The scurry of footsteps and waves of moans outside the bathroom signaled escalating confusion.

The hour was finally forced upon him and he was not yet ready to meet it.

He didn't want to die.

But what he wanted no longer mattered.

"You can go ahead." He held his hand up. He only needed a brief window of time to get away. "Need to wash my hands. I'll be out in a sec."

The scum did not budge.

"I assure you I don't need an escort," Dmitriyev demanded.

"I was told not to return without you," he said. "I'll wait."

Aleksey patted his face with the towel before drying his hands. "What's all the ruckus about? Somebody steal the vodka from the commissary?" he joked, chuckling uncomfortably. His nerves were like rip currents dragging beneath a calm surface.

"You'll find out soon enough," Filchenko said. "Let's go."

Filthchenko grumbled beneath his breath as he led Aleksey to the stairwell and down five darkened flights into the basement where the air was still damp from a burst pipe. He stopped cold before they entered the hall. The only possible meeting place was the room used to process walk-in volunteers from American and other foreign intelligence services. It was bugged with listening devices and cameras. More suitable for an interrogation than a gathering.

"Wait. There's no secure conference room down here," Aleksey said. "You must be mistaken."

He stopped and shook his head before continuing on his way. "This is where Komarov told me to bring you." He finally reached the door and pushed it open. He stepped inside first and held the door open to allow Dmitriyev to follow. "Have a seat. I'll be right back."

"What's this all about?" Dmitriyev said. "Do I have time to run and get my coffee?"

Filchenko smirked and turned to leave. "Trust me. You won't need it."

When the door slammed, a gust of air washed over his face. Although his stomach churned over, revolving in agitated spirals, he remained cucumber cool on the exterior in case the surveillance equipment was running. He might go down, but he refused to give in. He'd fight for every minute he had left.

His stomach jerked at the sound of the doorknob twisting. The Crooked Twins were the first to arrive. He greeted them and they responded with only head nods. Neither took a seat, rather they remained standing, flanking the door on either side. Inside, his steeled will begin to falter but he kept his back straight and his shoulders square.

"Ah. Back from New York, I see," he said, eyeing them from head to toe. "You don't look any worse for wear. I hear the Resident there is a real goat."

"We arrived this morning," one Crooked Twin said. "And he's more like a chicken running a coop full of foxes. That residency is shit."

"Bet that's what they say about Washington," he quipped. "I don't suppose either one of you has a cup of coffee on you. You know I'm dying for my morning fix. I could be back here in ten minutes. Yes?"

"No!" the other twin barked giving him the eye. His other half grinned.

He wondered how long it would be before they beat him to a pulp.

"Have a seat," he said, gesturing his hand toward the chairs in front of him. "I think we're going to be here for a while."

"I don't think so."

"Where is everyone?"

"Patience," Igor said. "They're on the way."

"Who is on the w—"

Three taps sounded at the door and quickly Aleksey returned to his seat. One of the Crooked Twins, who was positioned at the rear, pulled it open. One by one his soon-to-be interrogators filed inside. Grim-faced operational line chiefs circled the table. The Resident, Lana's father, and Filthchenko the scum, along with officers from the political, economic, science and technologies, and signals operational lines, took their seats and clasped their hands together, their glares burning through him like hot lasers. By the time everyone was seated, they'd blocked him in. Escape was now an impossibility.

Aleksey looked from side to side. "What's this? A staff meeting? Did I miss the announcement?" he asked Mikhaylov, who had filled the empty seat left open for him at the head of the table next to the Resident.

"No, I'm afraid not. Where have you been all morning?"

"I apologize for my tardiness. Bad stomach," he said. "Must've been something I ate."

The Resident glanced at Filchenko who nodded as if to affirm Aleksey's statement, stunning him motionless. At that moment, he was assured of his fate. The balance of power in the counterintelligence line had shifted in Filchenko's favor. It could only mean one thing.

"Today," the boss began, "is a disastrous day for the Service."

He paused leaving a thousand pounds of silence between them. Judging by the expressions on his colleagues' faces, some knew what was wrong while others, like Aleksey, were still in the dark and waiting for the great revelation.

"We've had a traitor in our midst for some time," Komarov said. The corners of his mouth turned down as he growled with disdain. "Fucking pig has jeopardized our mission, our lives, indeed our very existence in this country!"

Aleksey's stomach plummeted and his feet began to quake beneath the table as the Resident narrowed his eyes in Aleksey's direction. With guilt practically bursting through his pores, he traced the grain of the wood with his eyes to avoid the expressions bearing down on him. He couldn't look any of them in the face any longer.

"One of our own has indeed betrayed us. Someone in whom we've all trusted. Someone on whom we've relied. Someone we've all respected."

Aleksey feigned a disgusted expression. "Who is it!" he demanded. "We will take care of him the way men deal with pigs. The slaughter."

"Will you?" Komarov snapped. "I somehow seriously doubt that in this matter. It's why I've called you here today."

Chapter 47

CHAPTER 47

Friday Morning—The West Wing

J.J., Tony, and Six stood impatiently in the West Wing foyer entrance waiting on Kendel to escort them to their temporary office. After three days of interviews, Kendel's moment of truth had arrived. Attention had finally turned to the White House Chief of Security. J.J. tried to mentally prepare herself for Kendel's wrath. Six had just finished telling the crew he'd heard all kinds of attitude in Kendel's voice when he told her she'd be interviewed today. She accused him of concealing their planned interrogation. But she understood full well that failing to participate would be a direct indictment of her guilt.

J.J. took no pleasure in doing this part of her job. Interviewing law enforcement officers of any kind prompted a rare feeling of angst before questioning the suspect. They'd all made the identical pledge to one country. The dishonor of suspicion, the mere suggestion that an agent had broken his (or her) oath, was the worst kind of disgrace.

"Can you call her again?" J.J. said as she glanced at her watch and tapped her heel in an irritating beat against the pristine wood floors. "I can't believe she's playing games. Trust me when I tell you, she's going to have a long day."

"I've called her twelve times already, J.J." Six was clearly frustrated by J.J.'s impatience. "Short of beaming her up, I don't understand what else you expect me to do!"

"All right, you two," Tony interjected. "Maybe she had an unexpected meeting this morning. Let's give her a few more minutes before we go fully postal."

Hawk approached them with a confused look on his face. He eyed the three of them and said, "I haven't frightened you away yet?"

"Hawk, fear is a futile emotion and would suggest a level of interest in you that we don't have." She flashed a gritty smile then planted her hands on her hips. "Kendel Phillips was supposed to meet us here about thirty minutes ago. And we're not getting any answer at her desk."

"Uh, that's because she's not in today. Called in sick about an hour ago."

"Sick?" J.J. shot Tony and Six sideways glances.

"Not well. Yes."

"Well, would it be possible to speak with Sheldon Vance?" J.J. asked. "He's our secondary contact when she's not available."

He nodded. "Sure, he's here. If you'll follow me, I'll take you to his office."

He started up the hall as each of them trailed behind. Their eyebrows crinkled as they passed the stairway they usually took downstairs to Kendel's office. They crossed a busy hall with a sign marked "Administrative Section."

"Where the hell's he takin' us?" Tony whispered, his teeth clenched. "I thought he worked downstairs."

Six shrugged.

"Me too," J.J. said. She felt a little suffocated, as if she was walking in slow motion. She was confused, still trying to understand why Kendel didn't show up but afraid she already knew the answer.

Five doors down the hall on the left, he stopped at a door with the sign on it that read "Senior Staff." He twisted the knob and pushed it open, allowing the visitors to enter first. Inside the small room was a reception desk and a closed door leading to a back office, almost identical to the one they'd been borrowing downstairs in the Secret Service section. The guard walked to the inner door and knocked on it.

"Hey Sheldon, you in there? You've got company. FBI."

"Oh oh…okay. Just a second," he responded. His voice sounded small, feeble, much different than he had the day before. J.J. wondered whether the poor gorgeous man had caught a cold. It had certainly taken a toll if that were true. Before she had time to center her thoughts, a miniature black man with a receding hairline appeared. He wore Navy slacks, an argyle sweater vest, and a polka-dotted bowtie pinched him at the neck of his dress shirt.

J.J. craned her neck inside the office, still waiting for Sheldon Vance to appear.

"Good m-m-morning," he stammered. "How, uhhh, how can I help you?" J.J. studied him as his eyes shifted nervously between the three. He appeared jittery, almost scared. J.J. wasn't sure if his demeanor resulted from the usual intimidation most people experienced upon meeting FBI agents for the first time or something more.

"Who's this guy?" Tony blurted out, looking at Six and J.J. confused as hell. His face mirrored everyone else's…except Sheldon's.

J.J. took note.

"Uhhh," Six said. "I'm sorry. There must be some understanding. We're looking for *Sheldon Vance*."

His quivering lips turned up at the corners into a slight smile. "Last time I checked, I was Sheldon Vance," he said. "Been him all my life, at least that's what my mother told me. See? Says so right here on my identification badge."

He held up the card while they all hovered around the desk, leaning in to take a closer look.

"Ain't that a bitch!" Six yelled, unintentionally startling Sheldon. "It wasn't him!"

J.J. was suspicious at the level of his nervousness. The problem was more than the FBI's presence. No, he was scared and his fear had nothing to do with the people standing in the office. After some thought J.J. decided to play Sheldon's game. "Ummm, that can't be right. Some-one else introduced himself to us as you. Why do you suppose a person would go to such lengths?"

Sheldon looked down and his eyes shifted right before he let out a nervous laugh. "Tha—That's ridiculous. Who would…who would do such a thing?"

"It's clear you had nothing to do with this misunderstanding," she continued. "We've been grossly misled. Now that we've established that you're Sheldon Vance. The question is, who is the tall dark-haired guy who wears the designer suits? I think he has a circular birthmark thingy on the left side of his neck."

Sheldon shrugged. "I wish…I'd like to help you. But I can't. Sorry."

J.J. pursed her lips together and looked at Six and Tony through skinny eyes. Both appeared puzzled at first and then caught the hint.

"Well, you can't tell us what you don't know, right? I totally understand. We'll be on our way." J.J. let out a frustrated breath. "But before we go, I'm obligated to inform you that we are conducting a national security investigation. If I can be frank and cut through the bullshit for a second…"

"Sure, you can be frank…as long as I can be Sheldon," he said with a chuckle and a snort.

J.J. rolled her eyes. "Ha. Ha. Funny. If you think that's amusing you're really going to laugh at this," J.J. began. "If I cross this threshold and later find out you weren't completely forthright, you'll be doing your little stand-up routine for five years in Allenwood Federal Prison for every count of obstructing federal investigators I can dream up in my *funny little* head. And here's the kicker: I'll go to my grave ensuring you serve every second of your sentence. Now, isn't that hilarious, fellas?"

"Hysterical." Tony deadpanned. "By far, the best joke I've heard all week."

Six just stared at him with a cocky smirk and his head tilted to the side.

"Okay, guys. It's clear we're done here. Let's go," J.J. said, reaching for the doorknob. She twisted it open, pulled the door, and placed one foot through.

"Wait!" Sheldon leaned forward on the reception desk and rubbed his temple. Deep in thought. "Circular birthma…Ohhhh, the person you're talking about sounds like…Maddix. Maddix Cooper."

"Maddix Cooper!" they all said in unison. They spun around to face him.

Sheldon's forehead creased with worry. "Can you come back inside, please?"

J.J. closed the door as he walked from behind the counter. He lowered his voice in an urgent whisper. "He warned me you'd be coming around asking questions today. Said if I breathed one word he'd kill me."

"Is 'at right?"

"You gotta get him, before he comes back for me," Sheldon begged.

"What do you know about him?" he asked.

"He's a regular Don Juan. Flashy. Custom-tailored suits. He and Agent Phillips were an item for a while, but I don't know why they split up. I always wondered how he could afford his lifestyle. I mean I make more than he does," Sheldon said.

"Anything else?"

"I don't know why he would claim to be me. Who does that? But he told me if anyone came asking I was to deny knowing anything. As you can see, I'm pretty much in the dark."

"Trust me, you know enough. You've been a big help," Tony said.

"Could I have a minute to confer with my colleagues?" J.J. asked. "If you could step out of the office for just a second, I'd appreciate it."

"Son of a bitch!" Six yelled again after the door shut.

"No, this one's a daughter. And she's been playing us the entire time. She intentionally led us to believe Maddix was Sheldon."

"Kendel got a job at the White House first. Maddix followed her," Tony said. "She's dirty. He's dirtier. It's that simple."

"Whatever this case is, it's not simple," J.J. said. "If everything between them was so hunky dory then why would she break off the engagement? No, I don't believe she's the ringleader, but we can't discount her involvement. Sadly."

"So, what's next?" Six said.

"We gotta find Kendel and Maddix," Tony said. "How much you wanna bet he didn't show up for work today either? Bet they're gettin' ready to run."

"You can keep that bet. But, speaking of bets," she said, turning to Tony. "I want my twenty bucks back! This Sheldon looks *exactly* like a Sheldon. I think that makes you 0-3."

"Yeah, yeah, yeah."

"Now, let's get him back in here."

Six opened the door and waved him inside. "You've been very helpful this morning, Sheldon. Tell me, how can we find out if Maddix Cooper showed up today?"

"Oh, that's easy. I can just call down to the guard's desk. He comes in the same entrance every day and everyone here knows him."

"Great, great. I knew you were the man in the know," Six said, patting him on the back before resting his hand on his shoulder in a shameless schmooze. "One last thing. If you want us to get to him before he gets to you, we're going to need Kendel's and his address. And I mean fast."

He made the call to the front desk. No Maddix, of course. Then he paced to his computer. After typing his fingers feverishly on the keyboard he said. "She lives in Mitchellville, Maryland. 23145 Brock Court. He's in Fairfax, Virginia. 980 Swan Lane."

"Thanks, Sheldon. We'll be in touch." J.J. left her business card on the counter. "You call if either one shows up here…or if you need anything."

He nodded.

They exited the door and paced quickly through the hall.

"Where to first," Six asked.

"Kendel's place," J.J. said. "She broke up with Maddix for a reason. With Six there to push the right buttons, I know she'll talk."

CHAPTER 48

Friday—Irving Street

2 Days Left...

Lana paced in frantic circles consumed in her spiraling thoughts, unnerved by her disintegration into a mass of apprehension and distress. No passport. A week of hiding in plain sight, constantly looking over her shoulder. And an accomplice she was forced to trust, despite her own doubts. The stress had taken its toll.

She couldn't quiet her mind, no matter how much she drank.

Fucking Kyle Oliver. He still haunted her, the only man unfazed by her charms; the one man able to resist the primal urges that helped Lana dupe her victims into stupefied submission—and he knew it. Her sole failure. How could she know his wife would catch her in the act...and blame him? He swore he'd take her down.

Now running on adrenaline and three hours of sleep, the three shots of Stoli she'd gulped to calm her anxieties left her largely unaffected, except for the sweat beading at her hairline. As Santino's feet pressed against the steps, her heart began to beat a more frenetic pace. She dared not attempt to listen to his conversation with her former mentor. He had hearing better than her mother's schnauzer. One false move and Santino's lie would be as transparent as freshly Windexed glass...if he kept his word and didn't tip off Kyle.

She slipped her finger between the venetian blind, tugging down the slat just enough to survey the scene as Kyle and his new sidekick walked back across the street to Max McCall's house. Santino tapped on the door, startling her out of her panic attack. She sucked in quick relaxation breath as he opened the door and began to speak.

"Well, well, well, that was quite informative," Santino said. "With the hair and the eyes, I could barely recognize you. Gotta say, though, I prefer the blond."

"Took you this long to figure out who I was?" Lana said. "I'm disappointed. Gave you more credit."

"No, trust me, I had my suspicions," Santino said with a chuckle. "But that's some big talk from someone with a million dollar bounty on her head."

She turned head sharply toward him and narrowed her eyes.

"Don't worry. I ain't got no love for the Feds, and I'd take two in the head before I rat out my friends."

"Oh, so we're friends now?" Lana asked with a tenuous smile.

"You weren't saying that last night," Santino said. "Somewhere around midnight, I was big daddy."

"In your dreams," Lana said. "So, what did you say to him? Did he ask a lot of questions?"

"Relax. Relax. I took care of it," Santino said. "I did the last thing he expected me to do."

"Which was?"

"I cooperated. Told him he should come and take a look at you for himself because I'm not good with faces, once you return in a few days. Told him I'll call him when you get back."

She shook her head with approval. "Nice. Do you think he believed you?"

"I'm nothing if not a good liar."

She pursed her lips. "Mmm, exactly what I'm afraid of," she mumbled. "Anyway, you about packed up and ready for Sunday?"

"Yeah, except for one concern. Now that the cat's outta the bag so to speak," he said. "Uhhh, the hit on Sunday. This broad's not a fed, is she?"

"What do you care? You don't have any love for Feds, remember?"

"True. But I do love my life," he said. "Killing a Fed could bring all kinds of heat on the family if it could be in any way traced to me."

"It won't be."

"The hell it won't be," Santino said. "I gave myself away protecting you. Or maybe that's the way you wanted it."

"Don't' be ridiculous!" Lana said. "Everybody this side of the beltway knows that she and I hate each other with a passion. They won't suspect you for a second. They'll assume I did it. It'll take us five minutes to clean up the residue and your prints. And you can dump the weapon in any one of 100 rivers, lakes, or streams between here and Jersey."

"Meanwhile, you'll sipping Martinis in the south of France?"

"First of all, I don't sip anything. Secondly, I take my vodka in a shot glass," she said. "And yes, I'll be in France long enough to get transport Russia. The United States doesn't have an extradition treaty with France. If they figure out where I've gone, I'll be in Moscow before they can get through the layers of red tape necessary to ask the French to turn me over."

"You got it all figured out, huh?"

"I've had plenty of practice. It was once my job to figure it all out."

"So what're you gonna do if..." Santino looked down at the business card they handed him, "Supervisory Special Agent Kyle Oliver returns?"

"You'll handle that."

"What if your travel papers aren't there on Saturday?"

"That's not an option. If they have to draw them by hand, those papers will be ready on Saturday, or..."

"Or what?"

"You don't want to know. Neither do I."

CHAPTER 49

Friday Evening—Kendel's House

In the seconds she had to think, J.J. scrolled through her cover email account in the backseat of Six's Lexus sedan, his grown-up car, wondering why Aleksey hadn't contacted her. The investigation had been going at such a rapid pace that she hadn't had time to worry about his well-being to the extent that she should've. He was now her only high-level window into the Washington embassy and too valuable of a source to lose. She hadn't seen him since their unexpected meeting on the Ellipse. The time to panic was upon her. As soon as they wrapped up the Sit Room bug investigation, her first priority was connecting with him and finding out what embassy machinations had kept him out of touch at such a critical time.

"Are we there yet?" J.J. grumbled as she huffed and peered out the window. She noticed they hadn't yet turned off the beltway. "If my grandmother had carried us on her back we'd have been there ten minutes ago…and she's dead."

"Hey, don't make me reach back there snatch you up, young lady," Six said. After stealing a glance at J.J. in the rearview mirror, J.J. could see Tony's eyes burning on him. Six faced forward. "I'm not a chauffeur. I'm a spy. Besides, you know how the local cops are in this area."

"Enough said," J.J. replied.

After giving Six the stink eye, J.J. turned her attention to the scenery, taking in the string of McMansions with lush green lawns, perfectly manicured landscaping, cinnamon colored brick walkways, and expensive cars checkering the driveways.

"Sheesh," Tony said. "Maybe we need to jobs in White House Security. How much you think these houses run? Five hundred grand?"

J.J. said, "No, try seven or eight hundred. Couple million in the gated communities. Bunch of ball players live in the area. Redskins. Wizards. Even Sixes."

Tony turned to his left. "You got a spot out here?"

Six smiled as he turned into a large cul-de-sac. "Profitable investments. What can I say?" he said. "This is her house, the large white one on the left with the black shutters."

"Nice," Tony said. "Anybody check out her financials? She wouldn't be the first to sell out for money."

Six shook his head. "No, Kendel made a bundle when she sold her first condo which skyrocketed in value. Put down half and banked some. Whatever this is, it isn't about money."

J.J.'s telephone vibrated and she glanced at the screen. "Well, if this isn't some bullshit!" J.J. had had it up to her neck with Aleksey and his disregard for her rules or his own security. She wanted to hear from him, but not this way.

She faced Tony. "The fucking burn phone. I told him to get rid of it, yet here's the number flashing!" J.J. snapped.

Tony rolled his eyes in frustration. "Fucking moron. He's gonna get himself killed if he doesn't follow instructions. Answer it and give him hell."

J.J. allowed the phone to ring two more times before answering. "Speak."

"Uhhh, please don't hang up. This not a provocation and I'm in danger," the man said. He had a Russian accent, but his English was crisp and vaguely familiar. But he was not Aleksey, which sparked a whole new round of questions…and problems.

"O-kay," she answered tepidly.

Tony craned his body around in his seat and mouthed the words "Who is that?" She shrugged held up her index finger to gesture him to wait.

"Go ahead. I'm listening."

"Agent McCall." He paused, giving her a moment to digest the fact that he knew her identity. "I'm an intelligence officer. I just finished my tour in Washington and returned to Moscow last week. I have information that is of the highest value to the FBI—the identities Russian spies operating under deep cover and American government employees working on behalf of the SVR and GRU."

"Fascinating," J.J. said. She swallowed hard. "How'd you get the phone?"

"A mutual friend of ours. He gifted a pair of shoes to my son and it was hidden inside. I assure you it was not intentional, but a fortuitous accident in this case, yes?"

A friend in Washington. *Mutual?* J.J. had only one Russian "friend" in Washington and that friend only had ONE friend. The one who boarded his Aeroflot flight to Moscow last Friday. The one who'd been beaten within an inch of death based on false accusations and would have more than sufficient justification to seek revenge against his service.

"You know with whom you are speaking, yes?"

"I do," J.J. said. "Why are you contacting me? And what proof can you provide to demonstrate that you're not a double agent?"

"Do you not keep abreast of current events?" he asked. "Google me."

J.J. muted the phone long enough to say, "Tony, Google Russian security services. Check the news headlines."

He nodded and starting typing into his phone.

"I'm safe for now but not for long. I need passage to America, for me and my family. A new life."

"Where's your family?"

"Vacationing in Prague."

"Hmmm," she said. "Perfect timing."

Tony held up the phone screen and J.J.'s eyes bulged at the headline. *"Manhunt for Rogue Security Service Officer."* The subheading was even more explosive. *"One Dead, Scores of Secret Documents Missing."*

"Holy Shit," she said. Her mind raced, spinning with possibilities. This could be it—the mother lode. All the information they need to shut down Russian operations for years to come.

"Ahhhh, you're up to date, I hear."

"I'm not a position to make any promises. You understand bureaucracy. I'll need director-level approval from multiple agencies to pull this off. How can we contact you?"

"You won't. Notify your people. I'll contact you."

"I'm afraid that won't—"

A click sounded.

He hung up leaving a dial tone buzzing in her ear.

J.J. threw her head back against the seat and palmed her face. Her head was about to explode. Depending on what and how much information he clipped from the Center, he could very well turn out be one of the most valuable Russian volunteers in U.S. history. Some way to end her career. "This could be huge for all of us."

"Certainly sounds intriguing," Six said as he backed into the lengthy driveway and turned off the ignition. "It's not every day you get a Russian security officer to volunteer, but you can't trust them. Ninety-nine percent of them are doubles."

"Tony, show him your phone," J.J. said, knowing Six would be chomping at the bit to get his mitts in this case. Among his many professional talents, he was one of the top exfiltration specialists in the CIA and J.J. wouldn't trust anyone else.

Six grabbed the cell from Tony's hand and rolled his finger down the screen. "Have you been sprinkled with magic fairy dust? A thousand agents and clandestine officers would kill for this lead and it lands in your lap," Six said.

"Yeah, only because I have a source who doesn't follow instructions."

"He's still in Moscow?"

"Unfortunately, but his family's in Prague," J.J. said scanning the other houses in the neighborhood. "Let's table that discussion until later. Believe it or not, we've got even more pressing matters to attend to right this moment."

"That's debatable, but let's go," Tony said. "Six, you follow our lead."

"Why do I need to follow?"

"If someone in there has a gun, would you rather be in front of two armed FBI agents or behind us?"

"Good point," he replied. "Right behind you."

J.J. was half way out the door and up the driveway. Everyone exited and followed behind her.

"Her car's not out front," J.J. said, envying the bed of jasmine lining the flower beds near the front door. Somewhere deep inside J.J. was a little jealous. This is the life she wanted, a life she wanted with Tony. Two and a half kids. Sundays mornings—breakfast in bed. Sunday afternoons—football. It was a life that felt close enough to imagine, yet was still too far away to attain. "You think she's home?"

"She usually parks in the garage," said Six. "Protects the paint."

"A little habit she picked up from you, no doubt," J.J. said, remembering Six's fanatical habit of protecting the paint of his 911 Turbo. She stepped up to the entrance and rang the doorbell several times before noticing the door was already open. She immediately unstrapped her gun from the holster and gripped the handle with both hands. "It's unlocked. Six, call her phone."

He pulled an oversized Droid from his pocket and hit speed dial. Seconds later, J.J. heard a faint ringing. "Dragnet ringtone. Her phone's inside, door's open, and she's not answering."

"Kendel doesn't go anywhere without that phone. Something's wrong."

"All right. Let's check it out," Tony said, holding his gun in hand. He looked at J.J. "Will you do the honors?"

J.J. and Tony flanked the door as she gently nudged it open with her foot. She jutted her gun across the threshold, then stepped into the foyer. An airy and contemporarily decorated living and dining room sat on either side of the open foyer. She marveled at the 16-foot ceilings…and the chaos. Broken glass, vases, coffee tables and dining room chairs turned over and blood spatters on the pristine white custom slip covers. "Clear," J.J. said.

Six and Tony followed behind her and their eyes bulged at the destructions. "What the hell happened?" Six yelled.

"I'm gonna go out on a limb and say somebody had a disagreement."

"No shit," J.J. said. "I'll take upstairs. You guys look around here and in the basement. I'm afraid the only thing we're gonna find is a body."

J.J. padded up their stairs and opened up every door along the hall. The guest bedroom, bathrooms, and closets had all been left untouched. There was only one room left at the end of the hall, the master bedroom, which was marked by the double doors. She eased up to them and heard a low hum and bumping as if something was slamming against the wall.

"Special Agent J.J. McCall with the FBI! Who's in there? I can hear you."

She waited for a response, but none came. The bumping continued, now harder. The moaning continued, only now it was louder. In the background, the sound of Tony yelling, "Clear!" resounded from downstairs. J.J. stepped back from the door with her gun pointed straight ahead as she kicked it in…after three tries.

"FBI!" she yelled, her Glock at the ready. Clothes were dangling out of drawers as if the dresser puked. Somebody was looking for something. J.J. noticed a small empty Ziploc bag lying next to a powder-coated hand mirror and a small razor.

"Cocaine!" J.J. mumbled under her breath. "I knew it."

The bumping and moaning drew J.J. out of her thoughts and toward the closet. Was somebody having sex inside? Maybe that's why they didn't hear her. As she approached the cracked-open door a sliver of light shone through. "J.J. McCall. FBI. I'm coming in, and I'm armed."

"So am I," a small voice called from inside.

It was Kendel.

When J.J. pressed pushed the door open, her eyes opened as wide as her bottom jaw plummeted and her heart collided against her rib cage. Her hands trembled. Not from booze this time, rather from fear. No words could escape; they locked in her throat. She shook her head so feverishly she nearly collapsed from dizziness.

Kendel was there, on the floor in a sea of shoes, dressed in a large t-shirt and underwear, her back literally and figuratively against the wall, probably bruised from the banging. Black mascara streaked the length of her brown cheeks. Purple bruises in the shapes of handprints colored her arms. Blood trickled from her head. And the tip of a government-issued Glock was pressed into the curve of her temple.

"It's over," she cried. "My life is over."

J.J. eased toward her and in a whispery, gentle voice usually reserved for babies and angry dogs said, "Kendel, you don't want to do this. Nothing is worth taking your life over. Nothing."

She cocked the gun and put a bullet in the chamber.

"Stay there…or I swear I'll pull this fucking trigger."

"Ohhhkay." J.J. slowly tipped back to the doorway as if maneuvering through a minefield and yelled. "Uh, guuuuys? I need you upstairs…in the master bedroom…now!"

CHAPTER 50

Friday—Russian Embassy

Aleksey played stunned at the Resident's accusation. To suggest Aleksey was unable or unwilling to deal with a traitor in the service wasn't true, at least to the Resident's knowledge, unless...

"What do you mean this is why you've called us here today. I—I don't understand your meaning?"

"You will in a moment," the Resident said, staring at Aleksey for what seemed like an eternity. He sucked in a deep breath and rubbed his temples. "This morning I received an urgent cable from the Center. A Washington officer has betrayed us."

"A Washington officer?" Mikhaylov said. "But who could possibly—"

Komarov peered at the Crooked Twins and then said, "Stanislav Vorobyev."

Aleksey's mouth fell open and his chest rose and fell in dramatic heaves. It couldn't be. Why would he do such a thing? He was being framed. There was no other reasonable explanation. Aleksey had perhaps too hastily brushed off Vorobyev's fears and concerns that he was being hassled, probably a vain attempt to assuage his own guilt. He never conceived of the remote possibility that Stan would take matters into his own hands and resort to such drastic measures. He still couldn't. "No! Impossible! He would never betray his country. Never!"

"I thought you might react this way, but I'm afraid it's true," the Resident began. "He strangled one of our counterintelligence officers to death, General Stepanov, and took off with the crown jewels."

"Killed an officer?" Aleksey said. "This is preposterous. The Center has been watching too many spy movies. I can't make any sense of that."

*Filth*chenko huffed and rolled his eyes. "What do we expect from a friend of that swine!" he barked and then glared at Dmitriyev. "I'll be sure to convey your ridiculous sentiment to Stepanov's family."

"Wait, Stepanov?" he said. "You mean, Rasputin?" Aleksey said of Golikov's chief tattletale. He alone was responsible for the torture and deaths of more officers than hostile foreign services in recent years. "Are we really going to sit here and pretend he wasn't a piece of shit? He had more enemies in Moscow than Russia has citizens. Any one of a thousand officers would have done the same thing given the opportunity, including a few people sitting around this table!"

Aleksey had no doubt Vorobyev killed Stepanov in self-defense, a view he would hold alone judging from the expressions bearing down on him.

The Resident pounded his fist against the table. "Enough!" he said. "I want silence from all of you," he growled, glaring at Aleksey and the scum Filchenko in particular. "We have far more urgent issues to discuss than whom between Vorobyev and Stepanov is the bigger dickhead. Okay? Beginning with the fact that every single American operation is in jeopardy. We have no idea how much information he stole before he ran away like a spineless snake—but if the intelligence is in the hands of the Americans, decades of work has just been flushed down the toilet."

"Do we believe he got away?" Aleksey asked.

"It's hard to say," the Resident said. "We believe him to be hiding like a coward in the American Embassy, but right now he could be anywhere. Our watchers did not note any unusual activity or visitors last night. So, we simply cannot say."

"What…what about his family?" Aleksey asked, holding a straight face. Inside, he dreaded the consequences if they were stuck in Moscow following such a brazen betrayal, having had first-hand knowledge of similar pain for most of his childhood and early adult years.

"He sent them to Prague on the pretense of vacationing. He's now gone underground. The FSB has deployed every available resource to locate him. If he's in Moscow, he will not leave under his own power."

"I hope they bury him next to Osama Bin Laden," Filchenko barked.

"He should be so lucky," one of the Crooked Twins said, elbowing his sidekick with a chuckle. He stepped from the wall for the first time.

"By the time Golikov and Mashkov get through with him, there won't be enough of him left to feed a cat."

The chill in their voices iced Aleksey's veins. For everyone's sake, he prayed Vorobyev was in the American Embassy. If he were anywhere on the streets of Moscow, he'd be a dead man before he could ever reach safe harbor. Putin would rain down a steel curtain of security so thick his only means of escape would be the wings of an angel or face down in an unmarked grave with his soul destined for hell.

CHAPTER 51

Friday Night—Kendel's House

J.J. was relieved by the sound of footsteps padding quickly across the wood foyer as she tip-toed slowly back toward the door and peeked inside, watching from a safe distance as Kendel struggled with her demons in a fight for her life. The cavalry arrived in the hall outside the bedroom door and waited for J.J. to explain.

"Kendel's inside, banging her back against wall with what looks like her service pistol dug into her temple," J.J. spoke in a whispered tone, her somber expression speaking volumes above the dry tone in her voice. "And I think she's coked out. Found an empty bag on the dresser."

"Kendel? My Kendel?" Six said. "I knew that motherfucker was shady. Never thought he'd get her addicted to drugs."

"She's a big girl. Gotta take some of the blame," J.J. grabbed his arm firmly and looked him dead in the eye. "But Six, this is a critical situation and her life is hanging in the balance. Please, please, please don't go in there and be…"

His eyebrow scrunched. "Be what?"

"Yourself," she said. "I mean, be yourself, just the version of yourself that has, you know, a heart, empathy…*feelings*."

He snatched himself out of J.J.'s grip and started forward. J.J. snatched him up again, this time by the collar.

"Are you crazy?" Six barked in a loud whisper.

"No, *I'm* not. But clearly *she* is. And I have more experience with crazy women than you do. So give me a minute. When I signal, you come inside." He nodded in agreement and gestured for her to walk ahead.

J.J. returned to Kendel, keeping a non-threatening distance. "I'm going to trust you, Kendel, and in return, Lord knows I pray you'll trust me." J.J. held her hands in the air, including the one holding her Glock. Then she brought them down in front of her where Kendel could see, unloaded the clip, and rested both on either side of her after she sat

Indian style on the floor. "I can't help you if you don't talk to me. Is this about the drugs? I saw the empty bag on the dresser."

A slow sob erupted from Kendel's mouth as her body trembled in anguish. "How did I get here?"

"I want to talk about it," J.J. said. "But I gotta tell you, the sight of you with the you know, pressed against your temple is seriously freaking me out. I'm not asking you to put it down or hand it to me. Just please, take it away from your head."

Kendel turned to J.J. and glared, the life drained from her eyes.

"Please," J.J. said.

With her hand still wrapped around the gun's grip, she allowed her back and head to rest against the wall, and folded her arms across her body. Finally, the sobs began to subside; she rolled her face toward J.J. and spoke. "I blame you for this."

J.J. jerked her head backward in surprise. "Me?"

Through her peripheral vision, J.J. could see Six move toward the door but she gave him the hand. He stopped cold and backed up.

"I would've had a different life with Six," she said. "I never would've been susceptible to that low-life, degenerate, asshole Maddix Cooper. The fucking snake! Now, the life I've worked so hard to build, my career, my house…"

"For what it's worth, I had no idea you existed until it was too late," she said.

"I figured as much," she said, "because I know Six."

"Listen, I understand that—"

"No, no, *you don't* understand. *You will never* understand!" Her aggravation intensified with every word. Instead of taking two steps forward, she'd taken three steps backward. "I've met kings, princes, heads of state from countless nations, and I was on a first-name basis with the President of the United States…now, I'm nothing but a broke, drug addict destined for an 8x8 cell next to some of the very people I've sent down."

"He took your money?"

"Said he found an investment," she began, "said he would triple my cash even before I realized it was missing. And my dumb ass believed him. Ha! But why wouldn't I? We had the same security clearance. He was living the life I wanted…or so I thought. Nothing but window dressing.

"I'd already accepted his proposal. As far as I knew, I was investing with my husband, not just some guy I had a thing with once."

"How much did you give him?" J.J. asked.

"Two-hundred fifty thousand," she said. "Half the proceeds of my condo sale. The other half I sunk into this house."

"Oh my God," J.J. covered her mouth when she realized that was the exact amount of money Maddix had given Tomlin to buy the Devil's Rest. He stole money from his fiancé to get Tomlin on the hook. J.J. couldn't help but think that if she was Kendel, she wouldn't be holding a gun to her own head. Maddix, on the other hand, wouldn't be so lucky.

"Oh yeah. Story gets worse. Months later Maddix informs me that he's lost every penny. When I tried to take out a second mortgage to pay off my debt, I found out my house was underwater."

"Worth less than you owe…"

"A lot less. So, I depended on Maddix for every penny I needed to stay afloat."

"Right where he wanted you." J.J. seethed inside, fuming at Maddix's manipulation. "What about the coke?"

"It's not obvious? I was at the lowest point in my entire life, trapped with a man who I hated, beholden to a man who personified everything in humanity that I despised," she said. "He offered me a ride up from the abyss and I took it. But a ride with the devil is never free. And accepting that ride can only lead to hell. Found out later, too late, that he cut it with crystal meth…"

"Oh, God. To increase the addictiveness," J.J. responded, her voice soft with empathy. "Kendel…"

She nodded. "I knew about the contracting, thought he used *those* proceeds to afford his lifestyle. I swear on my father's grave I knew nothing about the bug or the scanners until Walter identified the problem. Never thought they'd stoop to that level."

"No?" J.J. asked, feeling the slight sense of an itch for the first time during their entire conversation. It'd become quite clear to J.J. that Maddix's kind of low had no limits, no bounds, no respect for what was right—and no loyalty. And Kendel at the very least *suspected* that he was the scum he turned out to be. "Where's he now?"

She shrugged. "I dunno. Said he had a date with the devil first thing in the morning," Kendel replied. "Tried to make me leave with him. When I didn't agree, well, you can guess what happened given the state of my living room. Wherever he's going, he's limping!"

The Devil's Rest. He was planning to hide in the boat…or set sail. If he decided to run, he wouldn't get far.

"You ever experience the pain of losing everything, J.J.?"

She shook her head. "Can't say that I have."

"Well, guess what?" she asked. "I'm not going to either."

"No!" J.J. screamed.

Kendel's eyes glazed over as if her soul left her body. She returned the gun to her temple. J.J. sucked in a deep breath. She leaned backward out the door, far enough to stick her hand outside, and she flapped it back and forth urgently waving Six inside.

"Don't!" Six urged. He folded his hands together and pleaded with her to put the gun down. "You don't want to do this to yourself. I'm the one who deserves it. Do it to me."

J.J.'s eyes bulged open as she moved aside and allowed him to enter. J.J. had hoped he'd serve as a distraction, not a target. Six asking anyone to take a shot at him for the wrong he'd done was akin to suicide.

Kendel wrapped both hands around the butt and pointed the gun at his head. "Don't tempt me! Now, back the fuck up. I mean it! Stop moving!"

Six ignored her and continued to tip slowly toward her with the confidence of a jungle cat. He was still out of her arm's reach, but he'd moved closer than J.J. dared to tread. "Don't you see that despite everything that has happened between us, I still love you? I will always love you. Don't you understand? Do you think I could live with myself if anything happened to you…*because of me?*"

J.J. marveled at his sensitivity. She had never seen him be so kind so loving toward another human being. Not even her. She dismissed the slight feeling of jealousy at the relief that he had managed to move even closer. Despite Kendel's constant refusal, she wanted him near her. J.J. could relate to that.

"I swear to God, if you take one step closer, I'll pull the trigger," Kendel screamed. "I swear I will!"

Six fell to his knees in front of Kendel. J.J. swore she saw a stream of tears washing down Six's cheek. Was he really crying?

"Please forgive me," he said, gently caressing her cheek and wiping the tears from her eyes all while the Glock shook in her hand. Then he pulled back his fist and cold-cocked her in her dead in the jaw. Knocked her flat with one body-shaking blow. The gun was now lying on a pair of red Jimmy Choos.

"What the hell, Six?!" J.J. yelled in abject horror. Her jaw dropped into her lap at the sight of Kendel's forced slumber. "Jesus, I need some chocolate. Where's my purse?"

Tony heard the resounding thud of Six's sucker punch and ran to the doorway. "What happ—are you kidding me?"

"What? She's no longer a threat to herself or others, and in case you hadn't noticed, *we're* the others. So, sue me." He stood to lift her limp body from the floor. "I'll get some clothes on her. Anybody got 'cuffs?"

"But…but…I thought you…" J.J. stammered. "Forgive me, for five minutes I thought you'd actually heard me when I said have heart."

"I did hear you. Just didn't listen. Better for me to put a fist on her jaw than for her to put a bullet into her head, right?" he asked. "Now, what are we going to do with her? Don't forget we've still got a subject to take down."

Tony looked at J.J. "She's looking at a possible obstruction charge. We don't have enough to hold her for more than 24 hours, but I think we gotta try to put her into protective custody until we can get her some help. Last thing we need is for her to put one in her temple…or take header off the Wilson Bridge."

"Call Washington Field and let them pick her up. Let them know what's going on," J.J. said as the sound of thunder rumbled in the night. "In the meantime, with this weather, Maddix isn't going anywhere tonight."

"Yeah," Tony said. "We've got time to slow him down. If we give that douchebag the slightest opening, he's goin' underground. And he's got enough money to stay under for a long time to come if we don't catch him first."

CHAPTER 52

*Saturday Morning, November 14th—Rock Creek Park
1 Day Left…*

"Blue leader, this is Jiggy." He spun the steering wheel sharply to the right as he pulled into the parallel parking space. He'd found an alternate area adjacent to Mikhaylov's Rock Creek Park drop location. "I'm moving into position."

"Roger that," Cannon responded. "Standing by."

The pouring rain had slowed to a light drizzle by the time Jiggy arrived. The lookouts had called Mikhaylov out of the Russian embassy compound an hour earlier, giving Jiggy plenty of time to find a spot to cover down ahead of his target's arrival.

It was only 8 a.m. and the wet weather had deterred the usual exercise crowd. He parked further away and started on foot to the nearby woods so he wouldn't be spotted by the Russians. His task was made difficult by the shedding trees which left wet leaves blanketing the landscape in noisy rust and golden colored mounds. Static buzzed in his earpiece transmitting to the radio. Something was causing interference.

Twitch and Cannon were posted at stationary positions nearby in case Jiggy got into any trouble, but they may as well be on the moon if they couldn't hear him.

"I'm taking up a position in a bush about 15 meters off the trail. Hopefully, I picked a good spot," he said, stomping around the area and kicking leaves to the side to frighten squirrels, or any other wildlife that could potentially blow his position.

"You got any idea where the drop site is?" Cannon asked.

"Not a clue."

"So, uh, how do you know you're not standing in it?"

Jiggy paused for a minute. His heart thumped. He froze and scanned the park. "I don't, but I wouldn't put a site here. Too far off the trail. Stand by."

He hated that Cannon was such a know-it-all, but he did have a solid point. Jiggy was clueless and had nothing to go on except a little experience and a lot of intuition, standing on a strip of asphalt in a tunnel of identical trees. He reluctantly trekked back to the trail, his eyes nervously darted toward every random piece of trash and the incidental mark. The rush of wind heightened his sense of time whisking by. With that he pushed up the path, scanning from side to side, his eyes dancing through layers of trees and brush tangled in a wooded web, looking for a mark, a symbol, or anything resembling anything.

He wandered and wandered and saw nothing.

In the midst of his descent into the bottomless pit of panic and despair, a white man in a jeans and a brown bomber jacket appeared from nowhere and appeared to be heading directly for Jiggy, whose eye was drawn to the bright red cap on his head with royal blue lettering. As the vaguely familiar man neared him, he pulled out a pack of cigarettes, which struck Jiggy as odd for a health nut on the walking trail.

"Excuse me, do you have a light?" he asked, hanging the cigarette in the corner of his mouth. The man's eyes were clearly drawn to the twisted earphone cord running into Jiggy's ear.

Jiggy looked at him askance while pulling down knit cap to conceal his ear a moment too late. More importantly, the glint of an accent rang in the man's voice.

As Jiggy patted down his pant pocket searching for a lighter or matches, it struck him. The man's identity. It was Aleksey Dmitriyev. His eyes bulged as he stuttered "Sorry, I-I-I don't smoke."

The man glanced over his shoulder and glared at Jiggy again. "You recognize me, yes?"

Jiggy nodded, peering over the man's shoulder to keep an eye for cars arriving in the parking lot. They were still the only two people around.

"Good," he said. "What you're looking for is a few meters up the trail, on the left. The tree with a braided trunk. You don't have much time. Send my regards to Agent McCall."

He tipped the bill of his cap with his index finger and disappeared down the trail, returning his cigarette to his pocket still unlit.

Jiggy paced quickly up the still deserted trail, using his binoculars to scan for the signal. After a few minutes of shifting his glance he finally spotted it, near a large tree easily distinguished by the braid of branches twisted around the base. Of course, that was the tree. It was distinct yet hidden in plain sight. He hiked into the woods about ten yards until the sound of car tires popping over rocks jerked him out of his thoughts. He again used his binoculars to peer out to the lot.

Russian plates.

Had to be Mikhaylov. Jiggy settled back into the bush stooping low to the base, roots from a majestic oak nearby poked into his stomach and ribs and the soggy ground soaked his clothes. He held his breath as Mikhaylov's shadow broke the sunlight and moved rapidly from the clearing into the woods, tree branches snapping under his feet as he moved off the path. The sound of harried footsteps drew uncomfortably close. Jig shifted his gaze slightly upward to get a clear view through the underside of the bush when a low hiss emanated from his side.

Hiss.

Above him, a jaunty squirrel on a long branch rattled the tree as acorn fell and pelted him in the face. The only thing that scared Jiggy more than snakes was squirrels. He struggled not to grunt, tightening his lips and laying as still as possible, but he could feel something moving against his lower leg.

Hiss.

It was the perfect storm. His every fear came to fruition in one brief, fleeting moment. He thought, *"The FBI doesn't pay me enough for this shit!"*

Hiss.

Jiggy's every instinct told him to scramble to his feet and bolt back to his car like Usain, vowing to never volunteer for park duty again— ever. But he could not allow his fear to ruin the Bureau's best chance at Lana. If he could just stay still for sixty seconds more, he could wait out Lana's father and get his hands on the package.

In a stroke of unadulterated luck, a cavalcade of cars began to flood the lot, stopping Mikhaylov cold. He froze and turned long enough to survey the lot. Jiggy guessed it was the senior exercise group again. Nosy old ladies—an intelligence officer's nightmare. Mikhaylov scurried to place the wrapped package in an indentation in the soil about a foot away from the tree. He kicked leaves over it until it was covered and placed a small strip of duct tape on the base of the tree, where it would go unnoticed by anyone not looking for it. He then scuttled back to the path and disappeared into the parking lot. Jiggy listened intently until he heard Mikhaylov's engine fire up and roll out.

Hiss.

Jiggy snapped his head toward the sound. And there it was. Scaly and black with bands of white circling its skin every few inches. Jiggy trapped the scream and jumped to his feet with the speed and grace of a grizzly bear. The sound of rustling leaves drew the attention of the old bitties who'd just begun their morning walk.

"Stalker! Stalker!" the woman in front screeched, angrily thrusting her walking stick toward him.

"Marg, call the cops! The stalker's back!"

"Oh shit!" Jiggy yelled. Park Police would soon arrive and they weren't fond of FBI anything. Especially not the Gs. His mission was to photograph the contents and return the package as close to its original state as possible, but with the police on the way he might not have enough time.

He pressed the mic on his radio. "Twitch, I'm gonna need a ride outta here pronto!"

"What's going on?"

"Some old lady thinks I'm a stalker. The police will probably be burning up the road in a couple minutes."

"You find the package?"

"Yeah, I've got eyes on it, but I don't have time to talk. Just get your ass over here."

He hurried to the tree and dropped to his knees, digging the drop from beneath the leaves. From his backpack he pulled out a box cutter and sliced the garbage bag open. He had another bag and more tape to repackage it. A large manila envelope filled with hundred dollar bills. Fifty grand if there was a penny. A letter written in Russian. He photographed it. A second white envelope inside contained something squarish, stiff.

He opened it.

A passport.

The picture looked like Lana and yet it didn't. Black hair suited her and disguised her well. The Bureau assumed she already had the passport and yet he was holding it in his hand. Even though he was told to photograph only, his stomach curled at the thought of leaving it behind. A feeling in the pit of his gut told him he couldn't risk allowing her to get it in her hands. With travel documents in her possession, there was a decent chance she could getaway. With the travel documents in the Bureau's possession, traveling outside the U.S. would be next to impossible. He started to request authorization but changed his mind. The police were on the way and he had to go.

So, he called an audible.

J.J. always told him it better to ask for forgiveness than permission. She also reminded him when he made mistakes that he was an FBI employee and it would take the government at least three years to fire him for incompetence.

His hands trembled with nerves as he dug inside his backpack to find the trash bag and duct tape he carried with him. He quickly re-wrapped, sealed, and buried the money, threw the passport and letter in his backpack, and grabbed the strap as he sprinted to the edge of the woods, avoiding the parking lot altogether. He regretted the four Heinekens he guzzled the night before as he wheezed to his destination. Twitch or Cannon better be waiting for him where the brush met the exit road as he told them. As he cleared the trees, Cannon's car streaked past him in a blaze of gold, while sirens blared in the distance.

Jiggy screamed in the earpiece. "Hey, hey! You passed me!" He stood in the lane waving his hands frantically until the brake lights flashed red. With the road clear, Cannon threw his Charger in reverse and floored it until Jiggy saw his face through the passenger window. He hopped inside just as the Park Police car zipped by them and let his head fall back against the headrest.

"Whew!" Jiggy said. "Damn that was close. They're gonna be all over this park for the rest of the day. But Lana won't be traveling any place anytime soon."

Cannon gave him the side-eye. "How do you know?"

"I've got this," he said, holding up a small plastic bag containing her ticket to freedom.

"Aw, man! How in the hell did you manage to find the package, you lucky bastard?"

"It didn't have shit to do with luck. I can tell you that." Jiggy shook his head in disbelief, still in shock at the exchange. "I had some unexpected help."

"Help?"

"Yes, help. J.J.'s never gonna believe this."

CHAPTER 53

Saturday—The Devil's Rest

The sun was still concealed beneath the horizon when J.J. and Tony arrived at the boat dock in Fort Washington. She radioed Money T to ensure he was in position with the equipment at the ready; now it was time to get the show started. The rain sliced sideways and the brisk wind rocked the boats in the crowded pier, as they crept along the deck of the Devil's Rest and made way for the cabin.

Bryer Scott appeared more than happy to turn over the keys when Tony called to inform him that Maddix had planned to steal it. With a 600 mile range, he could make himself difficult to find if he managed to get away. J.J. and Tony had arrived while the rain was still pouring, believing he wouldn't leave until the weather cleared. Fortunately, their guess paid off.

Tony tip-toed toward the cabin door and opened it as J.J., who was rain-drenched from hair to heels, flipped her jacket hood over her head and tightened it.

"This was a really good idea, Tony. I can't see two feet in front me and the water pooling in my shoes is making my feet squeak."

"The mission required us to get here before he did," Tony said. "So, quit your yapping."

J.J. chuckled as she followed him down the steps into the cabin. She almost had to catch her breath as her foot landed on the deck floor. Looking around, it was the picture of luxury—a bone colored, J shaped sofa covered in lamb-soft leather sitting to the left, a galley kitchen with granite counters and bench-style dining area to the right, draped in the same material. Teak wood covered the floor of a narrow hall leading to the master and guest staterooms in the rear; each had its own bathroom—or as Tony called them—the heads.

"Man, this is sweet," J.J. said. "Too bad it wasn't bought with espionage spoils. We could seize it and buy it in an auction."

"We?" Tony smiled. "Anyway, we'd better get into position. I'm gonna squat down here in the galley. You get back in the stateroom."

"Why me?"

"Because I'm bigger than you."

"And? I saved you."

"Okay, I'm also bigger than *him*."

J.J. shrugged. "Which is why it's better for him to see me first. You can get the drop on him and he won't even notice you're coming." She stopped and craned her ear toward the ceiling. "You hear that? The rain has stopped. Let's move. He'll be here soon."

Tony rolled his eyes—as if he hadn't just said the same thing.

J.J. crouched down in the kitchen area to the right of the stairway. He wouldn't catch sight of her until he reached the floor. By then it would be too late for the piece of shit. Fury simmered in her belly, ready to bubble up and erupt with volcanic strength as she waited for Maddix's arrival. She was pissed at him not only for what he did to his country, but also for what he did to Kendel. All J.J. needed was a reason, not even a good one, to fill him with more lead than a #2 pencil factory.

"Won't be long now," she said to herself.

In the instant she tried to settle her thoughts, the boat rocked and footsteps padded across the top deck. She leaned back against the cabinet doors, narrowed her eyes, and gripped the Glock with both hands. No sound could be heard except the lapping water…until the cabin door opened and her phone vibrated.

A text from her father.

Okay to cancel dinner tonight. Brunch tomorrow instead.

She rolled her eyes and mouthed the word "Fuck!" She knew Maddix had heard the reverberation. The entire eastern seaboard could've heard her phone's rumble in the quiet of the early dawn.

The cabin door opened and a shadow appeared on the floor. That's when she noticed her biggest mistake of the day. Water. She and Tony tracked it inside and forgot to wipe up behind themselves. The only question was how he would react.

"Bryer? You here?" he called out.

A rustling sound jarred her. She studied his shadow as he tipped down the stairs. He reached the last riser and the barrel of a gun protruded from the end of his outstretched arm, aimed and ready to fire.

She held her breath and waited for him to take the last step into full view. The sound of his heavy breath left the hair on her arm standing on end. His hard swallows betrayed his fear. He sounded scared and just twitchy enough to make a brash move that could get them both killed.

He took the last step down and his body appeared. From his black leather jacket to his deck shoes, he was Ralph Lauren clean. Although he still looked hot, his dark glasses and slicked back hair would not change his fate if he so much as sniffed the wrong way.

"FBI! Freeze! Put the gun down!"

He slowly turned his head toward her, took his finger off the trigger, and *raised* both hands in the air above his head. "What the hell's going on here?"

"I said down, goddamnit! Not up!" J.J. yelled. "I know you saw me on the news last week. He was my friend. You're nothing to me, you piece of shit."

As he bent forward to put his weapon on the floor, Tony emerged from the bedroom and hurried to collect it.

"I don't understand," he said. "What did I do?"

"Amnesia much?" J.J. snapped. "You know exactly what the hell you did. You shady bastard. And at 9:00 a.m. Monday morning, a federal judge will be using the information to deny bail."

"You have nothing on me!"

"We have a federal agent who is prepared to testify."

"Who Kendel?" Maddix asked.

J.J. rolled her eyes. "Your mama!" almost slipped from her lips but she suppressed the urge. "Yes, Kendel Phillips. You know…your former fiancé, the one whose $250 grand helped finance this boat?"

He blew out a hard breath and smirked. "Hmph. You haven't heard? There is no more Kendel."

J.J.'s eyes nearly bulged out of her head. She glanced at Tony whose mouth was gaped open.

"The fuck are you talkin' about?" Tony growled. "She's in federal custody."

"Afraid not," Maddix sneered. "She was released under her own recognizance. And as she was leaving, she was struck in a hit and run accident, killed on impact."

"Oh my God!"

"Shame," he said with a broad reptile-like smile. "The crack head might've made someone a decent wife once she cleaned herself up."

J.J.'s body shook, trembling with anger. "You son of a bitch!" she shook her head in utter astounded amazement. "How could you?"

He shrugged and snidely said, "Easy. Pressed on the gas and kept the steering wheel straight."

With no forethought, her finger increased the pressure against the trigger. Another eighth of an inch and his blood would be splattered across the pristine white lambskin leather couch. A volcano roared inside her; her gut finally reached its peak. Her cheeks burned like hot charcoal briquettes. She didn't necessarily want to kill him. But in her most primal sense, where eyes were for eyes and teeth were for teeth, she wanted him dead.

The idea of allowing Maddix to walk the earth while Kendel was under it left J.J. brimming with the urge for revenge.

Then something inside her snapped. She couldn't tell you the moment it happened but her motive was clear.

"Where's his gun, Tony?" J.J. barked. "I want it, now!"

Maddix's nose crinkled in confusion. "What're you doing?"

J.J. had already rested her Glock on the countertop and was squeezing her hand into plastic gloves retrieved from her pockets seconds earlier.

"What are you doing?" Maddix asked again.

When Tony hesitated to give it to her, she tromped over to Tony, pulled Maddix's gun from the small of his back, and fired two shots at the hull, right in the spot where she'd taken up her original position.

"Are you crazy?" Maddix yelled.

"Yep," she replied. "As a motherfucking fox. Stand up right now! Stand up!" she ordered.

Terror filled Maddix's eyes as he followed her every move. "She's gonna kill me and make it look like self-defense!" Maddix turned to Tony. "Are you gonna let her do this?"

"Do what?" Tony asked. "I'm in the bedroom. I can't see a thing."

"You're just going to leave me defenseless in handcuffs?" he whined, sweat pouring from his brow.

"Oh, no," J.J. said, her voice Mary Poppins sweet. "I'm going to take them off after you're dead so I can put your gun back in your hand."

She laid his gun on the counter and lifted hers, shifting her aim from his head to his chest, and back to his head again. She cocked it to put one in the chamber and asked, "Now, how do you want to die?"

Maddix shook his head feverishly. "No, please. Don't do this, please!"

"At least I'm giving you a choice," J.J. said. "That's more than you ever gave Kendel. This is my last time asking, how do you want to die?"

"You don't even understand what's going on." He stopped as his voice got choked up. "You don't want to do this!"

"Oh, I *so* want to do this. Nothing in my life has felt better than the prospect of *ending you*!" she growled.

Tony chuckled at Maddix's pathetic pleas. "All of the sudden this guy's Chatty Cathy. The fuck are you talking about?"

"Stop! I—I give up I'm responsible. It's all my fault," Maddix yelled. "Please! Just put the gun down!"

The crotch itch struck, permeating through her back and legs, leaving her knees wobbled. It couldn't be. This was the truth. Yet, her body told her it was a lie. Maddix admitted fault and yet his statement was untruthful. He wasn't completely responsible after all, as all evidence she had access to at present suggested.

A paper doll.

He was a cut-out protecting the true culprit. Before she could figure out how to explain to Tony, her mouth opened and words slipped out.

"You lying son of a bitch! Who are you covering for?"

Tony's head whipped toward J.J. and he threw his hands up in confusion. "J.J., are you freakin' nuts?! The man just confessed! Isn't this what we wanted?"

J.J. shook her head no. "We want the truth! This doesn't end if we don't get the truth," J.J. yelled. "You've got to trust me on this one, Tony. He's lying. He's covering for someone else."

Maddix stood there in shock…and then he got cocky. "Shoot me and you'll never know the truth."

J.J. walked over to him and pressed the tip of her gun to his temple. "Wanna bet? An investigation of your accounts, assets, phone contacts, and emails will tell me everything I want to know about you, you piece of shit," she dragged the tip of the gun from his temple to his lips and wiped the metal across so he could taste death. "I don't *need* your confession. But if you want to see tomorrow you will give it to me."

Maddix's breathing was short and labored. Sweat poured from his forehead and burned his eyes, causing him to blink nervously. He sat there pondering her proposition as if he had a choice as if he had a real decision to make. Then he cleared his throat and began to speak. "He wanted access and help cleaning the evidence. I gave him access and cleaned up the evidence. That's all I did."

"Who?"

"Gary…Gary Mosin," Maddix said, rolling over on his partner like a dog playing for treats. "You know him…he goes by Hawk."

J.J. and Tony glared at one another. "Are you fucking kidding me?" she exclaimed. She gasped and her mind began to replay their every interaction. In the Sit Room, at the entrance. His seemingly unjustified bitterness toward her. Always in the right place at the most opportune time. And Hawk was telling the truth when Kendel said he was locking the Sit Room after the fire alarm went off. He knew he'd ordered Maddix to clean it up before ERT arrived. Of course it was Hawk, the one person off her radar. The one person who was so unassuming that they'd never have ID'd him as a key cog in Lana's network. People like Hawk made the best spies because they were the least suspected.

"Where is he?"

"Half way to Russia by now."

"Of course," J.J. said. "Left you here as bait while he escaped. I'll bet you were the one who set off the alarm in the West Wing and sanitized the Sit Room so we couldn't find any evidence, didn't you?"

He looked away. "I … I had no choice. He threatened to expose me, said he would kill me if I didn't."

"What's he got on you?"

Maddix dropped his head. "It'd be easier to tell you what he doesn't have on me. Drugs…and many other less than legal activities. I was looking at 20 years."

"Well, now you can double that and subtract the parole," J.J. said, pulling the radio from her back.

"Fuck you!" he spat. "Kendel's dead. It's your word against mine. You've got nothing!"

She pressed the mic button beneath her shirt and said, "Hey Money, you get all that?"

"Loud and clear!" he responded, the volume high enough to be audible to the room. "Digitally recorded for posterity…er, I mean prosecution."

"You were bluffing the whole time? You set me up!" Maddix yelled, stunned that *his* ride with the devil had just landed him in jail.

"No," J.J. said. "I just pressed the gas and kept the steering wheel straight."

"All right, WFO is on the way," Tony said. "Listen, you think you could wrap this up on your own? I need to make an important stop before we meet Director Freeman."

CHAPTER 54

Saturday Evening – Irving Street

Santino cradled his cell phone in one hand while sipping a Campari and soda from the high ball glass on his nightstand. He wrangled with the urge to call Tony and invite him over for a chat about his roommate every time he looked at the screen and didn't see a call or a text from "Katherine."

"Where the fuck is she?" Santino mumbled as he stood to his feet again. He'd nearly paced a groove in the floor between his chair and the bedroom window. With his initial reluctance now justified, he'd loaned his car to Katherine hours earlier and now felt like a fucking moron for trusting that she would ever keep her word. His momentary stupidity left him vulnerable in a way he'd never allow if he didn't owe Nicky Mumbles 25 Gs by Monday; apparently he was wrong when he assessed she needed him more than he did her. Just as he pressed his hand against the first cell phone button, he heard a car pull up in front of the house. He exhaled and walked to the window and grumbled.

"Mother-fuck!" he yelled as he tamped out his cigar in the ashtray. He stuffed the cellphone in his pocket, tromped down the steps and opened the door before his unexpected guest could knock.

"Wondered when you were gonna show up," Santino said.

Tony stood silently with his eyes narrowed.

"So what?" Santino said. "You gonna let the grass grow under your feet or you comin' in?"

Tony strode across the threshold and Santino closed the door behind him. Ten years had passed since their last meeting, but there they stood, face to face, mirroring one another in size and stature, staring each other down. With a lightning quick strike, Santino yoked Tony at the neck and jammed him up against the wall. Through clenched teeth he growled, "You've got a lot of nerve showing up here, after everything that happened."

Tony pulled out his Glock and pressed the tip into Santino's temple. "You got two seconds to let me go or I will blow your fucking brains into Christmas."

Santino tightened his grip as Tony put a bullet in the chamber.

"You're lucky I don't put two in the back of your head for Jimmy Toots," Santino said, releasing his grip. "Make it quick. I was on my way out."

Tony looked Santino up and down and narrowed his eyes. "Shorts and a T-shirt in November? Yeah I can see that."

"Who are you? Donatella Versace, you fucking rat?"

"You don't even know what you're talkin' about! Bet you still believe in the Tooth Fairy and the Easter Bunny too, huh?"

"Hey, when only one side's got the balls to do the talkin' whadaya gonna do? What they have to say sounds a lot like right to me."

"You know as well I do, nobody—not Jimmy Toots, not Nicky Mumbles, not even my father was going to listen to me after I became a Fed. They couldn't hear shit over this badge," he said, pointing to the golden metal dangling from his belt.

"That's true," Santino said.

"So what? I should do rectal gymnastics and jump through my ass tryin' to make 'em believe me? Hell no. I just steered clear," Tony said, taking a seat on the steps. "But think about it, you've known me since we first caught the bus together to P.S. 128. You know what I know. You've seen what I've seen. I'm a such a freakin' moron that I'm gonna target somebody in my own father's family when there's four other families I coulda hit? That's crazy. Oobatz!"

"Sounds like bullshit to me."

"I don't give a rat's ass how it sounds. This is how it is," he said. "Why am I in D.C. chasin' Russians instead working undercover, trying to worm my way into the family? It ain't like they didn't ask. I'm not in New York because I made a choice not to be a part of that life…on either side."

"He got pinched right after you left for the Academy and you're tryin' to tell me you didn't have anything to do with it? I dunno, Ton'. The timing was awfully coincidental."

"Was it?"

Santino's eyebrow scrunched. "What're you trying to say? We got a rat in the family?"

"Think about it—who gained the most by pinnin' this shit on me? That's the question you should be asking yourself. For my money, I say Nicky Mumbles. Rrom what I heard, he moved up to capo when Jimmy Toots got pinched. All those fucking so-called Einsteins in the family, and yous couldn't figure that one out?"

Santino sucked in a deep breath, scraped his fingernails across his scalp, and shrugged. Tony had a point. Everybody knew Jimmy Toots was gunnin' to become capo regime. But even if Tony was a fed, it would take some pretty hefty stugats to pin the blame on the boss's son. On the other hand, Tony had never been a liar.

"I dunno what to tell you. I ain't got shit else to say."

"How about you tell me what brings you to D.C.? Nothing significant in your world's happenin' here."

"Needed money," Santino said. "I was ordered to pay restitution to Nicky Mumbles. Owe him 25 Gs so I'm finding creative ways to pull the money together."

"Restitution? What is he, Judge Judy? For what?"

"The boss made the deal. For…Rosa."

Tony nodded, glanced around the room, and noticed a woman's jacket hanging on the coat tree. "Who's stayin' here with you?"

Santino allowed the silence to linger before answering. The bus Santino had been waiting all day to throw Katherine under had just pulled into the station, primed and ready to thrust her body beneath it, the backstabbing bitch. "What business is that of yours?"

"Who is it?"

"My goomar. She's visiting from Jersey. We're heading back tomorrow," Santino said. "Now get outta here. I've got some place to be."

Tony took one last long look around the house. "All right, all right already. I'm leavin'. Just make sure you keep your nose clean until you get outta town," he opened the door and stepped outside. "You don't have my back…I don't have yours. We clear?"

"Fine with me," Santino snapped. "Everybody knows you can't trust a Fed anyway."

As he peered out the window and watched Tony drive away, Santino's mind churned over everything Tony had said. Could that snake Nicky Mumbles be responsible for the lie that put the wedge between Tony and his family? Thinking back to when they were kids, Tony told the truth even when confessing was to his detriment. Honest to a fault, drove Santino nuts. How could he convince Tony's brother Dante or his father that they'd been wrong about him all along? They were as stubborn as Tony was forthright, but they needed to understand what Nicky Mumbles was capable of. He might make a move on the boss next.

Since he was already downstairs, Santino wandered into the kitchen to grab some food from the fridge. He bought some nice prosciut' and bread from a little Italian bakery in Arlington, Virginia. It wasn't like home, but it was good enough to make a snack. No sooner than he pulled the handle, the front door opened. The sound of footsteps was followed by a loud thump that shook the floor. He poked his head into the hallway and saw Katherine's body sprawled out, face down; she moaned like a dying cow, either sick, in pain or both.

"Ow!" she groaned, struggling to turn onto her back. Then she kicked out her foot to shut the door. "Ugh. I don't feel so good," she said, her words slushed and slurred together.

Santino ran to her and kneeled beside her, the whiff of liquor so strong he thought she'd been swimming in it. "Holy Mother of God, what've you been drinking?" He fanned his hand in front of his face.

"The bar. All of it," she replied. "Do you smell that?"

"If you mean the booze, yes. You are seriously hammered."

"No, the smell of quicksand. I'm up to my eyes in it," she said, with her words running together. "It's over. My life's over. You're over. I'm over. It's all over."

"What the hell are you talking about?" he said.

"Look in thish package," she said. Her body wobbled as she emitted a loud, acrid belch. She struggled to sit up but didn't have enough arm strength. "Look and shee for yourshelf."

Santino peeked inside the package and saw the stacks of money, more than enough for him to pay Nicky back. He didn't understand the problem. "Money's in here."

"Yep. But no passa-porta," she said, attempting to mimic an Italian accent. "I'm stuck in this godforsaken country for-fucking-ever!"

"Can't you just tell them you need a new one?"

"No, I marked the signal telling them that I received everything okay," she said. "They're standing down operations assuming that tomorrow I'm on my way to France. Now, I'm trapped here. And if I can't leave, I can't give you money to pay back your people either. To put it in porn terms—we're seriously fucked."

"Shit!" Santino said, letting his head fall in frustration. If he didn't pay Nicky back by Monday, he was as good as dead. Both of their death warrants would be signed. No, he needed to get a passport as much as she did. And fast.

Santino calmed his thoughts long enough to think of who to call. He had a few contacts but would any of them have access to one ready to go by the next day?

"Here, let me help you upstairs," Santino said, gathering her limp body in his arms and lifting her from the floor. Like Superman, he'd come to her rescue yet again, maybe not for the reasons she suspected. He carried her upstairs, only banging her head against the railing once or twice. Then he moved into her bedroom where he gently laid her on the bed and pulled the trashcan over to catch the inevitable vomit spree.

"What am I gonna do?" she moaned, suddenly releasing a crushing round of sobs. "I want to go home. I want to go home," she cried.

Santino gazed upon her face. Never before had he seen her so vulnerable, so helpless. Yet, she had never been more attractive to him than she was at that moment either. He wanted her in what, for him, was the worst way. He wiped the tears from her eyes. "Stop crying. I'm gonna make a couple of calls. I think I can find you a passport, but it's probably going to cost ya ten Gs at the very least."

She bolted upright from the bed and pressed her hands against her head as if keeping it from exploding. "I've got it. Whatever. I can pay it." Then she grabbed Santino's hands and gazed in his eyes. Her face brightened with hope. "You're not kidding me, are you? I mean, you have a legitimate contact?"

He nodded and smiled. "Let me make the call. You should take a shower and get some rest. We're probably going to have a long day tomorrow."

She caressed his cheek and leaned forward to kiss him but he pulled back.

"After your shower," he chuckled as he stood to leave.

He walked to his room and closed the door behind him, then scrolled through his phone to find the number to the D.C.'s most connected middleman. Santino figured that's how he got the nickname "D.C." He'd only met the guy a couple of times, but had left a strong positive impression. Certainly didn't hurt that Santino was Italian and *The Godfather* was his all-time favorite movie.

The Jack of all Trades and master of none, if D.C. didn't have direct access to what you needed, he could point you in the direction of who did. Then he made a nice commission on whatever service he provided and kept his hands clean. He hoped this single call would be the only call he had to make. "Yo', D.C. This is your *Godfather* friend. I need a favor. A big one."

"My man, Castellano!" he said in his usual upbeat voice. "Leave the gun, take the cannoli."

Santino chuckled for D.C.'s sake and rolled his eyes. "Listen, I need a passport…not for me. Let's just call her Italian. You think you could hook me up? I need it tomorrow by 10 a.m."

"Hmmm. A passport for a woman?" D.C. replied. "I might have something for you. But it'll cost you eight Gs and a kickback for express service."

"Don't worry. I've got it. Knew you wouldn't let me down."

"Email her photo and vitals to this account," D.C. said reading off a Gmail address. "We can meet at the usual spot tomorrow."

He hung up the phone just as Katherine poked her head in the door. Suspicion in his gut told him the call was too easy. He questioned whether D.C. should've needed more time to call some people and get back with him later.

"Any luck?"

"Yeah, yeah," Santino said. "Which makes me wonder…I thought it would've been tough to find something at this late hour."

She nodded. "It should've been. I think we both know how the FBI operates. When something sounds too good to be true, somebody usually winds up in Supermax." She held up her index finger. "Give me one second."

Katherine disappeared from the doorway and reappeared a short while later with a canvas blue bag the size of a large envelope and a roll of aluminum foil.

"What's at?"

"A trick I learned in my old job," Katherine said. "I need the passport even if it's FBI made."

Santino agreed. "I know."

"Fortunately, I've got a plan to ensure we got both get the hell out of here as scheduled. When he calls you back with the meet location, we'll take a ride."

CHAPTER 55

Late Saturday Night—FBI Headquarters

Director Freeman labored to draw in a deep breath. The stress was taking a greater toll each day, but he'd slotted a check-up into his schedule next week. Exhaustion filled him to the core of his bones, but the night wouldn't end for at least another hour. However, he'd almost begun to regret his decision to call in Kyle, J.J. and Tony for an update on their cases.

With the Russian National Security Director expected in just a couple days, he couldn't afford an international scandal due to FBI operations, not when he'd been ordered by the President to cease activity. As a last resort, he could stand firmly on the grounds that political machinations had no bearing on critical national security issues—a spy and FBI agent killer on the lam and a bug in the Situation Room, planted by Russian intelligence—and he could not wait for a "convenient" time. Even though his reasoning was concrete firm, he wanted to avoid the necessity if possible.

"So, you believe Mr. McCall is safe for now?" Freeman asked.

Kyle nodded. "Absolutely. J.J.'s brother's a cop and taking a leave of absence to stay with him. In the meantime, we're waiting on the CJIS facial recognition analysis. We should have something by Monday at the latest," he said.

"Facial recognition isn't an exact science, so I hope we're not putting all of our eggs in that basket."

"No, sir. I've also got an informant on the lookout for white females trying to purchase fake passports," Kyle said. "Since Jiggy retrieved Lana's passport from the drop, it's only a matter of—"

Kyle's phone buzzed. He unclipped it from the belt holster and stared at the text screen. He slapped his knee and yelled, "We've got her! Goddamnit, we've got her."

Everyone sat at attention. "Some guy, Castellano, requested a passport. He wants to pick it up in the morning. The passport he's exchanging is the one I gave him and it's got a GPS tracker in it."

"Castellano?" Tony said, sitting up at attention. His voice shot up an octave. "Who Castellano?"

Freeman looked at Tony askance and then at Kyle.

Kyle shrugged. "I don't care if he's the son of the Pope John Paul. When he picks up that passport he's leading us straight to Lana Michaels and I'm taking them both to jail. That's all I care about."

"Here, here!" J.J. added. "You need me and Tony?"

"Nah, you two have had a long couple weeks. My team will take this from here. Should be a one-two punch. We've got a tracker in the passport. All we need is a couple of G-teams on surveillance, and one Tac Team to support the arrest in case things get out of hand."

"Sounds good to me," Director Freeman said. "I want a call the second Michaels is in custody."

"Me, too." J.J. glanced at Tony and appeared concerned by his blank expression. "Tonight we're supposed to meet with the Task Force and drink to closing this case. Tomorrow's Sunday Brunch with the family. After missing my father's birthday yesterday, he may disown me if I don't make it."

"Okay, now if you'll excuse us, Kyle," Freeman said. "Agents McCall and Donato are briefing me on another case before I get out of here."

"Okay, sir," Kyle said, standing up from his seat and moving quickly toward the door. "We'll call tomorrow when the op is over. You have a good evening."

Freeman nodded and smiled as Kyle closed the door behind him. "Now, tell me more about what happened with this Mosin character. Just thinking about him gives me a headache."

J.J. and Tony explained the entire case to him, going into granular detail about the Paper Doll clues left by Jim Cartwright, the former assistant director and FBI mole who was killed by Lana, Kendel's involvement with Maddix Cooper and the role Gary Mosin and MCM Construction played in the operation. Gary, like Lana Michaels, was the mole in a separate but linked network and he used Cooper and Kendel the same way Lana had used Chris Johnson and Jack Sabinski.

"We blew this one," Tony said. "Based on Lana's case, we should've known Maddix Cooper was just a cut-out for the real mole, but he covered Mosin's tracks well."

"Worst of all, he's probably half way to Moscow by now—and based on what Cooper says he's got a box full of intelligence on American operations that, in the hands of the Russians, will not only significantly damage U.S. national security, it will prove very embarrassing diplomatically. We've got to take him down."

"I agree. That's why I've already contacted the CIA Director," Freeman said. "What I'm about to tell you is closely held …but, on emergency orders from the National Security Council, they've mobilized every black ops officer west of Siberia to intercept Mosin before that information gets to the FSB."

"Wow. The world must be coming to an end. Can't believe you got the CIA to agree," J.J. said, covering her mouth in surprise. She'd never seen the agencies come together and agree on such a swift, decisive action.

"This isn't cooperation on their part," Freeman said. "It's self-interest. If the information he's carrying gets out, Moscow Station will be gutted. They have more to lose than we do. The decision was easy."

J.J. nodded. "I guess the only thing left is to figure out what we're gonna do with Vorobyev. He's got files in his possession that could certainly even up the score in our favor. This man has been operational for twenty years and his family's outside of Russia—at least for the time being. We're never going to get a better chance at helping him defect."

"Except one thing, J.J.—the man is still *inside* Moscow, a city with more FSB officers than ants in the Everglades. He's not even in the U.S. Embassy yet," Freeman said. He felt his hair turn grayer by the second. "Not only will we have to put CIA operatives at significant risk to get him *into* the Embassy, we will have to find a way to transport him across Russian territory, without getting caught, so we can exfiltrate him back to the United States. I don't even want to think about the amount of resources and time this will cost the Government. But we do take into account that the value of his information will far outweigh the risks, which is why we're working on it."

"We understand, sir. He'd have been better off if he had just turned over while he was still in Washington … then again he couldn't have accessed the intelligence that could end these mole investigations for good," Tony said.

"Even with the intel, we're still screwed. Between Golikov and the FSB, he's almost better off dead," J.J. said. "Thank God Dmitriyev pulled a major one out for us in helping Jiggy find that passport, but we still need the leverage now more than ever."

"I know," Freeman replied. "Which is why I'm attempting to work out a solution with the DNI and CIA. We've all got our best exfiltration experts on this. I'm hoping like hell we'll figure something out soon. The longer he stays in Russia, the more our risks increase and the poorer our chances of getting him out become. In the meantime, we've got another pressing matter to deal with."

J.J. and Tony glanced at each other and then turned back to Freeman.

"The Secret Service Director made it very clear during an extended rant that he wants the bug removed from the Situation Room…and I mean *yesterday*. Apparently, the President prefers not to have a Russian listening device in the walls of his office and is less than happy, to put it mildly, that we've stonewalled them on this. So if you can't think of any justifiable operational reason to keep the thing in place. It's out. Bright and early Monday. Are we understood?"

J.J. pursed her lips and let out a heavy sigh before nodding in agreement. "Okay, okay. Just seemed like a prime opportunity to throw a sucker punch; we don't get the chance to do that very often. We'll ensure it's removed and have Washington Field place it in evidence."

"No argument from Agent McCall? Hmph, there's something new and different," Freeman said. "Now if that's all, scram so I can go home. I've successfully averted divorce for two weeks straight—and I'm going for three."

"Yes, sir," J.J. said as she collected her things. "Please let us know if we can do anything to assist in the Vorob—" J.J. froze in her spot, her eyes wide and lips slightly parted. Then she slapped herself in the forehead. "Oh my goodness. I can't believe I didn't think of it before!"

"Uh oh, I know that look," Tony said.

"Unfortunately, so do I," Freeman said to Tony. "What is it, Agent McCall?"

"I've got an idea about how to get Vorobyev out of Russia safely," she said, her glance volleying between the two. "Don't you see? We've got to kill him!"

Tony's and Director Freeman's eyebrows scrunched in confusion and both shook their heads. Then Freeman said, "Excuse me? Let me get this straight. You're suggesting that the FBI should kill a Russian intelligence officer... in Moscow?"

She shook her head no and looked at him as if he'd lost his mind. "Of course not, Director Freeman! I mean, we aren't the CIA for goodness sakes," she said. "I was thinking more along the lines of getting the President...and the National Security Council to murder him in the White House."

Tony felt her forehead and he and Director Freeman shared a hearty laugh at her expense. "J.J., you've really lost it. You want the President...along with members of the NSC to kill a Russian intelligence officer," he chuckled. "What should they use? Professor Plum with a candlestick in the study? We're going to get you some medication for your condition."

"No. The President—with a bug—in the *Situation Room!*" J.J. snapped, crossing her arms across her chest. "Listen, no matter what we tell the Russians, they will never believe we're not hiding Vorobyev."

She paused to let the idea settle on them before continuing.

"But if they hear about Vorobyev's untimely death from the President during Gusin's next visit to the Ellipse, they will believe every word."

Both Tony and Director Freeman looked at each other in shock and then at J.J., conceding with deferential head nods. Her idea not only had merit, it would solve a couple of problems—if the President approved. And given he and Putin were not seeing eye-to-eye in recent days, they had every reason to expect a "yes."

"Hmm. Silence. Who's laughing now?" J.J. sang in a joking voice. "In chess terms, I believe we call this a checkmate."

. . .

J.J. and Tony spaced out their arrival at the District Chophouse, a retro downtown steakhouse and brewery, by thirty minutes. Tony arrived earlier. J.J. admired the rich mahogany décor. The place was a throwback to the 1930s post-prohibition era, where agents and spies could toss back handcrafted beers. She weaved through the L-shaped walkway toward the expansive bar, only to see Gia wearing a dress cut to every man's satisfaction, beaming her bright licentious smile intimately close to Tony's two-timing mug. Apparently, Gia was taking advantage of her time alone with Tony until J.J., Six, and Walter arrived.

A snarl choked J.J.'s throat as she tromped up to them and sliced him in half with a wicked glare.

"Well, well, well, gang's all here," J.J. snipped. "You two are looking *awfully* cozy."

"J.J.! You're…here," Gia said, her face scrunched in disappointment. "Didn't think you'd make it."

"Apparently not."

Tony gave J.J. a "c'mon" look and cleared his throat. "Uhhh, I'm going to hit the head. When I return, we'll all chill out, relax, and drink to the end of a long successful week. Hai capito?"

J.J. pursed her lips and nodded, as she watched him walk away. She appreciated his rear view as much as the front.

"Beautiful man, isn't he?" Gia said, also taking in the sights.

J.J. shrugged, stifling her anger, as she played down her response. "Eh, he's okay if that's your type."

"You'd have to be dead for Tony not to be your type, wouldn't you?" Gia said with a gossipy giggle, her tongue loosened by the spirits emptied from the three glasses in front her. "Umph. That ass. Those lips. So soft."

J.J. almost responded with a "Girrrrrl, I know that's right!" when the question hit her—*how the hell does Gia know how soft his ass and lips are?*

"Soft?" she said with an unnatural calm. "You guys have gotten friendly, huh?"

"Mmm, yes. We kissed at Gordon Biersch last week when he met me for drinks after work. But his mother called and he had to rush out."

"His mother, huh?"

Gia nodded with a far-off stare and a smile eating up her face.

J.J. mustered every ounce of strength she could gather to maintain her composure. She wanted nothing more than to stomp a mud hole in Tony's ass, but she refused to allow her emotions to best her in front of Gia.

Tony strolled up behind her. "Are we ready for another round?"

J.J. turned to him, face to face. The hurt weighed her eyes thin; she hoped he could see the pain in them. "I'm gonna head home," J.J. said. "I'm a third wheel. But if *your mother* phones while you're kissing Gia again, I'm free to take the call."

Tony's eyes bulged and his jaw dropped, his glare shifting between J.J. and Gia.

"If you both will excuse me," J.J. said, quickening her pace toward the door.

"J.J. wait!" Tony called from behind her as she whisked through the door. "Let me explain…I didn't know…"

"What, Tony? You didn't know you loved me before you kissed her…or until after I told you I loved you?"

"Please, listen…"

"No! Gia told me everything I need to hear," J.J. snapped, her jaw clenched. "Revenge tastes sweet, right? Gia's waiting. Get your ass back inside. Drink up!"

The death glare J.J. shot at him left Tony with no doubt and prevented him following her. He knew it was a bad idea. Chocolate couldn't soothe the beast that wanted to punch Tony's face in, but it was a better place to start than Belvedere...or her fist.

CHAPTER 56

"I'm leaving the Anacostia Metro right now," Santino said, talking to Katherine through his Bluetooth for the entire trip. "I should be at the Big Chair in a few minutes."

"Remember, timing is everything," she reminded him. "I'll see you back here within the hour."

Santino exited the subway station and caught the bus a few blocks down Martin Luther King Avenue to the meet locations—D.C.'s choice. Although quiet that Sunday morning and clearly in the midst of revitalization, it was still a part of town you visited because you had to not because you wanted to. Neglected old row houses and empty lots with fallen fences still lined the newly paved streets leading to the renovated freeway entrance, and the only people on the streets were homeless men wrapped in charity blankets and churchgoers bopping their heads to the gospel as they passed by on the way to the early service.

Santino wore jeans and a pair of seen-better-days Nikes; the dark glasses and a black hood from his reversible jacket exposed too little of his face for anyone to get a solid ID. Not even his hair color could be seen. The canvas satchel Katherine had prepared for him to transport the passport was clenched under his arm. His most distinguishing feature was his height. It wouldn't matter once he boarded the bus. If he pulled off Katherine's plan, he'd lose his tails before they got get within five feet of him anyway.

Up ahead of him in the parking lot next to The Big Chair, Santino saw D.C. pull up in his black Cadillac Escalade that sported no-view tinted windows and a set of rims more expensive than Santino's house in Jersey.

Santino scanned the area slowly, spotting the guys she called "the Gs" exactly where Katherine said they'd be. She told him not to flinch, to keep his eyes forward. They wouldn't pop him there. No. Santino's purpose, in their eyes, was to lead them to America's Most Wanted. So far she was right. Not a single one moved. He checked the time and settled down, slowing once he got a few feet from D.C.'s Caddy.

As Santino approached his car, D.C. turned down the window. "Castellano! In your Sunday's best, I see."

"Hey, dressed for success," Santino said with a smile. "You got it?"

"Right here," D.C. said, holding up a manila envelope. "Birth certificate's in there too. Here you go."

Santino grabbed the package, examined the contents, dropped the package inside the canvas bag, and handed D.C. an envelope thick with cash. "Birth certificate? Since when do you believe in charity?"

"Where I come from ten Gs ain't charity. Comes with the package," D.C. said, "Now I gotta run."

Santino looked down to the end of the block. Nothing. His transportation was running late so he stalled. "No Godfather quotes this morning?"

"Hmmm, let me think. Oh wait, I've got one. Check this," he said. "'I spent my whole life trying not to be careless. Women and children can afford to be careless, but not men.' Wise words wouldn't you say?"

"Indeed," Santino said as he watched the bus pull around the corner. "Ahhh, here's my ride. Thanks and, uh, you be *careful.*"

Santino boarded, paid his fare, and headed to a seat in the back corner. There were only three riders. From inside his jacket, he pulled out a beige baseball cap, which he reversed to the navy blue on the inside. Once he exited at his next stop and made his moves, he'd be free and clear in no time. If Lana was right and the Gs had expected him to drive to the meet, then they would be unprepared to follow him on foot. As long as he got a small window of time when they lost sight of him, he could get himself in the clear and finish this job. Nicky Mumbles, Jersey, and the life he'd been forced to abandon were only a few steps away.

CHAPTER 57

Sunday Morning—Surveillance Detail

Kyle found it difficult to disguise his nervousness. This wasn't the kind of neighborhood that welcomed cops of any flavor but especially Feds. In this world, snitches got stitches. And disrupting a federal case was a badge of honor. One misjudged glance at one wrong person and the entire op could be blown.

Kyle ordered his two G teams to establish a box perimeter surrounding the Big Chair; he set up the iPad to monitor the tracker inside the fake passport he had made especially for Lana. He and Hopper took up the lead position on V Street, which gave them direct line of sight to D.C.'s meeting with the devil's gatekeeper – the man buying the ticket to Lana Michaels' freedom. And like a breadcrumb trail to the witch's house, he'd lead the FBI straight to her. As soon as this Castellano person collected and delivered the goods, they would be on the way to toss her in Supermax.

Hopper glanced down at the iPad and then at Kyle. "Should be here any minute. D.C. sold him some story about being a punctuality fanatic."

"Talk about a whopper. D.C. doesn't even breathe on time. He's late for everything," Kyle said, his eyes locked on the street ahead. He heard the low hum from a bus rumbling down Martin Luther King Avenue. It stopped and moved again, its load lightened by one. When it pulled away, a man in a dark hoodie carrying a canvas bag under his arm trotted across the street. He turned sharply and positioned himself facing toward Kyle and Hopper's car for a moment too long to be coincidental.

"He caught the bus? I thought he'd drive."

"Depends on what he drives. In this neighborhood, maybe he was afraid it'd get jacked."

Kyle cut him a sideways glance, still amazed by Hopper's level of green, his inexperience. "No, something doesn't feel right," Kyle glanced over at the iPad.

The radio buzzed and Cannon, one of the Gs positioned around the perimeter, said, "Heads up. Possible subject. White male, six-two, dark hoodie, jeans, and sunglasses, approaching the meet location. A black Caddy SUV's pulling into the parking lot. Stand by."

"You got the tracker map screen up?" Kyle asked Hopper.

"Roger that. It's activated. D.C.'s car is parked by the chair right now."

The radio buzzed again. "They're making the exchange. The target has the package. Looks like he's putting it inside the canvas bag."

Kyle took a deep breath and started the car. It was time to pursue. Time to meet Lana face-to-face. Hollow point-to-face if he had his way. No matter what, she would pay for killing his best friend. She would pay for the loss to Kyle's godchildren, Jim's children.

"Black Caddy is bugging out," a voice called over the radio. "Subject's moving toward the bus stop. Westbound bus approaching. Subject is boarding."

Hopper turned to Kyle, his expression panicked, his face red. "I-I-I don't know what happened. We lost the signal!"

"What?" Kyle said.

"It's gone! Just disappeared."

Kyle leaned over the steering wheel in frustration then bolted up and slapped it. "Jesus H. Christ! It didn't just disappear. It's the bag. He's jamming the signal. Gotta be Lana. She knows we're onto her," he grabbed the radio. "Cannon. Get ahead of that bus and have the foot team board at the next stop. Tracker's disabled. We need eyes on the target now!"

Kyle turned the ignition and pressed the gas to the floor, the wheels turning and screeching until the smell of burnt rubber lingered in the air. "If he gets on the subway, we're going to lose him. He'll run us in circles all fucking day."

After a short pause, another update.

"Blue leader, this is Cannon," he said. "Cham's on the bus…and target's gone."

"Gone?!" he and Kyle yelled. "What are we, fucking Keystone cops? Unless you want to file for unemployment tomorrow morning, you'll find him."

"All units are sweeping the area and we've got a foot team entering the Metro. Standby."

Kyle sped down MLK Avenue, grumbling under his breath. "Goddamn, Houdini. They stashed a car down here."

"How the hell did he get in the black," Hopper asked, his glance flicking from side-to-side, scanning for logical escape routes. Then he spotted it. "Pull over! Look right there?"

Three blocks away two large vans, parked illegally, blocked the view to the bus stop. He could've easily slipped out of the rear entrance and between the trucks unnoticed while the Gs boarded in the front, a shrewd move no doubt coached by his partner-in-crime.

"That's it," he said. "That's got to be it. This case just went to shit. No way we're going to get them today unless one of the Gs gets lucky."

"Don't give up yet," Hopper said. "If anyone can find them, they can."

With a defeated expression, he waited for a clearing in the traffic. He whirled the steering wheel to the left when he felt his phone vibrate. He glanced at the caller ID. An FBI Headquarters number he didn't recognize.

"Oliver. What can I do for you?" he said in a snide voice that said he wouldn't be doing any favors.

"No, sir," Sunnie said. "It's what I can do for you. We got the results of your facial recognition analysis from the lab."

"What did they come back with?"

"Okay. Looks like a negative on the facial recognition for Lana Michaels. Doesn't mean it wasn't her. Just means that they could not confirm the ID based on the analysis."

"Well…damn," he said.

"The good news is they did get an ID on the car. It was Jersey plate FVB 23K."

Kyle sat upright from his formerly slumped position and whispered to Hopper telling him what was going on. "I'll be damned. Who is it?"

"One Santino Castellano. He's a known Bonanno associate with no criminal record. We did a full work up, and he temporarily forwarded his mail to a D.C. address on Irving Street—2131."

Kyle gasped. "*Santino* Castellano on Irving Street?"

Hopper turned. "Hey, that's where we interviewed that Sonny guy! You mean Lana was there all along?"

Kyle slammed on the gas and hit the sirens. "We've still got a chance to beat him there. Or at least meet him. And when we do, Lana is mine!"

CHAPTER 58

Sunday Brunch—Irving Street

J.J. took the elevator down to her condo lobby to meet Tony and Six. They all decided grab a bite at her father's and head to Alexandria to interview Maddix Cooper. They needed every piece of information they could get to catch Gary Mosin, and Six was in need of company, still quietly reeling from Kendel's death.

Meanwhile, J.J. seethed over Tony's behavior from the night before. Ogling Gia like some horny teenager. His attraction to her was clear to everyone. And every time she pictured his tongue in Gia's throat, she vomited a little in hers.

J.J. loved him, with all her heart she did, but she'd be damned if she played second fiddle to some barefoot and pregnant cultural fantasy ingrained in him since he weaned off his mother's boobs. And Gia seemed all too eager to trade in her day job for Tony, a set of Calphalon pots, and a nursing bra.

J.J.'s clear sense of self helped her understand that she was simply not made from housewife stock. She didn't obsess over biological clocks ticking or wedding bells ringing. Only handcuffs clicking and sirens blaring resonated with her, but she also envisioned Tony beside her every step of the way…until now. Damn Task Force. Damn Gia.

J.J. had the resignation letter in her pocket, she was ready to quit. And even Tony himself didn't want her to go. Now, he seemed to desire the green grass in the yard next door, rather than the one he'd helped plant and cultivate himself. An interesting turn of events, indeed, but she refused to give him the satisfaction of letting him know he got to her, especially with Six in the car. No, she decided to stay tight-lipped, get through brunch and the interview, and then spend the rest of the evening considering whether a future with Tony was even in the stars. Whether he indeed cared for and loved her as he professed. Did he really have her best interest at heart?

As she exited the main entrance, Tony's car was parked at the curb and Six was already inside, seated in the back. She slipped in, exchanged a quick cold greeting, and stared out the window, determined not to utter a word about what happened, especially while Six was sitting in the back seat. He was like a giant chocolate sponge ready to soak in any information hinting at a rift in their relationship in order to exploit it to his own advantage. But Tony refused to let the possum play dead.

"J.J., you know I can't do this. Let's just be adult about this and clear the air."

She slowly rolled her neck until she faced him and snapped, "The air is just fine from where I'm sitting. If you ask me, you're the one in this car with breathing problems." She placed her hands around her neck and pretended to choke. Heaven knows she wanted to take him up on his offer. So many heated words were simmering at the tip of her tongue, ready to spill out and fill the car, but she restrained herself. "If you want peace to exist between us, you'll leave this alone."

Tony threw is head back in disbelief. "There ain't nothing peaceful about what's going on here. So just spit it out so we can friggin' move on."

J.J. bit her bottom lip. They weren't far from her father's house now, only a few miles away. Oh, how she was tempted to let him have it, but if she was a lie detector, her father was certainly an anger detector. No matter how she tried to mask it and put on a smiling face, he'd know by her strained expression that they'd slipped around in the muckety-muck. She wondered if she shouldn't unload before she lugged their issues to the brunch table.

"Go on. If you're feeling froggy, take a leap. Nobody in here's stoppin' ya."

She inhaled deeply and then let it rip. "Since you insist on forcing the issue," she began, casting a glance over her shoulder at Six whose ears were ready to receive every syllable. "The next time we go to the…*store*…keep the Hershey bar out of your basket if what you really want is the…peanut brittle. That's all I'm saying! There will *always* be someone who wants a Hershey bar…over bony ass peanut brittle."

"Hershey bars are my favorite; I'll take it over peanut brittle every day and twice on Sunday," Six yelled from the back seat.

"Really?" Tony said, directing his remarks to Six. Then he turned to J.J. "It doesn't matter if I look at the peanut brittle, okay? I wanted the Hershey bar. I put the Hershey bar in my basket. I paid for the Hershey bar. And when I got the Hershey bar home, I loved it so much that I ate the hell out of it."

J.J.'s face turned warm and flush, while Six belted out a deep cough.

Tony continued, "I put my money where my mouth is. So it doesn't matter whether or not *I happen* to look at friggin' peanut brittle or a friggin' KitKat or a friggin' bag of Skittles!"

She snapped her head toward him with glossy eyes. "It matters to the *Hershey Bar!*" J.J. said. "And if you can't keep your lips off the peanut brittle, the Hershey bar will find a buyer who will respect its feelings."

"You mean the one in the back seat?"

"I mean one that *prefers Hershey Bars* over peanut brittle," she growled.

"You gotta be kiddin' me," Tony said, as he turned onto Irving Street and pulled the car to an empty space by the curb so they could finish before he reached the front of the house. "You're blowin' this completely out of proportion. Turning a molehill into a mountain the size of Mt. Vesuvius. We gotta be adult here because there is no way I can stay away from the peanut brittle. Whadaya want me to do? Quit going to the store?"

J.J. got quiet. Truth was, he was right. They'd be forced into each other's presence until they wrapped up the cases. She had to trust him…or let him go. There was no two ways about it—and one difficult choice.

"You gotta trust me. And we have nothing without trust. You think you could try that?"

She wanted to, but he had no clue about her level of insight into his mind; she believed he'd allowed his feelings for her to take a backseat to lust. God knows she didn't want to know. She wanted to live in blissful ignorance and believe he only had eyes for her. But she couldn't shake the memory of the crawling sensation that permeated through her entire being when she asked about his feelings for Gia. Or the smirk on Gia's smug face when she shared news of their kiss. Perhaps he was lying to himself, but he was certainly lying to J.J. The man she once trusted with all her might had failed her at the worst time, and in the worst way. Because no matter how hard she tried, she could never be Sicilian. She could never be Gia.

"Well?" he asked.

"We should get inside. Dad's waiting. Maybe we can finish this up later."

"Maybe," he said, reaching out for her hand.

She pulled it back and craned her neck around the left and right to scan the street. "Malcolm's car is here…for a change."

"Still on daddy duty," Six said.

She and Six made their ways to the sidewalk and waited for Tony lock up the car. Before she could turn to head up the stairs, she glimpsed a flash of movement in the corner of her eye. She glanced across the street and saw a bony dark-haired woman standing just off the curb in front of Mr. O'Leary's. The woman just stared, her eyes eerily stone and cold. She looked vaguely familiar, but J.J. couldn't immediately place her face. And something, besides Tony's behavior, didn't feel right.

J.J. took careful steps to the end of the curb as Tony stepped by her side. He followed J.J.'s gaze toward the woman and froze.

He grabbed J.J.'s arm to hold her back and whispered, "It's Lana."

In a rabbit quick movement, J.J. gripped the holstered Glock resting in the small of her back, snatched it out and aimed the front sight directly at Lana's head. The scene felt familiar. A little more than a week before she'd been in the same position, a gun pointed at Jake's head, only Lana eventually got away. This time would be different. This time J.J. was stone cold sober. This time her hand was steady and her finger was tight to the trigger. "Feels like déjà vu all over again. You better hold your breath because if you so much as sneeze, I will blow a crater right between your eyes."

CHAPTER 59

Late Sunday Morning—Irving Street

Santino had to admit that Katherine's plan was a good one—to stash his car along the route. He was gone before the Feds had a clue. Sunk deep in his thoughts, Santino glanced out of Lana's bedroom window as he waited for his target to arrive, some broad.

What did he care as long as he could pay his debt?

Ice water ran through his veins as he anticipated the deed. For him, it was no big deal, no different than any other hit, except this time he neither knew the identity of nor gave a shit about his intended victim. In the flash of a second, he could pay off his debt and go back home where he belonged.

He'd packed his bags and stashed them in the trunk of his car which was parked a quick jog away on an adjacent street accessible through the back alley. He decided to use part of the cash he would pocket to buy a cheap hooptie so he could ditch the 'Stang. The guys in his crew would give him all the alibis he needed, so he could just lay low in Jersey until the heat died down.

He grabbed his sleek, black Winchester rifle and attached the extended silencer to the silver barrel so it would fire whisper quiet. By the time anyone figured out shots had been fired and where they'd come from, he'd be out the back door and half way out of town. With no witnesses except for Lana, he could get away clean, wouldn't even be a suspect.

"You about ready?" Lana's voice called from the doorway. "I can't believe the day has finally come."

He spun around; his eyes met hers. "Me either. I'm ready get to back to Jersey. But to tell you the truth, I'll miss being here, you know, with you." He'd rendezvous with Lana overseas when she got settled. He couldn't believe his feelings for her had grown so intense in such a short period. But for the first time in a long while, he trusted a woman. She followed through on her word, did everything she said she was gonna do. In his world, women like that were hard to come by.

As she walked to him, he leaned his gun against the wall. She wrapped both arms around his waist and held him so tight he thought he'd lose his breath. Then she pulled back and looked up at him through a tearful gaze. "After what happened to my husband, I never believed I'd feel this way again," she said. "After what we've shared, my life…it will never be the same."

"I don't want to let you go," he said. "Maybe you could come with me to Jersey."

She shook her head no. "As much as I'd like to, I can't. I miss home…I miss my father. I cannot feel whole so far away from my country and I'll never have peace here. No, I have to leave. But you can visit me often and stay as long as you like. You'll love it there."

He nodded and smiled. "I unda'stand. And you better believe I'll be there as soon as I can."

"Good," she replied. "Now, where's the car parked?"

"On Kenyon Street. Bags are loaded and we're ready to go."

She let out a long sigh of relief. "You know I wondered if you'd come through for me. I know I can trust you with my life," she said then quickly shifted to business. "Now, when they arrive, I want you to wait for my signal. I'll raise my hand; that's when you shoot *them*."

"Them? I thought you wanted me to hit some broad," he said.

"I found out the man involved in my husband's death will be with her. I want them both gone." She looked at him curiously. "What does it matter to you? It's just a second bullet."

He shrugged. "You're right. Makes me no nevermind. As long as I get my money, it's all good. Where's the cash anyway?"

She pointed out the knapsack she'd tossed on the floor.

He stroked her hair down to the small of her back and then cupped her face in his hands before planting the softest of kisses. He wanted nothing more than to stand there and linger in her gaze, her lips, her grip, forever. But too soon, duty would call.

Their heads snapped toward the window when the sound of a car engine drew closer. Santino released Lana and glanced outside; he recognized the car as Tony's and turned to Lana. "No, that's not the car. Maybe they're running late."

"No, she's never late," Lana said, stepping up behind him. "What do you mean? That's the car. They're here. Get ready."

"*That's* the car?" Santino said, his voice raising in pitch. "Looks like there're two dudes in the car. You want me to shoot the black, right?"

"No, the white one who's driving. And make sure you kill him first. I want her to see his dead body before she dies. And I want her soul to rot in hell knowing I'm responsible."

The blood drained from Santino's face. Tony was the son of a made man, a boss. But he was also the same cocksucker who everyone believed had sold out his family. Still he had second thoughts. Nicky Mumbles knew where he'd been stayin'. Nicky might put two and two together, but then again he might not care as long as he got his money. "Wait," Santino said, "you mean that guy…the one right there. Dark hair, black leather jacket."

"Are you a fucking moron? Yeah, that guy right there!" Her eyes narrowed and through clenched teeth she hissed, "If you don't kill them, I will hunt them down like rabid dogs! And you will regret this pathetic betrayal for the rest of your life!"

Santino stiffened. Her words went from sugar to knife shanks. He'd warned her to watch her tone. Apparently, she still hadn't gotten the hint.

"What the fuck did you say to me?!" Santino snapped. In their time together, he'd never seen her go quite this far off the bitch cliff and he'd prefer never to see it again. "Threaten me and you'll be snacking on your fucking teeth for dinner, you cunt," Santino snapped.

"It's not a threat," she said in a softer tone. She glanced down at the rifle and back up again, expression softened, her voice calmed. "As long as you pull that trigger like I'm paying you to do, I'll call you whatever you want. I don't want to fight you."

Santino looked down at the knapsack and nodded. "Okay." He shrugged and then threw his hands up with open palms of capitulation facing her. "Whatever you say. It's your show."

"Thank you, my darling." She flashed a tentative smile and kissed his expressionless face. "Just give me a couple of minutes. I've got something to say to her. When I raise my hand, you fire."

"Got it," he said. "You raise your hand, I'll fire." A reluctant grin sliced through his lips and he nodded once more.

As she descended down the steps and headed outside, Santino cracked the window just wide enough to accommodate the barrel. His mind churned over her words and his conversation with Tony. Blood might be thicker than water, but without the money, blood was of no consequence because he was dead. No, he couldn't leave without the money. He could take the shot, or he could get shot. There were no other choices.

He grabbed the knapsack, unzipped the main compartment, and counted out 20 stacks of $100 bills. It was all there. He'd been paid. Now, there was only one thing left to do.

He moved back into position, lifting the rifle and preparing to aim.

Katherine was there, standing between two cars on the near side of the street. After an angry exchange, she took off her jacket. Everyone went silent. He positioned the butt against this shoulder and aimed the barrel through the crack. He locked his eyes on Tony, who after scanning the street, looked toward Santino.

Tony's mouth fell open, as if he was ready to yell. The black broad scanned the street and found Santino's window. She aimed her gun directly at Santino…before Tony saw her and forced his body in front of her. Santino's stomach tightened. He couldn't believe what Tony did.

Then the old man from across the street ran out.

Santino peered through the sight, pressed his finger against the trigger, and fired—twice.

Two silenced shots; his target was struck.

He'd done what he needed to do.

He dismantled the rifle with a soldier's speed, preparing for his escape before the police arrived. With the woman's screams and bodies sprawled on the ground, someone would call the police soon.

He returned his rifle to the case and quickly searched her dresser. He needed to ensure no evidence had been left behind before running out the back door. One after the other he pulled the drawers open and shut.

Nothing.

He was almost out the bedroom door before he had the second thought to check the closet. The space was empty with the exception of a few hangers. He ran his hand along the top shelf and his fingers were stopped by a small stack of papers. He pulled them down and gasped.

"That fucking cunt!"

The stack contained page after page of background information about him, several news articles covering Rosa's accident and the suspicion surrounding Cappi Merendino's death, his home address and those of the other guys in his crew, everything the cops would need to find him, right there on her closet shelf. She'd been playing him like a fuckin' violin in a string quartet all along. He stuffed the papers in the knapsack and dashed out the bedroom. As he started down the stairs to head out the back door, he was stopped by an unexpected presence.

Santino's eyes narrowed. "You've got some fucking nerve showing up here!"

CHAPTER 60

Sunday – Irving Street

J.J. stared down the barrel of her gun, waiting for Lana to make the move that would end her life.

"Gimme a break. Your aim was never that good," Lana scoffed. "Besides, I'm not armed." Lana took off her jacket and let it fall to the ground. She lifted her shirt to expose her waist and spun around. She pulled her pant legs toward the knee and exposing her bare foreleg. Then she approached the middle of the street palms out.

"Oh, don't worry about that! We keep a .45 in the car," J.J. said, mockingly. "If you force me pull this trigger, trust me, you'll be armed by the time the police get here whether you brought it or not."

Although it was clear Lana had no weapons, J.J. still felt uneasy, as if they were standing in a trap.

She suddenly remembered Cartwright's letter and Lana's words— *"American arrogance astonishes me. So smug that you cannot see the thief who waves hello with one hand while picking your pocket with the other."*

J.J. felt her pocket being picked.

She scanned the street left and right, up and down. Rooftops and open windows. She saw nothing out of the ordinary. "Six, check the cars. I'm not getting the warm and fuzzies here."

He nodded and proceeded to jog down the sidewalk, closely eyeing the passenger-side windows up and down the block.

"What the fuck are you doing here? What do you want?" J.J. asked, her eyes darting around the area looking for any unusual movement. There was nothing. The street was still.

"I'm tired of running," Lana said, her voice cracking with manufactured emotion. "I'm gonna turn myself in, but first I have a question I need to ask you."

Tony and J.J. looked at each other skeptically before the crotch itch struck. The piercing sting caused her legs to buckle for a moment, but she quickly recovered.

It was clear Lana was lying. J.J. didn't know if she had some sadistic plan or accomplices hunkering nearby, but a lie could mean nothing but trouble. J.J. lowered her aim from Lana's head to her chest so Lana would think she believed her. "What is it?"

"Do you remember Jake? Does the vision of him lying in his own blood haunt you at night?"

A rush of emotion shook her. God knows she'd been haunted every day and every night. The mere thought caused her mouth to water for Belvedere. Not a single day had passed that she didn't want to forgo her newfound sobriety to wash the pain away. "He was my friend. I didn't want to kill him. He gave me no choice."

"Oh, you had a choice. You just chose to save your precious Tony. With friends like you, who needs friends?"

Six ran up beside J.J. and flanked her on the side opposite Tony.

"All's clear," he said, slightly out of breath.

"Will you get the fuck on with it, Lana?" Tony barked. "We've got some place to be."

Lana's voice trembled as she started to cry, stunning J.J. into silence. She didn't know witches cried. "You robbed me of everything, my future, my life. It's over," she swiped her sleeve over her eye and clenched her teeth. "And now I'm going to return the favor. Take a look at your precious Tony," she said, an evil grin slicing her lips. "This is the last time you'll ever see him alive!"

She slowly raised her hand in the air, sending J.J. into a wave of confusion. Her eyes darted door to door, window to window, searching the area.

Then she saw it.

The blinds moved in the upstairs room of Mr. O'Leary's house. When the glimmer of the barrel protruded from the window, her eyes widened. She pointed her gun to the window and glanced at Lana, whose eyes widened to the size of milk saucers.

"What's going on here?!" Max's voice called from behind her.

J.J. turned to look over her shoulder and saw him walking toward the steps. "Dad get in the house…now!" she yelled.

She turned back to the window and aimed once again before Tony looked at her with a panicked expression and screamed "Get down!" as he threw his body in front of J.J.'s.

Two barely audible shots sounded. Within seconds, her body collided against the ground under a heavy weight. A limp body.

She got off one shot before her arm lost its aim.

A second later, her head exploded. A sharp pain bolted into her temple like the fiery sting of a lightning strike.

Her eyes lost the light and into darkness she fell.

Chapter 61

Sunday – Irving Street

"Tony?" J.J. whispered, buried face down under the weight of the body covering her. She felt a stream of liquid drift from her forehead down the curve of her cheek. She had no idea whether he was still alive, sending a wave of panic through her entire being.

He'd thrown his body in front of her, to protect her with the ultimate sacrifice—his life. He loved her in a way that no other man had, except perhaps her father and brother. He loved her.

She huffed, gasping to draw air into her lungs. Everything happened so fast. Seconds passed in double time. Her heart raced as she attempted to push him off, but he was too heavy. "Tony? Six?" She grunted as she tried shift under the leaded mass. Finally, a movement.

"Tony?"

"Shhhh…" He rolled off of her and whispered, "don't move. Don't make a sound until I give you the all clear."

"Okay," she whispered back. Her every sense was heightened. She could smell smoke in the air from a wood-burning fireplace. Harried footsteps padded around her, but she could see nothing. She patted her hand until she felt the cool grip of her Glock against her fingers.

On all fours, Tony crawled to the edge of his car bumper and scanned the area. "Looks clear. Shooter's gone. You okay?"

"I think so." She pressed her fingers against her face and felt a warm ooze emanating from her temple. Her fingertips dripped with blood. "Gash in my head, but I'm okay."

Tony jumped to his feet, pulled his gun from the holster, and ran toward the sprawled body.

Six who had stood beside J.J. only moments before the shots were fired, was now in the street. He knelt beside Lana and checked for a pulse. "She's dead."

"You stay here. Call 9-1-1 then Washington Field," Tony said to Six. "I'm goin' after the shooter."

J.J. shot up to her feet, casting a callous glance at Lana before hurrying to reach Tony, who was already half way up Mr. O'Leary's steps.

"Stand by!" he said as he busted the glass with the butt of his gun, reached in, and twisted the doorknob. Then he stepped beside the doorway in case the gunman fired. After a soundless few seconds passed, Tony led the way inside, J.J. on his heels. He gripped the butt with both hands and pointed the barrel upward as he headed up the stairs. No sooner than his foot hit the riser did a familiar face appear at the landing.

"You have some nerve showing up here," Santino barked, clearly ready to run.

"The fuck are you still doing here?" Tony said, lowering his weapon. His chest rose and fell at a rapid pace. "Thought you skipped town."

J.J.'s head volleyed between the two, her expression reflecting the confusion "You know him?" J.J. asked.

Tony looked at J.J. and nodded. "Yeah. He's my cousin. Works with my old man."

"Suzy Googotz out there offered me twenty-five Gs to put a couple in the back of your head…this one too," he said, jutting his head toward J.J.

"Hmph," J.J. said. "That explains why she approached me unarmed."

"Safe to say, the only thing she's hittin' now is the bottom of a fuckin' six foot pit. I mean, you may not be 'family'…but you're still *family*," Santino said. "Now unless you're plannin' to throw me a ticker tape parade, I need to get the fuck outta here before the cops come."

"I *am* the cops," Tony reminded him.

"You know what the hell I meant. You takin' me in or what?"

J.J. glanced at Tony, his expression asking a question she was unsure of how to answer. She thought for a moment and shrugged. "We're FBI agents and we have jobs to do, but we should maybe ask ourselves what Freeman would do to a man who saved the lives of two FBI agents and took America's most wanted agent killer off the streets?"

Tony motioned his head toward the back door. "You get pinched, you're on your own."

"Once a fed, always a fed. Don't loyalty mean anything to you?"

"You're a real piece of work, you know that?" Tony said. "Yeah, it means somethin' to me. That's why you're *running* out the *back* door…and not doing a *perp walk* in handcuffs out the front. Now get the fuck outta here before I change my mind."

J.J. and Tony stepped aside and turned their backs as Santino disappeared into the rear of the house and a door slammed. Before Tony could grab the doorknob, sirens blared. J.J. and Tony looked at one another curiously and ran into the street where an ambulance arrived, followed shortly by an unmarked FBI car.

J.J. could see Kyle and Hopper inside.

"Looks like the cavalry's arriving. You better call in a BOLO on Santino, so our story looks legit," she said, referring to a be-on-the-lookout alert to notify law enforcement that a subject was on the run. "We're going to have enough questions to answers as it is."

"I'm on it," Tony said, as Kyle and Hopper approached. He stepped out of earshot, leaving J.J. to handle the impending inquisition.

Kyle glanced down at Lana as the EMTs checked her lifeless, soulless form and prepared it for the body bag. "We get her?"

J.J. shook her head no. "She got got—but unfortunately the pleasure wasn't mine. A sniper took two shots from up there," she pointed to Mr. O'Leary's upstairs window. "The one on the right. Both struck Lana—two in the back. He must've run out the back door. By the time we ensured the area was clear and got inside, the shooter was gone."

Kyle turned toward Hopper. "You think it was Castellano?"

J.J.'s eyebrows popped up before she could catch herself. "Castellano?"

"Yeah, he picked up Lana's fake passport today," Kyle said. "From the looks of things, something went wrong. My guess is Lana's mouth. I always told her it'd get her killed one day."

"Well, he made tracks pretty quickly. Left it clean. But we've called ERT in to collect evidence and Tony's calling in a BOLO right now. If he's still in D.C. we'll get him," J.J. said.

"Left it clean, huh?" Kyle said with more than a hint of doubt in his voice. "Sunnie tells me he's related to Donato."

"Yeah." Her stomach sank as she attempted to improvise. "Cousins. From what I understand, they went to school together, but since Tony split from the family, he hasn't exactly been welcomed with open arms. He can't go within a hundred miles of New York or Jersey without risking his life."

"Apparently. Gotta love family," Kyle said.

"Tony spoke to him yesterday, but he said he was skipping town. He had no idea all this was going down."

"Well, there's plenty of time to find out what Tony knew and didn't know. In the meantime, we need to draw straws on who's gonna go brief the director first thing in the morning. We're going to have a late night cleaning up this scene."

"Oh, please. Let me do the honor," J.J. said. "Nothing could make me happier than informing him in person that the wicked witch is dead."

Chapter 62

"Are you okay, Director Freeman?" J.J. had nearly talked herself hoarse as she conveyed to Director Freeman the events of the past week. He appeared pleased, but unwell somehow. America's Most Wanted was dead, and a covert black ops manhunt was in full gear to find that piece of shit traitor Hawk—Gary Mosin. Task Force Phantom Hunter had cut off the head and the tail. Now, it was time to target the heart, the source of the money—Troika Technologies. Once the New York office took the Mashkov organization down, it would be only a matter of time before the entire network imploded.

He gripped his left arm and shoulder. "I'm fine. Think I strained myself lifting weights yesterday. I've got an appointment to get it checked out after my meetings this morning."

She sighed with relief and stood to leave. "Well, we can wrap this up then. I think we've hit all the high points."

"You have," he said. "But I have not. Have a seat."

"What's going on?" she asked, returning her butt to the chair.

"I want you, Donato, and the rest of the task force—save one—in New York. I've already cleared it with the SAC and the DNI. They're expecting you Friday. Nobody knows how this network operates better than you. You have the lead on the investigation—New York is supporting."

J.J. lurched forward in her seat. "But, sir, Tony can't...you know his history. If he goes to New York, he may not make it back to Washington, at least not alive. I can't risk putting him in harm's way, not for this case." She thought to herself, not for any case.

"The threat is legitimate?"

"Oh, it doesn't get much more real than this."

He sat back in his seat, rubbed his temples, and leaned forward on the desk. "Okay," he said. "The rest of you should take a couple days off and then get ready to go."

"But, sir, you said, 'save one,'" J.J. said. "Who isn't authorized to go?"

"Grayson. He's one of the best exfil experts in the CIA, and he developed some very critical contacts during his last tour. We need them. So, we're sending him to Moscow to help get Stanislav Vorobyev back to the United States."

J.J. felt a conflicting sense of relief and consternation. She wouldn't trust Vorobyev's impending exfiltration to anyone more than him, but going to New York without Tony or Six was like Princess Leia without Luke and Hans Solo. She'd be stuck with…C3PO and R2D2.

"So, it's just me, Gia, and Walter?" she said. "No offense, sir, but they're not exactly top cover."

"FBI New York is 2,000 strong. You'll have plenty of support," he said. "Now, if that will be all. I'm going to get myself to the doctor and get this arm checked out."

J.J. hesitated for a moment. For the first time she was alone, without Tony or anyone. And she wanted to ask him about her mother's case. He was in a position to get her all the information she needed.

"Is there something else, Agent McCall?"

"Well…no," she said as she stood to leave. She turned toward the door and suddenly found the courage to ask. "On second thought, sir…"

When she turned to face him, Director Freeman was slumped over his desk, clasping his chest, barely breathing. "Director Freeman?!"

Her mind blanked. She couldn't think. Her every action was driven by autopilot. She rushed to him and pressed two fingers against his throat to check for his pulse. "Mrs. Whitehouse!" she yelled. "Call 9-1-1!"

She stretched him out on the floor. He was still breathing…but barely. She couldn't do CPR, not unless his heart stopped. There was nothing for her to do but tilt his head to ensure he could breathe and wait in desperation. She grabbed his hand and held it tightly. "Help is on the way, Director. Help is on the way."

"Listen…*Nixon*," he struggled to say in a barely audible whisper. "Be….caref…."

Fear washed over her as the Headquarters nurse burst through the door and ordered her to stand back. "Nixon?" she called out from the distance. "I don't understand…what—" she began as emergency personnel whisked in.

As they wheeled him out on the gurney, he reached out for her hand.

"Tell his wife to meet us at the George Washington University Hospital emergency room. I'm riding in the ambulance," J.J. called back to his secretary.

In the midst of the flurry of thoughts flittering through her mind on the way to the hospital, she wondered why Freeman warned her about Nixon. He headed the good old boys club that counted Jack Sabinski as a member, but J.J. had never taken him for a racist. His problem was something else she couldn't quite put her finger on. One thing was certain: Freeman's illness had thrown one more monkey wrench in her ability to operate freely in New York.

She didn't know what Nixon had against her, but whatever it was she felt certain he would make her life at the FBI impossible until Freeman returned to office—or she found out what it was.

CHAPTER 63

Monday Afternoon—The Russian Embassy

Aleksey was stunned by the turn of events. Never expected for even a moment that Svetlana would be killed, even though he hoped like hell that she'd get caught. But he felt no guilt. None whatsoever. The hardest part for Dmitriyev was pretending as if he cared.

Continuous film loops of the crime scene replayed on every news channel at least twice hourly to fill the otherwise slow news day. He was thankful the Resident shut down most operations to give the residency time to mourn their fallen. He strode down the hall to Lana's father's office and found him glaring at the television screen with cracked bloodshot eyes and a steely, empty glare. His usually pale face was sullen and plum with a dangerous mix of anger, frustration, and grief for his lost joy.

Aleksey struggled to find words of comfort and solace, something that lacked the typical trite expressions of sympathy. Mikhaylov's pain was one he hoped never to experience in this lifetime or any other. "Brother," he said. "I have no words. I'm here for whatever you need."

He bowed his head in appreciation and gestured for Aleksey to fill the empty chair in front of his desk. Aleksey obliged.

"She was so young. Had her entire life to live for. All wasted." He tried to keep his voice from cracking but failed. Then he turned sharply toward Aleksey and though clenched teeth declared, "She will not die in vain. But the son of a bitch who did this will."

"I don't understand," Aleksey said. "You know the identity of her killer?"

He reached into his desk and pulled out thin stack of papers and then pushed them across the desk toward Dmitriyev. Told him they were copies of documents Lana had found to finger the mobster responsible. "She sent these to me only days ago. Told me if anything happened, I should find him. He would have answers. The news reports may indicate his identity is unknown, but I know where he is, and I know where to find him."

"So, what will you do?"

"Golikov's men have already returned to New York. Mashkov's people are already searching the streets. They will find him...and they will kill him. For me. And for my Solnyshko."

Aleksey was taken aback. He had no idea Mashkov, Golikov's most sadistic and vicious henchman, was connected in the United States, let alone New York City. He had a gnawing feeling that if handled sloppily—as Russian organized crime usually handled such matters—the fallout would compromise the residency. But attempting to reason with Lana's father while he was in this torrid emotional state was pointless—he'd avenge the death of his only child. Unfortunately, he didn't realize he'd also just sold his soul to the devil.

"I will leave you to your thoughts, but if you need anything at all. I'm here. We're all here," Dmitriyev said.

Mikhaylov's cheeks trembled as he fought back the tears. He couldn't choke out a thank you. Only managed another nod in appreciation.

As Aleksey stood to leave, a streak in the hall blasted by him as the sound of heavy footsteps pounded toward the residency leadership offices. He stuck his head out of the door and saw the panicked figure burst inside the Resident's door.

It was Gusin. The Resident had authorized him to monitor RAPTURE before the self-imposed operational stand down. He figured Svetlana's death would be briefed at the highest levels and wanted to find out what the Americans knew...and didn't know.

What he gleaned must've been significant.

Aleksey lingered in the hall, until the Resident's door flung open moments later. The Resident tromped into the hall pointing out officer after officer—all leadership. Aleksey called for Lana's father and followed Gusin and Komarov downstairs to the basement meeting room. Once everyone was seated, the Resident addressed the captive audience.

"Comrade Gusin has collected some valuable information this morning," he said. "According to our unwitting sources at the highest level of the American government, that traitorous, backstabbing, pig Stanislav Vorobyev…is dead. Piece of shit had a heart attack."

Several loud gasps erupted around the table before a moment of stunned silence. Once the news settled in the room, everyone exploded in cheers. They celebrated his death like New Year's Day or Christmas. Vorobyev had betrayed his country and he would betray no more.

Dmitriyev's mouth fell open and he squeezed his eyes shut before he regained enough awareness to join in the cheers with his comrades. Anything less would signal his guilt. But his heart hurt for Vorobyev's family. He couldn't help but feel responsible. Absent the chain of events that led to his interrogation, his friend would never have reached a level of desperation that would induce him to betray his beloved Russia. He died a victim of circumstance, one of both his and Dmitriyev's making.

Aleksey forced a fake, hearty laugh. "Serves him right. It's too bad the Government will have to waste taxpayer dollars to throw his decomposing body face down in a shallow grave."

The Resident shook his head no. "He is an American problem now. Let the American taxpayers waste resources to bury a man who was too dead to deliver the goods. What do we care?"

In that instant, Aleksey had learned one thing that tempered his solemn mood. First, Stan's body was still in American custody. Second, the FBI knew about the bug and would only share information they wanted Russian intelligence to hear. That meant this story about Vorobyev was probably a fabrication aimed at misinforming Moscow.

He reached into the small liquor cabinet. The occasion called for a bottle of single-malt scotch—Oban. He poured a cup two fingers high and then held his cup high in the air. "This moment calls for a toast. To our fallen comrade, Stanislav Vorobyev," he said facetiously. "May his soul find a home exactly where it belongs!"

CHAPTER 64

Monday Night—J.J.'s Condo

J.J. stared out the window and basked in the quiet of the stolen moment. She and Tony had been running at 200 miles per hour since the Sit Room case began. There'd been little time for anything other than investigating. But after Director Freeman's heart attack, after spending five hours in the waiting room with Rayna Freeman, after watching her stew in worry while the fate of her husband's life hung in the balance, J.J. found the time to remember love. The not-so-subtle reminder jolted her, shifted her focus to what was really important in life. Reminded her that nothing, no case, no investigation, no spy was more important than her health and happiness, further steeling her resolve to stay off the bottle and shifting her evermore close to quitting. She'd reaffirmed that her life was finally moving in the right direction, with Tony beside her, around her, behind her, in and outside her.

Yet, still she eyed the letter from Jim Cartwright—work was never far away...

"Two spies down and three more to go," J.J. said, sunken into her couch with her feet kicked up on the coffee table. "I'm really worried about Nixon being in charge until Freeman gets back on his feet. The director warned me for a reason. Something hinky's going on there."

"I agree. Somethin' definitely ain't right there. But I don't want you to worry your pretty brown head about anything. I have people who hurt people for me," he said. "Besides, when you take down the financial network, I've got a feeling this investigation's gonna be all downhill from there."

"I was thinking about calling Director Freeman to tell him to allow the New York office to take over the investigation. I can't do anything they can't do. And they know the streets better than I do."

"You're not fooling me. You just don't want to leave me behind," Tony said. "But you and I both know you'd go nuts sitting back here on the sidelines. They may know the streets, but nobody understands how the Russians operate better than you."

J.J. let out a long sigh, set the letter on the table, and grabbed Tony's hand. "You're right. I know you're right. Curse me and my work ethic," she said. "You gonna miss me while gone?"

Tony wrapped her in the comfort of his arms for the first time in too long. "You know it, my little Hershey bar," he answered. "Wish I could go with you, babe. But you can call me anytime. If I can't help you, I know people who can."

"What if I need some *personal* servicing?" J.J. asked. "You gonna send someone for that too?"

"Oh yeah, right after I kill 'em," Tony joked.

J.J. chuckled and then her expression turned serious.

"About Gia," she began, her voice exposing her vulnerability. "It's just been a long time since I've allowed anyone to get close to me, and I'm not going to lie, it scares the shit out of me. But I'm beginning to realize I'd rather live with the fear, than live without you."

Tony turned to J.J. and locked his eyes on hers. "You have nothing to worry about. Ever."

J.J. smiled and stroked his face. "I know, my sweet Antonio," she said with a wry smile. "because your little girlfriend Gia's going to New York with me where I can keep an eye on her bony ass!"

They dissolved into laughter before Tony added, "And two-and-a-half will be in Moscow."

"What's the half for?" J.J. laughed, wiping giggle tears from the corners of her eyes.

"Because he's a half-brain, half-wit."

J.J. kissed him. "And not even half the man to me that you are."

"Is that right?" Tony said, in his sexy tone. "Well, the lower half of me really wants to get into the lower half of you."

He wrapped her up in a passionate kiss, when his cell phone rang. He let it go to voicemail and it rang again. And again.

He pulled away from J.J., exhaled in frustration, and glanced at the caller ID. "It's a Jersey number. Lemme get this." He picked up the phone and swiped his finger across the screen. "Santino? Why are you calling me?"

He listened for a moment and bolted upright in the bed. J.J. watched his face transform, his ears reddened, and his voice quivered. "What the fuck happened? Is he okay?"

Tony kicked his feet over the edge of the bed and sat up, leaning forward on his knees. He scraped his fingers across his scalp. J.J. sat next to him and rubbed his back whispering, "Is everything okay?"

"Son of a bitch! Cocksuckers!" He gave her the hand and scooted himself away to give himself some space. She could hear the frantic voice rattling off of some story that sent Tony into a tailspin.

"No, no. I'll call my mother and get Uncle Paulie to drive her to the city tomorrow," he said. "Lemme make a few calls and I'll get back to you later."

He hung up and took a deep breath.

"It's my brother, Dante," Tony said. "He's been shot. Twice. In the back. He's in bad shape. They don't think he's gonna make it."

J.J. gasped and covered her mouth in shock. "What…how did …who did it?"

"Word on the street is that it was a Russian group. Dante and Santino were meeting in Brooklyn, and they hit Dante by mistake. They look more like brothers than Dante and I do."

"W-w-why would they want to hit Santino?" J.J. asked. "You don't think it's revenge for Lana, do you?"

Tony nodded. "That's exactly what I think…and everybody thinks. The group is linked with Mashkov. And we know something my family doesn't—that Mashkov has direct ties to Russian intelligence…and that her father is probably the one who ordered the hit."

In an instant J.J. was deflated. She felt like a truck tire with a slow leak. She hated to see the hurt on Tony's face and only wanted to make it go away. "What can I do to help?"

"Understand that what I'm about to say is not up for debate, J.J.," he said. "I'm going to New York. This is my family…and the enemy is bigger than me now."

"At least you hope so." How could J.J. argue with that? Especially after what she'd gone through with her own father when Lana had only threatened to kill him. Tony's brother lay in the hospital dying. She couldn't expect Tony to listen to reason or act within it.

"I'm afraid if we don't' find a way to bring calm to this situation, my family is going to war. A lot of bloodshed."

"I understand, Tony," J.J. said. "But I don't want a drop of it to be yours."

"Then just be there for me."

"You never have to worry, Tony," J.J. said, as she grabbed his hand and kissed his palm. "I'll always have your back."

J.J.'s mind whirred in confusion and despair. Her entire world shifted in a matter of seconds. Instead of going to New York to shut down the financial source of an Illegal's network, she was potentially putting herself in an all-out war between the Russian and Italian organized crime. The moment felt surreal and out of control, just like the potential for calamity if a tit-for-tat grudge match played out on the streets.

If she couldn't find a way to de-escalate the situation, she stood to lose something a lot more important to her life than her case.

STAY TUNED FOR THE NEXT EXCITING
INSTALLMENT OF THE SERIES…

A No Good Itch
(A J.J. McCall Novel)
Book 3

Sneak Preview Ahead…

Sneak Preview - Prologue

"THE SUPREME ART OF WAR IS TO SUBDUE THE ENEMY WITHOUT FIGHTING." ~ SUN TZU

Fear, failure, and the fear of failure turned enemies into friends like nothing else in the convoluted world of intelligence and spying. No doubt the reason FBI representatives had been summoned to the Russian Embassy in Washington.

The Minister of Foreign Affairs reeled after a reported "heated discussion" with the U.S. Secretary of State; she promised harsh and swift diplomatic sanctions following the successive wave of embarrassing Russian intelligence blunders resulting in FBI and Secret Service agent arrests. The tense political situation had outraged their now tight-lipped government contacts in Washington and New York and dried up critical sources of American intel. The stone silence threatened to paralyze the SVR's intelligence mission across the United States unless they quelled the fury. Thus, the come-to-Jesus meeting called by the SVR Resident was inevitable and necessary.

FBI Special Agent J.J. McCall marveled at the embassy's ornate grand lobby. Rich white and dark European marbles accented by cardinal red carpet runners, a stately winding staircase crowned in gold, and paintings of lush landscapes brightening the halls and sitting areas; J.J. placed it among the most beautiful embassies she'd visited. The sight was impressive and a stark reminder of the country's willingness to spare no expense when it came to putting up deceiving fronts and paying American traitors.

"We'll need a dump truck for the bullshit about to be heaped on us today," J.J. whispered to her co-case agent, Tony Donato. As the lead case agent behind the ruckus, she'd been ordered to attend the meeting, listen, and respond to nothing.

"Shhh," Tony whispered in reply. "The walls have ears."

Resident Andrei Komarov, the Russian equivalent to the CIA Station Chief in Moscow, led J.J., Tony, and Assistant Director of Counterintelligence John Nixon through the hallowed embassy halls until they reached a well-appointed conference room. It contained mahogany-paneled walls, large open armchairs, and an oversized table large enough to seat Komarov's ego and attitude, both massive in her past experience.

The group, all dressed in their services' uniforms—pin-sharp woolen suits in late fall hues concealed under beige all-weather overcoats—was met by the only other declared SVR officer in the Russian Embassy, Security Officer Aleksey Dmitriyev.

Jolted by his presence, J.J. avoided his gaze, kept their handshake and greeting brief. The last time they met, he was not working for her. Now, he was—and the only other person in the group aware of his status was Tony. Butterflies rolled in her stomach as everyone took their seats, and the meeting began. She forced a poker expression and prepared herself for the barrage of lies.

Komarov settled in at the head of the table, his face reddened and contorted. It was as if every word he was about to speak, no doubt carefully selected by the Foreign Minister, would sear his throat and exit his lips like sharpened razors carving him from the inside.

"We've all met before and are quite familiar with one another," Komarov began, shooting a slicing glare through J.J. Her aggressive targeting of SVR officers for recruitment was legendary...or infamous, depending on which side of the table you sat. She suppressed the awe she felt. He was the personification of the Russian James Bond in looks, dress, and devoid of any semblance of accent. "So, I'll feel free to dispense with the introductions and pleasantries since we all understand why we are here today."

J.J., Tony, and Nixon exchanged strained glances before she took a deep breath to brace herself. Komarov was about to progress through the four steps of surviving a massive operational failure.

Step 1: Admit nothing.

"There has been a spate of unfortunate and seemingly unfounded reports regarding the activities of our foreign intelligence service inside the United States," he said.

Her birthright, her gift, the ability to detect lies, sent the sensation of an army of crawling ants through her fingertips and up the length of both arms. She clenched her teeth and prepared for *Step 2: Deny Everything.*

"We have no information to substantiate the many reports circulating in the media nor can we speak to the involvement of any of our staff. However, I can assure you that if such activity occurred it was orchestrated by rogue officers conducting unsanctioned operations. If ever discovered, they will be dealt with accordingly. This brings me to my next point..."

As the lies continued, the annoying sensations intensified. The itch stretched through her back and up into her neck. She shifted in her seat and tensed her body to suppress it.

A moment of relief would come with *Step 3: Demand Proof.*

"If your Secretary of State persists in her current path and continues to threaten sanctions against our diplomatic corps, we must require access to the evidence used to justify these unfounded accusations against our government or we will be forced to reciprocate and target the U.S. embassy in Moscow."

They always demanded proof because they knew the FBI couldn't provide the most critical elements, at least not so early in the investigations. Such provisions risked revealing FBI sources and methods, potentially compromising the Russian Embassy recruit sitting across the table from J.J. It would also expose the FBI's knowledge of the listening device found in the White House Situation Room, an announcement the President had postponed for reasons unbeknownst to her.

Nixon cleared his throat. "It's forthcoming," are the only two words he offered, which was two too many in J.J.'s book. He said, "Continue with your little speech, please," in his typical condescending, patronizing way.

From the pinched expression on Komarov's face, he took the comment in the spirit in which it was intended, just as J.J. would've. This certainly contributed to *Step 4: Make counter-accusations.*

"And if your government should bring forth any evidence against the Service, we may be required to present our own proof that these arrests are merely a provocation to discredit Russia and increase hostilities within the international community given U.S. opposition to our security operations in the Ukraine."

Bullshit. But J.J. gave credit where it was due—the guy was good.

"We're not here to debate the validity of your political and military agenda," Nixon replied. "The FBI's primary concern is securing the homeland from terrorists and spies. So, if we could cut to the chase, why have you requested our presence here today?"

J.J.'s eyebrow arched. She'd never known Nixon to be a man with backbone. He usually preyed on the weak rather stand up to the strong.

"Ahhh, yes," Komarov said, relaxing his tone and posture, he leaned his back against the chair. "We brought you here to extend an olive branch if you will. I've been asked to assure you that the Service is not controlling any operations targeting citizens inside the United States.

Negotiations regarding the specifics of the new plans are underway within our executive channels and will demonstrate our proposed new era of cooperation. We would like to collaborate on issues, such as terrorism, which would be of great benefit to both our countries."

By now the itching sensation had permeated J.J.'s entire being. If the human body contained over a billion nerves, every one of hers had been stimulated in the worst way. She clenched her legs together and strained not to dissolve into a scratching frenzy.

But the truth had been revealed. They wanted to purchase conciliation with terrorism intelligence. J.J. felt relieved. With FBI Director Russell Freeman at the helm, U.S. national security could never be bought at so cheap a price.

Chapter 1

Monday Afternoon — Alexandria Jail

The U.S. Attorney's Office had stacked so many charges against Maddix Cooper, the next time he set foot outside of prison would be to take the pine box dive into a six-foot pit. Mandatory sentences for espionage, conspiracy, first-degree murder, and obstruction of justice. The list of traitorous offenses had left FBI Special Agents J.J. McCall and Tony Donato in a major predicament: How to convince a man with zero motivation to divulge information contrary to his best interest – without the use of torture? This question plagued J.J. as she and Tony crossed through the barbed-wire fence into the detention facility. Within a few minutes, they'd be face-to-face with the lowest form of human in existence; the answer wasn't coming fast enough.

The stench of confinement, an unsettling combination of despair and delinquency, permeated the cushy looking fortress on the outskirts of Northern Virginia and turned J.J.'s stomach. She'd spent more time in this hell hole over the past month than in her entire career, and she didn't care if she never saw it again.

Her last visit was at the behest of her then jailed boss, Supervisory Special Agent Jack Sabinski. Framed for committing espionage by his Jezebel, the dead Lana Michaels, Jack summoned J.J. and pled for her help in proving his innocence, a feat she accomplished despite her longstanding contempt for his mistreatment of her.

Now, J.J. focused her mind on interrogating the newest offender—Maddix Cooper, who, to her delight, was on the verge of becoming some inmate's bitch. He'd already ratted out Gary Mosin as the second member of Lana Michaels' Russian sleeper agent network during their showdown on the Devil's Rest. He also spilled that Mosin had disappeared off the grid and was fleeing to Moscow—but left out the details of Mosin's travel route, facts they needed to know in order to intercept him.

Never had an interrogation been so pointless from J.J.'s vantage point. No way in hell would Maddix divulge the details of Mosin's escape plans. The only reason he confessed their connection in the first place was to escape the bullet from J.J.'s gun. Now, tucked behind the bars of Virginia's premier correctional facility for newly arrested spies, he awaited a conviction that would guarantee if he died twice and came back to life, he'd still have to serve forty years. As far as he knew, a plea bargain might do little more than eliminate only one of his many life sentences. He had no viable reason to reveal another word. Certainly not out of the goodness of the cavernous pit where his heart was supposed to be.

The Sheriffs walked J.J. and Tony through a series of security doors until they reached the interrogation room. They left their overcoats with their escorts and tugged their suit jackets straight before entering. The sight of Kendell Phillips' murderer shrouded in orange and shackled at the hands and feet gave J.J. a burst of pleasure she hadn't felt since her early morning romp with Tony. A reddish blue bruise circled his eye and spread to the cap of his jaw. His gaze disintegrated under the weight of her glare and fell to his twiddling thumbs. She prepared to speak when an overwhelming scent jarred her senses—the smell of contemptible swine.

"Figured you two would show up sooner or later," Maddix said, his arrogance soaking up the little-remaining tolerable air in the room. It was a small box with dirty white cinderblock walls and a two-way mirror on the back side. He scratched the five o'clock scruff seeping from his square jawline. Red cracks peppered Maddix's penetrating steel gray eyes, and Lipton-sized bags bubbled from beneath them. His first few nights behind bars had left him sleepless and worn, an inconsequential justice for a scumbag who offed his fiancé to ensure the survival of his spy ring.

He locked his eyes on J.J. and all but ignored Tony. "Hope you enjoy the view because I've got nothing to say to you…or your little partner here." He jutted his chin toward Tony.

"My, my, my," J.J. said to Maddix. "What an ugly fall from grace. Too bad they don't make an Armani perp suit. You used to wear him so well."

Positioned across from Maddix, Tony scanned the rat's face and looked at him with a pained expression. "Rough night, eh? Did they forget to put you in solitary? Looks like you've been mingling with the locals."

"Nothing I can't handle," he said with a shrug. Then he leaned back, spread his knees wide, and placed his hands in his lap. "So, this is the reason you came all the way to Shangri-La? To gloat?"

J.J. savored his misery and then vexed him with a tight smile. "We're here to discuss your comrade in arms, Hawk—Gary Mosin."

The usual good cop/bad cop routine would have zero impact on Maddix, the former Secret Service agent. For him, the routine would be a day at the office. The puppet show held no mystery. The little information he'd dribbled to date wouldn't help a dog find bone. Even with the odds stacked against her, taking down Mosin before he found comforting shelter in the eager, waiting hands of Russia's FSB was an imperative, not an option. He'd hatched what appeared to be a fool-proof escape plan before defecting to Russia, but even the best-laid plans had vulnerabilities ripe for exploiting.

"Newsflash, doll." Maddix forced out a grating laugh, overplaying his weak position just a smidge. "You get nothing from me, not without a deal. I want immunity."

"Immunity?" J.J. blinked in rapid motion. After rolling her neck and eyes, she folded her arms over her stomach, lifted a single eyebrow, and prepared to kill any dream he'd concocted of shaking his bid. She'd arrived with the intent to take the path of least resistance, but his crassness suggested he sought the off-road experience. "First of all, my name is J.J. or Agent McCall, not doll. Secondly, if you ever deign to—" she started. Tony rested his arm on hers to stop her rant and signal he'd take over. He understood better than anyone that the bees-to-honey approach went out the door with the word "doll."

"Listen, you ain't gotta make this difficult. We didn't come here to pick a fight. Give us the information we need, and you can go back to counting the tiles on the ceiling . . . or whatever it is you do on the inside." Tony contrived a calm demeanor as he reached into his pant pocket and pulled out a pack of Marlboro 100s and a book of matches. He slid them to the middle of the table until they stopped beside a plastic ashtray. "Our treat. Enjoy. But if you choose to stay on the difficult route, we can reverse course any time."

Maddix cupped his hands and with no show of gratitude, pulled the offerings to the table's edge, his shackles jangling with his every move. He folded back the foil on the corner of the pack and knocked the open end against his wrist until a cigarette emerged. Then his brow drew together, furrowed in confusion. "You don't have a clue, do you?" His gaze ping-ponged between J.J. and Tony before he shook his head. "*That's* why you're here. You don't know!" With a slight air of cockiness, the corners of his mouth edged upward in a sneer; he eased back against the chair. "At the rate you're going, *The Washington Post* will get the scoop before you do."

"The fuck you talkin' about?" Tony's gruff New York attitude released like the Kraken. His face reddened as the sound of his grinding teeth emitted a low hum. Maddix's arrogance stoked his anger, affecting Tony as easily as J.J.'s. "What part of 'you ain't gotta make this difficult' did you not understand? You're already testin' my patience. I promise you that's not a smart move, not for someone in your position…which in…" he glanced down at his watch, "about an hour will be bent over for some booty bandit."

Maddix took a slow drag from his cigarette and allowed the smoke to swirl around his lips before resting the cancer stick in the ashtray. He again shifted his cocky gaze between the two. "The great and powerful J.J. McCall. Just as ignorant as he is, huh? Man, I should tell both of you to go screw yourselves. I don't need *you*. You need *me*."

J.J. caught a glance of Tony's fist which had curled into a tense ball. She pressed her hand to his arm to dissuade him from any impulsive actions. Like an electric current coursing through her brain, the touch sparked an epiphany, brought to light the answer to the question she posed to herself earlier. The solution to her Maddix predicament was simple. How do you make a man divulge information against his best interest?

You don't.

About the Author

S.D. Skye is a former FBI Russian Counterintelligence Program Intelligence Analyst and supported cases during her 12-year tenure at the Bureau. She has personally witnessed the blowback the Intelligence Community suffered due to the most significant compromises in U.S. history, including the arrests of former CIA Case Officer Aldrich Ames and two of the Bureau's own—FBI Agents Earl Pitts and Robert Hansen. She has spent 20 years in the U.S. Intelligence Community.

Skye is a member of the Maryland Writer's Association, Romance Writers of America, and International Thriller Writers. She's addicted to writing and chocolate—not necessarily in that order—and currently lives in the Washington D.C. area with her son. Skye is hard at work on several projects, including the next installment of the series.

www.ingramcontent.com/pod-product-compliance
Lightning Source LLC
Chambersburg PA
CBHW071917130726

47909CB00014B/2054